The Viscount Who Lived Down the Lane

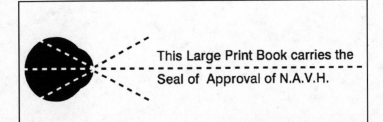

This Large Print Book carries the
Seal of Approval of N.A.V.H.

THE VISCOUNT WHO LIVED DOWN THE LANE

ELIZABETH BOYLE

THORNDIKE PRESS

A part of Gale, Cengage Learning

GALE
CENGAGE Learning·

Farmington Hills, Mich • San Francisco • New York • Waterville, Maine
Meriden, Conn • Mason, Ohio • Chicago

GALE
CENGAGE Learning®

LIBRARY OF CONGRESS CATALOGING-IN-PUBLICATION DATA

Names: Boyle, Elizabeth, author.
Title: The Viscount who lived down the lane : rhymes with love / by Elizabeth Boyle.
Description: Large print edition. | Waterville, Maine : Thorndike Press, 2016. | © 2014 | Series: Thorndike Press large print romance | Series: Rhymes with love
Identifiers: LCCN 2015051126| ISBN 9781410489234 (hardcover) | ISBN 141048923X (hardcover)
Subjects: LCSH: Large type books. | GSAFD: Love stories.
Classification: LCC PS3552.O923 V57 2016 | DDC 813/.54—dc23
LC record available at http://lccn.loc.gov/2015051126

Published in 2016 by arrangement with Avon, an imprint of HarperCollins Publishers

Printed in Mexico
1 2 3 4 5 6 7 20 19 18 17 16

To the Skyway VFW Post 9430
and to Chad Hasseberoek.
For all your
kindness and dedication to
the special-needs Boy Scout Troop 419.
They are blessed to have your example
and leadership in their lives.
For your generosity of time
and sponsorship,
as well as the brave service
you have given to our country,
I thank you.

PROLOGUE

London, Hanover Square
November 1810

"What is it, Haley?" Lord Charleton asked, sparing a glance at the door of the breakfast room where his secretary stood, hovering about like a nervous sparrow. "Is it Rowland? Tell me he hasn't landed in the suds yet again."

"No, my lord."

The man's brow furrowed a bit. "Couldn't be Wakefield."

"Certainly not, my lord."

The baron glanced up. "Wouldn't mind if it was. Demmed waste having him mope about, locked up in that house of his."

"Indeed," the secretary replied, and if Charleton wasn't mistaken, there was a note of irony to the man's declaration — one he chose to ignore, instead pinning a glance on the impudent fellow.

Under the scrutiny, Haley's jaw worked

back and forth as if the words were stuck there in his craw.

"Well?" Lord Charleton prodded. "Out with it. Before my kippers grow cold." As it was, the baron shoved his plate forward and set down the paper he'd been reading.

Mr. Haley cleared his throat and held out a letter. "I've come across a small debt your wife owed —"

There it was. That cold stillness that came every time someone had the nerve to mention Isobel's name. How Lord Charleton wished he could forget her passing so this wrenching pain would fade from his heart. Yet, still, even a year after her loss, it was a sharp ache he woke up with, one that haunted him even after he closed his eyes at night.

Now here was his secretary bringing her up when he'd quite forbidden the matter.

"Pay it," he ordered in a tone that said he wanted nothing further to do with any reminders of her.

"But, my lord —" Haley shuffled about.

Lord Charleton removed his glasses and slowly cleaned them. Then once they were perched back up on his nose he stared coldly at the fellow. He was a good man, Haley. An excellent secretary, but why the man continued to bring up Lady Charleton, the baron could not understand. Speaking slowly and deliberately, so there was no mistaking the matter, he said, "You know what to do. Take care of it and leave me be."

"If you insist, my lord . . ." Haley's voice trailed off tentatively. It wasn't so much a reply as one last prod.

Truly? He was going to ask yet again? If he wasn't the most thorough and honest fellow the baron had ever hired — well, actually Lady Charleton had found him and insisted he be hired, but that wasn't the point. Haley had become rather cheeky of late and Charleton wanted nothing more than to fire him on the spot.

But Isobel wouldn't have approved, and so Charlton inclined his head, reined back his ire and said with a final note, "Just see to it as Her Ladyship would have wanted." Then he went back to his paper and ignored Haley, who stood for a few more moments in the doorway.

And if the baron had looked up, he might have seen the wry, wily smile that had led Lady Charleton to hire Mr. Haley in the first place.

CHAPTER 1

London
Six months later
Areowwwwww! The unholy complaint filled
the carriage.

"You should have left that foul creature
back in Kempton, Miss Tempest," Mrs.
Bagley-Butterton complained for about the
hundredth time.

Which equaled the number of times Hannibal had let out that ear-piercing yowl from
the basket in which he was trapped.

"He doesn't like being penned up so,"
Miss Louisa Tempest said in defense of her
cat. "And I couldn't leave him behind."

There was a sigh of resignation from
beside Louisa. Miss Lavinia Tempest, Louisa's twin, made a very deliberate show of
looking out the window. She wasn't about
to rise to Hannibal's defense.

Never would.

Louisa suspected her sister shared Mrs.

Bagley-Butterton's exasperation and wished poor Hannibal back in Kempton as well.

"I only hope your godmother is an understanding sort," the matron continued, shifting in her seat in the carriage and eyeing the large basket on Louisa's lap with an air of disdain and suspicion. She had protested vehemently against the cat being brought along, but she could hardly prevent the matter when the carriage conveying them to London belonged to the girls' father, Sir Ambrose Tempest. "I know I wouldn't have that cat in my house." She sniffed loudly.

"Then it is fortunate that we are staying with Lady Charleton," Louisa replied. "She is so kind and generous." She smiled as she said these words. Lavinia kept her gaze fixed out the window, though it was obvious from the way her shoulders shook that she was having a terrible time keeping from laughing at the implication.

"Yes, quite. How kind she is to offer to bring the two of you out . . . well, without . . ." Mrs. Bagley-Butterton sniffed yet again, Louisa's slight going right over her head, and unable to say quite what she wanted.

Whatever was this Lady Charleton thinking, bringing out two unknown misses of such dubious lineage?

Then again, it wasn't like Louisa hadn't heard the aside Mrs. Bagley-Butterton had made to their housekeeper before they'd departed Kempton.

"Does this Lady Charleton know?"

"She'll learn the truth soon enough, ma'am," Mrs. Thompson had replied. *"So will all of London, poor dears. Secrets always seem to have a way of winkling out, now don't they?"*

Yes, the horrible, awful secret.

Louisa pressed her lips together and stared out the window as the brick and stone of London began to surround them. Perhaps, just maybe, by some bit of chance, the truth wouldn't come "winkling out" as Mrs. Thompson avowed, and Lavinia could have the Season she'd always wanted.

At least this was what Louisa hoped as she looked at the gray and foreboding walls surrounding them.

Oh, this wasn't Kempton, with its green hills and grand oaks.

How she wished she were there in that dear little village. She would be if it hadn't been for two things: the recent marriages of three spinsters from their once-accursed village, and their godmother's invitation to spend the remainder of the Season in London.

Had the world gone mad? Kempton

13

misses didn't get married (unless they wanted to run the risk of going mad or, worse, seeing their groom meet some horrible and tragic fate), and godmothers didn't just suddenly remember old promises.

Yet here they were, she and Lavinia, arriving in London to do just that: have a Season and if Lavinia was lucky (or unlucky, as it might be) find someone willing to risk life and limb to marry her.

If only Louisa could explain her unwillingness to marry to her sister. But that would mean telling Lavinia the truth Louisa had only discovered by chance. Even Papa had been deaf to her concerns, brushing off her worries that "such old business will hardly concern the tabbies of London."

So Louisa kept her silence, and hugged Hannibal's basket a little tighter, glad to have him with her. Her one-eyed, half-an-ear-missing, mangy tabby of a tom seemed to be the only one who listened to her of late.

And right on cue, Hannibal let out another terrible yowl.

Yes, well, his opinions weren't always well timed.

"It is most kind of you to come with us to London when Papa was prevented from doing so," Lavinia interjected quickly, probably hoping to stave off another complaint by Mrs. Bagley-Butterton.

"Fortune has a way of smiling on me," Mrs. Bagley-Butterton declared, her disapproving gaze fixed on Hannibal's basket. "Your father's accident was my blessing. Now I will be in Town for the arrival of my first grandchild. As I should be. These London midwives will only make a muddle of things — and I doubt they will have eggs as fresh as these," she said, nodding to the basket of provisions that took up most of the seat next to her, "to make a good healthy coddle for my son's wife after she delivers. She's a London girl." This was also said with a suspicious sniff. "Yes, yes, indeed, your father's broken leg was a most fortuitous event. If he hadn't tumbled over that stile, I might not have managed to arrive in time."

Louisa doubted very much that Mrs. Bagley-Butterton's son and daughter-in-law shared that sentiment, but she kept her opinions to herself. As much as she was loath to admit it, she'd had an equally uncharitable thought when the footmen had carried her father home the other day.

Finally! Something that would prevent them from leaving Kempton.

15

But she hadn't realized the extent of Lavinia's determination.

Not go to London? Her sister had been horrified. They were already a bit on the shelf — and to wait another year? Lady Charleton might not feel so obliged then to bring out a pair of spinsters well into their decline, Lavinia had argued.

Louisa's arguments to the contrary — that their dear papa needed them — had fallen on deaf ears. The Society for the Temperance and Improvement of Kempton would be close at hand if Sir Ambrose needed anything, Lavinia declared.

Of course they would, Louisa knew. Every single member over a certain age had been delighted to offer her assistance.

Help the poor, widowed Sir Ambrose while his daughters were in London? Why, there had been a veritable stampede of ladies, baskets in hand, all willing to give up their time to sit with the ailing (and eligible) scholar.

It seemed Louisa was the only spinster in Kempton who didn't want to get married.

And yet to explain the truth to her sister the horrible secret even she wasn't supposed to know, would mean breaking her sister's heart. So Louisa had tried another tack.

"Lavinia, you know we cannot go out in

16

society," she'd argued on the morning before they'd left. "Neither of us can dance a single step without blundering about."

"We will learn," Lavinia had said with every ounce of stubborn determination she possessed. "Never fear, there will be two gentlemen in London, or somewhere, who won't mind if we . . . if we aren't . . . perfect."

And that was where her sister had stopped. For a moment, Louisa had almost dared ask if Lavinia knew the truth — yet to ask her sister would mean having to drag that horrible, awful secret out for a full airing.

The curse that was all their own.

Though, given Mrs. Bagley-Butterton's comments to their housekeeper, it seemed their affliction was no secret in Kempton. Then again, there were no such things as secrets in a village as small as Kempton.

"In London, no one knows us and I am certain any number of ladies arrive without knowing a quadrille," Lavinia had added. "Good heavens, if Tabitha Timmons of all people can find a duke — a duke, Louisa — and Daphne Dale can marry a Seldon, and Harriet Hathaway can become a countess — our Harriet, married to an earl — well, certainly we can be afforded two under-standing gentlemen. Nothing so grand as a duke, but I think a viscount or even a baron isn't too much to ask for."

A viscount, indeed! Not for all the viscounts in England would Louisa step foot in society if it meant . . .

But it was too late now, for the carriage slowed as it rounded a corner and then came to a stop before a grand house.

"This must be Hanover Square," Lavinia announced, nearly tumbling out of the carriage in her haste to get going on their "grand adventure," as she called it. Lavinia would have suffered plague-ridden battlefields (as if three days in Mrs. Bagley-Butterton's company wasn't a close second) if only to arrive at Lady Charleton's house and be launched into society.

Hannibal, hearing the door open and having no desire to be left in the carriage, let out another ferocious yowl. Louisa eyed the basket and shuddered. Oh, he was going to be one vengeful tomcat when he was finally released. Looking up at the elegant residence before them, with its fine white stone and elegant railing, she hoped Lady Charleton had some old chair or sofa that she didn't mind being mauled.

Or a carpet that needed to be replaced. Sooner rather than later.

"I suppose this address is proper enough,"

Mrs. Bagley-Butterton declared as she glanced up at the fine house that took up the corner of the square. "They'll have room for you, and for that beast as well, if Her Ladyship doesn't send it back to Kempton with the carriage —" Her pursed lips and raised brow said all too clearly how she wanted to finish that sentence.

Or have it drowned in the Thames as it ought to be.

"Whatever do we do now?" Lavinia asked Louisa as the coachman and his assistant began unloading their trunks and settling them down on the curb before the house. The cases and boxes quickly began to block the sidewalk, and passing Londoners glared at them as they dodged through the hodge-podge of traveling cases.

"I suppose we knock," Louisa said, resolving to do just that. She marched up the steps and gave the bellpull a firm tug, reminding herself to make her introduction sound sincere no matter how much she wanted to turn around, snatch up Hannibal's basket, tow Lavinia back into the carriage, and order John Coachman to dash back to Kempton as quickly as possible.

But whatever she planned on saying — or doing — was interrupted by another yowling fit by Hannibal. The murderous complaint made it sound as if he were being skinned alive — loud enough for a poor old cart horse in the street to rise up in its traces and nearly bolt, and a nanny with her charges to bundle the children close and tug them in the opposite direction.

"Silence!" Mrs. Bagley-Butterton declared and gave the basket a swift kick.

She watched in horror as Hannibal's prison overturned and its contents spilled out. "No!" Louisa cried out.

Hannibal, meet London. London, meet Hannibal.

Needless to say, Hannibal was not impressed with his unfamiliar surroundings and let out yet another deafening howl of complaint.

Now, up and down the street, doors were opening and curtains parting, not that Louisa had much time to notice. She knew she had to get ahold of her unruly cat before he bolted in a mad dash.

She raced down the steps, but it was too late, Hannibal had seen the light of day and wasn't about to surrender his freedom. Not easily. Not anytime soon.

He went dashing out into the street — through the legs of a horse pulling a fancy curricle. The owner cursed and most likely would have added an ungentlemanly hand

gesture if he wasn't at the moment struggling to control his high-strung horse.

Louisa would have followed into the busy
street, but thankfully at that point, Hannibal reversed course and ran toward the
house — right past her and up the steps.

Except it was the wrong house.

And at the very worst moment, the door
opened and Hannibal streaked past an
imperious-looking butler.

"Oh, no," Louisa gasped as she made an
equally mad dash to follow her cat.

"Louisa Tempest! Don't let him ruin
everything," Lavinia cried after her.

*Better Hannibal returns us to Kempton in
disgrace than the world discovers the horrible,
awful truth . . .*

At the top of the steps, she collided with
an elderly butler, only pausing for a second
to offer a rushed "I am so sorry."

It wasn't that Louisa was apologizing for
her uninvited arrival into the house, but
rather for what was about to happen.

She paused in the foyer to get her bearings and all too quickly had them, for up
the stairs there was almost immediately a
very loud crash. Followed by a triumphant
yowl of conquest.

True to his name, Hannibal was ready to
pillage.

Crash!

Pierson Stratton, Viscount Wakefield opened one eye and shuddered.

If the infernal racket echoing through his house was any indication, he had to assume that Napoleon had crossed the channel and Mayfair was under siege.

That, or his French chef was skinning a cat for breakfast.

Which would no doubt be served burnt or half done like everything else the fellow "cooked."

Outside his darkened room there was another cacophony ringing through the halls. *Crash! Yowl!*

Pierson sat halfway up and cringed. His head pounded furiously in protest at this early awakening, and as the noise came closer — boots coming up the stairs, another yowl and the cry of a voice he didn't recognize.

"Hannibal! You get back here, you bad cat."

Good Lord! Who was in his house? Since none of his family dared cross his threshold, and Tiploft knew better than to let anyone enter, it had to be thieves or the French.

Either way, it would be the last time

whoever it was committed such folly.

Struggling out of bed, he ignored the pain in his head, winced at the familiar ache in his wounded leg, and threw his wrapper over his shoulders, giving the tie a half hitch as yet another piercing howl ripped through the halls.

This was exactly why he kept his household so small.

So he could live in peace.

Catching up his walking stick and plucking his pistol from the drawer of his nightstand, he crossed his bedchamber as quickly as he dared, then yanked open the door, pistol held before him.

In his blurry-eyed state, he saw the rush of someone coming down the hall. "No further," he ordered. "Not one step further or it shall be your last."

It was then that Pierson truly opened his eyes.

Thankfully before he fired.

For there before him was a doe-eyed minx, her beribboned bonnet askew and a tumbling mess of brown hair falling out from beneath it.

No, not brown. More like mahogany. If one was inclined to look a bit closer.

Which, bleary-eyed as he was, Pierson did. Look, that is.

23

Yes, definitely mahogany.

And definitely a miss as his gaze fell lower over a curved shape that could only be female.

In his house, no less.

The viscount yanked his gaze away from the chit. "Tiploft! What is the meaning of this?"

His butler, who had hurried up from behind the lady, had his horrified gaze fixed down at the viscount's feet and Pierson glanced down as well.

Then he knew without a doubt he was still drunk. What the devil sort of vermin was this?

The mangy ball of fur let out a sort of meow, except it was more guttural, like a *rrooowww,* as if the creature was prone to indulging in too many cigars and cheap brandy.

Something Pierson knew a bit about. However, not the cheap brandy part. He couldn't abide the stuff. And thankfully he was wealthy enough that he could keep a decent cellar.

Rr-ooowww, the animal repeated, eyeing the viscount as if he were measuring him — one beast to another.

Pierson wasn't even sure the creature was a cat — for it was missing one eye, most of its tail and a good portion of one of its ears.

It rather looked like his former batman — Russell — a boxer of some note, and a fellow known for his temper and rash judgment. He and Pierson had gotten along famously.

Until he, like so many others, had fallen on the retreat to Corunna.

Poor demmed bastard. Russell had gone down cursing and died in the agony of an infection.

The viscount shut his eyes against the memory and wished for his brandy bottle — the one that kept such instances at bay.

But there was no chance of that, not with what felt like half of London in his house.

In. His. House.

That was enough to coax his eyes open. "What the devil," he muttered as the creature, the one as yet to be determined if it was a cat, began to wind around his legs, its tattered coat brushing against him.

Then the animal had the audacity to roll around in front of him as if it was his — the viscount's — duty to pet him.

"You had best scratch him. Quickly," the lady advised, nodding down at the beast that looked capable of taking a few fingers and a good part of the rest of his hand.

"I never," he told the beast.

Not that it listened, for it proceeded to wind its way beneath Pierson's wrapper, rubbing against his legs, and then popping out again, only to start coughing.

"Oh, no," gasped the young lady.

And then he saw why.

The cat proceeded to cast up its accounts right in front of the viscount's bare toes.

"I warned you," the lady said, sounding hardly sorry for the mess on the floor.

What the devil? She'd warned him? Of all the impudence.

Besides, he'd felt a bit queasy when he'd gotten up, and this display before him didn't improve matters. Good heavens — who knew a cat could hold so much inside.

"That's most likely the worst of it," she was saying, with a practical resignation as if invading strangers' homes and allowing her cat to . . .

Oh, hell, Pierson couldn't — wouldn't — look down again.

Nor was she waiting for him. She lunged at the last moment to catch her pet, but the wily feline had anticipated her move and dodged her, going under the hem of Pierson's wrapper.

Not that this deterred the miss. She nearly collided with Pierson, reached under the robe and gathered the unholy creature into her arms, all the time offering a rambling explanation. "He's been locked up in a horrid basket the entire trip from Kempton, and he's overwrought. If you would just get me a . . ."

She paused there for a second, right in front of him and his barely closed wrapper. Then there was a sharp intake of breath. After another moment, she straightened, cat in her arms and sporting a bright pink hue on her cheeks.

Apparently he should have done more than tie his robe shut with a half hitch.

But if he thought an unsightly display would send her fleeing from his presence in a maidenly display of embarrassment, he was entirely wrong.

This miss with her pretty pink cheeks and luscious mahogany hair — which led to yet another revelation — how long had it been since he'd been with a woman? — wasn't done with him yet.

"As I was saying, I am most sorry about Hannibal. It's just that he's rather unpredictable around new people."

This was not an explanation. Or an apology. The gel was actually chiding him.

"And houses, it seems," Tiploft muttered, glancing over his shoulder at the remains of a vase.

"My sincerest apologies about that, and the other one as well," she said to Tiploft, as if it was his butler's vase to begin with. "And that other thing —"

"The statuary from Italy, miss," Tiploft informed her.

"Truly? That was Italian? I do hope it wasn't all that dear. But you should know that the statue wasn't Hannibal's fault, more mine." She bit her bottom lip and frowned at her cat. "I went to catch him and . . ." She looked from Tiploft to Pierson, and then hastily swung her gaze back to his butler. "I suppose the particulars don't really matter at this point." She bit her lips together and glanced back over her shoulder at the path of destruction she'd brought to his house.

Pierson gaped. "Where the devil did you come from?"

She turned toward him and blinked, as if she had quite forgotten he was there. "Kempton." There was an unmistakable certainty to her statement that implied the answer should be obvious.

Even to him.

"Should I know that?" he asked his butler. For he wasn't all too sure that he wasn't still drunk and she was a figment conjured by the Madeira.

Mahogany-haired misses, indeed! This was what came of drinking from the back of the cellar.

His butler coughed slightly. "I don't believe it is relevant, my lord."

"It is relevant if you are from there," she replied tartly, shifting her cat from one side to another.

Safely ensconced in his mistress's embrace, the creature didn't seem quite as hellish.

No, if Pierson were being honest, he thought the demmed creature appeared quite smug about his superior position up against her breast.

Oh, he might still be half-seas over, but he wasn't so bosky that he couldn't discern a feminine shape that begged to be explored — though she was obviously doing her best to hide it beneath the plain gown she wore. She might even be a proper bit, if it weren't for the path of ruined crockery in her wake.

That spoke of an impulsive and passionate nature. A dangerous mix in a pretty miss that begged to be unleashed in a different way. Say, in a man's bed.

Rrooooww, the cat hissed in warning, as if sensing the viscount's line of thought.

One tom to another.

"Hannibal means no harm," she said, putting her hand over the cat's face. She stole a glance at Pierson, her gaze dipping down toward the opening in his robe, and again her cheeks flushed deeply and her gaze fled in any direction but his.

It was an uncomfortable moment, and Pierson realized that if he was a decent sort, he really ought to see to adjusting his robe.

But then again, she'd invaded *his* house. If she didn't like the view . . .

Tiploft cleared his throat and tossed a significant glance at the vase.

Her teeth bit at her lower lip as she surveyed the damage as well. "Yes, oh, dear . . . I suppose I could see to it that your vase is repaired . . . *my lord.*"

She made that last bit sound like she doubted his place in *Debrett's.*

Then again, she was in good company. Most of London looked at him askance.

But for some reason, from her, from this pushy, unlikely intruder, it irritated him that she found him unworthy.

He was, but that wasn't the point.

Pierson wrenched his gaze away from her tantalizing mane of hair, and that embarrassed flush on her cheeks — ignoring the hot flush of pride at having put it there — and looked over at the multitude of pieces

30

that had once been his mother's favorite vase.

And this chit thought to see it fixed? Unlikely. The thing was good and smashed.

Rather like his life. Conquered not by Hannibal or trampled by one of his legendary elephants, but torn to pieces by the French bullet that had shattered his leg, by the lives lost — ones he had watched in despair be picked away by French snipers — on the long road to Corunna.

"If you have some glue —" she was saying.

Pierson had heard enough. There was no fixing that demmed vase, just as there was no way to fix his life. "Out," he told her, forgetting he still held his pistol and waving it toward the stairs.

"Well, I never!" she said, both affronted, and worse, not moving. "I was only trying to be neighborly. If you haven't any glue, I can return once I am settled and see to putting things to rights —"

Pierson couldn't have heard her correctly. *Come back?* God only knew what sort of things she'd uncork, what sort of plague and pestilence she'd bring — or worst of all, that unholy cat of hers.

Right then and there, he should have known that the better part of valor would be to retreat back into his bedchamber and leave this entire mess, well, *all* of the messes, in Tiploft's capable hands. However, something about her left the viscount a bit off-kilter.

And all too angry.

This chit with her mahogany tresses and horrified glances reminded him that the rest of his days would be spent just as he had since he'd returned from Spain.

Alone. Bitter. And hiding away in a bottle. As broken as the vase on the floor. As foul a mess as whatever it was her cat had coughed up.

Nor was it one that could be "fixed," as she so blithely offered, with a pot of glue and a sunny disposition — which he feared she might possess.

No, this miss held up a mirror he didn't want to gaze into. One that terrified him more than the nightmares that plagued his sleep.

"GET OUT OF MY HOUSE," he bellowed, a sudden rush of temper boiling over. "Get out now," he told her, pointing again toward the stairs with his pistol.

Her dark blue eyes widened like a pair of saucers, and she whirled about and fled. Until, that is, she got to the head of the stairs and took one last glance in his direction.

It would have been kinder if she hadn't.

For the big, round tears in her eyes held not fear, but pity.

And in Pierson's opinion, a bullet would have been kinder.

CHAPTER 2

Louisa dashed out of the man's house, tears threatening to spill from her eyes. "Whatever am I crying for?" she asked Hannibal.

The cat blinked as if he hadn't the vaguest notion why they were in such a rush to leave.

"How can anyone be so horrible?" she whispered into Hannibal's one whole ear.

After all, she'd only offered to help, as any young lady from Kempton would, and the wretched man had all but threatened her.

Get out!

No one had ever shouted at her like that. Not even Papa when she'd accidentally tossed his favorite shirt in the charity box.

Blindly, she went down the steps and hurried toward her original destination, but only managed to bump into a gentleman who was hurrying along the sidewalk.

"Have a care!" he huffed.

"So sorry," she offered, pulling Hannibal closer.

Good heavens, she'd barely set foot in London and already she'd made a mess of things. And here she'd been quite convinced it was Lavinia who would make a muddle of their debut. They weren't twins for nothing. Why, in Kempton, Louisa was considered graceful in comparison to her sister.

Which wasn't saying much for either of them.

Dear heavens, what disasters would they find themselves in when she and Lavinia entered society? With two broken vases and a smashed piece of statuary to her credit, and having only just arrived, Louisa wanted to despair, yet her practical side rallied and gave her a moment of pause.

In her defense, she'd never met a man wearing only a robe.

And nothing else . . .

Oh, never mind that she'd tumbled into those antiquities *before* she'd met *him.*

Having met the man, she supposed she should just be thankful she and Hannibal had gotten out alive.

And unscathed. Well, for the most part.

Much to her chagrin, she shivered as she thought about him, standing there with his pistol waving about, roaring like some wild

beast. It wasn't fear that had her quaking —
well, a fear of sorts. She felt . . . well, she
felt so . . . undone by the entire encounter.

However could a man be so utterly unkempt, so undressed, yet be so utterly
fascinating at the same time?

Perhaps it was the way he'd stared at her.
He'd looked her over and most likely found
her wanting, but there had been a moment
when he'd looked at her with something
akin to hunger, or so she thought . . . like
he'd wanted to devour her.

Oh, heavens, she didn't want to consider
such a ridiculous notion, because when she
did, she went right back to a vision of his
bare legs.

Naked legs, indeed! A pair of muscled
limbs covered in crisp dark hair. Whyever
would that make her heart tremble so
oddly? Especially when his manners had
quite the opposite effect.

But still, she took another glance at the
house and wondered what it would be like
if he weren't so beastly.

Oh, bother! Whatever was wrong with her?
Surely the last ten minutes had proven that
she was entirely unfit for London.

But whatever was she to do now? Standing as she was before Lady Charleton's
house, there was nothing left to do but

continue forth.

Especially since John Coachman had already abandoned them.

She marched up the steps and into the foyer, where their bags and trunks had been deposited. She spied Hannibal's basket and before he could protest, whisked him inside and tied it shut.

"Before you cause more mischief," she scolded. "Besides, we want to make a good impression."

For as long as we can manage, she mused. A hope that didn't take long to come to fruition as a voice bellowed from a room at the end of the foyer.

"Provide a Season for a chit I've never met? Over my dead body!"

Louisa moved toward the door and peered inside. When she spied Lavinia near the entrance, she slipped inside and went to her sister's side. "What is this?"

"Ssshh," Lavinia warned, her finger to her lips, then taking another look at her sister, quickly went to work to set her to rights, straightening her bonnet and tucking the ringlets that had fallen free back up into their rightful place. After one last critical glance, Lavinia turned back to the tableau before them.

Louisa assumed the man behind the huge

desk must be Lord Charleton — his iron gray hair, commanding presence and domineering manners certainly suggested he was a nobleman. Besides, the younger man to his right was too plainly dressed and had the resigned air of a secretary about him.

She assumed this fellow must be Mr. Haley, the man who had written Papa with Lady Charleton's instructions.

Still, Louisa's gaze remained fixed on their host's choleric expression. Whyever was Lord Charleton in such a pet over their arrival? Surely he must have known.

"Underhanded, Mr. Haley. That is what I call this. I should have you removed," Lord Charleton ranted, pointing at the door.

Apparently not.

"As I tried to explain, my lord, her ladyship's instructions were quite specific —" the secretary was saying.

It was then that the baron noticed Louisa's arrival and his face went from choleric to nearly explosive. "What the devil! There's two of them? They're multiplying like rabbits before my eyes. I won't have this, Mr. Haley. I won't, do you hear me?"

"Good heavens," she muttered as Lord Charleton went back to lambasting poor Mr. Haley, "is every man in London so ill-tempered?"

"Every?" Lavinia whispered back. "What do you mean?"

Louisa shook her head and replied, "I'll explain later." Not that she wanted to, for it would mean telling her sister about her encounter with Lord Charleton's neighbor.

And the vase. Oh, and the statue. And the gift Hannibal had managed to cough up. And what a horrid beast he was. His Lordship. Not Hannibal.

Quite frankly, when he'd been yelling so and waving that pistol about, she'd thought she was going to cast up her accounts.

But then it occurred to her that perhaps the man next door wouldn't be so wretched if he wasn't so unkempt. However could a man be in a decent humor if he was to be found prowling about in the middle of the afternoon in his altogether, as if he'd just gotten up?

At least she suspected as much considering his feet and calves and . . . oh, good heavens . . . *higher* had been bare beneath that blue silk wrapper.

She drew in an unsteady breath. Certainly she'd seen the masculine form before — Lady Essex kept an Italian statue of Mars in her second drawing room that Mrs. Bagley-Butterton liked to call indecent and improper.

A Roman god in marble was one thing, but seeing the same distinct lines in the flesh was quite another.

Louisa felt the now-familiar rush of pink to her cheeks, for a few inches higher and she might have glimpsed . . .

She looked down at the floor. No, a lady didn't think of what was higher beneath a man's robe. She just didn't. Not even if she might have dared a glance at the aforementioned Mars when Mrs. Bagley-Butterton wasn't looking.

Still, she couldn't help wondering if Lord Charleton's well-formed neighbor was *that* scandalous.

Up there, that is.

Not that any lady was likely to discover such information. What with that temper of his and his ill-kempt house. Whatever was wrong with the man — besides the cane that he'd leaned on so heavily — that he chose to live thusly?

Perhaps he wasn't getting regular meals, she mused. The man had looked a bit drawn. Lady Essex always said that the only way to keep a man in line was to keep the devil well fed and properly tended to.

Well, if the dusty house, what with all the Holland covers and dirty corners, let alone his ragged appearance, was any indication, he wasn't being seen to.

Not properly, that is. Perhaps he just needed . . .

In a rush, Louisa saw the man, shaved and trimmed and properly brushed, wearing a fine wool suit and polished boots — yet she didn't think he would look proper even then.

He was far too dark — inky black hair and swarthy looks that left him resembling a pirate of old, or some Spanish grandee. And her vision of him shifted, so he was striding down a wooded path, in a white shirt and breeches, carrying a bouquet of wildflowers and smiling, a knowing glint sparking in his eye the moment he spied her — waiting for him.

And that look, that smoldering glance, was meant just for her.

Louisa closed her eyes and chided herself.

She'd come to Town to help Lavinia find a husband and then she was returning as quickly as possible to Kempton.

Where she belonged.

And it seemed they might be going sooner than expected.

"This is blackmail," Lord Charleton declared, slamming his fist down atop his desk. "Nothing less."

"It is nothing of the sort," came the firm

and commanding reply from the doorway. Into the room strolled an elegantly dressed woman with a steady, quiet beauty about her. She came to a stop before Mr. Haley and Lord Charleton, but not before she spared a curious smile at the sisters.

Lord Charleton, for his part, glared at the new arrival, but rose as good manners dictated. Still, his speech was anything but welcoming. "What are you doing here?"

"I was summoned," the lady replied, nodding in greeting to Mr. Haley.

"You and the rest of England," he blustered.

Louisa leaned over. "Is that Lady Charleton?"

This brought a mist of tears to Lavinia's eyes, and right then, Louisa realized her sister had been crying.

"No," she replied. "Oh, Louisa, Lady Charleton is dead."

"Dead?" she gasped. "I don't understand. How can this be?" She glanced around the room, where there was no crepe, no black. No signs of mourning.

It was Mr. Haley who answered her questions, though it was more in response to Lord Charleton. "My lord, when Her Ladyship became ill, she was quite resolved to see all her unfinished obligations completed."

Three pairs of eyes turned and stared at Louisa and her sister and they both shrank back a bit to be the subject of all this vitriol. But after a moment, Louisa remembered one of Lady Essex's most often made admonitions.

Stand up straight, girls.

So she did, rising to her best posture and meeting the examination with a noble expression of cool nonchalance. She wanted to appear every bit the lady, and certainly no one's obligation. After all, she and Lavinia were the daughters of Sir Ambrose Tempest — hardly paupers or beggars. This earned her an approving smile from the unknown lady.

But what that was worth was yet to be seen.

"Lady Charleton was most conscientious of her promise to Lady Tempest to see that her daughters were brought out in society," Mr. Haley continued.

"And such an obligation ends when one is no longer around to see it completed," Lord Charleton replied, wagging his finger at his secretary.

Mr. Haley was apparently made of sterner stuff. "Not in Lady Charleton's estimation, my lord."

"Nor in mine," the lady offered, and, perhaps having a better measure of the situation, settled into a chair before the desk, though none had been offered. She looked over her shoulder and nodded for the sisters to do the same.

After a moment, Lord Charleton sat as well, frowning, but apparently more comfortable atop his throne.

Mr. Haley sighed, probably with some relief to have the tension in the air deflate, even if by only a tiny measure. "Lady Charleton," he said, continuing his story, "true to her generous nature, asked for me to send for the young ladies when they reached a proper age —"

"Proper?" Lord Charleton blustered, eyeing the sisters. "Why, that pair is too long in the tooth to be of a proper age. How old are you, gels?"

Louisa wavered for a moment. They were too old, but it was hardly their fault. The curse on their village had only just been broken — but she doubted this was the time or the place to bring up *that* bit of history.

Instead, she did as Lady Essex had always instructed and held her ground. "Four and twenty, my lord."

Beside her, Lavinia flinched.

Perhaps she should have been a little less forthcoming.

"Egads, Haley, you've missed the mark by four years," Charleton said with a snort that sounded a bit victorious. "Waste of time and money to bring them out."

Lavinia turned to her and gave her a look that said all too clearly, *Now you've done it.*

But not quite.

"Too old?" The lady turned in her chair and examined the girls, smiling encouragement at them. Her eyes sparkled a bit and they crinkled at the corners as she turned to face Lord Charleton. "Don't be such an ogre, Charleton. You know very well indeed that I was two years older than these sweet-faced dears when I married Aveley."

Charleton snorted. "Harrumph! You didn't need to be brought out when you came to London. Had half the town mad for you before you stepped out of your carriage."

Louisa watched as the lady's expression flickered for a moment; something bittersweet and lost seemed to flit across her waning smile.

"Yes, be that as it may," the lady said, having recovered from whatever bit of nostalgia that had plucked at her armor, "I am still unsure as to what my role is in all of this.

Mr. Haley, why have you summoned me?"

"Oh, yes, my lady. I apologize," the man said, as if snapped out of a trance. "Her Ladyship left each of you a letter." He patted his jacket and then reached inside and fished out a beribboned packet that he proceeded to untie and then hand out — one for each of them.

Notably, Lord Charleton set his letter down on his desk and then, as an added measure, pushed it to one side.

The lady, most likely Lady Aveley, for she had the air of rank about her, proceeded to open hers, defying His Lordship. She glanced over her shoulder at Louisa and Lavinia and nodded for them to do the same.

Well, it wasn't as if Lord Charleton could get any more annoyed with them, she decided, so Louisa did as she was bid and slid her fingernail beneath the wax seal.

My dear Louisa,

I am most saddened that I will not be the one to see you out into society. I had such grand plans for you and your sister. Alas, my plans have had to change. You have by now been introduced to Lady Aveley, who is as dear to me as your mother once was, and will do nicely in my stead. She found a perfectly wonderful marquess for her own daughter.

I suspect you are here at Lavinia's behest, and that you are most reluctant to marry, given that rather old-fashioned curse that still holds Kempton in its thrall. But a curse only has power if you believe in it. Trust me, you shall not go mad if you marry — though there are days when any man, even a good one, will tempt a lady to reach for a fire poker.

Find a man who loves you as deeply as Charleton loved me. As much as your father loved your mother, despite all her faults.

I know my dearest George is probably being quite a bear and very ill-tempered about your arrival, but trust me in this, he is a man of good heart. Find a similar gentleman and you will never regret a single day of marriage.

All my fondest wishes to you,
Isobel Rowland, Lady Charleton

P.S. Do you play chess? I thought I recalled from one of your father's letters that you are a skilled player. If Charleton continues to be horrid, set out the chessboard in the library. Just set it out, the rest will follow.

47

She glanced up and found Lady Aveley still reading her letter, a pensive expression settled on her brow.

When she looked at her sister, Lavinia appeared horrified by the contents of her letter, for when she finished reading it she promptly stuffed it into her reticule.

Good heavens, whatever could Lady Charleton have written her?

"My lord," Mr. Haley was saying, "if you would but read your letter —"

"I will not," Lord Charleton huffed, rising from his seat, the letter still unopened on his desk. He looked over at Lady Aveley. "What shenanigans has she enlisted you into?"

Lady Aveley, who didn't look as if she'd ever shenaniganed in her life, folded her letter carefully and then glanced up. "She simply asked me to stand in her stead and sponsor the girls for their Season."

He gave a short, curt nod. "Then do what you will. You and Haley. I will have nothing to do with any of this." He waved his hand toward Louisa and Lavinia. "Best take them with you."

"Take them where, Charleton?" she asked.

"To your house. Can't have them here."

The lady rose from her chair and faced

the baron. "I have no house to take them to."

"Whatever do you mean? You have a perfectly good house on Berkeley Square. Plenty of room."

"I have no such thing. The house to which you refer belongs to my son, the current Lord Aveley."

"Your son, indeed. Sounds like an ungrateful pup if he can't manage to find a spare room for his own mother and a pair of chits. You won't take up any room at all. Take yourself off to his place and leave me be." With that, Charleton began to leave the room as if this was the end of it.

"I cannot and I will not," Lady Aveley told Charleton in no uncertain terms.

The lady's firm announcement stopped the baron at the door. Ever so slowly, he turned around.

"My son is newly married," she continued. "I promised him when he wed I would not impose upon him and his new bride. And I will note, this is all Isobel's doing, not mine."

As the two glared at each other, as if waiting for the other to budge, Mr. Haley waded in, clearing his throat and saying, "I have seen to having the entire west wing of the house readied for the ladies, my lord."

Everyone in the room turned and gaped at the poor secretary. It was one thing for Lady Aveley to poke at Charleton like a bear at the circus, but quite another for Haley — whose very livelihood depended on his employer's goodwill.

"Without my permission?" Lord Charleton's iron brows rose to lofty points.

Mr. Haley straightened, following Lady Aveley's example. "With, my lord."

"With?" the baron blustered. "When the devil did I agree to such an overreaching obligation?"

"In late November," Mr. Haley said. "I mentioned to you that I had discovered an outstanding debt of Lady Charleton's —"

Louisa watched the baron's eyes narrow as he plucked at his memories for a hint of this fateful conversation. When his expression furrowed, she guessed he recalled the exchange and was not overly pleased.

"You might have been a bit more forthcoming —"

"I attempted to be," Mr. Haley replied, with a firm recollection to back up his claim. "But you were quite explicit in your instructions. You told me to handle whatever it was as I saw fit. As Her Ladyship desired. So I have."

Checkmate.

Not that Lord Charleton was one to concede easily. "Then you can continue to do so, Mr. Haley. Handle it, that is. Just leave me be." Then he turned and stormed out into the foyer, and moments later the front door banged shut.

Mr. Haley turned to Lady Aveley, mouth pursed in a worried line. Now that Lord Charleton had washed his hands of the matter, the poor secretary looked a bit adrift. "Your Ladyship, I do hope —"

"Never fear, Mr. Haley, Lady Charleton's letter was quite eloquent. I can hardly turn down Isobel's last request any more than I could have done when she was alive."

"Where would you suggest we begin, my lady?" he asked.

The pair of them turned toward Louisa and Lavinia and examined the girls with critical gazes.

"Shopping," Lady Aveley declared. "We shall start tomorrow, first thing."

"Most excellent," Mr. Haley agreed. "Indeed, that was the second item on Her Ladyship's list."

Louisa had to wonder, as they were hustled up the stairs toward their rooms, what else was on their wily godmother's list?

Pierson tried returning to bed but found

51

himself unable to get back to the dreamless void that had become his refuge.

Certainly he preferred the darkness to the infernal sunshine that was even now peeking through his curtains, a persistent nudge that there was an entire world beyond.

A world he was determined to ignore.

But today it seemed impossible to escape, so after an hour or so of tossing and turning, he rose again, and pulled the bell for Tiploft.

"My lord?" Tiploft asked quietly as he tentatively entered the room. "Are you unwell?"

"I'm unsure," he replied. "I had the most alarming nightmare."

"Indeed," Tiploft replied, moving inside and getting to the business of setting everything to rights.

Tiploft wasn't much for elaboration or great shows of emotion.

In other words, he was the perfect butler.

"Indeed. There was a cat and miss in my house." Pierson paused and looked up from where he stood before his closet. "At least I believe it was a cat." He had no doubts the other creature had been a miss. Her enticing mahogany locks and the notion of what they'd look like unbound had been what had kept him awake.

Tiploft paused in the middle of retrieving a shirt from the floor. "So you do remember, my lord. I had rather hoped —"

Yes, his butler would hope as much. "— that in my usual state I wouldn't have any recollection —"

"One can hope, my lord."

Pierson glanced again over his shoulder. Was that Tiploft's idea of a joke? "Yes, well. She was fetching, wasn't she? I didn't dream that much, did I?"

"Quite fetching," the older man agreed.

A bit too readily.

"Oh, don't get any ideas, Tiploft," Pierson told him. "If you think letting pretty little minxes into my house is going to bring me 'round — like my mother and sisters are always chiding me to do — I won't have it."

"Of course, my lord. It was hardly the conspiracy that you suspect; rather her cat was frightened and ran into the house. Miss Tempest merely followed it."

"Yes, of course. The cat. How could I have forgotten that creature? Ugliest thing I have ever seen. Are you certain it was a cat?"

"No, my lord."

Pierson nodded. "Wherever did she come from?"

"The cat, my lord?"

He glanced over at his butler again. Perhaps it was Tiploft who was going mad. Making not one, but two jests in a single day.

This was what happened when one arose too early. One discovered one's butler wasn't quite himself before four in the afternoon.

"The chit, Tiploft," he replied. "The fetching one. Miss —"

"Tempest, my lord. Miss Tempest."

Well, the name fit. She'd arrived like a whirlwind. Her and her demmed cat of doubtful origins. *La tormenta,* as the Spanish said.

"Yes, yes, Miss Tempest. Where the devil did she come from?" He tried asking this with an air of nonchalance. For he didn't care in the least where the gel came from, just so long as she didn't come back.

"Her mother, I would surmise."

A third jest? Pierson needed to check on the brandy supplies. And here he'd always thought it was that high-handed French fellow his sister had insisted he hire to cook for him who was siphoning off a good portion of his liquor cabinet.

"Very amusing, Tiploft. And after her mother, where do you suppose she might have ventured from?"

"I believe she went next door, my lord. To

54

your uncle's residence."

"Charleton's?" Pierson managed. Now he was going to check the brandy supply. And the whisky. "No, no. You must have it wrong," he insisted, going to the window and parting the curtains. His gaze swept up from his uncle's neatly kept gardens to an upper window of Charleton's house, and to his astonishment, he spied a young lady framed there — and as if by some unknown magic, she turned at that moment and looked over in his direction.

"If you say so, my lord," Tiploft was saying. "Is that all?"

Dropping the curtain, Pierson turned around and faced his butler. Now he wasn't so sure of anything. What the devil was his uncle doing with some doe-eyed chit?

Tiploft looked at him with a blank expression, but the viscount wasn't fooled. The man was being deliberately vague, and Pierson knew why. His cagey old servant hoped his master would drop everything and go over to call on Lord Charleton — if only to see what the devil was going on.

And perhaps even run into that fetching little bit of muslin. What with her wide eyes and tumbled mahogany hair.

Oh, hell. He should never have used the word *fetching*. Not in front of Tiploft. He'd gotten the man's hopes up.

"My lord?" the butler prompted. "Is there anything else?"

"Breakfast, if you can muster it. And ask that fellow —"

"Monsieur Begnoche," Tiploft supplied, his nose pinching at the mention of the cook. He hadn't approved of the man since he had been foisted upon them by the viscount's sister, Lady Gamston.

A French cook is the only proper way to see a kitchen managed, Margaret claimed as she'd deposited the fellow in their foyer, after old Mrs. Withers had quit in a huff.

"Yes, yes, Begnoche. Is it possible for that man to cook my eggs so they aren't burnt? That might be the French way of doing things, but I prefer mine done with an English turn."

"I shall pass those instructions along, my lord." Tiploft turned to leave, but paused at the door and Pierson had the sense that the man had more to say.

And the viscount was just as certain he didn't want to hear it, so he rushed to add, "And Tiploft —"

"Yes, my lord?"

"No more misses. And definitely no more cats. Or beasts. Or whatever that devil's spawn might be."

Tiploft nodded. "As you wish, my lord."

As he'd suspected, that wasn't at all what Tiploft had hoped to hear.

For the viscount's eggs arrived burnt *and* runny.

"Shopping! And in London," Lavinia declared as she fell backward onto the narrow bed. "I will not be able to sleep a wink tonight. New gloves, new gowns, new bonnets, new —"

Louisa stopped listening for she had paused at the window and realized that this room of theirs afforded her a perfect view of the house next door. Turning her back to the window, she set Hannibal's basket down and opened it up. The cat stalked out, all haughty disdain, as if he hadn't caused a terrible ruckus earlier, nor was he the least bit ruffled at finding himself in yet another strange room.

He leaped up onto the window ledge and looked at the house and garden across the wall and then glanced over his shoulder at Louisa, as if to say, *Isn't that where* he *lives?*

"Yes, unfortunately," she muttered without thinking.

"Unfortunately?" Lavinia repeated, having stopped somewhere between new shifts and new stockings. "Louisa, whatever has come over you? Did you not hear Lady Aveley? We are going *shopping*."

That should have cheered any young lady immensely, but without thinking Louisa's gaze drifted toward the window. Yes, she would be quite pleased with the notion of going shopping if she hadn't become convinced that all the men of London were quite dreadful.

Starting with *him*.

Nor had Lady Charleton's words of encouragement helped matters . . . *A curse only has power if you believe in it.*

Unfortunately, Louisa did believe.

But it wasn't the Kempton variety of blights that had her at sixes and sevens, but a nagging disquiet that she shared more with her mother than brown hair and blue eyes. And such a knowledge was of little concern when one lived in Kempton and there was no hope of testing that belief.

Safe and sound in her little village, she would never be faced with a man who might have the countenance or charm to tempt her, to stir within her any evidence that she might carry the same wanton, disastrous inclinations.

At least she hadn't any indication until she'd encountered *him*.

Him. That pirate in his silken robe. He'd

58

stood there like some Ottoman sultan, trying to decide whether to have her tossed in his harem or fed to the wolves.

How was it a man could look at a lady with such disdain and still leave her so . . . so . . . Oh, bother, she didn't know what she was.

But she did, and Louisa hugged her arms to her chest to stop the tremulous hammering inside.

Good gracious heavens, if one ill-mannered beast of a fellow could prompt her heart to patter at such an alarming rate, what would one who was properly done up — say, a rake of the first order — do to her?

She didn't want to know. She had to stand firm in her conviction not to allow herself to fall prey to love's dangerous folly.

Meanwhile, Lavinia was nattering on about tomorrow's promised adventure. ". . . we'll finally be able to get proper gowns," she was saying. "Fashionable, but respectable."

That word stopped Louisa. *Respectable.*

Even Hannibal's ears twitched at the word.

Oh, not this again! Lavinia avowed that if they behaved in a respectable fashion, models of propriety, no one would notice . . . well, notice . . . the broken antiquities. And crockery. Or vases.

Louisa sighed. Her sister went so far as to keep a list of respectable things. Proper outings. The right social events. Improving books.

Louisa knew only too well that her sister wouldn't find Hannibal's near destruction of the man's house or her own tumble into antiquities all that respectable.

Then again, Hannibal would never make it on to Lavinia's list.

Nor, Louisa suspected, would the man next door. Not a man who'd come bolting out of his bed stark . . . Oh, dear, she couldn't say the word.

Not without her imagination getting the better of her.

Naked.

Louisa closed her eyes. Yes, she was quite certain meeting one's neighbor in his altogether did not fit on Lavinia's list of respectable things.

No, Lord Charleton's neighbor was certainly not respectable. Or proper.

Respectable. Proper. Louisa glanced up. That was it. "Lavinia, I don't think any of this is a good idea. We should go home at once."

"Go home?" Her sister sat up and gaped at her. "Before we've gone shopping?" In

Lavinia's estimation, anything that involved new gowns couldn't be anything but decidedly proper.

"How can it be respectable to stay here when Lady Charleton has gone to her reward? Shouldn't we be mourning her? It is hardly proper to come to London and make merry when our godmother has . . . has . . . gone to her reward."

Since Lavinia strived with all her being to appear the epitome of proper, Louisa thought this argument would be foolproof.

But she didn't know her sister as well as she thought.

Or at least how far Lavinia would stretch her own rigid standards to have a Season. "Didn't you hear Mr. Haley?" she countered. "We are not to be blamed for not knowing about Lady Charleton's death. The baron refused to have notices published because he was so bereft with grief. The poor, dear man."

The same poor, dear man, Louisa would point out, who wanted them out of his house.

"However could you think of refusing Lady Charleton's dying wish that we have our Season. Her *dying* wish, Louisa."

As if *that* made a difference.

"How can we think of ourselves," Louisa

61

asked her, "when we should be wearing black?"

"She's been gone for over a year. And you heard Mr. Haley, even Lord Charleton refused to wear black for her — he couldn't face her loss. If he loved her so much how respectful would we be if we scorned her bequest?" Then, as if she sensed her impending victory, Lavinia hammered her arguments home. "I daresay even Lady Essex would approve of us staying. Especially if it meant we might be of some assistance to Lord Charleton."

Louisa glanced up, recalling Lady Charleton's words.

If Charleton continues to be horrid, set out the chessboard in the library. Just set it out, the rest will follow.

Which left her wondering what Lady Charleton had written Lavinia. But before she formed the words to ask, her gaze strayed out the window to the other house, and in a blink, one of the curtains fell back into place. As if he'd been looking over here and thinking of her.

Any thought of Lavinia's letter was forgotten as Louisa quickly turned her back to the window.

Oh, goodness gracious, what a preposterous notion, she chided herself. If that man was looking out his window, he was most likely surveying his yard to consider which corner might be best to bury her or Hannibal in.

Which was precisely why the situation over the garden wall was none of her business. The last thing she wanted to do was tumble into another encounter with *him.*

Or any man.

Meanwhile, Lavinia had risen from the bed and come closer, her gaze narrowed as she studied both her sister and her cat — who at the moment appeared all innocence, sitting on the sill, calmly cleaning his face with one of his striped paws. "Louisa, whatever has gotten into you? Did something happen when you went to fetch Hannibal?" Her sister paused. "What did he do?"

All that was missing from that statement was the word *now.* As in, "What did he do *now?*"

"Whatever do you mean?" Louisa asked, looking anywhere but at her sister. And not at the window. Definitely not at the window.

Lavinia's gaze narrowed. "When Hannibal went into that house, what did he do? Ruin a carpet? A sofa? Oh, heavens no! Not something expensive?"

Louisa flinched, knowing the only thing to

be done was to tell her twin sister everything.

Yet once she confessed the entirety of it
— there were no half truths with Lavinia,
she'd ferret them all out one way or another
— Louisa knew exactly what her sister
would advise. Insist upon. Demand.

And it was the last thing Louisa wanted to
do.

CHAPTER 3

The next day, Louisa woke up early, her sister's words still ringing in her ears.

Oh, Louisa! This will never do. You must make things right. What if he is a man of influence?

She looked over at the window and shook her head. She doubted their next-door neighbor was an arbiter of society, or even a man of consequence, even if he was a viscount — information Lavinia had wheedled out of one of the maids.

Louisa sat up and looked out the curtain at the tangled garden and the dirty windows across the wall, all of which begged for a neighborly turn. She was about to look away when she spied something else.

A striped cat going over the garden wall and into the jungle beyond.

Hannibal! Oh, how the devil had he managed to get out?

By making himself utterly unwelcome

below stairs, she guessed. He did have a way of getting what he wanted — even if it only added to his always-growing list of transgressions.

"Oh, bother," she whispered, and got up, dressing as quickly and quietly as she could. If she knew her cat, he was going after the curtains he'd failed to climb and shred yesterday, or worse, to see how His Lordship's leg might do as a scratching post.

His Lordship. That gave Louisa pause. Not just a rake or a recluse, but a nobleman.

Viscount Wakefield.

Even more startling, he was Lady Charleton's nephew. Lavinia had managed to obtain near enough to an encyclopedia of information about the man. The only son of Lady Charleton's brother, the previous Lord Wakefield, Pierson Stratton had been wounded in the war. Sent home in a terrible state. Never quite the same.

Further, he'd also brought home a terrible temper. Was considered unpredictable and generally avoided.

The latter part had come as a warning, but that hadn't stopped Louisa from dreaming about the man. How could she not? She'd never met anyone who so resembled a pirate — what with his dark glances and outlandish mane of hair. And in her dream, he hadn't been on the deck of a ship, but in a ballroom — wearing only his blue silk wrapper — and from his dangerous smile, she'd been shocked to realize she wanted to dance with him just like that — knowing he had nothing on beneath — her hands sliding beneath the silk where . . .

She'd jerked awake at that moment, and chided herself for her foolishness.

She never danced. But she did have a cat to go retrieve before she found herself back in his company.

Wearing God only knew what.

Tugging on her boots, Louisa stole a glance at Lavinia, who was still sound asleep — thankfully — and snuck out, leaving her sister to her peaceful dreams.

But before she closed the door, she spied the hamper they'd brought along as a gift for Lady Charleton. In the chaos of yesterday it had never been unpacked. Louisa tiptoed over to it and stole a pot of strawberry jam from inside.

Lady Essex always said that a spoonful of their strawberry jam could solve just about any problem.

With Hannibal, the entire pot might be the best way to start. Especially if he managed to breach the viscount's house yet again.

She went down the back stairs and out the door that led into the garden, where the morning was bright with sunshine. Truly, Lord Charleton's garden made it hard to believe one was actually in London — a delightful arrangement of formal plantings complete with graveled paths, rosebushes and a knot garden in the middle — more like something one would find at a country manor. Yet once she made her way down the path to the door in the wall, the contrast between the two yards became all too clear as she found her entrance blocked.

Oh, the latch moved, but the door in the wall only wiggled a bit at first and then held fast.

Since Louisa knew that a failure now on her part might have significant ramifications later — images of a limping and bleeding Lord Wakefield parading himself through Mayfair as a cautionary tale to all eligible men to avoid the Tempest sisters haunted her — as surely as Lavinia would haunt her for the remainder of her days if it was Hannibal who left them ruined.

So she tried again, and while the door gave a little, it got caught up in the thick tangle of overgrown grass and weeds on the other side.

"Faith! Couldn't the man bother to at

least trim his lawn a bit," she muttered, glancing around for another avenue. Certainly she could clamber over the wall as Hannibal had — for it wasn't that high — but it would hardly further her and her sister's entrance into proper society as "elegant young ladies" if she were seen climbing a garden wall like a thief.

Or tumbling over the other side, as would most likely be the case.

So it was through this door or nothing.

With one more determined shove, it groaned loudly enough to wake up the rest of Mayfair — but worse still, and to her horror, one of the rusty hinges popped loose, leaving the door barely hanging on.

So much for a stealthy entrance and unseen departure with Hannibal well in hand.

She closed her eyes and wished herself for the hundredth time back in Kempton. Why was it these disasters always happened to her?

But it seemed no one had heard her, and since there was no one about, she continued into the other yard, squeezing through the opening. Once she had, she wished she hadn't — for immediately she began cataloguing the list of things that needed to be done. The climbing rosebush trimmed. The hedges cut back. The beds weeded and tilled. The lawn — good heavens, was there even a lawn beneath all this?

This is not yours to manage, Louisa Tempest, she told herself.

Find Hannibal, leave the pot of jam for the poor beleaguered butler — Tiploft, she thought his name was — and then get back home.

"Hannibal," she whispered. "Come out, you naughty beast. Come out here where I can see you."

Rrrroew.

She spun around at the familiar cry. No proper meow for Hannibal. It always sounded like he had a putrid throat.

Which rather fit his temperament and looks.

"Come on, kitty," she cooed. "Where are you?"

Rrrroew, he howled even louder.

Louisa blanched and looked over her shoulder at the house. The last thing she wanted was the lord and master to come blazing out of the house, brandishing that wicked-looking pistol and threatening to shoot her again.

Then to her horror, the door began to open, and in a panic that it might be the owner of the house, she dashed behind the lilac bush, and then felt overly foolish for having done so, for it was only a servant.

She was about to make herself known, when the gate from the mews squeaked open, and into the garden came another man — this one a rather shady-looking character.

"What's ya got for me today, Bludger?" the man asked the fellow who'd come from inside the house.

The servant, Bludger, grinned, holding up a bulging sack, his beady eyes all squished up like an overly fat pig. "Oh, it's a grand haul today, Tommy. A grand one. A ration of bacon, eggs, a bottle of that wine, and some good butter. Oh, and some candles I was able to nip, along with another spoon. This lot will fetch a pretty penny, I'd say."

Louisa's mouth fell open. Lord Wakefield's servant was stealing from him? Then she paused and looked at the man again. *Bludger?* Whyever was that name so familiar? As if she'd heard it before.

But where, she couldn't remember.

Meanwhile, the pair continued their pattering as they traded goods and coins. "They on to you yet?" Tommy asked, sparing a glance at the house.

"Oh, that old butler might suspect I ain't French —"

"Or a cook," Tommy laughed.

Bludger laughed as well. "But as long as that crippled nob continues to —" He held his hand up and tipped it like he was drinking from a bottle. "I'll have that house emptied afore he notices."

"Better spoils than what we could pinch on the *Nemesis,* eh Bludger?" the man said, now holding a good part of Lord Wakefield's breakfast. He nudged his cohort in the side with his elbow and laughed softly.

Louisa drew in a deep breath. *Bludger.* Of the HMS *Nemesis.*

The very same ship Harriet Hathaway's brother Benedict served upon.

And hadn't he written Harriet a year earlier that the ship had been well served,

. . . since their thieving cook, Mr. Bludger, has deserted. Though his loss isn't so keenly felt — for he was always burning our breakfast despite all his claims that his mother was French and she taught him to cook all proper. But he's deserted, him and one other of the fellows — who was suspected as well of thievery. When they catch Charlie Bludger — which one day they will for he has a tattoo on his arm much like mine — they shouldn't hang him

72

for leaving, but for false claims that he could actually cook.

She and Harriet had read Benedict's letter more than a half a dozen times, laughing over his account of the man.

Louisa glanced up, more than shocked. For here he was, the very same Charlie Bludger. It must be him. She was certain.

Heavens! The man was a deserter, and worse, no cook.

With their transaction completed, Tommy scurried off like a rat and Mr. Bludger grinned as he pocketed the coins he'd gained.

Why, no wonder Lord Wakefield was in such a foul temper. His own cook was stealing from him.

And most likely burning his breakfast.

Well, that would never do. And forgetting her own admonishments of not getting involved, she stepped out from behind the lilac bush. "Mr. Bludger?"

The man whirled around. "Who the devil are —"

Louisa straightened and pointed toward the mews. "I think it is best if you leave, sir."

Those piggy eyes narrowed. "I ain't going nowhere, missy. Who the devil do you think you are?"

"Who I am matters not. But what does is that you will leave," she told him, pointing toward the mews. "Or I will summon Bow Street. Or perhaps an officer from His Majesty's navy."

Yet even as she issued her threat, she realized a clear flaw in her plan.

Without Bow Street or an officer about, or even a respectable fellow at her back, she hadn't much authority.

Actually, none whatsoever. Nor any protection, for that matter.

"Now see here, you bossy wench," Bludger snapped like a snarling dog, wading through the weeds, a twisted and mean look on his face. "You can't order me about. I'm staying put. But you —" He caught her by the arm and took a long look at her. "Now you'll fetch a pretty penny." He clapped his hand over her mouth, and then called after his fellow thief. "Tommy, ho there. I got something else for you."

As much as being part of the Society for the Temperance and Improvement of Kempton was learning how to be a proper lady, their kindly mentor, Lady Essex, had also imparted one very important lesson — how to manage an ill-mannered rogue.

A lady must never allow a man the upper

74

hand, she liked to say.

Well, it wasn't so much an upper hand.

Louisa rammed her knee into Bludger's privates and was rewarded with a loud yelp. Yet even as he let go of her, Tommy returned. She thought for a moment she'd only made the situation worse, for now Bludger wore a murderous expression and the other man had the look of a large rat having spotted an easy morsel.

She was backing away from the pair of them when from the house, the kitchen door groaned as it was flung open.

"Whatever is the meaning of this?"

Louisa glanced up and there he was. Lord Wakefield. He might have appeared most heroic if he hadn't looked more like death warmed over.

He was yet again unshaven, his hair in an untidy queue, and his wrapper barely on — for one sturdy bare leg stuck out.

She was starting to think the man didn't possess a single stitch of decent clothing.

"Miss Tempest?" He gaped at her as if he thought he was imagining things.

Louisa pressed her lips together, for she had rather hoped he hadn't noticed her. Lavinia would probably sell her into Mr. Bludger's care if this turned into something ruinous.

Then she glanced back at Lord Wakefield's bare, well-muscled leg and her heart gave an odd sort of leap. Well, she supposed it already had.

Turned rather ruinous, that is.

Meanwhile, the viscount turned his dark countenance on the pair of miscreants. "Monsieur?"

It was no question, but held all the air of a threat.

Louisa, screwing up her courage, wasn't about to let this foul fellow talk his way out of his misdeeds. "I fear, my lord, Monsieur was just leaving. For good." She sent a haughty, threatening glance of her own over at Mr. Bludger, as if daring him to countermand her.

Especially now that reinforcements had arrived. She took a quick glance at the viscount. He wouldn't wash his hands of her by handing her over to this scoundrel, would he?

Given his dark expression, she couldn't be certain.

Oh, this was a fine kettle of fish!

Mr. Bludger's hands fisted at his sides as if he wanted nothing more than to knock her teeth out, but he could hardly do so and not find himself in Newgate. Or hanging from the nearest yardarm.

"Oui," he muttered instead, stalking toward the house and brushing past his — former — employer as he went inside. A few moments later, he came out, a rough sack in hand.

Tommy, had, like a rat off a doomed ship, already slipped from sight.

"We'll cross paths again, miss," Bludger hissed as he passed her. "Mark me words." He banged the gate shut as he left and there was a scurry of feet as the former cook and his partner hightailed it down the lane.

Gladdened to see the man good and gone, she turned around and found herself out of the fire.

And in the frying pan, as it were.

"Miss Tempest, am I correct in assuming that not only did you awaken me yet again, but you just relieved me of my cook?"

She cringed a bit. She supposed she had. "I am ever so sorry —"

"What is all this, my lord," Tiploft said, having come out of the house to the steps. "Oh, my! Miss Tempest! You've come back." The man smiled kindly at her.

"Yes, not quite my reaction," Wakefield remarked dryly. "And you might have an entirely different opinion, Tiploft, when you find out she's gone and run off Monsieur Begnot —"

"Begnoche," Tiploft corrected.

"Yes, yes," Wakefield said, adding a dismissive wave of his hand. "It hardly matters now. The fellow's gone."

"And good riddance, my lord," she told him. "He was —"

"— my cook, Miss Tempest," the viscount said. "And now I have no one but poor Tiploft to burn my toast."

Both men stared at her, and Louisa knew that even the argument that their "French" cook wasn't anything more than a naval deserter and a thief would hardly remedy the situation.

Or even smooth it over like a layer of jam. *Jam.*

She glanced down at the ground where the crockery had fallen unbroken into the tangle of weeds.

That was it.

What the entire situation needed was a bit of strawberry jam.

"I do believe I can remedy this," she told him, catching up the pot and marching determinedly toward the house when a protest arose from underneath the lilac bush.

Rrrroew.

All three of them turned and Louisa reversed course, climbing down through the weeds until she spied Hannibal tucked beneath. Moving quickly, she scooped him up. "Bad kitty," she chided her cat, who she swore was grinning at her. "Actually this is why I was here in the first place — Hannibal came over the wall and —"

She left off the remainder of that sentence since it was rather redundant. *And I feared he'd wrought more damage.*

As her father liked to say, "Any sentence that begins with 'Hannibal' always ends with an apology."

But that was neither here nor there, for it had been she, Louisa, not Hannibal who had been the cause of all the problems, though one might argue she'd done the viscount a good turn by sending his felonious cook packing.

Wading through the overgrown vegetation, she handed the pot of jam to the viscount, doing her best to appear ignorant of the fact that the man was probably wearing nothing beneath his wrapper.

She also did her best to ignore the delicious shiver that ran down her spine.

Though that didn't stop her imagination from giving the image a thorough going over — a pirate of a lord *naked* beneath his silk wrap.

Dear heavens.

"What is this?" he asked. No, more like demanded, as he looked down at the crockery in his hand.

"Strawberry jam," she told him. "As a way of apology for yesterday."

"There is no need —" he began.

"Of course there is, my lord. We are neighbors and neighbors do for each other." She smiled at him in hopes of persuading him to move aside. When he didn't, she resorted to bribery.

"Besides, the jam shall go rather famously with your toast, my lord."

When he glanced again at the pot in his hand, she used the distraction to whisk past him. Without his leave or his permission, she strolled right into his kitchen, bold as brass, hoping she could bluff her way through this mire — at least until she came up with a plan to repair the damage she'd wrought.

Pierson realized, as Tiploft helped him into his jacket, this was probably the first time since he'd come home from Spain that he was actually getting dressed before noon.

And more to the point, because of a woman.

Well, more like a busybody handful.

Glancing out the window, he realized the

garden door was hanging by only one hinge. *La tormenta,* indeed.

"Females," he muttered, more to himself.

"Yes, my lord," Tiploft replied as he handed the viscount his cane.

"That girl and her cat are a menace," Pierson continued, taking a glance in the mirror. His old coat hung loosely from his frame and he realized he needed a shave and a haircut.

Not that he cared, nor did he want to, he reminded himself.

"Whatever is Charleton thinking, inviting some young miss into his house?" Pierson asked.

"I have no idea, my lord." Tiploft held up a razor and towel, a not-so-subtle suggestion that a shave might be in order.

The viscount shook his head and Tiploft set them aside with all the air of a martyr. Pierson suspected his butler knew exactly what Miss Tempest's connections were to Lord Charleton, but the crafty fellow wasn't about to give his reclusive employer an easy answer.

Probably wanted him to limp over to his uncle's house and discover the truth for himself. Which wasn't a bad idea — if only to ascertain when Miss Tempest was *leaving* London.

Hopefully that was sooner rather than later.

Speaking of which . . .

"She can make my breakfast, then she is out of the house, Tiploft. Do you hear me? Out with her!" He'd gotten to the door and paused, his stomach growling at yet another early awakening. Over his shoulder, he asked, "Do you think she can cook?"

It was his experience that the prettier the miss, the more helpless she tended to become.

And Miss Tempest was very fetching. Which didn't bode well for his breakfast.

"She has an air of management about her, my lord," Tiploft replied. It wasn't really an answer, but an observation.

There was no arguing, this Miss Tempest was a bossy minx. And he didn't need some pretty busybody reordering his life; he had his sisters for that, and he'd nearly managed to get them to leave him be.

Yes, *that* was exactly what he wanted. To be left alone.

So he could discontentedly sulk about his house with no one to point out his deficiencies. Remind him of his failures.

He took a step and a familiar pain ran up his leg.

But this time it seemed to lodge in his

heart with a deep, burning ache. Just as it had when he'd first come home from Spain.

Broken.

Still broken, he would remind anyone who dared to interfere in his life. That was exactly why Miss Tempest had to go.

And it wasn't because she was pretty — which only a fool couldn't see. No, it was because disaster and ruin seemed to swell up in her wake. Good Lord! She'd had a twig stuck in her hair when she'd gone marching past him like an empress.

The chit needed a keeper.

And a new cat, he thought, as Hannibal went dashing up the stairs past him, something clenched in his teeth.

"Dear heavens," Tiploft exclaimed as the feline disappeared down the hall with his prize.

"One interloper at a time, my good man," Pierson told him as he turned to enter the dining room and came to an abrupt halt in the doorway.

Before him the entire table gleamed, and at the head was set a plate, and silver — polished silver that sparkled in the bright morning light winging in from the window.

Good heavens, she'd not only opened the drapes, but cleaned the window, allowing the bright spring sunshine to fill the room.

But the real glory was the plate — with two eggs and a slice of ham. Not only that, the toast rack sat before it, filled with perfectly browned pieces of bread.

Pierson tentatively made his way to his seat, for he wasn't too sure that the sight before him was real. It was the sort of lure that rose up in his dreams from time to time.

Of what his life had been meant to be . . . A cozy home, decent meals, a bright, pretty face across the breakfast table from him. And yet the sunshine coming into the room had the opposite effect, for it illuminated the dusty corners, the faded furnishings and all the other ways his life had gone astray.

But even that he could shuttle aside. Ignore, as it were. For he did that every day and it had become second nature to him.

No, what did him in was the saucer of jam beside the toast. All bright and ruby, promising a sweet finish to his repast. It was the promise of summer bottled up to brighten darker days.

And as he took a step closer, tempted to dip his finger in and steal a taste, like one might dare a kiss from a pretty maiden, that old pain shot up his leg.

A stark reminder of something he knew only too well: that darkness always won.

It was to Miss Tempest's misfortune that

she chose that moment to poke her head in from the servant's door and ask, "Is everything to your liking, my lord?"

Unfortunately, he realized, it was more than that. It was a blatant reminder of everything that was missing from his life, and everything he'd lost in Spain.

Everything he'd never have. Especially that demmed saucer of strawberry jam. For it was the very same color as Miss Tempest's lips.

Sweet, rosy and so very kissable.

And how he longed for lips such as hers to smile at him, to call to him, to beg him for yet another kiss.

Something else that would never happen.

And in that moment, the black tides in his heart won.

Get out of my house!

Louisa flinched as once again the viscount's explosion of fury echoed through her thoughts. Even now, hours later, his furious expression, his hasty flight from the dining room, and his butler's apologetic words as he showed her out the door.

Please do not think ill of His Lordship. He isn't himself.

Dear heavens! Whatever had she done? She'd managed to get all the burnt bits scraped off the toast.

And then later, from her room, she'd watched him come outside, Hannibal in his arms. She had feared the viscount meant to toss her cat over the wall, but instead, he'd set the unruly feline down with all due care, and then, after having glanced around, gave the old tom a scratch behind the ears, which left Hannibal lolling about his bare feet like a kitten.

Not quite the fearful beast she supposed. Either of them.

So lost in thought, she didn't even notice Lady Aveley calling to her, until the matron was right beside her.

"Miss Tempest," Lady Aveley said, "there you are! Has something finally caught your fancy?"

Louisa blinked several times as the woman's words drew her back to the task at hand. Shopping. Which was hardly a task, but rather a rare treat.

And yet, Lord Wakefield's earlier ill humor and then his kindness to Hannibal had left her at sixes and sevens, a quandary of unfinished business.

And if there was anything that Louisa detested, it was something going wanting. And right now she'd left poor Tiploft, and, she supposed, Lord Wakefield, in a bit of a tangle.

When she turned toward Lady Aveley, she bumped into the counter and nearly overturned the bolts of silks stacked up there.

She caught them just in time, but earned disapproving glances from several well-heeled customers as well as a sigh of exasperation from Lavinia, who was deciding between a blue muslin and an apple green print.

As Lady Aveley helped her to straighten the bolts, she asked, "Is there something amiss, my dear?"

Biting her lip, Louisa stole a glance over at her sister. For she hadn't told Lavinia what had happened. "Yes, well —" she began. "Oh, heavens, I've made a terrible muddle of things."

Lady Aveley caught her by the arm and gently steered her to a corner, well out of the hearing of the other shoppers. "My dear child, what is it?"

Taking yet another glance at Lavinia, she knew exactly what her twin would tell her to do. *Remedy this mess.* Before it turned into a greater problem.

But that would mean facing down that beastly man once again. And yet . . . perhaps she could fix everything — with Lady Aveley's help — and never have to see him again. Just fix this one small thing and then she could wash her hands of the man.

For once and for all.

That hopeful thought had her screwing up her courage, enough so that she waded back into the mire. "Lady Aveley, how does one hire a cook?"

CHAPTER 4

Rrreowww.

The unearthly yowl yanked Pierson awake.

Rrreowww.

The second one had him sitting up and opening his eyes, only to be greeted by a wretched bit of sunshine flitting through a slight opening in the curtains. The shaft of light cut across the room like a spear to his temple, daring him to just try and ignore the brilliance the day offered.

Rrreowww.

"Bloody hell," he muttered as he got up. He wasn't too sure what the order of the day was going to be, but for now he had a rather sketchy list of immediate concerns.

Close those damned wall hangings.

Drown that cat.

Go back to bed.

But once his feet hit the cold floor and he stumbled his way across the room, he knew there was no returning to the void of dreams.

So there he stood, naked and cold and hungry. And just a bit hungover.

Well, a lot hungover.

Rrreowww.

He blanched as the noise cut through his skull. "Drown the cat" rose rather quickly to the top of his list, and he caught up his wrapper as he went.

All things considered, where Hannibal went, Miss Tempest most likely wasn't far behind.

At least he bloody well hoped so. He had a few choice words for the miss. About her cat. Or rather, former cat.

"Good God!" he exclaimed as he pulled open the door and immediately took two steps back.

Hannibal himself was always a bit of a shock, but there he sat on his haunches, battered ears twitching and his one eye looking up with pride. The demmed feline had brought a grand offering with him. A rather large rat. *Rrreowww,* the cat repeated, and if Pierson wasn't mistaken, with all the puffery of one of His Majesty's naval officers.

Then the cat came strolling forward, rubbing against the viscount's legs, before making a beeline for the now-emptied bed. He hopped up and came to a stop right where Pierson had been sleeping moments before. Turning a few circles, he finally seemed satisfied with his choice and plopped down to begin cleaning himself.

"Now see here!" Pierson protested, not that Hannibal even deigned to notice.

"Yes, well," he managed, taking another glance at the rat to assure himself it was good and dead. Turning back to the bed and the interloper, he said, "Don't get too comfortable," as he tugged on his breeches and a shirt.

If he had to get up, he might as well get some breakfast. But what that might be, he couldn't imagine. Tiploft had managed, with the help of the nearby inn, to pull together a manageable supper, but it wasn't the same as having one's dinner hot from the kitchen.

Not that his former cook had been anything to brag about, but the meals had always been hot.

More often than not burnt, but heated nonetheless.

Catching up Hannibal and sidestepping the rat, he stalked down the hall, his stomach growling.

Rrreowww, the cat complained. *What the devil is the matter with you? I brought a rat.*

"I think I'd prefer roasted cat," Pierson threatened. But it was obvious this sort of prospect hardly dinted Hannibal's nerves. Most likely he'd heard it before.

Probably daily.

Cat in one hand, cane in the other, he managed the stairs slowly, and considered what might be had this morning. Some toast and butter, perhaps?

Though some ham and eggs wouldn't be all that bad either.

But no jam. None of that, he thought with a shiver.

For while he'd made a great show of storming off the previous day, he was rather sheepish to admit — after she'd left — well, fled, actually — he'd returned like a beggar to the table and eaten every morsel. Including the jam, until he'd realized the flavor was something akin to summer and bright promises — rather like the chit herself.

The viscount shook his head like a dog, tossing any image of the pretty minx out of his thoughts. No, that decided the matter — he needed to find a cook immediately.

Perhaps he could enlist his man of business — but after a moment of consideration, Pierson discarded that notion. The overly cautious fellow would want to make a careful search, if only to assure that the viscount got a proper replacement.

Again, time was not in his favor. Or rather his stomach's.

And while Pierson knew the matter could be quickly expedited with a note to his mother or his sister Margaret, that was the last thing he wanted to do.

It would be akin to running up a white flag, giving his female relations all the evidence they needed to prove his life wasn't as perfectly ordered as he declared it to be.

Mother, Margaret, and most likely, even Roselie — for she never liked to be left out of her share — would descend upon the house and start putting things in order, and then after that, they'd insist on doing the same to him: meddling and "setting him to rights," as Margaret often said.

He shuddered and decided a few cold plates of greasy meat from the public house could be borne if it kept the females in his life at bay.

And Miss Tempest as well. She was rather like that annoying ray of sunshine that had divided his room — reminding him of all that was bright and beautiful, everything that the world had once offered him.

Well, it was his world no longer. And all he needed was someone who could manage to put a good char on a beefsteak, cook a rasher of crisp bacon, and perhaps send along a pot of tea that wasn't cold.

How hard could it be to find someone capable of a few decent dishes?

He hauled Hannibal through a dark and cold dining room and continued down the back stairs to the kitchen, where a puzzled-looking Tiploft was surveying the stove.

Which was also cold.

This did not bode well for the prompt arrival of his breakfast.

Pierson sighed. "What is it, Tiploft?"

"My lord!" The butler looked up, plainly surprised to see him up and about so early in the morning. "I can't seem to get the stove lit this morning. Confounded new contraption. Your sister insisted —"

"Say no more." Pierson sighed, leaning against the doorjamb. When he'd come back from Spain, his mother and Margaret had taken advantage of his convalescence and "modernized" as much of the house as they could before he'd regained his ability to walk and discovered what mischief they'd been about.

The fancy stove, which was the devil itself to light, was just one such example of their meddling.

"I do hate to add to your woes, Tiploft, but Miss Tempest's cat has returned and left a rather large rat in the hallway."

Tiploft sighed. "I shall see to it, my lord."

"How did he get in?" Pierson asked as he made his way toward the back door.

"He bolted in when I opened the door earlier. I didn't realize he'd brought something with him."

"For future reference, my good man, this foul beast always brings an entire host of disasters with him — undistinguishable piles, dead vermin, Miss Tempest —"

Even as he invoked her name, there was a sharp, determined rap of someone demanding entrance at the kitchen door.

Knock. Knock. KNOCK.

Apparently a rather brave soul with a limited amount of patience, who was, given the viscount's mood, about to meet his demise. He dropped Hannibal to the ground and yanked the door open.

Before he could utter a word, a substantial woman came bustling in. "About time," she blustered as she barreled in, nearly toppling Pierson in the process. The woman was not so much large of girth but tall and strongly built. And certainly not the sort of woman a man naysayed easily.

She stopped in the middle of the kitchen, her mouth falling open at the state of affairs around her.

Pierson had to admit, the place was a shambles. Dishes and pots stacked up in the sink; Tiploft sporting a face smudged with ash; and him, the master of the house, in nothing more than his breeches and a loose shirt.

And given that he hadn't put on any shoes, he could also assure her the floor needed a good scrubbing.

But he doubted this woman needed to be told that.

She spun around and glared at him. "Who are you gaping at? Never seen a woman before?"

"I . . . uh . . . uh," Pierson stammered, for he'd never been berated so — especially not in his own house.

Save by his sisters.

"Harrumph," the woman replied to his stammering and turned to Tiploft, dismissing him just as quickly. "A useless, shiftless lot if ever I saw one. Now it appears I've come just in time, but mind you —"

Pierson hadn't served under Wellington not to know when to pluck up his courage and stand his ground. "Madame, who the devil are you?"

The woman turned slowly around, eyes narrowed. "Cheeky fellow aren't you? I'm the new cook, if you must know. And don't

96

be calling me 'madame,' I'm Mrs. Petchell to you. No talking fancy, or flirting, or trying to charm me is going to get you out of your responsibilities around here. Nor is being lame. This is my kitchen and I am in charge and you'll work like everyone else, cripple or not."

What had she just said? Flirting with her? Pierson didn't know whether to laugh or run. She was at least twenty years his senior.

But the woman wasn't done with her extraordinary pronouncements. "Well, now, what a mess. That miss wasn't wrong about that. And here I thought she might not know the difference between a pot and kettle like most of these fancy ladies —" Her steely gaze swept over the room once again, " 'Pon my husband's grave, I owe that gel an apology."

What gel? he was about to ask, only to find the lady continuing her speech. Or rather, tirade.

Having finished her quick inspection of her surroundings, Mrs. Petchell heaved a large sigh. "I can see rightly that I am needed here. Yes, indeed, this kitchen needs Matilda Petchell's touch, it does." She shrugged off her cloak and shoved it at Pierson. "Now I hear from the miss that the master's a regular devil of a brute, but I don't blame him. Not in the least. I'd be in a perpetual pet if my meals were coming out of this ruin." She continued into the kitchen and then stopped, and looked over her shoulder at the still-open door. "Well good thing I gots my Bits and Bobs with me," she declared, jerking her head in a nod, that brought with it more arrivals.

A pair to be exact. Yet they came no farther than the door. Two wide-eyed mites viewed the kitchen like one might a cell at the Tower. The scrawny little girl, with her bright red hair tied in pigtails, bit her lip and looked ready to bolt, while the other one, a boy with a smile that showed a few missing teeth, and an equally red mane, winked at Pierson, trying to look older than his narrow frame implied.

Mrs. Petchell tapped her foot with a staccato beat. In fact, everything about the woman was impatient. She seemed to quiver with nervous energy.

And it came spilling out each time she spoke. "Bitty, you get those dishes sorted out. Bob, you see to that stove." Then she caught up the coal scuttle and shoved it at Pierson. "Well, what are you waiting for, Hopping Giles?"

Tiploft gasped at the woman's use of the vulgar slur.

She shot a glance at the butler. "Oh, aye, I'm not one to mince words. And aye, he's lame, but I don't mind it a bit if he works for his keep. I don't cozen anyone laying about and expecting to be fed, nor will I hold my tongue for anyone who don't know their place." Nodding as if that was the end of the discussion, she prodded Pierson again with the coal scuttle. "Be useful, you shiftless vagrant. Go fetch some coal and a bit of kindling from out back so Bob can get that stove going — something you might have thought of doing afore I arrived."

She poked him once again with the bucket until he truly had no choice but to take it. For one wild, fleeting moment, he thought she meant to clout him with it if she had to "ask" one more time.

"Don't gape at me like a mackerel, get moving," she told him as she shooed him out the door. "I've got His Lordship's breakfast to make and not much to do it with from the looks of things."

As the woman continued to order her troops about, Pierson Stratton, the fifth Viscount Wakefield, backed down the steps and found himself in his own garden, having been routed from his house.

More to his shame, he'd raised barely a defense. Flanked and defeated before he could fire off a shot.

Suddenly, it occurred to him that he was exactly as she'd claimed, nothing more than a shiftless vagrant, for he hadn't any notion of how to reclaim his own castle.

Taking a wary glance back inside the kitchen, he spied Mrs. Petchell interrogating Tiploft like his very position was at stake — enough so to give Pierson pause.

Certainly she couldn't recall his letters patent, but he wouldn't put it past this overbearing Amazon not to try.

Yes, perhaps fetching the coal was the better part of valor. For quite honestly, he was a bit wary of returning without it.

Even if he was lord and master of the house.

I am the lord and master, he reminded himself as he glanced around and tried to discover where the coal was kept, or even a scrap that might serve as kindling.

From behind him, the garden gate groaned as if it hadn't moved in years, and it was followed by an added complaint.

"Oh, bother these hinges."

Pierson cringed. For it wasn't the censure of his broken garden door that had him balking, but the voice.

He glanced first toward the kitchen and then back at the still-shuddering garden gate. Now it all made sense.

Mrs. Petchell's "gel."

And the newfound bane of his existence.

As he turned around, he discovered Miss Tempest, her back to him, caught in a tangle of rose canes.

A rose trapped by thorns.

If the front of Miss Tempest was enticing, her backside was even more so. It showed a decidedly feminine figure, with curves and soft angles that could tease a man into believing the lady was just as pliable.

And any man who thought that, Pierson reminded himself, would be a fool.

If only to prove matters, she continued her complaints.

"Oh, bother," she sputtered as she tried to extract herself, but only managed to catch not only her hair, but her gown. "Why doesn't that man hire a gardener for this tangle?"

"Have you considered that perhaps he prefers a tangle, if only to keep busybody misses on the other side of the wall?"

She stilled. There was a moment that Pierson felt the unlikely desire to laugh, but when she turned her head toward him, he thought better of it. "Well, why are you just standing there? Do something!"

His first thought was a rather uncharitable

one — having to do with pushing her into the roses and leaving her there, but one look at those lips, pursed together and so in need of . . . Well, he didn't want to consider what this lady needed, though a thorough kissing did come to mind . . . and, despite his misgivings, he found himself moving forward to help her.

As he drew closer, towering over her, she leaped a little, as if in panic, and managed to get herself further imbedded.

"Oh, dear," she gasped, swiping at the unruly canes and getting her sleeve caught in the process.

"Hold still," he ordered, and to his amazement, she did. "However do you manage to find trouble so quickly, Miss Tempest?" he asked as he leaned closer and very carefully plucked the first branch from her hair.

She glanced quickly at him, her eyes wary. "I'm hardly in trouble," she replied. "Just caught."

Caught. He wanted to laugh, but as he freed her from yet another cane, the thorns pulled a strand of her mahogany hair from its tight, perfectly wound chignon, and the silky tress fell into a rebellious wave alongside the curve of her chin.

And there it was. The moment that changed everything.

For suddenly it was Pierson who was caught — with an aching desire to reach out and set the damage to rights, to brush the errant strand away and in the process, graze his knuckles against the silken temptation of her fair skin.

He swallowed and tried to look away, but there they were, her lips, that tempting pair of ruby jewels, parted just so, and begging a man to come explore.

His gaze fled upward, where he found her staring at him, a starry light to her eyes. It seemed that, along with his own good sense, that practical, tart-tongued chit he'd just met was gone, and in her place stood a lady whose wiles and passion had found a way past his defenses.

You've been alone too long, my good man, he told himself as he tried to wrench his gaze away from that dangerous light, away from the wayward strand of hair that had ignited this blazing spark inside him.

All these years — first in Spain and then home — spent alone came haunting forward. How could he have forgotten how something so purely female could lead a man to forget the very simple fact he was a gentleman?

Well, supposed to be, he mused as he leaned closer, his senses filling with the unmistakable air of roses and Miss Tempest. His eyes closed as he heard her soft intake of breath, and he let his fingers tease that curl back over her ear. He didn't need to see what he was doing, for he could feel her trembling beneath his touch, so he knew he had the right of it.

The rake he'd once been would then have followed with his lips, letting them explore the very same path. Then, inch by inch, he'd free her from her thorny prison and take her captive in his arms.

That is, until he opened his eyes and all his fantasies took flight, for the lady was gaping at him as if he'd suddenly gone mad — or worse, she knew exactly what he was thinking . . .

They stared at each other, both suddenly wary. So very lost in that fragile, dangerous moment.

Not that he had any idea what to say — for he didn't quite understand what had happened.

Not that Miss Tempest seemed to be at a loss for words — though they came out in a whispered, halting jumble.

"I — I — I . . . that is, I think . . . I'm undone," she told him, glancing away as she tugged the last cane off her sleeve and slipped past him.

Right about then, her devil of a cat came bolting out of the house. After a hasty flight down the steps, he came to stop beside Pierson, settling down on his haunches with an air of feline disdain.

Hannibal, meet Mrs. Petchell.

Apparently the cat got along with the cook as well as he did with everyone else.

"Oh, Hannibal, what have you done now?" Miss Tempest exclaimed.

"He brought me a peace offering," Pierson explained, looking down at the one-eyed tom.

"He did?" she asked with a wary note.

Obviously she knew her pet very well.

"A rather large rat," he told her.

Miss Tempest cringed a bit before she asked, "Was it —"

"Dead? Yes, rather," he replied, and then for the life of him, he didn't know why, but he added teasingly, "You might want to inform that beast of yours I prefer strawberry jam."

The teasing words came out before he could stop himself, and she appeared as surprised as he was.

Strawberry jam, indeed! What had gotten into him?

Miss Tempest, that was it.

This chit was going to be his death. Or

rather his undoing. Still, his fingers wound tightly around the handle of his cane and he took a step back, tamping down the unfathomable rush of desire that had flooded his limbs.

All of them.

With that thought came a shiver of recognition, and if he were a suspicious sort he would have called it what it most likely was: a portent, a warning.

If there was ever a lady who could find the odd crack in the curtains of his life, throw back the hangings, and allow the sun to flood into his world once again, it was this one.

Miss Tempest would dare where no one else would tread. He could see it in her eyes, in the set of her chin.

In her choice of cats and cooks.

And that very notion frightened him more than Mrs. Petchell in the kitchen with a coal scuttle.

"Yes, well," Miss Tempest stammered a bit. "I saw Mrs. Petchell coming up the mews and thought I would come over and see that she was properly settled," she said as she brushed her hands over her skirt. "That, and Hannibal was missing."

That answered his previous question. Not that Pierson had really had any doubts as to who the "gel" was who had thrust Mrs.

Petchell into his kitchen.

"My lord?" she prompted, this time wading further into his garden, seemingly unafraid that she faced — oh, what had Mrs. Petchell said? — oh, yes, "a devil of a brute."

That she thought him a brute bothered him more than he cared to consider.

Perhaps he had been a bit churlish before, but demmit, it was his house and his life in which she was so blithely interfering.

He'd had everything perfectly ordered before she'd tumbled — quite literally — through his front door.

Well, mostly.

And now . . . and now . . . well, she had him considering reckless, foolish notions like kissing her — and if there was anything that would upset his precarious and precious routine, he had to believe kissing Miss Tempest would be disastrous to his closely kept sanctuary.

Yet as churlish and brutish as he'd been, here she was, daring to venture into his garden, nay, his life, yet again. "Miss Tempest, have you nothing better to do than interfere in my life?"

Much to his chagrin, she didn't take it as an insult, not in the least. She blinked once or twice and then managed a sturdy, determined smile. Oh, the determined part was the most vexing. "No, not at the present," she told him. "Luckily for you."

Luckily for him?

He was about to give her an entire litany of all the ways he was anything but lucky, but she had already sidestepped him and was snatching up the abandoned coal scuttle.

"Oh, dear, let me do this," she said, making her way to the coal shed. "How kind of you to help Mrs. Petchell as she gets everything in order." She deftly filled it and then handed it to him. "I do hope everything is to her liking." Then she leaned in close, close enough that Pierson could detect those spicy hints of, what else, roses once again. "I must warn you, Mrs. Petchell is rather particular about her kitchens, but she comes highly recommended by Lady Aveley."

Had the chit bothered to ask him if any of this was to his liking? Or by his leave? Rather, she was worried about Mrs. Petchell's sensibilities?

And when he looked up again, he found that she'd started toward the kitchen and was glancing back at him, as if surprised he wasn't following in her sunny wake. "How do you like her?"

"Not. At. All."

That put a decided crimp in her smile.

And while that, he thought, should be a victory for his camp, it brought none of the familiar glow that came from routing an enemy. So he sallied forth, lobbing yet another shot to send her packing. "Whatever possessed you, Miss Tempest, to hire a cook for me?"

Her hands fisted all too quickly to her hips at his challenge. "Because you needed one."

Well, she had him there. But there was a better point to be made. "And why did I need one, dare I ask?"

She blushed at this, though only slightly, a hint of dusky pink rising on her fair cheeks. "That hardly matters," she told him. "Besides, Mrs. Petchell comes highly recommended."

"So you've already said."

Her lips pressed together.

If only they weren't the color of strawberry preserves. Sweet. Delectable. Tempting.

His better judgment clamored for a hasty retreat. Yet with his enemy in his sights, he stalked forward. Boldly.

Not because those delectable lips of hers tempted him, but because he had her cornered.

Or so he thought. Foolishly.

Towering over her yet again, he fired his best sally. "And who recommends that harridan you've foisted upon me? Newgate?"

To his chagrin, she laughed. "A harridan? You're being quite the grumbletonian today." She paused and then added, "Even for you."

What did she mean by that? *Even for you?* Rather than give it much thought, he continued on. "Your cook thinks I'm a footman. Called me a 'Hopping Giles,' and sent me to fetch coal."

Miss Tempest, rather than being shocked at such a state of affairs, shook off his complaints and replied, "You must have mistaken her."

He held up the coal scuttle.

Unwilling to raise a white flag, as any honorable combatant would when defeated, she continued forward into the fray. "Plainly, you were improperly introduced."

"Improperly introduced?" he nearly exploded. "The woman was set on me."

Miss Tempest pulled her skirt back and swished past him, heading toward the kitchen. "Set on you! I never! Lord Wakefield, considering all I've heard of you, it seems you are also afflicted with a terrible flair for the dramatic. Set upon you, indeed. She was nothing of the sort."

And if Pierson thought that was the end of the matter, he was sadly mistaken.

The chit whirled around and came stomping back to face him, thorns at the ready. "And why wouldn't she mistake you for some layabout when that is exactly how you appear this morning?" She waved her hands at his hastily donned ensemble.

Well, it wasn't like he was expecting callers.

He never had callers.

Until now, apparently.

"If you are determined to live your life looking like a common ruffian, then you had best be comfortable being addressed as one." She walked around him and sniffed. "No wonder poor Mrs. Petchell confused the matter." Then she was off toward the kitchen again. "Well, come along, let's set this to rights."

"There is nothing to set to rights," he told her, holding his ground. "You can take her back where she came from. Her and those imps she brought with her."

Again, that incredulous expression that spoke volumes. "You don't mean to keep her?"

"No, I do not. Not unless she knows how to roast a cat."

Back she came down the steps yet again,

and he regretted his words immediately, for she brought with her that air of roses. Sharp and determined to overshadow anything else — including his better judgment. "I'd wager your monsieur was adept at that recipe."

Most likely he was. There had been more than one dish that Pierson hadn't dared ask what it was. Better to think it chicken and leave it at that.

Nor was Miss Tempest done roasting him. "You cannot let Mrs. Petchell go. She's a widow with no other means."

Pierson wondered if the woman's marital state was because the former Mr. Petchell expired out of self-defense.

He thought he might have to follow suit, since Miss Tempest hadn't finished ringing a peal over his head. ". . . and furthermore, those children are orphans. Her sister's children. The dear lady has taken them in."

"I am not running a charity, Miss Tempest."

"Those children have no one else but their aunt."

He set his shoulders. "And how is that *my* problem?"

For a time, and before he'd inherited, he'd fancied the law and had even studied it for a bit. After all these years, there had been one sound piece of common sense that he'd never forgotten.

Never ask a question to which you don't want to know the answer.

And now he'd gone and strayed from that very sound advice.

Miss Tempest leaned in close and lowered her voice. "Their father perished in the flight from Corunna. I would think that you, of all people —"

Corunna . . . Pierson heard nothing more.

That one word was enough to stop the air in his chest, bringing with it a slate of horrible, bloody images.

His garden disappeared and he saw nothing but the road, awash in blood and mangled bodies, men writhing in the throes of death. And the horrible, helpless feeling that there was nothing to do but keep marching. Running.

Now here were more casualties from that mayhem being laid at his doorstep.

"Not again!" he said, stabbing his cane into the ground and leaning heavily against it as he tried to breathe.

Whatever she'd been saying, her words came to a quick halt, giving him time to stalk past her, ignoring the sharp pain that such a quick movement sent through his leg.

"Not another word," he growled in warning when she went to open her mouth.

Like a brute might. But at this point he didn't care. He wasn't about to wade into another bloody ditch. Not ever again.

And then he got inside the kitchen.

His kitchen, he reminded himself.

It was all still a chaotic mess — which only served to rattle his shaken nerves all that much more. Yet as he drew another deep breath, he could see that the girl had organized the dishes in the sink, while the boy — by some miracle of happenstance — had gotten the stove lit and now a kettle was atop it and starting to steam.

Across the room, Mrs. Petchell and Tiploft were nose to nose having quite a row of their own.

Mrs. Petchell whirled around at his arrival. "So this one," she began, jerking her thumb at Tiploft, "says you're the master."

"I am," Pierson said, rising up, and for the first time in ages, wishing he looked more like one. But there was more to being noble than a well-cut coat and polished boots. He tucked his chin up and glared at her.

But if he was expecting a bit of remorse or even a demmed apology for her high-handed ways, he wasn't about to get anything like that.

Not even close.

"Harrumph!" she managed, and shook out her apron. "We'll see about that." Then she pointed at the door that led up to the main floor. "If you're the master, what the devil are you doing in my kitchen? Get out with you."

From behind him, he heard a choking little cough from Miss Tempest. Whether it was dismay or laughter, he couldn't tell.

Not that it mattered.

Nor was Mrs. Petchell done. "Oh, but first, the Bits and Bobs have something to say." She shot the children a pair of pinning glances. "Don't you now?"

"Aye," the little boy began.

"Yes, milord," the girl said, her lower lip trembling. She turned to Pierson but didn't look up at him. "Thank you, sir," she mumbled, more to the floor than to him.

"We'll earn our keep, milord," the boy added, to which his sister nodded emphatically.

"Oh, aye, they will. I'll see to it," their aunt declared with a no nonsense huff.

And in that moment, Pierson felt that crack, that bit of warmth from earlier slice across his heart, opening it a bit more.

No. No. No. He didn't want any of this.

Especially responsibility for the welfare of two scrawny orphans.

War orphans, Miss Tempest would add.

He didn't bother counting Mrs. Petchell. Pierson suspected she could do for herself in the furthest reaches of Russia with nothing more than a penknife and an apple core.

But when he glanced up, firm in his resolve to cast the entire lot of them out, he spied Miss Tempest standing in the doorway, sunlight now flooding in around her, illuminating her, and her gaze shining with a misty veil.

One that defied him to be anything but the brute she thought him to be.

Even Hannibal, now perched in his mistress's arms, cocked his head to let his one eye give him a good look at the viscount. *I didn't waste a perfectly good rat on you, did I?*

"Yes, well," he muttered. "See that you do." Then he nodded to Bob and said, "There's a dead rat in the hallway upstairs courtesy of Miss Tempest's cat. Please fetch it for her, with my compliments."

Then he fled upstairs, each step echoing one determined thought.

I am the master of this house.

I am.

But he suspected he was the master of

little else.

After Lord Wakefield fled to his domain above stairs, Mrs. Petchell turned her sharp gaze on Louisa.

She had to suppose there wasn't much that escaped the irascible cook's notice — and right now she felt exposed and bare — as if the cook could see inside the dangerous tangle of desire still roiling inside her.

"Harrumph!" Mrs. Petchell snorted, as if she knew the answer, but wasn't about to share her opinions.

Thankfully.

"Off with you, miss," the cook said, shooing Louisa down the kitchen steps and out into the garden. "I've got work to do." And with that, she slammed the kitchen door shut.

Louisa paused in the overgrown garden, just stood there like a statue — save for the uneven rhythm of her heart — and wondered at what had just transpired.

It had seemed a simple task: having spied Mrs. Petchell coming up the mews, Louisa had hurried over to ensure the lady got a proper introduction.

Then she'd come through the garden gate . . . she'd come through and . . . and then . . . well, everything had turned upside down.

She glanced down at Hannibal. "I got caught," she whispered to him. By the rose canes and by . . . *him.*

Cornered by that beast of a man. When he'd come storming across the yard, she had thought at first he meant to toss her back over the garden wall, but then he'd stopped before her and . . .

"I thought for a moment he meant to —" she confessed to her perfect confidant. Say what you might about her less-than-amiable pet, he was a good listener. "I thought he might . . ." She began to tell him, but stopped. She couldn't confess *that,* not even to Hannibal.

Wasn't it every girl's dream to be kissed?

Picking her way through the tangle of rose canes, she slipped through the opening in the wall. Faced with the thought of seeing Lavinia, she stopped yet again.

Her sister would see through any dissembling on Louisa's part, so she settled down on a bench, setting Hannibal free to roam about Lord Charleton's perfectly ordered garden, while she collected her composure.

For all she'd called the viscount a ruffian, she found herself entranced by him. He was a puzzle of contradictions.

And if there was one thing that could needle at Louisa, it was a tangle that needed unraveling.

Yet here she was, still firm in her conviction not to marry, yet she couldn't stop herself from thinking of him, of his chin — dark with stubble — and how, heaven help her, she'd wanted to run her fingers down the strong line of his jaw.

She'd longed to untie the hasty queue of his hair and run her fingers through it until he resembled a pirate in all his untidy, most ruffian ways.

So when his hand had reached toward her, when he'd pushed that wayward strand of hair off her cheek . . . she'd wished, she'd wanted, so much more.

She'd wanted him to cradle her chin in one of his great, large hands and turn her face up so he could steal a kiss.

As she'd tried to breathe, tried to stop thinking about him carrying her off in some rakish manner, she'd looked up and into his eyes and seen something there that had left her utterly unsettled.

A need so deep, she'd been afraid of falling into it. Afraid it reflected the turmoil raging inside her — the one that had nearly prodded her into rising up on her toes, catching hold of him and bringing his mouth to hers.

The toe of her boot gouged into the gravel path, sending the rocks scattering.

"Oh, bother," she muttered as she dropped down and went to work gathering them back into place, setting it all to rights.

If only the stark, ragged desire inside her could be dealt with so easily.

"I wanted him to kiss me, Hannibal," she told her friend when he came to inspect her work. "He must think me quite the country goose."

For worse yet, in that naked moment of awakening, what foolish thing had she'd said?

Oh, yes, she remembered. Blushed at the very memory.

I think I am undone.

She'd all but told him that she was willing — how utterly mortifying was that? — and yet had he taken advantage of her?

No. He'd let her slip away. Let the moment pass without comment.

The heat in her cheeks blossomed and left her chest tight and aching. She'd come ever so close to making a complete cake of herself.

"It won't happen again," she told Hannibal. "I vow it won't."

Hannibal made a bit of a shrug and walked away, tail flitting back and forth.

"He isn't the proper sort, not in the least," she added.

Hannibal had no comment. For they both knew that wasn't true.

For even when she had been utterly convinced that the viscount was a complete beast, he'd gone and surprised her. She'd have wagered every bit of her pin money that he'd intended to march inside his kitchen and send Mrs. Petchell packing.

But he hadn't. He'd looked down at the Bits and Bobs, a pair of orphans as lost in the world as he, and given them a place in his home.

Oh, bother the man, she thought, sitting back on the grass. It was impossible to detest him now. He was rather like that lion in the children's story. The one with a thorn in his paw.

That was Lord Wakefield to a tittle. A dark-maned lion with a thorn in his paw.

Whatever would he be like if it was plucked free?

Taking one last glance over her shoulder at the beast's lair, with its garden lost in time and the windows covered with curtains that told the world quite clearly he wanted nothing to do with anyone, she wondered who Lord Wakefield truly was, and why a man who could be so kind should want to hide away from the world.

And live in such a shambles.

Hannibal returned, and she reached out to scratch his one good ear. If this were Kempton, with the society behind her, she'd shoo away all the cobwebs and dusty corners of his world so he might be tempted to come out.

"But this isn't Kempton, Hannibal."

And if she was to discover who the man behind the wounded veneer might be, she would have to do it all on her own.

Louisa shivered again.

That is, if she dared.

CHAPTER 5

Pierson woke late the next day to find that Hannibal hadn't even bothered to announce his arrival.

He was stretched out on the coverlet beside the viscount, sound asleep. And taking up a good portion of the bed. Presumptuous wretch!

The viscount went to get up and then remembered the quantity of brandy he'd had the night before and paused to get his bearings.

Usually he consumed that much to forget the horrors of Spain.

Now he'd added Miss Tempest to his list of matters best blotted out.

If he didn't evict the chit from his memories, he'd be spending more nights like the previous one, pacing about his study, his fingers flexing as he recalled the silk of her hair as he'd brushed it off her chin, unrequited desires leaving him restless.

Demmit! He should have just kissed her and been done with it . . .

That notion got him moving out of his bed, with Hannibal making a discontented *mew* at being disturbed.

Once again there was a bit of sun piercing an opening in the curtains. How was it that every morning since that chit had arrived he'd been greeted in such an unholy manner? As if nudged awake by Miss Tempest herself. And he'd sworn that he'd closed those drapes tight last night before he'd gone to bed.

He reached for his cane and then stomped about the room, getting his clothes pulled on, for he knew exactly what must be done.

Get that minx out of his life. *For good.*

Given the determined tilt of her brow and that teary-eyed glance of gratitude she'd shone upon him when he hadn't sent Mrs. Petchell packing, he'd wager his next quarter's rents that she'd be back.

Rather like her cat.

He went downstairs and found a splendid breakfast laid out on the sideboard. Taking an appreciative sniff, he conceded that having well-cooked meals certainly was an improvement. But that was the last of Miss Tempest's changes he would tolerate.

A new cook and two children were

enough. But he drew the line there. No more improvements.

And no more thoughts of kissing . . .

Once his breakfast was finished, he gathered up his cane and rang for Tiploft.

"I need my coat and gloves," he told his astounded butler. "Oh, and tell that lad to toss Miss Tempest's cat into a sack for me. He'll find the beast on my bed."

"Yes, my lord," Tiploft replied.

"It is time I set this all to rights," he added.

The wry glance from his butler suggested the viscount could try, and good luck with his endeavor.

Well, Pierson would show him. He was the master of this house and his life.

A sentiment he intended to repeat half an hour later when he was shown into Lord Charleton's library.

Much to his chagrin, he found not his uncle there but Lord Charleton's heir, Mr. Alaster Rowland, ensconced on Charleton's imposing chair and helping himself liberally to the brandy bottle.

No matter that it wasn't yet noon.

"Tuck," Pierson said, using the nickname he'd given his former friend when they'd been but lads. "Whatever are you doing here?" He didn't look Rowland in the eye.

He never did. Not anymore.

"Summoned," Tuck drawled, propping his long legs up and settling his boots atop the desk. He cradled the now-brimming glass in his hands and smiled, a slight, lazy tip of his lips. "I suppose you were as well, cuz."

Cuz. He started to argue the matter — for just because his aunt and Tuck's uncle had married, that didn't make them . . . Well, no matter.

"No, I was not summoned," Pierson replied, eyeing the reprobate with disdain. It hadn't always been so between them — once they'd been as close as brothers. Him and Tuck, and . . .

Pierson stopped there. He didn't like to think of that third name. So instead, he upended the sack atop Charleton's desk, right next to where Tuck had his boots propped.

When Hannibal came out, hissing and spitting, Tuck nearly toppled out of Charleton's chair to avoid being swiped. "Good God, Piers, what the devil is that?"

"If you weren't already foxed, you could see that it is a cat."

"So you say," Tuck replied, warily moving around the desk and taking a stand across the room. "And I am hardly foxed. Only mildly bosky. I'm not such a fool that I don't know what is going on around here

— show up half-seas over and I'll wake up in the parson's trap — that's what would happen."

It took Pierson a moment to follow the logic of Tuck's complaints, yet when he did, he had no love for the conclusion.

Not one bit.

The very thought of Miss Tempest being matched to Tuck tightened like a knot inside Pierson's chest.

And worse was the furious thought that sprang forth with that unholy image.

Over my dead body.

"Do you know what the devil is going on?" Tuck continued, then apparently changed his mind. "What am I doing asking you? Probably don't even know that Charleton's gone into the matchmaking business. The word is all over Town. He's been hoaxed into this mess by some leftover debt of your aunt's." The man groaned. "If you'd deign to show your face, you might know these things. Uncle is going to try to snare one of us into this marriage folly — I'd wager my next quarter's allowance on it."

"Haven't you already wagered that away?"

Tuck was always at least two quarters behind with his debts. If not three.

The man paused and then grinned, ever unrepentant and hardly ever slighted. "Suppose I have. No matter. Then again, you said you weren't summoned. Might want to take that creature and make a dash for the country before Uncle remembers you're still alive." Tuck took a long glance at Pierson's coat and ensemble. "Well, mostly." He heaved a sigh and went back to warily watching Hannibal.

Thankfully, Charleton made his appearance just then, and Hannibal took the opportunity to streak through the open doorway, making his escape.

"Wretched beast," the baron muttered as he watched the cat go. "Ah, Alaster, right on time." Then the baron looked up and noticed the room's other occupant. "Wakefield?"

The viscount nodded in return. "I know I am intruding upon your meeting, but my business won't take but a moment." He shifted uncomfortably. It hurt like the devil to stand about like this, though he'd never admit as much.

Certainly not in front of Tuck.

"Yes, well, come, sit," Charleton said. "I see you've already helped yourself to a libation." This was directed at his heir.

Tuck tipped his glass, an incorrigible grin on his face. "Yes, well, it seemed fortification might be necessary."

"Harrumph," the baron snorted, and made his way to his chair.

As the baron dropped into his place, Pierson took the other chair. Tuck remained standing, taking an insolent stance near the door.

Probably so he could beat a hasty retreat if it came to that.

Pierson turned his back to his old friend and got directly to the point. "Sir, I implore you, keep that chit out of my house and out of my life."

"Out of your house?" This incredulous statement came blurting out of Tuck, and the other two turned to him.

"Not a word out of you," Charleton threatened, adding a wag of his finger to emphasize his point.

That seemed to be enough for the reprobate. Tuck turned his attention back to his brandy glass.

Not that Pierson was fooled for a moment. But he wasn't about to leave just to return later so he could have a private word with Lord Charleton. He'd managed to get this far, so he'd conclude his business and get back to his house.

His castle. His sanctuary. Well away from loafing fools like Alaster Rowland — who only served to remind him of the past —

and well away from bothersome chits who prodded him to think only of the lonely days that lay ahead.

"Yes, well, my lord," the viscount said, sitting up. "You must rein Miss Tempest in. She's interfering in my life."

Charleton barked a laugh. "Get in line." Then after the moment, he glanced across the desk. "Though, I must say, if anything, I commend her — she got you out and over here. When was the last time you came calling?"

Pierson sat back, for he hardly saw how that mattered, but something about his uncle's hard expression suggested it did. To him. And that took the viscount aback — for he just assumed most people preferred not to see him. Not to be reminded of the ugly toll a war can take.

Besides, his limping about was hardly fashionable.

So as to his social calls, he had only one thing to say. "I hardly see how that matters. I simply prefer to keep my own company."

"Yes, the bleary eyes, pale features and grimace every time you move confirms as much," Tuck muttered.

Pierson took a deep breath. The sooner he got this interview over, the quicker he could leave. "Sir," he continued, shifting his chair so he faced Charleton directly, "if you can just keep her out of my house, I would be most appreciative."

Charleton glanced up. "Which one?"

Which one? A wary chill ran down his spine. "You mean there is more than one of them?"

"Yes. Two," Charleton replied. "Louisa and Lavinia."

There was a low whistle from Tuck. When the other two turned to glare at him, he grinned. "I'll be as still as the grave."

"Happy day that," Pierson muttered.

"Yes, well, which one is causing this misery, my boy?" Charleton asked.

Pierson paused and let a momentary flash of alarm fade a bit. He could hardly say the one with the strawberry-colored lips.

He glanced over his shoulder. Not in front of Tuck.

"Does it matter which one?" he said, with a shrug of indifference. "Ban them both if you must. And that beast of hers — why, he's practically moved into my house."

Charleton's brows quirked. "Hannibal? So you've had the pleasure."

"I don't know if I'd call it that —" Pierson began before his uncle barked a laugh.

"Better your house than mine," Charleton said. "While Louisa avows her cat is harmless, one of the maids quit just yesterday. Swore the beast had beset her with an evil eye."

"Probably didn't like cleaning up after him," Pierson noted.

"How's that?"

"That cat toppled one of my mother's Italian vases. And left a rather indistinguishable pile on the carpet. Not to mention he has a penchant for bringing in gifts."

"Gifts?" Tuck asked.

"Dead rats," Pierson told him, then returned to the more pressing matter at hand. "I just want the chit and her cat out of my house. I'm tired of her unexpected arrivals."

"Sounds like my sort of gel," Tuck added gleefully.

"None of that!" Charleton barked at him. "Those girls are Lady Charleton's goddaughters. Their father is a respected scholar and gentleman. They are innocent young girls, *ladies,* you devilish pup, and will be treated as such. Lady Charleton's wishes were explicit in this matter, especially since their mother died when they were young. Isobel promised Lady Tempest they would have . . . Well, she left instructions with Haley that they be . . ."

And as it always did when it came to his wife, Charleton came to a blundering halt and he glanced away, his grief still as fresh as the day Lady Charleton had been lost.

A twinge of something — guilt, perhaps — nudged at Pierson. Not that he'd done anything to help his favorite aunt's husband. Hadn't even gone to her funeral.

All he could do was glance away and try to ignore his own shame.

"Yes . . . well . . ." Tuck said into the awkward void. "Where were we? Ah, yes, banning Uncle's stray misses from your house, wasn't that it, Piers?"

The viscount gave a tight nod.

Tuck wasn't done. But then again, he did like to wade in where he wasn't wanted. "And what grievous offense has this chit managed — besides getting you to lower your demmed drawbridge? That she dared venture into your lair says much for her. Brave one, this gel."

Pierson turned slightly so he could look Tuck in the eye. "She fired my cook."

That brought Charleton out of his grief-stricken reverie. *"Louisa did what?"*

"Fired my cook," Pierson repeated, only after he silently tested her name. *Miss Louisa Tempest.*

No, that wouldn't do. To think of her with such familiarity would only lead to trouble. Miss Tempest she was, and troublesome

Miss Tempest she would remain. "After she sent him packing," Pierson continued, "she felt the need to go find a new one. Foisted some harridan off on me. Monstrous woman. Mrs. Picton. No. Mrs. Pettle."

He didn't know why he was complaining. If the meals he'd enjoyed since yesterday were any indication, the woman could cook. But that was beside the point . . .

Tuck came and sat down in the chair next to Pierson, gripping the padded arms. "You don't mean to say Mrs. Petchell?"

"Yes, that's it. What of it?"

Tuck sat back, raking his hand through his hair. "Aveley's Mrs. Petchell?"

"I don't know whose she was before, but now I've got the bother of her. But now that you say that, I do believe Miss Tempest mentioned that Lady Aveley helped her find the woman."

"Good God, man!" Tuck exclaimed. "Mrs. Petchell! In your kitchen, no less." He let out a low whistle of disbelief. "I want to see Aveley's face when he finds out. Nearly divorced his wife over the entire matter. Foolish chit fired the old gel so she could get herself some haughty French fellow."

Well, Pierson knew that scenario all too well. But still . . .

"What did this Petchell woman do that

Aveley's wife let her go? Poison someone?" he asked, not putting it past the rough woman to tamper with his kippers.

"Poison?" Tuck shook his head. "Oh, no, nothing so drastic. Rather, that spoiled miss Aveley took for a bride thought a French chef would lend their household entertainments a certain cachet — I do say, it's just one more reason not to marry — these Bath gels come along and take a well-ordered, sensible bachelor house and turn it upside down."

And even when one hasn't married them, Pierson fumed silently, thinking of Miss Tempest and the determined set of her strawberry lips.

Nor was Tuck done extolling the virtues of Mrs. Petchell. "Oh, you've stolen a march on Aveley, that's for certain. Mrs. Petchell is extraordinary — she can cook a beefsteak to a turn." He let out a sigh of envy, as if the plate was before him and he was allowed only a sniff. When he recovered, and he did so quickly, he continued. "You'll find out soon enough — and you'll be the envy of London. She turned down half a dozen offers, refused work from some very lofty addresses. Can't see why she'd come work for you, but that's to my benefit."

The man sat back, hands folded over his

stomach and his long legs stuck out in front of him.

Pierson didn't like the sound of that — nor the sight of Tuck making himself at home. "What the devil do you mean?"

"Now you have to invite me to supper. I won't be deprived, and don't worry, I hardly ever stand on ceremony. Nothing special — just half a dozen or so dishes and a good steak. Oh, and that port your father always kept. You haven't drunk it all down, have you?"

Pierson flinched at the implication. His drinking was his own business. "I don't host suppers."

Tuck leaned back in his chair. "You do now, cuz," he said with his usual confidence. "And I don't see why you are over here complaining about this Miss Tempest to our uncle. That gel managed to get Mrs. Petchell into your kitchen. Mrs. Petchell, of all wonders." He smiled and met Pierson's gaze. "What you should be doing is proposing to this paragon."

"Proposing?" Pierson sputtered as he sat up.

Tuck nodded, almost solemnly. He turned to Charleton. "Is this Miss Tempest a fetching bit of muslin? Might consider the gel myself if she's pretty. Is she?"

"No!" Pierson shot back, having regained his wits.

"No?" This question came from the baron.

"Not in the least," Pierson insisted.

"Well, is she or isn't she?" Tuck asked, his gaze moving from his uncle to Pierson as if he knew something was afoot.

Of course he did. Tuck could find mischief in an empty sack.

And that was the problem. Pierson didn't know why, but he didn't want Tuck — or any man with such a reputation — anywhere near Miss Tempest.

"Fetching? No. Not particularly. Rather plain in my estimation. Reminds me of a sparrow," Pierson replied.

This seemed to deflate Tuck's interest in her. For now. "Yes, well, you do have an eye. Or at least you did. Your Melliscent was fair enough. And if you say this Miss Tempest isn't —"

"Not in the least," the viscount asserted. "Quite plain. And worse, a harridan in the making." To emphasize his point, he screwed his brows together and frowned at their uncle. "Heaven help you, Charleton, when you foist her off on some unsuspecting rube." He shuddered for good measure.

For his part, Lord Charleton said nothing, watching their exchange with a bland

137

expression, though if Pierson didn't know better, he suspected the baron was bemused by the viscount's dissembling.

Well, there was a fragment of truth in all of it.

The gel was going to be the death of some man — just not him.

And most decidedly, not Tuck.

Plain? Louisa reeled back from the doorway. *A harridan in the making?*

She didn't know which one offended her more . . . or why she even cared.

"Louisa Tempest! What are you doing?" Lavinia's horrified question spun Louisa around.

Good heavens, her sister's timing couldn't be worse.

"Ssshh," she replied, and nodded toward the door.

Her sister frowned. "Come away from there right now," she whispered, catching Louisa by the crook of her arm and trying to tug her away. "What if someone catches you?"

She'd considered such a consequence when she'd walked past and heard Wakefield's unmistakable tones coming from inside. But that same voice had lured her closer, just as the possibility of his kiss had before.

She slipped from her sister's grasp. "But it's *him.*" Despite how her pride rankled at being called a harridan, or rather "one in the making," for some reason she wanted to hear more of Wakefield's opinions.

Even if he thought her a ruinous match.

Well, she had her own opinions of him. Awful beast of a man.

"Him?" Lavinia repeated, then the dawning light of understanding widened her eyes. "Oh, *him.*" Lavinia looked from the door to her sister. "Are you certain? Lady Aveley says he never leaves his house. I swear, Louisa, if you have gone and ruined —"

"No, no, it is nothing like that," Louisa said, even if it had sounded very much like that.

Oh, bother, it sounded *exactly* like that.

I just want the chit and her cat out of my house. I'm tired of her unexpected arrivals.

Yes, well, at least he'd already levied that charge before Lavinia happened upon the scene.

And apparently the unprecedented arrival of Lord Wakefield changed her sister's disdain for eavesdropping, for now it was Lavinia with her ear pressed to the door.

"Who's the other gentleman?" she asked,

getting straight to the heart of the matter. Lavinia might not approve of eavesdropping on principle, but that didn't mean she was unaccomplished in the act.

Louisa shook her head. "I'm not certain. Lord Charleton called him Tuck."

After a moment of consideration, Lavinia came up with the answer. "That would make him Mr. Rowland, Lord Charleton's heir. The son of Lord Charleton's brother. Lady Aveley told me all about him. He's barely received — a terrible bounder." She shook her head with dismay, for such a man would never do in Lavinia's estimation.

Respectability. Loyalty. Sensibility.

Those were the traits her sister wanted in a marriage partner.

Having met Lord Wakefield and listened to this Mr. Rowland, Louisa was starting to believe her sister would be better served by getting a pug than seeking a husband in London.

"Whatever are they going on about?" Lavinia whispered as she strained to hear more.

"Mrs. Petchell," Louisa supplied, ear back at the crack in the door, and having caught up with the subject being discussed inside. When her sister appeared puzzled, she continued. "The cook. The one Lady Ave-

140

ley suggested."

"That might explain this," she said as she dug into her pocket and produced a note, handing it over to Louisa before manning her position once again.

Louisa glanced down at the note written in a rough, bold hand.

A word with you, Miss Tempest. Immediately.

M. Petchell

Louisa nearly groaned aloud. This didn't bode well. Not in the least.

"Go on, see what she wants and make sure that everything is managed," Lavinia whispered, shooing her toward the back stairs. "I'll take a full accounting for you." And with that, she pressed her ear back to the door.

CHAPTER 6

Pierson left his uncle's study some time later without a sense of accomplishment. If anything, he was more out of sorts than when he'd arrived.

"She's hired you an adequate cook," Lord Charleton had told him with a dismissive wave of his hand.

"More than adequate," Tuck had added — though no one had given his comment any notice, for the baron was already continuing on.

"Be that as it may," the baron had said in a tone that wasn't to be brooked. "She's done you a favor and there is no reason to be over here finding fault with a fat goose. The matter is closed."

Before Pierson could complain, the baron added with a firm conviction, "Besides, my boy, Lady Aveley will soon have those two chits far too busy for either of them to spare a moment meddling in your affairs."

"Or lack thereof," Tuck had added.

With that decided, there had been nothing left to be done but take his leave — which he'd done before Tuck could add any more of his insulting observations.

Gathering up his hat and coat from the butler, Pierson stomped his way home, wishing he could share Charleton's conviction that Miss Tempest's interference was over — given that she'd soon be out in society and haven't any time for such foolery.

Indeed, he should be overjoyed in the knowledge, yet there was a lingering part of him that was more than put out that Tuck had been summoned for just that purpose — aiding in the sisters' imminent launch into the marriage mart.

And he, Pierson, had not.

It wasn't as if he wanted any part of London society. He'd been through that social whirl years before. Even been betrothed to the most sought-after lady in all the *ton*.

Melliscent.

How odd of Tuck to bring her up — for he'd never approved of Pierson's pursuit of the Original and had warned him continually of her failings. Not that Pierson believed him — not until he'd returned from Spain and the perfect and lofty miss who had promised so faithfully to wait for him had departed his bedside in a whirl of silk skirts and disdain.

How can I be held to you? I never promised to marry half a man.

Not that he'd cared at that point. Still, Tuck had been right.

Bother the man.

Pierson heaved a sigh and wished he could stand behind popular opinion that Alaster Rowland was London's laziest, most useless, careless, feckless, ne'er-do-well who had ever lived — his entire existence hinged on his expectations of inheriting his uncle's title — living off Charleton's largesse, his mother's unfathomable patience and, more to the point, his notorious charm.

But he couldn't. He knew Tuck too well.

And unfortunately that knowledge was mutual. Which was exactly the reason he couldn't, nay wouldn't, look his old friend in the eye.

Still, it would be so much easier if he could dismiss Tuck outright. But seeing him brought forth all the memories he so longed to forget.

Still, whatever had Tuck been thinking? Calling him 'cuz' and mocking his solitary existence.

"If you'd deign to show your face," Pierson muttered, repeating Tuck's admonishment. Go about Town? Madness! It was all stares and curious glances as he hobbled past, followed by heads shaking in dismay at his reduced state.

Why on earth would Tuck even suggest such a thing? That he go out for display, a curiosity like one of the elephants in the Tower?

Of course that never occurred to Tuck, who went everywhere. Was welcomed everywhere.

Well, nearly everywhere.

Pierson paused, and not so much because he now had to manage the steps up to his own front door, but because of a more wrenching realization.

He was jealous.

Jealous to the core of Tuck and his capering ways. His freedom.

Worse, when he looked at Tuck he saw his own life — the life he'd once had and would still if he hadn't been caught in a rush of patriotic fever and bought a commission in the Tenth.

Seeing Tuck reminded him all too clearly of the other life that had been lost in that decision. The one that haunted Pierson every waking moment.

And, as always happened with those memories, the ones perpetually lurking about the periphery, waiting for that weak moment when he hadn't the wherewithal to send them scurrying back into the shadows, they stormed his thoughts, just as the French had come after Paget and his brigades as they'd raced to the coast.

Just as Poldie had rashly rushed into the path of the bullet meant for him.

Poldie. Pierson reached out and caught the railing in a tight grasp as an overly familiar sense of panic and nausea rushed over him.

Different. Everything would be different if *Poldie* hadn't followed him — into the Hussars, into the war. Then he, Pierson, would be the one buried in an anonymous grave in Spain and Poldie would still be capering about Town in Tuck's wake or married and living in the country, breeding horses and hounds.

Poldie, I'm so sorry.

And for some wry reason, he swore he could hear his old boon companion whisper back, *Don't pity me, pity Tuck.*

Pity Tuck, indeed! Pierson thought. *For what?*

As he went to go up the steps, setting his cane as he went, he had his answer.

146

If he wasn't lame and, as Miss Tempest so eloquently put it, "a rare beast," he'd be in much the same straits as Tuck right this moment — with Lord Charleton insisting that he do his share in escorting and squiring the Misses Tempest about Town.

Possibly being leaned upon to take one of the sisters in marriage.

What the devil was his uncle thinking? Not even the most desperate of *cits* was likely to dangle a daughter in front of Alaster Rowland, and yet here was Lord Charleton doing just that.

Pierson ignored the fit of pique that flared up inside him. It wasn't like he could dance attendance on any woman.

Couldn't dance, for that matter.

But it also occurred to him that for all his assertions that Miss Tempest — at least *his* Miss Tempest — was a plain harridan, a practiced rake like Tuck would eventually find his lie amusing . . . and worse, draw unsavory conclusions as to why Pierson had told such a Banbury tale to begin with.

Especially since the gel was an all-too-temping bit of muslin.

No, he wouldn't put it past Tuck to court Miss Tempest if only to add salt to Pierson's ever-present wounds.

Demmed bastard.

Tightening his hold of the railing, he hauled himself up the stairs, grimacing with each step, but managing it. By the time he got to the top, Tiploft had the door open and looked to say something, but the strained expression on the viscount's face kept his butler from uttering whatever was on his mind.

"I'll be in my study," he muttered as he handed over his coat and hat and gloves.

"Very good, my lord," Tiploft replied.

Pierson started down the hall, but found his way blocked — someone had left one of the closet doors open — and he was guessing it wasn't Tiploft. Probably one of Mrs. Petchell's brats. He shifted under his walking stick so he could reach out and close the door, yet as he did, a bolt of pain ran up his leg, bringing with it his all-too-familiar ire.

But this time it was more than just the discomfort — it was Tuck and his gallivanting ways, it was the slight of his uncle not asking him to dance attendance on a pair of chits, that he wasn't good enough to court some country miss, that he'd lost everything when Poldie had stolen his fate, and suddenly, the very small thing of finding the closet door wide open when it should be shut propelled his anger forward like a champagne cork prodded from its prison.

He exploded.

"Demmit!" he bellowed, and shoved his shoulder into the door.

Only instead of the satisfaction of hearing it rattle in its casing as it slammed shut, there was an indignant yelp from inside and the door came rounding back on him, hitting him squarely in the chest.

Sending him toppling over in an indignant heap.

Louisa sighed as she got up on her tiptoes and surveyed the array of mismatched linens on the top shelf of Lord Wakefield's linen closet.

Dear heavens, however could a house be run amid such chaos?

Certainly she didn't blame Mrs. Petchell in the least for being in such a pet; the kitchen, well, the entire house, was a disorganized mess. No wonder the poor lady had asked her if she, meaning Louisa, could spare an hour and do something to bring some sort of order to the linen closet — so when Mrs. Petchell sent Bitty for some rags, the poor child wouldn't fetch some fancy doily meant for the dining room.

This sentiment was echoed by Tiploft, who apologetically explained, as he showed her into the large walk-in closet that held all the tools of household cleaning, that the management of such things quite escaped him.

He was a butler after all, and what was needed was a housekeeper, but until His Lordship would agree to hire one, well . . .

Having been raised in Kempton, she could hardly refuse. The lessons of neighborly kindness had been drilled into her since the tender age of ten, when she and Lavinia had gone to their first meeting of the Society for the Temperance and Improvement of Kempton.

As Lady Essex always said, *A lady never shirks her duty when asked for help.*

No matter if the recipient of such kindness thought her plain and a harridan.

Louisa paused in her sorting as her thoughts flitted back to what she'd overheard.

Fetching? No. Not particularly. Rather plain in my estimation.

She huffed a bit and reached for another stack of linens. If anything, knowing his true sentiments made it easier for her to continue thinking him a beast — even if she'd nearly changed her opinion of the man when he'd begrudgingly allowed Mrs. Petchell and the children to stay.

As she'd watched him capitulate — seen his face soften as the children had offered their promises to him — she'd thought for a moment she'd glimpsed the man Lady Aveley had hinted was beneath all the bluster and beastly manners.

Yes, well, she wasn't sure she wanted to know who this other Lord Wakefield might be — if he was kind and caring and a gentleman, that only made his terrible assertions to Mr. Rowland that she was plain all the more stinging.

And whyever would he say such dreadful things? Especially when just yesterday she'd thought . . .

Oh, bother, she didn't even want to remember what she'd thought.

That he might kiss her . . . and that she wanted him to.

Oh, it was all so ridiculous. Why would she want such a wretched beast to kiss her?

Well, she wouldn't be led astray, not by him or any other man, she thought as she tossed several well-used towels into the rag bin, hoping her errant thoughts would follow.

But she couldn't forget the brush of his hand on her cheek, warm and sure. Gentle, even. Which rather belied the overbearing man she'd come to know.

Instead the viscount had touched her and plucked desires from the shadows of her heart as easily as one might pluck the petals from a daisy — each one a wish and a prayer.

Kiss me. Devour me. Take me.

No. No. No! Louisa added another frayed towel to the rag bin — as frayed as her nerves. Proper ladies didn't become entangled with gentlemen.

Not. Like. That.

She'd vowed to spend the Season helping her sister find a nice, respectable match with a gentleman who had a proper, respectable, orderly household in the country, far from gossips and where a bit of breakage wouldn't be an issue.

Nor would he mind that his wife was a bit madcap. And ungainly.

Louisa paused. For that very image of a proper gentleman suddenly seemed all too tame and, quite frankly, boring.

Her vision of an overly patient paragon came to a sweeping end as a pirate of a man stormed through her thoughts, a man who would capture her in his arms and carry her up the stairs of his dark and dangerous lair and . . . well . . . make her feel as she had before . . . when she'd thought the viscount meant to do just that.

Ravish her.

And when this pirate growled about and acted ever so beastly, Louisa never minded because just as quickly he would remember that he had better things to do and would return to plundering her heart.

As it was, she barely gave any note to the sound of the front door being opened, or the thudding of boots on the stairs.

That is, until she heard an indignant curse and the closet darken as the door came slamming shut.

In her defense, Louisa would note, she wasn't overly fond of small, enclosed spaces to begin with, but the very notion of being locked in a dark closet sent her into a panic.

"Dear me, I am still in here, Mr. Tiploft!" she cried out and pushed the door back — no, more like frantically shoved it — which was then followed by a wrenching curse, the clatter of something hitting the floor and then a large thud.

Followed by a truly awful groan.

A beastly one.

Louisa flinched, her eyes screwed shut. Oh, no. *Lord Wakefield.*

If only it were possible to wish oneself well away from a disaster.

Not that she hadn't been in this predicament before. The small fire at Wheldale. The bunting incident of '07. The punch bowl last Christmas.

However did she always end up in these circumstances?

As she let the sequence of events unfold in her mind's eye — the door coming shut, her panic and push, the clatter of his walking stick hitting the floor, followed by the horrible thud of him, Lord Wakefield, landing akimbo — she cursed her ill luck.

Opening her eyes just a bit, she wondered if it would be possible to remain in the viscount's linen closet for an hour or so?

At least until he managed to gain his feet and his temper cooled a bit.

Then to her dismay, he cursed again as he made what sounded like another effort to right himself.

No, if his choice of vocabulary was any indication, it would be Michaelmas before she dared poke her nose out the door.

Yet when she heard him groan again, she could hardly remain still. Sighing in resignation, she peered around the door.

Only to find that it was worse than she thought — for Wakefield was completely sprawled out on the floor and his walking stick well out of reach.

"Oh, let me help you —" she said, hurrying around the door.

"You!" he growled, looking up at her. "I should have known."

Well, whatever did *that* mean? As if she went about bowling over viscounts as a matter of habit.

Shattered punch bowls were more her calling card.

"Are you determined to be the death of me?" he complained as he struggled to reach for his walking stick.

"I hardly meant to do this — you were about to lock me in a closet," she shot back, retrieving his walking stick and handing it to him — for which he rather ungratefully snatched it out of her grasp.

"Miss Tempest, you have a talent for being the most bothersome, meddlesome female I have had the misfortune to —"

And a wry part of her noted that he hadn't added *plain* to that list of sins.

However, as much emphasis as he put into his scold, when he began to get up — even with the help of his cane — she could see what a struggle it was for him and silently went to his side and caught hold of his arm, adding her own strength and will to his determined resolve.

Yet the moment she caught hold of him, she realized that as damaged as he might appear, as beastly as he most certainly was,

Lord Wakefield was entirely male beneath his ragged exterior, for her fingers wound around thick, corded muscles that bespoke of an unyielding power — as hard and unforgiving as the man himself.

Something about that buried, hidden strength left her oddly unsettled — her breath catching in her throat, her knees quaking. That, and she suddenly had an unfathomable desire to trace her hands up the length of his arm to his shoulders, to the planes of his chest, if only to see just how hard the rest of him might be.

Good heavens, whatever was wrong with her? Every time she got close to this man, she began thinking like the worst sort of jade.

Worse, her heart began thudding with an unsteady, unnatural tattoo — each beat like an enchanting, beguiling wish: *Draw closer to him.*

When she looked up, she realized he wasn't in his usual state of *dishabille* — his unruly brown hair was tied back, though his shave could only be called rough. Yet with that much of the stubble scraped away, she discovered just how strong (or rather, stubborn) his jawline was, and how the hollows of his cheeks lent him a hungry, piercing profile.

A beast still, but a strikingly handsome one without his ragged trappings.

Whatever would it be like to be desired by such a man? she wondered. Until, that is, she realized she was staring at him — well, gaping actually — and worse, clinging to him, even when he was up and standing on his own two feet.

She knew he no longer needed her support but she found herself unwilling to let go, pinned by his furious expression, trapped in the glare of his dark eyes.

Lost in the scandalous desire to be carried off.

That is until she remembered what he'd said about her earlier.

Rather plain in my estimation . . .

Louisa's hand dropped from the crook of his arm and she hastily stepped back — out of reach and well out of that dangerous sphere where Lord Wakefield was so . . . so monstrous, and came so close to being . . . something most tempting.

But that didn't stop her heart from twisting a bit, knowing that when he looked at her, he found her wanting.

"What are you doing in my house?" he demanded, his tone punctuating his disfavor with her, and thankfully lessening his appeal.

"I'm nearly done and then I'll be gone," she told him, retreating into the linen closet and wishing this task hadn't taken so long. She had hoped to be well and done before he'd returned.

To her chagrin, he followed her into the tight confines and with his commanding height and wide shoulders, he took up the remaining space.

He seemed to steal all the air as well.

"What are you doing in my house?" he repeated.

She drew another deep breath, one that barely seemed to fill her, and turned around, having picked up a stack of tea towels that had been mistakenly placed atop bed linens. "I think that would be evident even to you, my lord. I am sorting linens for Mrs. Petchell."

"That's not necessary," he told her, taking the tea towels from her and shoving them back on the sheets. His dark brows furrowed together and silently finished his statement with an emphatic *Get. Out. Of. My. House.*

Louisa took a deep breath. "It is most necessary — a cook needs to know which of the linens can be used as rags and which cloths can be used in the kitchen. This," she said, with a flutter of her hands at the tumbled collection of linens and sheets, "is a mess."

He took a skeptical glance at it all. "No one else has ever complained before."

"Then you haven't hired competent help."

His jaw set. "There isn't a finer butler in London than Tiploft."

Louisa stepped around him, her skirt brushing against his legs.

Long, hard legs, she recalled. Muscled and lean . . .

Quickly she set aside the memory of his naked limbs and went back to sorting tea towels. "Mr. Tiploft would be an excellent butler if he were allowed to do his job. Instead he must also be your valet and the housekeeper, all the while seeing to the shopping and managing the accounts. Worst, you've failed to notice that he is too old to be doing so much. He should have been retired years ago."

Her censure had no impact on Lord Wakefield — as if he hadn't the least notion how a properly run house was managed.

"I hardly see how any of this" — he waved his hands at the disorganized shelves — "is preventing Mrs. Petchell from cooking my supper."

"Lady Essex always says what you need should be in reach. Easily gained and quick to find. Take this for example," she said, holding up a beautiful linen tea towel, the edges decorated with a delicate and intricate embroidery of roses and vines and leaves. "Such a towel should never be used in the kitchen. What a disaster it would be if Bitty took this by mistake to mop up something —"

"— hideous your cat left behind?"

Louisa ignored his suggestion, turning the beautiful towel over. "This was most likely done by a previous Lady Wakefield in the days before she even knew she would be a viscountess. This is an heirloom, my lord. Made by a young lady for her glory box."

He scoffed at the notion. "An heirloom? I hardly see how. It's a towel. I'd wager you have stacks and stacks of this sort of frippery set aside for the day when you drag some man into the parson's trap."

Of course he would view marriage as a trap. Hadn't he done his best to send Mr. Rowland fleeing for the hills rather than be presented to her or her sister?

"Then that is a wager you would lose, my lord," she told him. "I haven't such a collection for it has never been my intent to marry. However, I can appreciate the time and effort another put into her dreams and hopes." She took the towel from him and carefully folded it, placing it on a higher shelf where it wouldn't be grabbed by Bitty in some mistaken haste.

The viscount crossed his arms over his chest. "Not marry? The devil you say!"

"The devil has nothing to do with it," she told him tartly.

"But Charleton says —"

"It is my sister who wants a Season, not me. I am here in London under duress."

Then something happened. The hard line of his jaw relaxed and his lips teased into something resembling a smile. "Yes, I can see that," he teased. "I suppose you brought that hellcat along with you just to drive away any unwitting suitors."

"Hannibal has his moments."

"Warn me before one of those comes along."

Louisa clapped her lips together to keep from laughing. Who would have known the man had a sense of humor?

"Let me guess, the real reason you have no glory box is because you've been too busy being a nuisance to some other gentleman to have the time to stitch up a stack of towels."

She flinched at his words, but wasn't about to rise to his bait. "I have no glory box because I come from Kempton. There was no point in using my time collecting such things when it was all but assured that I would never marry."

This seemed to take him aback. "Why wouldn't you get married?"

Well, other than being plain and a future harridan? she wanted to snap, but, remembering Lavinia's admonishment to maintain a civil relationship with the viscount, she took a deep breath and explained the obvious. Even as she said the words, she knew her explanation was only making her seem more ridiculous in his eyes.

"The village I come from, Kempton," she told him, "has been for some time — well, since forever — cursed. Well, not the village so much, but any lady born there. We are destined to never marry — and for the few who have dared, the marriages have ended rather badly."

Heavens, she'd never even realized how archaic and foolish it all sounded. Then again, she'd grown up surrounded by the Kempton curse — and never once questioned the soundness of such a belief.

"And yet here you are," he countered. "In London, and according to my uncle, seeking some unfortunate fellow to apparently curse. As if knocking me over isn't enough for you."

Bother the man. Sense of humor or not,

he was determined to mortify her.

"Yes, well, the curse has been lifted — or so it seems," she replied, taking up another stack of tea towels. "As of late there have been a flurry of weddings — the new Duchess of Preston, for example, and the newly wed Countess of Roxley, both of whom are from Kempton. Happily, no one has turned up dead, or mad, or . . ."

Or with a fire iron stuck in his chest. Which, Louisa mused, as she looked over Wakefield, might be well deserved.

Meanwhile, the viscount's brow was screwed into knots. "Roxley's married?"

"It was in all the papers," she told him.

"Whatever sort of harebrained gel would marry him?"

Louisa bristled a bit. "His bride, Miss Harriet Hathaway, comes from a most noble and illustrious Kempton family. Four of her brothers are in His Majesty's service. And she's not harebrained."

His gaze narrowed. "Hathaway — as in Lieutenant Hathaway?"

"Yes, Quinton. You know him? Oh, of course you would. Lady Aveley said you were in Spain."

The viscount gave a tight nod. "Yes." And that was all he said, having glanced away.

And yet she couldn't stop talking. Not as

long as he kept standing there in a moody silence. Perhaps if she explained it more clearly, he wouldn't look at her as if she was mad as a hatter. "So you see how there was no point to using my time for stitching up such fripperies, as you call them." Folding another tea towel, she added it to the growing stack. "In Kempton, ladies have traditionally put their time to more philanthropic uses."

This brought the viscount's piercing gaze back upon her, but she didn't miss the mischievous twinkle there. "Such as pestering their neighbors?"

"No one in Kempton ever complains when the society takes them under their wing," she shot back. Well, hardly anyone. There were a few exceptions. Sir Roger had always been a touch difficult, but they managed to see his house properly done every Christmas. And the widow Botton had never taken their help kindly. What with her collection of unruly cats and broken buckets that she thought the entire village was bent on stealing.

"The society?"

Truly, did he have to sound so suspicious? It wasn't like they were fomenting revolution.

She huffed a sigh. "The Society for the

Temperance and Improvement of Kempton. Lady Essex Marshom is our esteemed patroness."

The immediate look of horror on his face said all too clearly he knew who Lady Essex was.

"Whatever does this society do?" His question had an air of *Dare I ask*?

"Why, help our neighbors," she replied, taking one more look at the towels she'd gathered up — most of which were worn thin and needed replacing. Without even thinking, she handed the offending ones to Lord Wakefield.

"Aha! So you have a natural calling for this sort of thing," he said, looking up from the towels she'd handed him.

"Calling for what?" It was a question Louisa would nearly regret asking.

Viscount Wakefield leaned closer. "Driving men mad."

No truer words had ever been spoken.

Miss Tempest had the unwitting habit of driving him just that . . . mad.

In the three days since she'd come barging into his life, she couldn't have done a better job of upending it if she'd arrived with a barrage of cannon fire and a battalion behind her.

Certainly she'd done something to him — thinking of yesterday when she'd left him undone, tangled up with desire.

For a brief moment in the garden, he'd believed. He'd felt. He'd desired.

Yet, by what right did he have to live, to feel every bit of life, when . . .

Pierson drew back from the dark memories of Spain. No, he had no right to be living. To feel such desires. None whatsoever.

Yet here she was. Again. Like a clipped penny constantly finding its way back into his pocket — even when she thought him a complete beast.

So perhaps it was time for a different approach. If she was as proper as his uncle had said, then there was one way to send her off.

For good. Especially if she was as dead set against matrimony and men as she claimed.

No matter how wrong his method might be. A single kiss ought to do the trick.

Yet, when faced with the prospect, he realized he'd nearly forgotten how, even with Miss Tempest's pair of perfect lips luring him closer.

Yet as Tuck might say, stealing a kiss was nothing more than the turn of a card.

Easily done, Pierson mused, when there was nothing to risk.

And when the lady smelled as tempting as a summer breeze — beguiling and full of promise, he remembered how it was done like the veriest cardsharp.

Yet he wavered with indecision. Fear, one might even say. Perhaps he should just back away and show her the door — just order her out. *Yes, well,* an ironic sort of voice reminded him, *look how that has worked so far.*

But this might . . .

And for a man who'd been living in a self-induced winter for so long, the warmth of her lips and the promised delights of her lush body were too much to resist.

"Miss Tempest," he said, reaching out to gently pull a wayward curl from the confines of its pins, and letting it fall over her cheek. "Didn't Lady Essex ever teach you the dangers of linen closets?"

She backed up a step, but that was all the room left to her, and when her backside bumped into the shelves behind her, she let out a small, indignant yelp.

"Well, she did say once that a disorganized closet was a sign of . . . a sign of . . ." she began, glancing around him and looking ready to bolt like a fawn in the forest.

"A sign of what?" he asked, his hand reaching out and cradling her chin, stilling her movements.

He gave her her due — she chucked up her chin and met his gaze with a steely one of her own. "Lady Essex says untidy closets are a sign of darker troubles."

"Truly?" he mused as he leaned over her and inhaled deeply around the shell of her ear. "How dark?"

She might be doing her best to look unmoved, but he could see her pulse fluttering in her neck, see her lips part slightly, her lashes waver as they softly closed. "I haven't the vaguest notion —" she began, and stopped as his lips brushed against a spot right behind her ear. "My lord! Whatever are you doing?"

"Discovering your darkest secrets."

And true to his word, he caught hold of her with one hand and drew her up against him.

For a precarious second, he reconsidered. Realized the folly of turning over a card without knowing what was in one's hand. That is until she looked up at him, her lips open in a perfect moue of protest, which only left her open to him.

Enticing him.

While he might be out of practice, he knew when to forge ahead, and so he captured her lips with his.

Soft and yielding, she shivered in his arms. And for Pierson, he realized quickly that kissing Miss Louisa Tempest was like falling into a dream. His senses filled with her, roses and something so very feminine, a scent he knew, one that left him trapped with promises.

Her full breasts pushed against his chest, his hand rested at the small of her back, just above the rounded curve of her bottom.

This chit was the most delectable collection of curves and wiles and so he explored, letting his hands trace over her, until they came to her bottom and he let his fingers curve around her, hold her close.

Desire and lust raced through him as he continued to kiss her, his tongue sliding over those tempting strawberry petals, opening her up, and all he could think of was what it would be like to undo the rest of her.

Her prim gown, her tidy chignon — and leave her in the same state as his closets — in complete *dishabille.*

Naked and willing. His to do with as he pleased.

To devour, to make love to, bury himself inside her, stroke her until he was sated and senseless, and the only thing to be heard was her ragged sighs as she came shivering and crying out in release from beneath him.

Like a starving man, he deepened the kiss, his hand tucking her right up against him — against his arousal, her body fitting to his with exquisite agony.

This is what it will be like, he thought recklessly. Hot and tight. It was enough to nearly send him over the edge.

His hand roamed up, following the line of her curves, rounding over her breast, his thumb rolling back and forth over the tight nipple hidden beneath.

Around him, everything shifted as his body became consumed with desire. However had this happened?

She had done this.

Louisa.

Miss Tempest no more, he realized with stunning clarity.

This minx had unleashed him from his chains, undone the passions that he'd spent so much time tamping down, refusing to acknowledge.

In that moment his entire, hastily drawn plan to send her fleeing shifted.

He was supposed to be kissing her thoroughly, and then send her running for the safety and sanctity of Charleton's, but he'd forgotten what it was like to hold a woman.

A tempting one. He'd forgotten how close

and treacherous that line could be where play could turn to reckless, dangerous want.

His heart hammered a new tattoo. *Live. Live. Love.*

Love?

No. Not that. Never that.

Pierson wrenched back from her, trying desperately to catch a breath, still his hammering heart. Oh, good God, what had he done?

What had he unleashed?

The moment Wakefield's lips claimed hers, Louisa was lost.

Oh, not her usual kind of lost where she couldn't find her way out of the maze of halls at Foxgrove without someone pointing the way, but an entirely new sort of lost . . .

She wasn't herself anymore.

The viscount's kiss had awakened the lady within her.

Desires she'd never known burst free from their confines — how had she not known that this was what a kiss could be? Could do?

As Wakefield's lips covered hers, teased their way past her surprise, it was no mere brush of the lips, no staid and proper kiss from this viscount.

Louisa's heart hammered in her chest, her

breath lost as well, caught in a passion-filled sigh trapped in her throat.

A tangle of thoughts teased her. *Run your fingers over his barely shaved chin. Wind your arms around his neck.*

Touch him.

That one, so filled with need, nearly shocked her out of her slippers.

Touch him?

She didn't dare.

But it seemed he did.

Dare, that is.

His hand roamed down her back, leaving a delicious sense of wonder in its sure and deliberate wake. The viscount was no wary explorer — he boldly marched toward his conquest, skilled and confident in the path he forged.

And, having found his way, he caught hold of her — dear heavens, his hand was on her backside! — his touch warm and strong, and then he pulled her up against him.

All of him.

At least, she surmised, the important part.

Damaged and broken he might appear, but he was still a man.

He pulled her closer, hitching her up against him, so close, she teetered on the tips of her slippers and found her fingers winding into the lapels of his coat, if only to steady herself.

She might have toppled him over earlier, but now he was upending her world, and she couldn't do anything but hold on for dear life.

Still, the closer she came, the more she discovered. His lips had teased her mouth open, and now his tongue filled her, tormented her.

Touch him.

A shiver ran down her spine as she realized that this bit of passion was but a taste. A tease. A window to another world.

And windows, given Louisa's rambling luck, were something she generally tumbled out of.

The real question became, would he catch her?

As if he had felt her shiver, knew the questions chasing through her thoughts, he pulled her closer yet, so while there were still layers of clothes between them, it felt as if she'd been laid bare, that there was nothing between them but desire.

Louisa tried to breathe, willed herself to pull away, flee before it was too late.

But then his hand rose, tracing an intoxicating trail up from her hip, rounding her breast — her breast? — Never had she felt so perfectly a lady as his hand cupped her there, reverently, and then hungrily as his thumb rolled over her nipple.

The sigh that she'd been holding back rushing out in surprise. "Oooh," she gasped.

His finger teased again over her nipple and it hardened quickly in response.

And here she'd thought that love was all soft verses and lulling melodies.

No, indeed. Love, or rather passion, was hard and full of twisting, demanding desires that left one restless, anxious, frenzied and . . .

For a second his kiss deepened and then in an instant it was gone.

He reeled back from her, gasping, pulling air into his lungs like a drowning man having found the water's surface.

Louisa wished she could find the wherewithal to breathe as well, for she was dizzy and reeling in a whirlpool of desires.

Then she found herself cut adrift as he let go of her, as if she burned, and she reached behind and caught hold of one of the shelves, trying to steady the chaos whirling inside her. Find her footing. Her bearings.

For here she was as disheveled as his linen closet.

Ragged. Torn.

And in an odd way, made all the more beautiful for the discovery.

She'd never thought of herself as the sort to inspire passion.

Panic, mayhap, but not this blazing black fire that burned in the viscount's dark eyes as he gaped at her.

At least, she hoped that fire was fueled by desire.

But it was something else.

For, whatever he'd planned when he'd trapped her inside here, when he'd leaned close and caught her lips with his, it hadn't gone entirely as he'd desired.

Something had changed. For the worse.

Her hand moved to her lips. So whyever had he kissed her? "What are you doing to me?" he asked so quietly, so softly, she thought for a moment she might not have heard him correctly.

What was she doing? He was the one who had kissed her, she would point out, but that hardly seemed the correct answer considering the furious set of his jaw. "Nothing," she said, shaking her head. "I only came to —" Her words stumbled to a halt for she could see clearly the passion and desire she'd felt moments ago in his touch, in his kiss, had turned to something far more dangerous.

"Go away," he told her, his voice rising, pleading, while his hand — the one that had teased a gasp from her — now pointed to the door. "Can't you see what you are doing . . . what you're asking of me?"

Agony, deep and wrenching, blazed in his eyes. A pain so piercing, she feared it would overtake him.

"Nothing. I'm not —" she stammered, but realized he wasn't looking at her anymore, his face turned toward someplace far away, his eyes glazed over with a desolation that had welled up from some hidden recesses, a darkness only he knew.

Louisa reached out for him, but he flinched away from her touch and then dropped to his knees.

The man who'd kissed her so passionately was gone. Lost.

"Go!" he ordered. "I beg of you, leave me be."

Torn between her innate need to help but taken aback by this sudden change in his demeanor, she didn't know what to do.

Yet one thing was certain, the thorn was back in his paw, embedded so deeply, he roared with rage. "Get out!"

Louisa wasn't such a fool not to heed him.

She caught hold of her skirt and dashed from the closet, stumbling against him in her haste — but this time it was so very different.

His body was still hard and solid, yes, but it was shaking with fury and barely restrained anger.

And for a second, his pain, his fears were hers as well, and now it was she reeling back from him in shock.

She had done this. There was no other explanation.

Once out of the linen closet, Louisa dashed down the hall and made for the stairs, heedless of her course.

And for once in her life, Louisa Tempest didn't give a second thought or backward glance to the breakage she was leaving in her wake.

CHAPTER 7

*She is banned from my house, Charleton. Do
you hear me? Banned!*

The words still rang in Louisa's ears.
Heavens, they'd rung through Lord Charleton's house like one of St. Paul's bells.

For not long after Louisa had fled the
viscount's house, he'd arrived at Lord Charleton's door — for the second time in only
a day — and he'd made his sentiments
known only too loudly to the baron before
he'd stormed back to his lair across the lane.

Banned.

Now, hours later as Lavinia prattled on
from her narrow bed across their room —
something she'd read in the paper, a sale on
silks it seemed — Louisa fumed as she
stared out the window.

"Even though the money Lady Charleton
set aside for our Season is substantial, it
never hurts to be frugal, don't you agree?"
Lavinia asked.

"Hmm, yes, certainly," Louisa murmured, hoping that was the answer her sister was seeking. Thankfully Lavinia seemed satisfied as she went back to prowling her paper.

Out the window and over the garden wall, all Louisa could see was a single candle lit in one of the kitchen windows — the rest of the viscount's house stood silent, pitch black and unwelcoming.

Like the owner himself. Save when he wasn't holding her and . . .

She pressed her lips together and tried to look away, for she needed no reminders of what had transpired, how she'd left the linen closet.

Undone.

She ignored that word. It was rife with implications. Like the way her knees had wobbled the entire way home.

After all, she'd only been trying to help — that is until that dreadful man had come storming back into her path. Never mind that it was *his* house.

And now she was banned. She shuddered as she considered all the tasks that still needing tending over there — hiring more staff, a thorough cleaning of the cellars, and she didn't even want to consider how much dusting needed to be done. Oh, and she had to imagine that the attics were in a terrible state.

Let alone the terrible crime of leaving the linen closet only half sorted. Unfinished.

Oh, it was a terrible state to be in.

And she wasn't talking about the closet . . .

Lord Wakefield, she silently pleaded. *I am ever so sorry. I didn't know.*

The depth of his pain. His loss. Whatever had happened to him?

Something, she suspected, that had more to do with Spain than with a stolen kiss in a linen closet.

Yet that didn't stop her hand from going to her lips and wondering how one fixed that sort of pain.

It would take far more than a kiss.

Not that she'd ever find out. For Wakefield's sentiments had been clear.

I've told Tiploft I will sack him and anyone else who lets her set one foot inside my house, Charleton. Not one foot!

Oh, the shame of it.

Worse, the entire staff of Lord Charleton's house now knew the viscount's loudly made opinions about her "meddling" ways and penchant for "tampering with what isn't hers."

If only she could tell one and all that he'd kissed her first. Well, she'd meddled first, that was true enough, but he'd kissed her. Pulled her into his arms and kissed her. Right there in the linen closet.

Louisa didn't know if that made it even more scandalous — a linen closet, of all places!

Not that he'd seemed to notice. Nor had it stopped him from unraveling every bit of respectable decorum she'd woven around her life.

Unconsciously she closed her eyes, as if to blot out the rush of passion that welled up inside her, a well that until today had been quiet and unassuming, but now toiled and bubbled and threatened to boil over. Desire, raw and unbidden, and more importantly, unwanted, left her utterly confused.

She was supposed to be in London to help Lavinia find a respectable match — not let herself be led down a path to ruin. Then again, her situation could hardly compare to the agony she'd seen in his eyes.

Terrible, wrenching pain . . .

"Louisa? Good heavens! Are you listening to me? Which gown do you think would suit me better — this one, or the one with the slashed sleeves?" Her sister held up two fashion prints — one of which also featured a well-dressed gentleman standing attentively at the lady's side — not kissing her or referring to her as "a female horror."

"The one on the right," she told her sister as she hurriedly rose from the bed. Notably, it was the print without the gentleman. She paced to the door and then changed her mind, going to the closet.

No, not the closet, she decided, turning around yet again.

By now, her sister was gaping at her. "Whatever is the matter with you? Is it Lady Charleton's nephew who has you in such a state?" Lavinia set aside her fashion plates. "You can't let him inflame you."

Louisa's cheeks heated with mortification. Inflame? Was her secret that obvious?

"It isn't him. I just don't —"

Lavinia reached over and caught her hand. "Louisa, you worry too much. You'll be the most elegant lady in London. You need only concentrate. Remember what Lady Essex is always telling you — stand straight and watch where you're going — if you but do that you shall not fall."

Words Her Ladyship said every time Louisa arrived at Foxgrove. And went to leave.

Not that they had ever helped.

Lavinia gave her hand another squeeze and then went back to sorting fashion prints. Then she glanced up, her gaze narrowing as she looked her twin over. "There

182

isn't something else, is there?"

Of course Lavinia would notice that something was amiss. Her sister could spot a loose thread at fifty paces.

"No. Nothing," Louisa said hastily, looking around the room, anywhere but in her astute sister's direction. Oh, dear, this would never do. If Lavinia caught even a hint of scandal, she'd needle it out of Louisa with the precision of a diamond cutter. "I think I need to go downstairs. And check on . . ." She glanced around the room. "Hannibal. I need to find where Hannibal is."

"You shouldn't have brought him here," Lavinia called after her as she fled the room. "He'll only bring trouble."

He already has, Louisa thought as she hurried downstairs, fleeing not only the turmoil inside, but Lavinia as well. If she had to listen to her sister prattle on about their purchases and the gowns that were due to arrive, or which bonnet was better suited for her new day gown, or wonder aloud for the hundredth time if Lady Aveley had managed to secure vouchers to Almack's as the good lady had promised, Louisa knew she'd explode.

Or worse, tell her sister what had happened in the linen closet.

Louisa clenched her teeth together. She

just couldn't . . . And yet she and Lavinia never kept secrets from each other.

Without realizing it, Louisa found herself before the open doors of the library, where inside she could see a chessboard atop a table.

The line from Lady Charleton's letter came rushing forth.

If Charleton continues to be horrid, set out the chessboard in the library. Just set it out, the rest will follow.

It wasn't the lady's husband who was being horrid, rather her nephew, but it seemed much the same situation to Louisa so she went over to the board — an exquisite piece of inlaid ebony and ivory.

Glancing around, she spied a narrow drawer in the table and opened it. Inside lay the pieces — the pawns, the knights, the castles, the rooks, and the queen and the king — all resting in velvet.

Without a second thought, she gathered them up and set them to rights, facing each other in orderly rows, the little world atop the board ready for yet another conquest.

She stepped back, wishing the turmoil inside her could be as easily restored, when suddenly a shadow fell across the board.

"What the devil are you doing?" Lord Charleton demanded, his furious gaze fixed on the tabletop. He stormed forward and looked ready to sweep the pieces from the board.

"I . . . I . . . was looking for Hannibal," she offered, nodding where her cat lay sleeping. He was a beast most of the time, but occasionally he came in quite useful.

Though Lord Charleton apparently didn't think so. "And that gives you leave to meddle in my library?" His gaze fell hard upon the chessboard.

"I never . . . that is, Her Ladyship suggested —" Louisa bit her lip to stop the blustering flow of words.

"Lady Aveley is a busybody —"

Louisa flinched at the word, for hadn't Wakefield called her as much earlier?

Keep that interfering busybody out of my house —

Lord Charleton's tirade stopped as well, as if he was remembering the same heated exchange. "Yes, well, I suppose that word has been overused around here of late. But Lady Aveley overstepped when she told you —"

Louisa shook her head. She certainly didn't want the blame placed where it wasn't warranted. "Lady Aveley didn't suggest this, my lord," she told him. "It was Lady Charleton's idea."

This took him aback. "My . . . I hardly think . . . Whyever would Izzy . . ." The words came sputtering out as a mixture of emotions played out over his face. Confusion. Grief. Anger. And then he glanced over at Louisa.

She thought perhaps he would, as Wakefield had earlier, order her out of his house.

Which would suit her mood entirely. Out of this house. Back to Kempton. Back to where her quiet existence, her orderly life, made sense.

But instead, he shocked her.

Much as the viscount had — no, not by kissing her — by taking hold of a nearby chair and placing it behind the white pieces. Another he placed opposite and nodded to her. "I assume you play."

"Yes, my lord."

"Show me."

And so Louisa sat down, and with a sigh of resignation, Lord Charleton followed. She moved out a pawn and so the game began.

"Louisa, aren't you?"

She nodded. It wasn't often that people who had just met them could tell the sisters apart.

"Thought so," he said as he made his first move. "You don't prattle as much."

Louisa smiled, though she knew she shouldn't.

They continued to play, in silence, which seemed to suit them both. But after a time, the baron, without raising his gaze from the board, said, "How do you find London?"

"Not so well," she replied without thinking. "What I mean to say is, there is nothing to do here in the city."

"That's not how I hear it," he said, with much the same tone as Papa used when she or Lavinia overspent their pin money.

"My lord?" she replied nonchalantly. Occasionally feigning innocence worked with her father.

Not so much with Lord Charleton. "I've had a visitor today," he said. "In fact, he was inclined to come by *twice.*"

Louisa's cheeks flamed, but she didn't glance up. After all, everyone in the Charleton household knew about the viscount's visit, especially his second one. "I presume you are the one Viscount Wakefield came to see me about since his complaints also included your beast of a cat."

"Yes, I suppose I am," she admitted, the words still ringing in her ears.

Keep her and her demmed cat out of my house, Charleton! The viscount had bellowed loudly enough for everyone from the cellars to the attics to hear. *She's a med-dling, tiresome chit.*

The only redeeming part had been that Lady Aveley and Lavinia had been walking in the park during this unholy tirade and hadn't heard it . . . firsthand.

"He's my nephew, you know," Charleton was saying. "Wakefield, that is. Well, not by blood, but by marriage. His father was Lady Wakefield's brother."

"Indeed," she managed as she made her move hastily, and lost a knight in the process. "I believe Lady Aveley mentioned as much."

Then to her shock, Lord Charleton leaned back in his seat and howled with laughter. "Good heavens, gel, I don't know what you've done to put him in such a lather —"

"I didn't intend —"

He held up a hand to stave off her protest.

Louisa's lips snapped shut, while inside her, objections whirled about as if caught in a gust of wind.

I never meant . . . That is, it was all Hanni-bal's fault . . . I should never have brought him to London . . . I should never have . . .

Let Lord Wakefield kiss me. Or rather, kissed him back.

"No need to look so horrified, child," Lord Charleton told her. "Whatever you are doing, keep it up."

"My lord?" Louisa stammered, as she had visions of being once again in Wakefield's arms, his lips upon hers, his hands roaming over her body, and when she thought he was about to . . .

"Whatever you've done to wake that boy up, continue so."

She blinked — not sure what to say or even if she'd heard him correctly. "My lord?"

Continue kissing Wakefield? Why, it was an impossible notion. Ruinous. So very wrong.

Oh, if only it weren't . . . some very devilish part of her whispered.

Meanwhile, Lord Charleton continued on. "Wakefield hasn't been out of that lair of his in months. Now you've gone and lured him out. Twice." The baron shook his head as he chuckled. "Whatever you did to annoy him — well, if anything it got him out of his house. And his misery. Well done and keep at it."

Louisa bit down on her bottom lip. Oh, however could she explain this? Well, Lady Essex always said the truth, even in spoonfuls, was better than a lie. "You know that isn't possible, my lord."

Lord Charleton looked up from the chess

piece he'd been toying with. "Why not?"

Louisa only glanced at him before she went back to studying the game. "You heard him. Lord Wakefield has banned me from his house."

"That's unfortunate, indeed," the baron remarked. He leaned back and examined the board between them. "Did Lady Aveley tell you Wakefield was a terrible rake before he ran off to war? Him and that no-account heir of mine, Tuck." Charleton laughed a little. "No, I suppose she didn't tell you that."

"I hardly think —"

"It really isn't necessary to the story. But it does show how far he has fallen."

"My lord?"

"He came home and we all thought . . . Well, it matters not what we thought, for we were grievously wrong. He's locked himself away and nothing has moved him. His mother despairs over the situation."

"That house doesn't help matters," Louisa muttered without thinking.

"What is that?"

"Nothing, my lord."

"Nothing indeed," he scoffed as he made his move. "Whatever you've done you've worked a miracle. And there is nothing to be argued about it, you must continue."

"But you know that isn't possible." Louisa took his rook. Go back? Never. She never wanted to cause him such grievous pain ever again.

Yet what if you were the cure? A sentiment Charleton echoed almost immediately.

"Oh, bother his bluster," the baron told her. "I'd consider it a personal favor." He sat back from the table and folded his arms over his chest. "I'm asking for your help in this. Lady Charleton would be beside herself to see him thusly. She loved him like a son."

Louisa nearly groaned. She could hardly tell the baron her true reasons for not wanting to see Wakefield again. "I don't see how I can help. He has banned me."

"So he has. Hmm," the baron mused, placing a finger on his knight, and then drawing it back as he reconsidered his move.

"Which is most unfortunate," Louisa insisted.

"Why is that?" the baron asked, his hand having returned to the rook.

Then the words sort of tumbled out. "That house is in a dreadful state. There is so much that needs be done, my lord. A thorough airing. A good cleaning. A proper housekeeper. Maids. A few footmen." Those were things she knew she could right. Make good. "Why, the linen closet was nearly my

191

undoing," she said without thinking.

In more ways than one.

"The linen closet?" Lord Charleton asked, as astutely as he played chess. "What were you doing in Wakefield's linen closet?"

Louisa doled out her answer in the tiniest teaspoon of honesty she could manage. "Mrs. Petchell asked me to help."

"Hmm," the baron mused as he moved a pawn forward instead. He was leading her into a trap and she wasn't about to be caught. She took his rook instead and his brow furrowed in concentration.

"If only he would let me help. I do so deplore disorder. All that house wants is a bit of management."

As did the man himself, but it wasn't her place to say so.

"Yes, I suppose so," the baron agreed.

And like her sister, she began to prattle. "And the gardens, my lord. Oh, heavens, I look down at them from my window and it hurts to see roses in such a deplorable state."

"Deplorable?" he murmured as he gazed a bit mournfully at his lost rook.

"Yes. What I wouldn't give to take a pair of clippers to those bushes. And then the peonies! Why, they have no supports. They will be all toppled over by June and ruined in the first bit of rain. How can a man live amidst such horrible disorder?"

"How indeed," he agreed, though she suspected he was speaking in a wider sense.

"Yet there is nothing I can do, not when he's banned me from the house."

The baron paused and glanced up at her. "But not the gardens."

The next morning, Lord Charleton's footman, the fellow who also looked after the baron's gardens, delivered to her clippers, a spade and a large basket — with the baron's blessing.

And as much as she wanted to turn and run, when she found herself at the door in the wall, she couldn't shake that feeling that she'd left something very important undone.

After years of being part of the Society for the Temperance and Improvement of Kempton, such doubt, any niggling thought that a task wasn't completed, was nothing short of a sin.

Once the baron had made his request, his plea, there was only one thing she could do — agree to venture forth.

So Louisa defiantly pushed open the garden door and waded in.

Besides, there was a very wry part of her that wanted to prod the viscount a bit. He had, after all, called her "tiresome" loud enough for the entire Charleton house to hear.

"Tiresome, indeed, you wretched man," she muttered as she glanced around, her gaze straying uneasily toward the house. There was also the matter of whatever she'd broken when she'd made her heedless flight from the house.

Broken and undone.

Much as their kiss had left them both . . .

Louisa straightened. Besides, what sort of man declared a lady "plain" and a "harridan" and then ravished her in his linen closet?

She glanced again at the house — with its windows tightly curtained shut and that go-away milieu that hung from the attics to the cellar — and knowing full well that she'd left something far more important than a linen closet undone.

Undone.

A tangle of images and memories unraveled inside her. Wakefield's lips stealing over hers. His tongue tracing a delicate line over her mouth, teasing her to open up to him. And when she did, he'd opened more than her lips — he'd awakened a Pandora's box of desires.

Oh, that knowledge — of how a man's kiss

could leave you breathless, how a kiss could make your breasts tighten, your insides quake and grow heated, and oh, heavens, wet — could not be outrun.

Could not be straightened back up and tucked on the high shelf of a closet to be shut away and forgotten.

That moment, that kiss, would live in her heart for the rest of her life.

Leaving her, in a word, undone.

So if the linen closet was — like the man who owned it — unattainable and out of her reach, perhaps Lord Charleton's "suggestion" was the next best thing.

She could tidy up the garden.

Squaring her shoulders, she looked around and sighed. Bother! What an overgrown mess. No indeed, she wasn't about to spend another morning looking over the wall at this tangle.

Besides, unused to being so idle, she'd go mad sitting around all morning being proper. Oh, Lavinia might be in alt over their changed circumstances, poring over the newspapers, prattling on about this ball or that soirée, and weighing each and every invitation that arrived in the salver, but Louisa was not.

The notices that had begun as a trickle were now like a river, with notes pouring in.

Apparently the news of the deceased Lady Charleton's newly arrived goddaughters was being bandied about and they'd become something of a curiosity and therefore worthy of social inspection.

"So many opportunities," Lady Aveley had declared at breakfast.

For disaster, Louisa wanted to add as Lavinia had beamed happily.

Hadn't this morning's session with the dancing master, Monsieur Delacroix, been humiliating enough? And a most telling portent of things to come.

After thirty minutes of having his toes trod upon, he'd stormed out of the music room, telling Lady Aveley as he limped to the front door, "There is nothing I can do for mam'selles."

And bless her heart, the dear lady had taken Monsieur at his word, thinking that the sisters needed no further instruction.

No, it was much better out here in the garden, Louisa decided, where if she tumbled over her own feet, no one would call her "an abomination to the Graces," as Monsieur Delacroix had.

Sizing up where to start, she considered Lady Essex's best advice: start at the beginning. So she clipped at the tall rose canes that kept the garden door from opening easily, each snip a rebellious drumbeat.

Ban me, will you, she mused.

He ought to have, at the very least, called upon her and apologized, not ranted at Lord Charleton that she was a busybody.

Snip. Snip.

Even a note might have sufficed in such circumstances.

Dear Miss Tempest,

I most sincerely apologize for kissing you senseless . . . If I hadn't had my wits rattled when you knocked me over with the closet door, I might have behaved in a more gentlemanly . . .

Louisa's defiance grew more rooted with each rosebush she tamed. *Snip. Snip. Snip!*

Every clip of the shears, every cane she carefully tamed, she felt as if she were telling him that she was utterly indifferent to his kiss. And to his opinions. And his lack of manners.

He meant nothing to her.

Which was a terrible lie, but she hoped if she told herself as much, perhaps she'd stop dreaming of his arms around her, of his lips teasing hers open, of his hands curving over her . . .

"Ow!" she cursed as a great big thorn

stabbed her, bringing her back to the tangled mess that was Lord Wakefield's garden — and in nearly every way, her heart.

Pierson woke up to a persistent *snip, snip, snip* coming from his gardens.

And worse, there was a stubborn bit of sunlight tracing through an opening in the curtains and slanting right across his bed. A bright nudge of sunlight as insistent as the clatter coming from below.

Snip, snip, snip. Pound, pound, pound.

"What the devil," he muttered as he climbed out of bed and went to the window, tugging open the curtain.

At first the brilliant spring sunshine left him blinded, but he couldn't shake the suspicion of what he'd glimpsed.

Miss Tempest.

And when he looked again, yes, there she was. In his garden. Meddling.

Never mind that she looked quite fetching, he thought he'd made it quite clear to Charleton, and to his own staff, that the lady's presence was not wanted. And yet there, on closer inspection, were Bitty and Bob standing beside her, the girl holding a basket for the lady, while Bob energetically hammered stakes into the ground.

When the lad finished with his task, he

looked expectantly up at Miss Tempest and the lady smiled down at him, saying something that left the boy blushing and laughing, basking in her smile.

Pierson stepped back from the window as the oddest sensation needled down his spine.

Something as green as the stalks she clipped and as dark as the cellar.

It was utterly ridiculous, but here he stood wishing it was he receiving that radiant glance from the lady. That it was he basking in her delight.

For she had the sort of smile that could melt a man's heart. Make him forget himself.

Tempt him to forget his pain.

He whirled away from the window and cursed, catching up his breeches and tossing them on. This was exactly why he'd banned her. She had no business in his life. No right to interfere. He nearly tore the cambric shirt he yanked on, but his haste was being hurried with each annoying *snip*.

Snip. Snip. SNIP!

It was as if she was taking great personal delight in cutting each and every one of the careful ties he'd bound around his life to keep the world out.

Out, he would remind her. Not in. Like

199

the demmed morning light that kept finding its way through his curtains at whatever ungodly hour it was that it came up, despite having checked his draperies twice before he'd gone to bed.

He stormed down the hall with only a sketchy plan as to how he was going to toss her over the garden wall.

First, he had to figure out how he could do that and not touch her.

Not put his hands on those tempting curves and pull her close. He'd have to manage a way to look past those dusky lashes, those soft lips of hers, because that would throw his every intention of removing her from the garden into chaos.

She'd most likely end up in his bed . . .

Pierson skidded to a stop. His bed? Had he gone mad?

He stood there, halfway down the stairs, his hand gripping the rail.

No, if he'd gone mad, he'd be in the library looking up plans for a trebuchet. Then he could remove her without having to hold her.

Perhaps it would be the better part of valor to give this task to Tiploft — he could send Miss Tempest packing.

Coward . . . a voice not unlike Poldie's whispered up from inside him. The one that usually called to him in his nightmares.

Yes, well, he supposed he was being cowardly. Nor did he care. Even Sir John Moore had told them at Sahagún, *I've known for some time, we'll have to make a run for it.*

That wasn't cowardice, but common sense.

And facing Miss Tempest was akin, in his estimation, to facing eighty thousand of Boney's best troops.

He continued down the stairs to the kitchen. No, he wasn't about to go out and inform Miss Tempest that he'd ordered her off his premises. But certainly his servants weren't doing a very good job of enforcing his instructions.

Opening the door, he strode in, ready to lambast one and all for their failings — when he came face to face with nearly his entire staff: Tiploft and Mrs. Petchell.

Sitting comfortably at the table sharing a pot of tea. The scene was so domestic, so utterly quiet and peaceful, he nearly forgot his errand. And it occurred to him that having such a small staff was suddenly a disadvantage — for he felt rather a heel to have to order Tiploft up and out of this cozy comfort to go dispatch Miss Tempest.

And he hadn't the nerve to ask Mrs. Petchell to do it. Not when she had a kettle within arm's reach. Besides, she looked rather furious that he'd come this far into her domain.

"My lord —" Tiploft began as he rose to his feet, even as the garden door came bursting open.

"Oh, Auntie, can I have a rag? I got dirt on the new dress the beautiful miss gave me, and she says if I sponge it off quick it won't be ruined," Bitty said. Then she spied Pierson standing there and her smile faded as her eyes widened with fear.

Like he might pop her in the stove and bake her for supper — which was most likely the story Miss Tempest had been telling the children — a nightmarish tale of The Viscount Who Lived Down the Lane.

"Oh, gar!" the child gasped. "I weren't s'posed to mention it, not in front of you."

"And why not?" he asked, brows arched and feeling most imperious.

Right then Bob came stumbling in behind his sister. "Bitty, what's taking so — oh." His gaze widened as well.

He glanced at Bob and realized the lad had on new breeches. He could tell they were new because they actually fit the boy, and there wasn't a single patch on them. Pierson glanced over at their aunt.

"Another gift from Miss Tempest?"

"Yes, milord. And it was a kindness of her to think of them," Mrs. Petchell said without blinking an eye.

For her words really meant, *Miss Tempest saw to them when it should have been yours to do.*

"She told us not to tell you," Bitty rushed to add. " 'Cause she didn't think you'd like her helping us. Since you don't want her —"

Not like it? Of course he didn't. Because Mrs. Petchell had been right — even if she hadn't come right out and said it — it was his job to see to his staff.

Even a staff of ragamuffins.

Which only increased his vexation. The woman was winding her way into his life no matter what he did. Or rather, didn't.

So Pierson reiterated his instructions. "I thought I made my orders clear," he told them all. "I do not want that lady" — he pointed his finger toward the kitchen door — "in my house."

Before Tiploft could mutter an apology, Bob spoke up, "The miss isn't actually *in* the house, milord. She's in the garden."

That sounded to Pierson like Miss Tempest's argument and not one from the likes of Bob — so he let the boy off with only a piercing stare.

Which, to his chagrin, didn't even quell the little guttersnipe. Bob stood his ground like a knight guarding a fair maiden.

A willful, bothersome, headstrong one. She'd found a way to invade his castle without setting foot inside it.

"Is there anything else, my lord?" Tiploft asked. Not since Pierson had been a lad of four had his butler sounded so disapproving.

Pierson tried to open his mouth and form the words. *Get. Her. Out.* But when he looked from face to face, he realized he was outnumbered. Even if he did pay their wages.

Yes, Moore had been right. At times it was better to fall back.

Especially when faced with the tremble of Bitty's bottom lip and a sheen forming in her eyes. Having two sisters, he knew the signs of imminent tears when he saw them.

Oh, good heavens, he couldn't have that.

"Please bring my breakfast tray to the library," he told Tiploft instead. "And Bob, you follow me. I need some books from the top shelf."

If anything, he had to admit the addition of Bitty and Bob to the household had made his research easier. The lad could scramble up the library ladder like a monkey.

Much better than sending Tiploft up.

From outside, a distinct *snip, snip, snip* came echoing into the kitchen, leaving everyone still — and all eyes on Pierson. Again, he tried to form the words, but knew that there was no way he was about to go outside and order her off his lawn. That would mean facing her down. And quite possibly owning up to his high-handed behavior the previous day.

Or worse, apologizing.

Which he had no intention of doing. He had nothing to apologize for — since he realized in that moment of indecision there was something he did know to be an inalienable truth.

He had quite liked kissing her.

And such a notion was as insufferable as the infernal racket of her clippers.

Snip. Snip. Snip.

"Bob, with me," he ordered, and turned from the kitchen, moving up the stairs as quickly as he could and fleeing to the library, which was the one logical room in which he could hide and not look a coward — for it faced the square and wasn't anywhere near Miss Tempest.

But this time when he entered the cool dimness of the shuttered room, a sense of disquiet ran down his spine. Looking around, he saw it as if he hadn't been in it for ages. Everywhere — from the open, forgotten tomes, to his notes and papers on military strategies scattered about, all he saw was a disorderly mess. That, and every time he went to reach for a book, on Caesar or Alexander's conquests, or Scipio's cunning, they all seemed to have leaped up to the highest shelves, necessitating a call to Tiploft or Bob to gain his desired volume, say on Hannibal.

Hannibal. Pierson winced as he looked across the room. For all too predictably, there was his own Hannibal, having breached the house once again with the daring of his namesake, and curled up like a confident conqueror on the chair by the fire.

What was it every general, every tactician he studied asserted? Well-organized and disciplined troops were the key to any military success.

Bob, who seemed to sense his consternation, glanced around as well and huffed. "The fine miss says an orderly arrangement makes a task more easily done."

"Does she now?" Pierson replied. The woman was a modern Trojan horse, wheeling her way inside his walls without setting a single slippered toe inside.

"Aye. It seems to me you always want the

books that are up high, so why not move 'em all down where you can git 'em?"

Pierson was about to argue the point, that the volumes on military history had always been kept on the top shelf, but something about Bob's practical and stubborn expression — a look that said, *I'll keep climbing up there iffin you want me to* — nudged at the viscount's unwitting hold on the past.

It was much like Miss Tempest's practical observations about the linen closet.

What you need should be in reach. Easily gained and quick to find.

Then he glanced around the entire library and realized that most of the accessible volumes did not hold his interest — and were certainly not necessary to the tome he was writing on military tactics.

Damn her hide. It made perfect sense to reorganize the shelves.

"How long until Miss Tempest is done tampering with my gardens?" he asked the boy.

"A few days, I think," Bob said.

Pierson eyed the room. That would probably be how long it would take to reorganize the place. Of course, his sister would suggest hiring a librarian to do it all properly, but he'd had enough of new faces about the house without adding another.

Though perhaps a few footmen to guard the garden door might be a wise choice.

"Shall I fetch them books down, my lord?" the boy prompted.

"Yes, Bob. Let's get at it."

CHAPTER 8

It actually took five days, but by noon of that day, Pierson had finished putting the library to rights — shelving the books he wanted on the lower shelves, sending the more tattered volumes out to be rebound and consigning the poetry volumes and literary essays to the top shelf.

He had no need of flowery speeches and declarations of love so close at hand.

Bad enough he had a tempting miss trespassing in his gardens.

As for his papers, he'd culled and tidied them until everything in the library was orderly and lined up.

Like proper battalions, he mused as he gazed at the shelves, ignoring Hannibal, who was yet again curled up and napping on the chair by the fireplace. The wretched beast arrived each day, uninvited, and made himself at home — as if he found the viscount's muttering and curses soothing.

"Well, this is your last day to cadge about," the viscount told the cat, who looked up with his one eye and twitched one of his battered ears, a dismissive sort of wave.

If you think so, the cat seemed to say as he defiantly tucked his nose back into the curl of his tail and returned to his indulgent snooze.

"Yes, well, I haven't given up the notion of building a trebuchet," Pierson replied, setting aside any thought of Hannibal's mistress — who, he would note, was just as stubborn and defiant and in need of a good toss over the wall. Instead, he took another look around his library and, with a bit of jaunty pride to his hobbling gait, made his way to the dining room.

After days of avoiding the place — since it overlooked the gardens — the wafting odor of pie and something else as mouthwatering lured him away from his usual tray. But once there, the remarkable repast of ham, pigeon pie and — inhaling deeply — fresh tarts, awaiting him held little appeal as he found himself driven to the French doors.

And the garden beyond.

To his relief — as he stole a glance through an opening in the curtains — there was no sign of Miss Tempest, though her work was in evidence nearly everywhere he looked.

Without even thinking about it, he pushed open the doors, and wandered into the middle of the garden.

The side that bordered Lord Charleton's wall had been transformed. Beds spaded. Plants trimmed and tied upright. Even the path had been raked, the overturned stones no longer black with soot. The roses looked ready for their summer glory.

But the other half of the garden — well, that was still in its tangled state, standing in stark contrast to Miss Tempest's labors. But then again, it was going to take a carpenter to get the wooden arbor straightened, and the patience of Job to get the knotted herb garden back in its proper shape.

As for the lady, there was no sign of her.

"Given up, have you, Miss Tempest?" he said aloud, feeling a bit smug.

"No, not at all," came the reply.

He turned around and found her standing in the open gate. Where the old battered oak door had creaked, groaned and refused to open much more than to let a cat through, now it slid open silently and widely — enough to let in an interfering miss without so much as a warning.

She stood in the entrance, certainly not dressed for London, but looking, he imagined, as she did every day in whatever that small village of hers was, ready for a day of — oh, fustian, what had she said? Oh, yes, "taking people under her wing."

Or as he preferred, pestering them.

But he had to admit if he was going to be hectored by anyone, this miss — with her large straw bonnet, her dark hair coiling down her shoulder in a single long braid, and wearing a bright yellow gown as sunny as her smile — left him willing to be ordered about. For the time being.

Still, he'd let himself be taken to the rack before he confessed this, but she was utterly fetching like this — all simply done.

London, he realized, would ruin all that.

And that was a terrible shame.

"You've been remiss," he said before he could stop himself. "Neglecting your labors." Rebellious, unwanted labors.

He nodded toward the impossible-looking tangle of clematis and ivy — enough to make an army of gardeners weep, hoping they might deter her. Send her scurrying back from whence she came.

"I've had other obligations," she told him, strolling into his yard without so much as a by-your-leave. She set her basket down and began to dig into one of the beds. "Besides, you banned me from your house — not the gardens."

"So I was informed." When an uncomfortable silence settled between them, he spoke again, if only to say something other than the words he knew he should be uttering, *My apologies, Miss Tempest.*

Instead he continued quite blandly, or rather safely, by saying, "You've accomplished much here."

She glanced around, surveying her work, and then went back to her digging. "It helps pass the time."

"Shouldn't you be out shopping?" he asked, pulling forth his memories of his sister Margaret's Season. "Taking tea and charming patronesses for vouchers?"

To his surprise, she sort of shuddered at the suggestions. "I prefer to be useful."

Useful. The word struck a chord inside him.

He'd been anything but since he'd come home, much to his mother's dismay. Especially when he'd made it all too clear he had no intention of finding another match once Melliscent cried off. Instead, he'd buried himself inside his library, writing and compiling his research. Neglecting his lordly obligations.

Whatever else could he do? He'd come home broken and damaged. Why didn't everyone else see that? Understand?

Still, something about the longing in her voice plucked at a nerve inside him. "Yes, well, be thankful you can be that." He held out his cane. "I'm not so lucky."

She set down her trowel and gazed at him. "Whatever has your cane to do with being useful?"

There it was again. Her stubborn defiance. Yet this time, Pierson felt a slight chill run down his spine. Was it anger or something else, he wasn't sure, but he answered with nothing less than lofty indignation as he had so many times before. "I cannot ride. I cannot dance. I can't even climb up into my curricle, which makes me barely a gentleman."

She arched a brow. *Barely a gentleman, indeed.* But thankfully she did not wade through *that* door, and instead just shook her head and went back to digging.

Well, more like stabbing the dirt.

Nor was she done. "You can still speak, can you not?"

"Well, I —"

"And have opinions?"

"Of course, but —"

"And think for yourself?" But apparently not finish a sentence, for she stopped her labors and turned to face him. "And sit in the House of Lords? You can sit?"

He blanched a bit at this. Demmit, of course he could sit, but she didn't understand. And frustrated by her disbelief and her annoyance with him, he blustered into the verbal hole she'd dug.

"You don't understand," he said. "I'm not the same man I once was. I've made a mess of things."

"Then clean it up," she said with that inarguable no-nonsense advice that she gave so easily.

But he was ready this time. "That's impossible." His words came out in a tone that brooked no argument, for they came with the memory of Poldie dying. Bleeding from a wound that should have been Pierson's.

He couldn't bring back Poldie.

"If you say so," she said, shrugging her shoulders and glancing around for the trowel.

Her disbelief left him dumbfounded. Just like that she could so blithely dismiss his pain? He shifted so he towered above her. "Sometimes you cannot bring back what is lost. You just cannot."

And if he expected more arguments from her, he was wrong, for in that moment, his words fell upon her and the weight of them sagged her shoulders down in defeat.

"Yes," she said softly, winding her fingers

around the trowel. "Sometimes a thing is lost forever." She paused for a second and then went back to work, as if that was all she could do.

Anything he had been about to say fled in the face of her admission. Whatever had she lost? It was no trifle, that he knew. So what was it, or rather was it, who had left her words, her heart, so full of regret?

Regrets he knew only too well.

He paused for a moment as he got his bearings — the garden hadn't been this tidy for years and he'd nearly forgotten what was where — information he knew only because his mother had taken great pride in her small green space, bringing him and his sisters out to play while she worked among her "other dear flowers," as she called her beloved plants.

"What are you doing?" he asked as he realized where she was digging.

"Planting strawberries," she said over her shoulder. "They will do nicely here."

Strawberries? Tempting reminders of her lips sprang to mind, but he swept those aside. Stepping forward, he leaned over and took the spade from her hands — nearly forgetting his own rule of never touching her.

He straightened quickly. "You cannot dig

about wherever you may. Especially not *there.*"

"Actually, I already have," she told him, reaching up to take back the shovel and willfully stabbing the ground with it.

"There are tulips planted there," he told her. He didn't know much about gardening, but that much he did know.

"There were," she replied, as if digging up someone's garden was well within her purveyance.

Pierson drew a deep breath. "Were? Why you insolent, busybody —"

As he drew another breath, she glanced up at him. "I believe the words you are looking for are *plain* and *harridan.*"

That stopped him, for he had a fleeting memory of using those exact words the other day in Charleton's study. But however would she know that unless she'd been . . .

He glanced down at her and recalled this was the same minx who'd fired and hired a cook without his blessing, cleaned out his closets and dug about his garden as if it were hers.

Why wouldn't she eavesdrop?

And while she should be ashamed of such disgraceful conduct, it was Pierson who felt the pang of guilt. He'd called her that and worse. Plain. A harridan. All in an attempt to steer Tuck away from her.

For what end?

So he could kiss her . . .

Though right now, the only way he wanted to touch Miss Tempest was to wring her neck. How dare she destroy his mother's tulip patch. Meddle in his life . . .

Dig up memories he wanted no part of . . .

"Yes, well," Miss Tempest continued, "if you are done haranguing me, I have work to finish." Her implication was that he might not understand what that meant. And to prove her point, she stabbed the ground again with her spade, this time as if she were planting it into something more meaningful.

Like his back.

"Stop!" he ordered. "Those tulips — how could you?" His mother would be furious. More so than she already was with him.

"Good heavens, Lord Wakefield. If you don't want me —"

And there her words stopped. Either consciously or accidentally, he didn't know which. Not that it mattered.

For there they were. Right there out in the open.

If you don't want me.

She glanced up at him, those honest, open eyes of hers looking at him. Searching for something.

Most likely an apology. A confession. A declaration. For what she had said wasn't true. And perhaps they both knew it.

He did want her.

And when he'd held her, kissed her, listened to that soft mew of desire that had slipped from her lips and teased him more than her fingers winding into the folds of his waistcoat as she'd pulled herself closer to him, he knew she wanted him as well.

But as quickly as the moment had come upon them, it passed and she looked away, saying, "I haven't done anything to your tulips. I merely moved them." She paused and pointed to a bed directly across from the dining room windows. "Over there. You must plant things where they are meant to be — so they will flourish. Next spring, and every spring after, you will be able to enjoy them from the dining room instead of having them hidden away over here."

In his anger, he nearly missed what she was saying — for he was still trying to reconcile the fact that she had come into his garden and started moving things about without his permission. But those words, *Next spring and every spring after,* pushed forth a memory he'd long forgotten.

A memory that bloomed within him.

"My father said that once," he managed, more for himself than for her.

She glanced over her shoulder at him. "Your father?"

"He brought those bulbs back from Amsterdam — for my mother — before they were married, or even betrothed."

"He wooed her with bulbs?" Miss Tempest asked, her eyes alight with mirth. "A rather unconventional choice. I thought gentlemen were supposed to charm ladies with actual blossoms."

Pierson laughed, despite himself. "I didn't think romance was something you concerned yourself with."

Miss Tempest sniffed. "Just because I have no intention of marrying doesn't mean I'm blind to the process."

"But are you immune?" he asked before he could stop the words.

What he really wanted to know was if their kiss had affected her as well.

"Quite," she told him with a defiant glance, as if she wanted him to challenge her.

To kiss her again, to hold her . . . but, oh, it was too dangerous.

And she seemed to sense that as well. "You were saying about your father —"

He nodded in agreement. Not so much

about continuing his story but to leave that other subject, the unmentionable one, alone.

For now.

"It's more about my mother, I suppose," Pierson told her. "She was quite a beauty — still is quite striking, if all the old blades who propose to her every year can be believed."

"She sounds indomitable," Miss Tempest remarked.

"Something like that," he admitted. Stubborn and proud and had loved her husband too dearly to ever marry again.

"Why did she choose your father and his tulip bulbs?"

He nodded as he went back to the story. "She led a merry chase her first Season — with scores of suitors and proposals — but she had turned them all down. Just before the next Season, my father was called to be part of the delegation to Paris for the treaty — which left him stricken, for he was determined to have her and now all his rivals had a clear field. He returned just as it was rumored that my mother was to be betrothed to a duke who had famously declared he would have her hand. And when my father arrived, he went straight from the ship to my grandfather's house. And there in the foyer, filled with flowers from all her other suitors, he offered my mother a basket of bulbs — and declared that what he had brought her was a bouquet of flowers that would come to her every spring for the rest of her life."

And if it was possible, Miss Tempest appeared to be without a retort, for there in her eyes was a mist of tears.

She who proclaimed herself quite immune to romance. And as if to prove herself a most practical miss, she dashed the evidence away with her sleeve.

But now he knew the truth: she was as tender-hearted as Bitty.

At least so he thought.

"That is the most beautiful thing I've ever heard," Miss Tempest admitted. "Your father sounds quite the romantic devil." She picked up her basket and began sorting through the bits of roots and greenery she'd brought to plant. "You don't take after him much, do you, my lord?"

Louisa tried her best to bite back those impertinent words as they tumbled from her lips. Whatever was she doing?

Flirting. The word rose up like a promise and a caution.

She was flirting with Lord Wakefield.

When she'd opened the garden gate and

seen him standing there, surveying her work, she should have silently turned around and fled.

But she hadn't. She couldn't. For as much as she should be well and done with him and his shouting and his bluster, she couldn't help holding on to her suspicions that with time, his thorny paw would heal, and he'd find his way to be the man who scratched Hannibal's head when no one was looking.

Not for her, certainly. But for a lady worthy of his heart.

So she'd waded in, and now it seemed she'd dived headfirst into this folly.

Flirting with him. And somewhere, somewhere quite deep inside her, she knew why.

Because ever since he'd kissed her, pulled her into his arms and teased her awake, she'd been unable to think of anything else.

Other than his kiss.

She turned back to her basket of strawberry starts. Of course she wasn't flirting. She hadn't the least idea how to gain a man's interest.

Not unless one counted tripping over his boots.

And glancing over her shoulder up at the glowering figure behind her, she thought Lord Wakefield certainly wasn't the sort of man upon whom one might practice such an art.

He looked positively ready to dump her basket of starts atop her head.

Which would probably serve her right.

And then it happened.

He began to laugh. It started as a guffaw, and then he truly laughed. The sort that rolled freely from him.

And from his surprised expression, she suspected he hadn't made such a merry sound in a very long time.

The other part of his deep mirth was that it was entirely infectious.

And all too soon, Louisa was giggling — which then turned into a rather unladylike display that had her holding her sides, her basket and trowel forgotten.

"Oh, goodness, I've never said such an impertinent thing in my entire life."

"I doubt that," he told her as he settled down on the grass beside her, eyeing her with a wry expression. "Who would have thought you such a tease, Louisa —"

"I am no such —" She came to a blinding halt. Louisa? "My lord, you shouldn't —"

"What? Call you by your name? I have certain rights left, even if you are determined to usurp all of them." He smiled at her. "You may call me Pierson."

"I shall not," she told him tartly. That would never do.

"You will," he told her.

She sniffed at his presumption. Call him by his Christian name, indeed. It was too intimate, too forward.

Like kissing him in his linen closet?

"Still," he was saying, "you won't last long in London society if you speak your mind so freely. Take me, for example. It is only through the greatest of restraint that I haven't sent you packing over that garden wall. You and that dreadful beast you insist is a cat." He leaned closer and picked up a strawberry section that had fallen from the basket. He studied it for a moment, and then set it back with the others. When he glanced at her, he winked.

Cheeky devil! Who would have thought it? Lord Wakefield had a sense of humor.

"I have no intention of lasting in society," she told him, looking around for her trowel. "I'm only here to —"

"Yes, yes, I know. To see your sister well matched. But I would think that now that you've seen a bit of London, and with Lady Aveley's tutelage, you would have changed your mind."

Was he speaking of finding a husband or something else . . .

Like a kiss.

"Not at all," she told him with every bit of finality she could muster, and glanced around for her trowel.

As if that could stop the rogue. And just as Lord Charleton had said, Wakefield was a rogue. At least he had the bloodlines of one.

Bother her curiosity, for the other day she'd gone and looked him up in *Debrett's* — running her finger down the listing of the Stratton family line until there in the Elizabethan dynasty had been her answer.

One of his forebears had been the daughter of a Spanish diplomat, who was also rumored to be a pirate.

Louisa couldn't help wondering what other traits that reckless daughter with her beguiling Mediterranean manners and bewitching glances had brought into such a very English lineage — besides the searching dark eyes and bombastic nature.

Passion. Endless, deep passion, whispered her own desires.

Their eyes met, and for a blinding second, Louisa felt herself falling, thinking he might kiss her yet again.

But to her relief — and chagrin — he settled back. "Truly? Not even a thought of finding a husband?"

"Good heavens, no!" she said with more feeling than was probably proper.

Again, he laughed at her. "So you keep saying — but one of these days some gentleman is going to set his sights upon you and be stricken in love — then you'll be his problem and not mine." He grinned at her, reaching across her and into her basket, plucking out a large bundle of roots and handing it to her.

"Now who is teasing?" Louisa took his offering and divided it further and then tucked the plants into the ground. "I am hardly the sort to inspire such passion."

"You inspire me," he told her.

Now it was Louisa's turn to laugh. "Inspire you? To what, violence?"

"Well, I will admit, you vex me to no end, but I suspect Lady Aveley will have you off to Almack's soon enough, and then you'll become the next Original or Diamond or whatever it is that every fool chases after these days, and you'll have no more time for me. Therefore, I can afford to be generous today."

"As it is, we are off to Almack's this very night." She knew she should be giddy with joy over the prospect, but the idea only filled her with dread.

Nor had Lady Aveley's assurances of a

successful evening given her much comfort.
You'll meet all the best of society.

All Louisa could see was a sea of expensively trimmed hems waiting to be stepped on.

"Tonight?" Lord Wakefield laughed. "Isn't that right into the devil's snare?"

"Excuse me?" She'd never heard the hallowed hall called that.

"For a lady who professes not to want to marry —"

"I don't. It is my sister who is determined to find a match. And someone has to —"

"Yes, yes. Keep an eye on her." The viscount's lips turned up mischievously. "Is your sister as . . . as . . . ."

"As?"

"Cowhanded?" he asked with a laugh.

Louisa's mouth opened in a moue of protest, but she could hardly deny the matter.

Still . . .

"That isn't very polite —" she began.

"I have a box of broken vases and crockery that might disagree."

"Lord Wakefield, you are a dreadful tease," she said, going back to her labors. After a few moments she offered an answer. "She's worse."

He rolled back and laughed. "Serves my

uncle right. And Lady Aveley. Oh, Almack's will never be the same."

"Do they have a punch bowl?" she asked tentatively.

"A large one," he said, looking as if he was going to ask the next question: *Is it in danger?* But didn't.

He probably already knew the answer.

Mortal danger.

As she considered how she could avoid such a fate, she had another question. "You've been to Almack's then?"

The viscount shuddered. "Yes. More times than I care to count." He glanced toward her basket and began poking at the bundle of roots.

Louisa had the sense that there was more to this revelation, and once again heard Mr. Rowland's voice as it had come through the door when she'd been eavesdropping.

Melliscent was a rare beauty.

Had the viscount met this Melliscent there, at Almack's? Walked into the grand room, looked across the glittering array of ladies and misses and fallen in love with her "fair" beauty in a single beat of his heart.

Louisa could see the scene as if she were there — standing in the middle of the crush, a silent observer to a very private moment, only able to watch as Wakefield found a way to be introduced to the lady, when he asked her to dance, and that singular moment when the lady glanced up and into his dark eyes, her own alight with the possibility of love.

"Miss Tempest?" Lord Wakefield snapped his fingers in front of her. "Are you woolgathering on me? Dreaming of some perfect gentleman with tidy linen closets, no doubt."

She glanced at his bemused expression and then it was her turn to look away, fixing her attention on the task of sorting through the starts she'd convinced Lord Charleton's greengrocer to secure for her.

Yet it was nigh on impossible to decide which of them to plant and which to discard with *him* right beside her.

He sent her thoughts racing in a thousand directions. And in her mind's eye, it wasn't Melliscent he'd fallen in love with that night.

But her. Miss Louisa Tempest.

Standing in the middle of the crowded room, she was the only lady his eyes beheld. The lady who lit his heart. The one he'd come striding across the room and smiled The Viscount Who Lived Down the Lane 177 *upon. A man full of confidence and daring, before he'd become this stomping, snarling beast.*

She stopped herself right there before she envisioned anything else. Something ruinous.

Such thoughts were exactly what came of reading the *Miss Darby* novels Harriet Hathaway was always sharing with Lavinia.

Romantic drivel, she'd tell them with disdain, and yet . . . she always read them. Worse, she'd also snuck from the top shelf of Lady Essex's library one of her French books. The one with pictures . . .

Now when she looked at Lord Wakefield, she could easily understand why the intrepid Miss Darby strayed so often and so close to ruin for the love and affection of her handsome Lieutenant Throckmorten.

Perhaps Throckmorten had Spanish ancestry as well . . . tempting dark eyes and unruly waves of hair that begged a lady to reach out and brush those errant strands back into a respectable queue so he didn't look quite so piratical.

So utterly desirable . . . which led her thoughts to the French picture book.

Oh, good heavens, Louisa Tempest, she scolded herself, her fingers twitching to do just that. Brush that dark strand of his hair back off the side of his face, to run her fingers over the stubble there, to feel the hard lines of his lips before they came crashing down atop hers . . .

Instead, she rubbed her nose and went back to work. But her resolve to finish her task quickly diverted as she stole yet another glance at him as he too picked through the strawberry starts. All of a sudden she realized something about him was different.

Entirely so.

Here he was, sprawled out on the lawn beside her, and he was hardly snapping at her. And only mildly threatening to toss her over the wall. And he hadn't sent Mrs. Petchell and her orphans packing as he'd once threatened. In fact, he'd been teaching Bob to read, insisting that the boy be taught so he could be "of some use."

"If you have no desire to go to Almack's, don't go," he said with that air of authority — the one that a man who had led others and was used to being obeyed threw out so simply.

She shook her head. "I must go. Lady Aveley went to great lengths to secure vouchers."

"Must go," he repeated, and laughed. "You'll change your mind when you get there and all the fellows descend to scrape about at your hemline."

"Scrape at my hemline, indeed. Lord Wakefield, I am hardly the type to inspire such madness."

He tipped his head and studied her for a moment. "No, I suppose you aren't," he finally declared.

This took her back a bit. "Well, thank you," she finally managed, a small part — oh, bother, a rather large portion — of her heart quaking at his honesty.

"Oh, don't look so put out with me. I only meant that you'll hardly be reckoned a Diamond if you parade about with that smudge on your nose," he said, nodding at her, and then digging into the pocket of his jacket. With a handkerchief now in his grasp, he reached out and gently began to wipe the top of her nose.

His touch left her mesmerized. She didn't dare raise her lashes, allow herself the danger of looking up and into his eyes.

Still she could feel the weight of his stare upon her. And worse, by not looking up, all she could see of him was his lips.

Solid, hard, and turned in a tempting, mischievous, one might say devilish, line. And when they parted, his chin moving toward hers, her lashes fluttered open and heaven help her, she couldn't stop herself.

She looked up and into his eyes.

That was a mistake.

Lost. I am lost.

And this time, when Louisa Tempest tumbled, she fell headlong into something that could very well mean her ruin.

Pierson tried to tell himself this was folly even as he was moving closer, his head tilted, and he knew what was about to happen.

He'd kiss her. Right here on the lawn, in the garden. Where anyone could see them. And he didn't care.

For right now she was perfection indeed. And he couldn't help teasing her a bit. "You are hardly cowhanded now, Miss Tempest. Quite the opposite."

She'd put a light into his life, and it teased him to come closer. To live again.

She put her hand against his chest and stopped his forward motion. "Then perhaps you'll come with us tonight."

All Pierson heard was one word. *Tonight.*

Then the rest of what she was saying tumbled past his visions of her mahogany hair unbound and falling free. Her lips open and begging to be kissed. Her hands winding around him, pulling him closer . . .

"Perhaps if you came with us . . . to Almack's . . . then the punch bowl wouldn't end up . . ." She paused and bit her lips together.

Almack's?

"Never," he blurted out, sitting back from her. "I cannot." *I won't.*

"Why not?" she asked, sitting back as well.

"Because I can't . . . Don't you see that?"

"I don't see any such thing," she replied.

"Louisa, please," he said, reaching for her, but she drew back.

"Don't call me that," she told him. "It isn't proper."

But more to the point, he could see the hurt and confusion caused by his refusal to go to Almack's.

Better she'd prodded him into the House of Lords. But Almack's? He shuddered. 'Twould be like being tossed to the lions.

He leaned over again, thinking to kiss her, beg her forgiveness, find some way to explain his refusal, but he was thwarted in another way.

"Milord!" came the shout from the kitchen door. "Milord!"

Bob. Impatient and full of importance, he made his announcement with a full measure of his aunt's fierce determination, and, if Pierson wasn't mistaken, someone else.

Him. Is that what he sounded like? All bluster and indignation?

"Milord!" the boy repeated. "Aunt wants me to tell you your tea is growing cold, and

235

she didn't bake those tarts to go to waste."

Miss Tempest sat up, her cheeks heating as fast as the viscount's tea was cooling.

"Oh, gar!" Bob said. "I didn't see you there, miss."

But seen her he had. Right up close to the viscount. Nearly in his arms.

The boy blinked and then began to stammer again, for it was obvious he didn't know quite what to do.

But she did.

The lady got up. "You cannot come tonight? Not even for me?"

Pierson looked up at her. "No." Not even for her.

She nodded once and then turned and quickly crossed the yard, in great long strides and, before he knew it, was through the garden door. "Miss Tempest, wait!" Lord Wakefield called after her as he struggled to rise. "Oh, demmit, come back here," he ordered, once again all bluff and indignation.

But she didn't heed him.

And more to the point, he didn't follow her. He couldn't. He didn't dare. Why didn't anyone else see that?

CHAPTER 9

Pierson sat down for his supper later that day, his gaze straying to the French doors — out into the garden. After Louisa had left, he'd finished planting the strawberry starts she'd brought, with Bob's help.

And the lad — smart whip that he was — hadn't said a word about what had transpired.

Or rather, what hadn't.

Bitty had come out as well and the pair of them had raced about the yard in merry abandonment, their laughter tugging at his regrets.

More than once, he'd caught himself smiling at them, that and glancing at the gate hoping to catch sight of Miss Tempest returning.

Whatever was coming over him?

Worst of all, he felt a complete churl for not agreeing to go to Almack's as she'd asked. But couldn't she see how such a request was impossible?

"Most impossible," he muttered to himself.

"My lord," Tiploft intoned from the doorway.

Pierson glanced over his shoulder and immediately recalled Miss Tempest's admonishment about his butler.

He should have been retired years ago.

Retire Tiploft? Pierson couldn't fathom such a notion. He'd be lost without Tiploft. The man had been the anchor of the household since . . . since . . . Well, since Pierson had been in short pants.

And with that realization came a pang of guilt.

The man probably should have been pensioned off a decade ago.

"My lord?" Tiploft prodded.

"Yes, what is it?" Pierson asked.

"Mr. Rowland is here."

And before Pierson could order his butler to bar the door and send the vagrant packing, Tuck came strolling into his dining room with all the air of an invited guest.

"Get the hell out of my house," the viscount told him, pointing toward the door.

His old friend laughed and waved him off as if Pierson was joking. "Cuz! You, of all people, know I am never one to stand on ceremony," he drawled before he settled into a place at the table. He leaned forward and examined Pierson's half-filled plate and the chargers on the table — then lapsed into a wide grin. Apparently the offerings met with his approval. "Yes, well, it appears I'm late. No need for concern — I can catch up."

If it were possible, Tuck settled deeper into his chair.

Pierson knew from experience there would be no removing Tuck now.

At least not until he'd eaten his fill and drank up a good portion of Pierson's best Madeira.

"Bring him a plate, Tiploft," Pierson managed, hoping there wasn't a hint of hospitality in his words.

Not that such a lack of manners would bother Tuck, or even rise to his notice, for he was too busy examining the contents of every platter and dish, exclaiming with delight at the large beefsteak and inhaling deeply over the onion soup. "Indecent of you, Piers, to keep Mrs. Petchell all to yourself. Ah, Tiploft! Thank you, my good man!"

Latching on to the plate Tiploft had brought, Tuck wasted no time filling it and then diving into his supper with great gusto, waxing on about Mrs. Petchell's culinary skills.

Which might have made a true host happy, but Pierson knew it would only encourage Tuck to drop by any time he needed a good supper.

Which, it being Tuck, would mean nearly every night.

"What are you doing here?" Pierson asked, returning to his own meal before it grew chilled. He'd eaten enough cold suppers in Spain to last him a lifetime.

Tuck grinned as he carved himself a substantial portion from the beefsteak.

The one that had been meant for Pierson.

"Uncle's forcing me to go to Almack's tonight," he explained. "Dancing attendance on his country wards. An evening smiling at a pair of — what did you call them? Ah, yes, plain harridans. A man can't be asked to do that without some fortification, don't you agree? Speaking of which" — he turned to Tiploft — "is there any of that remarkable Madeira about?"

Pierson was about to shake his head and order his butler to deny its existence, but a sudden spike of panic ran through his veins.

Tuck was escorting Miss Tempest to Almack's?

His thoughts raced back to earlier. That

moment when he'd refused Louisa's request. What the devil had he done?

He looked up and found Tuck studying him and hastily returned to his own supper. While he tried to look calm and disinterested, his insides were a tangled coil.

The notion of a rake like Tuck anywhere near Miss Tempest had him at sixes and sevens.

More to the point, what was their uncle thinking?

"He's forcing me, you know," Tuck said, looking up from his meal. "Wants me there so someone dances with them." He shuddered with the very notion of it.

Dancing. Once again, Pierson's thoughts went to how it had felt to have her up against him, in his arms, warm and willing.

Would she dance like that? Fluid and seductive?

Well, he'd never know, would he? But Tuck would. He'd be there, all charm and gracious manners, ready to take advantage of the lady's country innocence.

Much as you did, his conscience pricked at him.

Yes, well . . . that wasn't entirely the same, he'd argue.

Which was as much a lie as his nonchalance over the subject.

Meanwhile, Tuck was prattling on. "—
then I suppose he'll be expecting me to
marry one of them —"

"Ma-ma-r-r-ry?" Pierson choked out.

"Oh, aye," Tuck told him mournfully.
"Not that I have any objections to a fetching miss with a large dowry. Easier to be
lured into the parson's trap by a pretty face,
don't you think?"

"Wouldn't know. I have no intention of
ever marrying."

"Lucky you," Tuck said, tipping his glass
in a salute.

"Refuse to go," Pierson advised, returning
to his supper and finding that his once
grand beefsteak now tasted like an old boot.

"Can't," Tuck told him between gulps of
wine. "He's gone and threatened my allowance."

"*Ah* —" Pierson hoped he sounded sympathetic, when in fact the notion of a broke
Tuck was worse than a Tuck in full possession of his quarterly allowance. Charleton's
heir would do whatever it took to keep his
income flowing.

And in that vein, Tuck continued on with
his speculations. "Do you recall what sort
of dowry these chits might bring? I seem to
recall Charleton mentioning something
about an estate —"

"No, I don't. I don't think they have any sort of money," Pierson rushed to remind him. "I do believe respectability is what Charleton wanted to impress upon you. Loads of it." He went back to his meal and didn't look up.

For fear his old friend would see the lie that had just fallen from his lips revealed in his wary gaze.

Tuck was just the sort who could spot a bouncer from across the park.

"Ah, yes. He did go on and on about that," Tuck nodded, waving his fork and, having emptied his first plate, surveyed the chargers once more. "Still, I can't help thinking that plain chits — they are plain, aren't they?"

Pierson nodded. He didn't know why he continued to keep up this farce, but he had to.

Not that Tuck wouldn't know the truth soon enough.

His friend shuddered. "Yes, well, plain it is. Still, it is my experience that plain ones always do seem to come with a decent dowry. There's an irony in that, don't you agree?"

"Yes, indeed," Pierson said, even as he was trying to figure out a way to keep Tuck from going to Almack's. Locking him in the cellar might work, but then, knowing Tuck, he'd spend the night happily drinking down the best vintages.

Nor could he suggest they head out for one of their former haunts. For then Pierson would have to go out.

Meanwhile, Tuck was still calculating the possible advantages of a plain miss. "— certainly makes them more palatable. A large dowry, that is. And if these chits are as unpleasant as you insist —"

And it struck him that no matter the dowry Miss Tempest came with, whoever gained her hand was getting a priceless treasure.

"Is money all you think about?" Pierson asked, setting down his knife and fork.

Tuck paused as well, his eyes narrowing, dangerously so. "I know what you think of me. And I could explain matters, but I doubt you would understand. Or care."

That last bit stung a bit. For once they had been close. As close as brothers. With Lady Charleton's encouragement, he and Tuck had grown up together.

Along with Poldie, that is, whose father's house was just across the square.

But all that had changed — the day Pierson and Poldie had bought their commissions, while Tuck had foolishly and recklessly gambled his money away in some Seven Dials hell.

At least so he had said the day he turned up at the docks to watch them sail away to their fates.

It had been an image — Tuck standing rigid and alone alongside the Thames — that had haunted Pierson for some time. Left him furious and unforgiving to this day.

Especially when that vision had been replaced by a memory far more haunting.

Yet even now he suspected there was more behind his friend's story than just a tale of a bad hand of loo.

He should ask. He should demand an explanation. But that would mean letting Tuck back into his life.

Forgiving him. Not that there was anything to forgive — but maybe if Tuck had kept his word, come to Spain with them, Pierson would have been able to keep the vow he'd made to bring Poldie home alive.

"I don't see why you came here," Pierson began, pausing for a second before adding, "other than for the beefsteak."

"Which is excellent," Tuck told him, waving the large piece stuck on the end of his fork before he popped it in his mouth and chewed it with all the gusto of a contented lion. Once he swallowed it and washed it further down with a large gulp of wine, he grinned at Pierson. "If you must know, I came to see if you would come as well. To Almack's, that is."

Pierson choked, for certainly he hadn't heard Tuck correctly.

Go to Almack's?

"Have you gone mad?" he blustered.

"I suppose I have," Tuck agreed, grinning at the bite of steak he was about to devour. "It is just that misery loves company and I couldn't think of anyone in London more miserable than you."

"It is just as I imagined," Lavinia said in breathless wonder as the sisters entered the hallowed ground of Almack's.

Indeed, it was well beyond the usual staid affair in Kempton. Not even the Midsummer's Eve Ball at Foxgrove could compare to the splendor before them. As waiters rushed by proffering trays laden with cakes and drinks, Louisa drew in a steadying breath to calm the flutters in her stomach.

Butterflies that had started the moment Mr. Rowland had joined their party as they assembled on the front steps of Lord Charleton's town house for the carriage ride to King Street. Rowland's brows had risen at the sight of them, and not, Louisa noted, with censure.

It was clear, from the wicked smile that had lit up the handsome features of Lord Charleton's heir, that Mr. Alaster Rowland found the Tempest sisters a delightful surprise, and had even gone so far as to say as much after their initial introduction.

"My dear ladies, however has my uncle kept you hidden this long? I am delighted I will have you all to myself before we reach Almack's, for once there, I suspect I will be swept aside by a rush of likely partners." Then he'd bowed rather unsteadily over both their hands, and Louisa had seen the censorious look Lady Aveley had shot Lord Charleton.

This is a bad idea, the matron's dark glance said all too clearly.

And as Mr. Rowland had made his way, swaying back and forth to the waiting carriage, Lavinia had sniffed her disapproval. "He's bosky," she'd whispered to Louisa.

But all thoughts of Mr. Rowland's disgraceful state were forgotten the moment they got to their intended destination.

Almack's.

They'd come in the doors, presented their vouchers and even now were crossing the threshold into a new world far from Kempton's country ways.

After nearly colliding with a footman, Louisa was ready to beat a hasty retreat, but Lavinia, having anticipated her twin's reluctance, slipped her gloved hand into the crook of Louisa's elbow and moved her forward without missing a step.

This time.

Lady Aveley, well versed in the ways of Almack's, walked in proudly and confidently on Lord Charleton's arm, and when she glanced over her shoulder at her protégées, she nodded at them and Louisa could almost hear the lady's silent assurance.

Smile, girls. Smile.

Louisa did her best to prop up her lips, while beside her, Lavinia all but glowed with radiant happiness at having finally made it here. To Almack's.

"Aren't you glad I talked you into having that gown made up?" Lavinia whispered.

"Yes, I suppose you were right," Louisa admitted. For her sister had been downright bullheaded over the matter and wouldn't leave the modiste shop until Louisa had agreed to something more elegant than the plain silk she'd picked out for a ball gown.

Back in the shop, the short-sleeved, delicate creation Lavinia had declared "perfect," along with a length of white crepe she insisted was "the only choice," had seemed far too extravagant, even for London, but now looking around at the colorful array of gowns, Louisa could see she'd been wise to listen to her fashion-mad sister.

Even if she felt nearly naked.

Nor was she alone. Most of the gowns being worn sported the same short sleeves that left one's arms bare down to where one's long gloves stopped at the elbows.

But it was the back of Louisa's gown that made it stand out — for it fell in a deep V, leaving her exposed nearly to the middle of her back, where a pink ribbon adorned the display, its long ties ending in a cascade of silk fringe that swayed as she walked. The white crepe gown ended just above her ankles, where the hem was decorated all the way around with silk roses in a variety of pinks, joined by a twined green ribbon that wound between them like the wild tangle of rose canes in Lord Wakefield's gardens.

And in a breathless moment, she was there again. In the garden. The smell of grass and earth and Lord Wakefield surrounding her. And she was lost.

No, entwined. Entangled. Caught.

Louisa stopped herself right there and drew in another deep breath.

She mustn't continue to let that man

invade her every thought. He was going to ruin everything.

Including her.

For there in the grass, she would have let him . . . let him . . . well, she wasn't precisely certain what would have come next, but surely it would have been ruinous.

And glorious, a wry part of her conscience whispered.

Yes, that as well. But that wasn't why she had come to London. She had braved this folly to see her sister well matched and herself bundled back to Kempton where she could quietly live out the rest of her days.

But quiet would be a difficult notion now.

How would she ever find peace with this restless curiosity, these awakened desires that Lord Wakefield had coaxed and teased from her?

Wasn't it bad enough that since their encounter in the linen closet, she'd woken up every night, tangled in her sheets, breathless and anxious from half-finished kisses, the memory of his touch leaving her quaking, longing.

Botheration, that man! How she wished she'd never met him.

"I suppose you two cannot wait to dance," Lord Charleton was saying as they waded deeper into the crowd.

"Dance?" Louisa sputtered, glancing over at her sister.

Lavinia looked just as horrified. "Oh, no, not tonight," she said, shaking her head.

The two sisters, without even thinking, curled their pinky fingers together and stole a glance at each other.

Promise?

Promise.

"I'm certain Mr. Rowland will insist," he said, glancing away. "And if a gentleman asks a lady to dance, it is rude to refuse."

"Not when he is bosky," Louisa muttered under her breath. She didn't like to naysay her host, and Lord Charleton was a dear man, but he had a terrible blind spot when it came to his nephew and heir.

"Well, I have been practicing," Lavinia said quietly, her gaze straying longingly toward the dance floor as Lord Charleton went over to greet an old friend.

"Practicing?" Louisa tipped her head and looked over at her sister, whose confession shocked her. "When?"

Even with all their appointments with the modiste, trips to the milliner and all the shops and rounds of visits that they'd managed in the last fortnight, Louisa was certain she would have noticed another dancing master coming to call.

She certainly would have heard him just as hastily departing in a whirl of French expletives.

"While you've been disappearing into the garden next door," she whispered back, her brows arching into two question marks.

But before they could continue — which was really the last thing Louisa wanted to do — Lady Aveley drew close and said, "Time for introductions, my dears. A successful Season is like a war. We need allies and high ground, and tonight we shall gain both. Come along, now. We shall storm the gates, as it were." She glanced over at Louisa. "And please, Louisa, try to smile."

Doing as she was bid, Louisa forced her lips up.

"Ah, there is the Countess of Heatley and her son, Lord Ardmore," Lady Aveley whispered, delicately tipping her fan toward a knot of guests not far from where they stood. "A perfect place to begin. Ardmore stands to inherit a fortune from both his father and an uncle. He's a paragon," she told them, letting the importance of this introduction weigh down upon them before she led them toward the matron and the tall, handsome gentleman at her side.

"He's elegant-looking," Lavinia whispered as they hung back just a bit.

"Indeed," Louisa agreed reluctantly. For suddenly she saw the enormity of what they were doing — Lavinia would meet someone and they would marry, and Louisa would return to Kempton. Their lives would be forever changed and no more would they be each other's constant companion.

Suddenly her future, the one she'd been so utterly certain of, seemed quite bleak. And very lonely.

She'd never minded the notion of keeping house for her father for the remainder of his days, but what then? What would she do when their aged father died, and Maplethorpe went to Lavinia's eldest son? What if he didn't want an old maiden aunt doddering about?

Louisa suspected she wouldn't be feeling this way if she hadn't met Lord Wakefield.

If he hadn't kissed her.

Given her a tempting taste of what she'd be missing.

And it was as if Lavinia knew of the turmoil inside her, for her sister nudged her and said, "See, you might be enticed to give up your ridiculous desire to die a spinster. Can you imagine being kissed by such a handsome man?"

Louisa was starting to think Lavinia was as bosky as Mr. Rowland. First dancing and now kissing!

Then again, Lavinia had spent most of the afternoon reading the newest *Miss Darby* novel, an endeavor that always made her a romantic wreck for a good fortnight.

So as Lady Aveley made the necessary introductions, and others — namely young gentlemen — joined their circle, Lavinia glowed with dreamy delight, but all the while Louisa's thoughts kept straying back to her sister's question.

Can you imagine being kissed by such a handsome man?

Kissed? When Louisa looked at Lord Ardmore, she only saw what was lacking. His expression was too soft. His hair tamed and oiled into place. His jacket perfectly cut and not a single thread out of place.

But his kiss? She tried to keep her nose from wrinkling. Not when the memory of Lord Wakefield's restless kiss still left her tingling, quivering . . . and in other, far more unmentionable places, aching.

And even while she'd sworn, as she'd rushed from his garden, that she would never stray into his path again, she found herself wishing she could look up and find him standing in the doorway. His gaze fixed on her and her alone.

Yes, if anything then she'd insist he apologize for leaving her in such a state.

But a small voice inside her mocked that sentiment.

Apologize for giving you a taste of every naughty, wicked fantasy you've ever desired?

Yes, well, there was that. How could one expect an apology for being given a glimpse of heaven?

Viscount Wakefield did what he always did after his supper — that is, after he'd sent Mr. Rowland packing — he retired to his study with his books and papers.

Yet when Tiploft arrived with the brandy bottle and glass His Lordship had ordered up, the butler saw his employer's papers abandoned on the desk, a book opened and forgotten. And, more surprising, His Lordship pacing about the room.

Actually pacing. Back and forth as if his leg was of no matter.

"He'll take advantage of her, you know," the viscount said, even before Tiploft had fully entered the room.

"He, my lord?" As if Tiploft had to ask.

But his nonchalance was answered with an emotional outburst. "Tuck! He's off with Charleton tonight. To Almack's. And with her, no less."

"Ah," Tiploft acknowledged. He no more

had to ask who this "her" might be than he had with regard to Mr. Rowland. This was the first stirring of interest the viscount had shown in the world beyond the four walls of this house since he'd returned from the war.

He knew the viscount spent most of his waking hours reading and rereading military theories and histories, but it was hardly a butler's place to point out that no amount of reading would reverse the past.

Nor would it bring back the lives lost on the retreat to Corunna.

So Tiploft said nothing more, only poured a measure of whisky for the viscount and handed him the glass.

The viscount frowned at the swirling amber liquid. "What does Charleton know of these matters?"

"Matters, my lord?"

The viscount set his cane aside and waved his hand in the air. "Bringing out gels into society. Why, 'tis madness. Evidenced by the very fact that he asked Tuck to assist him. Tuck!" He finished his emphatic pronouncement with a large swig from his glass.

"Indeed, my lord," Tiploft muttered. And then he did it. Dared to tread over the line that separated noble from servant.

He did the one thing a man of his station was never supposed to do: he prodded his employer.

Because Tiploft had known the Honorable Pierson Stratton since the day he'd arrived in this world, all red-faced and squalling, and had proudly watched the young master grow up — the son Tiploft had never had.

And when the viscount had returned from Spain, wounded, broken and despairing of life, Tiploft had believed that the viscount's heart would heal right along with his injuries, even when his betrothed had abandoned him in such a shoddy and ill-mannered fashion. (And good riddance to Lady Melliscent, Tiploft would have added.)

Yet the viscount hadn't rallied, as the butler had hoped.

Instead, Pierson had drawn the walls of the Stratton town house around him like a castle of old, scorned his friends, and refused to go out in society, blotting out any hopes Tiploft had of seeing yet another generation of Strattons arrive into this world.

Until now . . .

So in desperation born of watching the man slip away into the darkness he'd brought back from Spain, Tiploft prodded as he hadn't done since the viscount had taken his very first toddling steps across the front foyer.

"It does seem a situation fraught with disaster, my lord," Tiploft murmured as he straightened the glasses on the tray and tucked the cork back into the bottle. "And Miss Tempest is —"

He let his words trail off and the image of that beguiling lady sink into the viscount's imagination.

"Miss Tempest is a handful —" Wakefield told him after a few moments of contemplation. "And in need of a good chaperone."

Especially after the other afternoon, Tiploft mused. He knew exactly what had happened in that linen closet. He hardly approved of such things, but then again, if the lady could touch the viscount's heart, then Tiploft wished he'd locked them inside, instead of backing away and quietly making himself scarce.

"But then again, Almack's is not the sort of place where a lady can be easily compromised," the viscount mused, glancing at the decanter of whisky and then toward his scattered papers.

Tiploft hardly liked that direction and fired his best shot. "Though you've said on more than one occasion that one must never underestimate Mr. Rowland's ingenuity. Especially when it comes to the delicate sex.

Nor will Mr. Rowland be alone in his efforts — think of how many others who share his inclinations will be in attendance. And an innocent country lady like Miss Tempest . . ."

The butler sighed. Heavily. As if the ruin and misfortunes about to befall Louisa were a foregone conclusion.

That implication brought the viscount's gaze off his papers and notes and back to the conversation at hand. "Good God, you're right," he said, setting aside his glass. "I need to get to Almack's."

"Almack's, my lord?" Tiploft hoped he sounded surprised.

"Bloody hell, yes," the viscount said, heading toward the door. "What time is it?"

"Won't you need vouchers, my lord?" That stopped his employer, for Tiploft didn't want any of this to be *too* easy for Wakefield. And after a pregnant pause, he offered, "Though I do believe Miss Stratton is in possession of vouchers."

"Roselie?" The viscount blanched a bit at the mention of his sister — because with Roselie came their mother, and Tiploft feared the entire plan was about to unravel.

"I'm most certain Her Ladyship is out this evening, leaving your sister unescorted," he supplied. "Perhaps you could —"

"Yes, yes. Excellent suggestion, Tiploft."
He glanced at his butler. "And you say
Mother is out?"

"Her Ladyship is at the theater this evening."

"Good news, that," the viscount muttered.
"It will hardly be of note if I escort my sister
— especially with Mother otherwise engaged." This he said more to himself, again
glancing at the clock. "Dear God! Is that
the time? Send the boy over with a note for
Roselie, will you? I need to get changed."

"Indeed, my lord," Tiploft said. And for a
moment he let his hopes for the future
flicker anew, glinting like the forgotten
whisky bottle in the fading firelight.

"Louisa! There you are! At long last. I
thought I would never find you in this
crush." Lady Aveley appeared suddenly
through a slight opening in the crowd.
"Good heavens, no wonder I couldn't see
you — whatever are you doing, hiding
amongst the wall hangings?"

"I'm not fond of dancing," Louisa de-
murred, not daring to look the lady in the
eye.

Beside her, Lady Aveley stood fanning
herself, her gaze searching the room. "I suppose I wouldn't want to dance again if my

first foray had been with Lord Ilford." She finished this with a shudder and gave Louisa a searching glance. "My dear, I am so sorry — if I had known he was going to make himself known to you, I wouldn't have turned my back. He can be rather . . ."

"Dreadful?" Louisa prompted.

Lady Aveley bit her lips together to keep from laughing. "Exactly," she agreed. Then she stilled, her fan hanging in the air. "He didn't . . . That is, he wasn't . . ."

Louisa shuddered a little. After all, she'd promised Lavinia she wouldn't dance, but there had been the Marquess of Ilford, having come up to their party, a puffed example of importance, and he'd all but insisted Louisa join him in a dance.

With his hand outstretched, she had been in a rush to find some way to refuse him.

But she couldn't come up with a single reason — other than that he made her skin crawl a bit.

Not that he'd improved once he'd gotten her out on the dance floor.

"You are the daughter of Sir Ambrose Tempest, are you not?" he'd asked, a tip to his smile that looked more predatory than kind.

And was it her imagination, or had the man's grasp upon her tightened ever so slightly?

"Yes, my lord," she told him, glancing around and hoping to fix her gaze on Lady Aveley. But Her Ladyship and Lavinia were nowhere to be seen. Lord Ilford had managed to move them well across the room.

"Have I mentioned that my father knew your mother?" he said, with a nonchalance that left her off-balance.

Knew her mother? Her heart hammered. He didn't mean . . .

Yet he did.

In the blink of an eye, there was no mistaking the matter, for Lord Ilford pulled her closer and said, "I have high hopes you've come to London to follow in her footsteps." His once salacious smile turned licentious, and his hand began to stray.

That was the first time Louisa trod on his foot. With the heel of her slipper.

When the dance ended, and Ilford had limped away in a pet, Louisa had fled as far as she could, to the far wall where the ladies who never danced quietly retreated, and tried to still her pounding heart.

Lady Aveley drew closer and said behind her fan so no one else could hear, "That horrid man didn't say anything untoward, anything to upset you, did he?"

"I — that is —" she began, looking around

for something innocuous to say. Whatever could she say? *He wanted to know if I was a lightskirt like my mother.*

"Nothing of import," Louisa told her. After his first slight, he'd been too distracted trying to keep his glossy boots out of her way.

The lady sighed and nodded. "Heir to a dukedom he may be, but I've always found the man to be rather presumptuous. We'll just make sure you and your sister are not subjected to his company again."

Louisa decided it might not be best if she told Lady Aveley she'd already taken care of that.

But the other matter . . . Certainly Lord Ilford wouldn't repeat such malicious tidings? Her head spun. This was precisely what she had warned Papa about, and what had he said?

No one in London will care of such old news.

The matron fluttered her fan as if that was enough to dismiss the matter, and smiled. "Now let us find someone more worthy of your beauty."

"Oh, I don't want to —" All Louisa wanted to do was go home. To Kempton. Far from London.

Lady Aveley laughed at her discomposure. "Yes, you do. You just haven't met the right man yet. And when you do, you'll know."

The right man. Why was it when the lady said those words, Louisa was transported right back into Lord Wakefield's arms? Back in the linen closet where she hadn't felt ungainly and cowhanded, but quite desirable.

Then came an insensible, panicked thought. What if he heard of her mother's disgrace? Learned the truth about her? And Lady Aveley and Lord Charleton as well? They had been so nice to her and Louisa, and now would they be tainted by association?

And worst of all, Lavinia. Her sister had no idea of their mother's sins — and to find out in such a setting . . . Louisa looked for her and considered how she was going to tell her twin the truth she'd hidden for so many years.

A truth she'd only accidentally discovered.

"Miss Tempest, are you well? You look flushed," Lady Aveley said. "Or have I discovered your secret — you do have a beau!"

Louisa's mouth fell open and then snapped shut. "No! Not at all."

The lady laughed, and mischievously tapped Louisa's arm with her fan. "I was young once as well. And I know all the signs. There is someone, isn't there?" And before Louisa could add an insistent *No!,* the lady continued on, "Don't worry, my dear. Whoever he is he'll most likely move heaven and earth to be here tonight. That is if he hasn't got windmills in his head."

"Oh, he's not —" she began before she could stop herself.

The baroness held up her fan. "Aha! The truth. There is someone." She grinned with delight.

"It isn't like that —" Louisa began. *It isn't anything* was what she should have been saying. Oh, heavens, she didn't know what it was. But not that. It couldn't be that.

Lady Aveley continued blithely on. "Men! They can leave us all a tangle, can't they? I was in much the same straits when I was your age. I can see it in your eyes."

Hopefully Her Ladyship couldn't see what else Louisa was trying to conceal. The raw desire Lord Wakefield plucked from her so easily. With him, she felt wanton.

Certainly if Bob hadn't come into the garden when he had, there was no telling what she would have done next under Lord Wakefield's evocative caress.

Good heavens, she was no different than her mother — which would only spell disaster.

The lady moved closer and tucked Louisa's hand into the crook of her sleeve and led her away from the long row of wallflowers. "Tell me this, does he know you exist?"

Well, yes, she wanted to say. *He quite likes to bellow at me every opportunity he's afforded.* Instead, she once again began to stammer. "I — I — I —"

"Ah," Lady Aveley said, leaping upon that one word as if it confessed all. "Don't tell me he's in love with your sister?" When this elicited no reply, she continued. "A dear friend? Oh, I can't recommend that scenario. There's nothing more horrible than having to smile as you watch your love carry off another." The baroness glanced away, still with a smile on her lips, but there was a sad light to her eyes that prodded at Louisa's heart.

"But my lady, you married him after all, didn't you?"

She shook her head just ever so slightly. "No. I didn't."

Louisa's head swiveled toward the woman. For there was an important lesson here, a wisdom in her words.

Don't make the same mistake I did.

Yet how did one stop her heart once it was engaged? That mercurial, magical moment when it pauses and makes that decision.

Him.

For Louisa's distraction wasn't so much the kiss — yes, well, that had a lot to do with it — but more to the point was the man behind those lips, that touch, that solid embrace.

She suddenly realized the truth of what had happened over the last fortnight.

Lord Wakefield had done more than kiss her. He'd marked her.

But how? And when?

Bother, she'd just met the man and all he'd done was scold her.

And kiss her.

And show kindness toward Mrs. Petchell's foundlings. Then there had been that moment in the garden, when his usually wary gaze had been unguarded and she'd seen a depth of pain and suffering that pulled at her.

For she suspected whatever had towed the viscount into its dark clutches wasn't something that could be easily fixed or mended — like an untidy linen closet.

But botheration, she couldn't shake the desire to help him put his life back in order. Then she would run back to Kempton,

where she had her own demons to hide
away.

CHAPTER 10

As Lady Aveley led Louisa through the crush of Almack's, she continued her easy patter. "Ah, there is your sister. With Mr. Rowland. I suppose I should be relieved he is doing as Charleton instructed and dancing with her."

"Lavinia is dancing?" The question bolted out of Louisa's mouth and Lady Aveley slanted a questioning glance at her.

"Shouldn't she be?"

Louisa bit her bottom lip. Oh, dear, how did one say something so embarrassing about one's own sister?

Between the two of them, Lavinia made Louisa look like a ballerina.

"Miss Tempest?" Lady Aveley pressed, glancing back again at Mr. Rowland as he took Lavinia's hand and placed it on his sleeve. "Is it Mr. Rowland who has you concerned? Don't get me wrong, I could have wrung his neck when he acted as if

Charleton was asking him to perform the most onerous of obligations — but it is good for him to do something respectable. And at the very least, see to his duty to his uncle."

"Yes, well —" Louisa said, barely able to look over at her sister. "It's just —"

Lady Aveley looked over there as well and at that moment, Mr. Rowland stumbled a bit. "Oh, no. I had hoped he wasn't as —"

"He seems a bit unsteady," Louisa remarked, flinching slightly as the baron's heir wavered again.

"Unsteady? My dear girl, he's drunk." Lady Aveley looked ready to go fetch Lavinia off the dance floor, but right then the musicians began to play. The lady grimaced and turned her back to the dance floor. "Oh, I cannot watch!"

Louisa rather thought it a boon. Now if Lavinia stumbled over her own feet, perhaps everyone would blame Mr. Rowland.

"I should never have let Charleton insist on bringing him!" Lady Aveley declared, glancing over her shoulder at the couple, her mouth pursed into a tight frown.

"You don't approve of him?"

"No, I do not. Most days. Oh, how that man charms his way back into society's good graces each and every time he makes a muddle of things is nothing short of a miracle — but this is Almack's of all places! If only Wakefield had come along with him." She glanced heavenward as if she could conjure the viscount from thin air.

"Lord Wakefield?" Louisa asked, the name sending a shiver down her spine.

"Oh, you needn't sound surprised. Believe it or not, he used to haunt this place when he was . . . well . . ." she said with a sigh. "I nearly died when Mr. Rowland announced in the carriage that he'd asked the viscount to join us. I will give Charleton's heir this much — that took some nerve, bearding the lion in his own den, so to say. Still, it was cruel of him to ask, when he —"

"Cannot dance?" Louisa prompted.

"Yes, exactly."

"I don't want to dance, but that doesn't mean I can't enjoy the evening. I don't think Mr. Rowland was being cruel in the least."

After all, she'd asked him. And he'd refused her too.

"Perhaps. Then again, I don't think Mr. Rowland would ever be deliberately cruel to Wakefield. They were once inseparable. Larking about Town like brothers. Causing every mother and maiden no end of headaches."

Louisa could hardly imagine Wakefield

"larking." "Whyever is the viscount so . . . well . . . so . . ." she began, trying to form a diplomatic query.

"Beastly?" Lady Aveley supplied. "You needn't mince words over him. His own mother refers to him thusly."

This took Louisa aback. "His own mother?"

Lady Aveley laughed. "Yes. Lady Wakefield is quite plain on the subject of her only son. Especially after he tossed her out of the house."

He'd tossed his own mother out . . . Louisa tried to close her gaping mouth. "Has he always been so . . ."

"Terrible?" The lady shook her head. "No, not at all. He was very much like Mr. Rowland before he bought his commission and joined the Tenth." She glanced over at Lavinia and Mr. Rowland, where the man was wavering through the more complicated movements of the cotillion, and shook her head in dismay.

"What happened?" Louisa prompted, thinking of the mysterious Melliscent.

Her Ladyship heaved a sigh and continued, "Well," she began, pulling her gaze away from the dance floor, "he bought his colors and served quite admirably. Promoted in the field for bravery. Then came that dreadful business with Corunna."

"It must have been horrible," Louisa said, for she'd seen the pain in his eyes, the depth of his misery.

"I suspect what the papers printed and what Lord Wakefield survived are quite different. Yet for Wakefield, those weeks haunt him still," she said.

"That was when his leg —"

"Yes. Shot by a French sniper."

"Oh, dear. How horrible."

"Indeed. He nearly lost his life. And the leg." She stood a little straighter. "I suppose since he cannot dance, he sees no point in coming here. Or anywhere."

"That hardly matters," Louisa said, thinking of her own predicament. She couldn't dance, yet there she was. "There are other things a gentleman has to offer other than being a dance partner."

Like his lips. And his arms . . .

Louisa stopped herself right there. Heavens, she had to quit thinking of him like that.

Lady Aveley shrugged. "It isn't just his leg. Poor man gets shot by the French and then comes home and has his heart torn in two by the woman he was supposed to marry."

"Marry?" Louisa turned her full attention

273

to this news. Wakefield had meant to marry his Melliscent? And yet . . . "What sort of woman would cry off in such a circumstance?" She couldn't fathom such disloyalty.

Lady Aveley nodded her head across the room. "A woman just like that one. Lady Blaxhall." She added a tip of her fan in the direction of a tall, lithe beauty in a dove gray gown and with a tremendous arrangement of feathers atop her icy blonde hair. "That, my dear, is the real reason Lord Wakefield is wounded. The former Lady Melliscent Tendring." Her Ladyship made an imperious sniff. "And just about out of mourning for poor Blaxhall and already making the rounds here at Almack's from the looks of things. But I don't know why I'm surprised — after she threw over Wakefield, she married Blaxhall with all the indecent haste of a Covent Garden chorus girl."

Louisa knew she should be shocked by all this information, but she was too busy looking at the lady, this Melliscent, who had broken Wakefield's heart. Lady Melliscent was everything Mr. Rowland had hinted at.

Beautiful, in a cool, elegant way. Like a grand lily blooming in a garden. She even moved with a subtle confidence that seemed to allow her to glide through the room, as if waving gently on a summer zephyr.

More like a snake, Louisa thought uncharitably.

And it seemed a sentiment Lady Aveley shared. "If you ask me, Wakefield is far better off having not married that gel," she declared. "Still, Melliscent's desertion was a cruel blow. After she cried off, he closed himself up in his house and hasn't been out in society since." She made a *tsk, tsk,* and continued, "Barring his friends and family from seeing him. Sending anyone who dares packing." She shook her head. "That is why you will never see Viscount Wakefield at Almack's. Or any other dance."

"He loved her that much?" Louisa asked the question without thinking.

"I suppose so, but why, I will never understand — she's always seemed such a calculating creature to me. But, la! Listen to me," Lady Aveley said, "I sound as gossipy as my mother-in-law." She glanced over at the dance floor where Mr. Rowland was teetering through the dance steps and flinched slightly. Then she surveyed the room yet again. "Ah, now here is the perfect change of subject. A respectable prospect just for you. He asked to be presented and I wager he will give you second thoughts about this unrequited love of yours."

"Lady Aveley, as I said before, I have no desire to dance. Or marry. Please don't —"

For even if there was someone, soon enough they'd find out about her mother and then . . .

"Pish! You only say that because you haven't met the right man. And any man who hasn't followed you here tonight isn't worthy of your heart. Now smile, my dear, and meet a true gentleman."

Louisa drew a deep breath and turned around, and bother if she wasn't half wishing to see the viscount coming toward her. But instead it was another man — oh, he was handsome enough and very well turned out, but not . . . not . . .

Him.

"Oh, dear God, what was I thinking?" Wakefield muttered under his breath as he stood just before the ballroom doors.

He was stopped. Not by the crush of people. Or any assumption that he might be barred from being allowed inside.

For honestly, what patroness would turn away an unmarried gentleman with a title and fortune?

Yet he hardly felt like a gentleman. More like the beast everyone thought him.

His thoughts raced back to this afternoon — Miss Tempest's enigmatic smile teasing him to lean closer and taste the all-too-tempting sweetness of her lips.

For they had been sweet when he'd dared to do so in the linen closet — far more tempting than he could have imagined. In her kiss was both a mix of innocence and desire that left him staggered with the possibilities.

The proper miss on the outside hid a simmering minx within.

She'd kissed him back that afternoon with a passion that matched her name — Tempest — hell, she created a devilish tempest inside him every time he looked at her. He not only wanted to ride out the storm she brewed in his heart, he wanted to step into the eye of it and let it blot out every bit of the world around him.

This afternoon, it had been no different. He'd wanted to drown in her kiss and would have done so if it hadn't been for Bob's untimely arrival in the garden.

And with that opening, she'd fled from his side, fleet and quick.

As well she should have — his refusal to come with her had been loutish. And short-sighted, he realized. Would she welcome his arrival now, or would she tip up her pert nose just as the young woman crossing in front of them was doing.

Beside him, his sister, Miss Roselie Stratton sniffed. "Lady Honoria. Ignore her ill-manners, Piers. I do."

His fingers curled around the handle of his walking stick and he drew a deep breath to steady his racing heart. Louisa had been right to run from him. As he should turn and leave right now.

Taking a step inside would be allowing himself to believe he could have a life he didn't deserve.

"It is usually considered good form to attend Almack's inside the ballroom," Roselie pointed out from where she'd come to a stop, just beyond the grand double doors. She was looking back over her shoulder with that bemused smile she reserved just for him. It was a mix of oh-good-heavens-don't-just-stand-there censure and her own rare humor.

Taking a deep breath, Wakefield moved to her side, making that dangerous crossing over the threshold and back into society.

Not for too long, he promised himself. *Just to see that Tuck hadn't made a mare's nest of Charleton's plans and then return home.*

And to see her . . .

Pierson quickly set that thought aside. He

was only here to ensure that nothing untoward happened. To be Tuck's conscience, since the man professed to have none.

But he knew that was a lie. Oh, not the part about Tuck, but that he had to make sure nothing untoward happened to Louisa.

Which made him London's biggest hypocrite, since the only man she truly had to worry about was probably him.

And when he saw her . . . he'd . . . he'd . . .

He'd what? Declare his feelings for her? Ask her to dance? Both impossible notions. So what the devil was he doing here?

And when he couldn't come up with anything that resembled good sense, he panicked a bit and turned to leave.

"Oh, good heavens," Roselie protested, sounding very much like their mother. "I didn't get myself rigged up — and at your insistence, I might remind you — only to come this far. You'll make me an object of gossip." Her brow quirked up. "Besides, I'm in the mood to dance."

"I'm not dancing."

"Be seen dancing with my brother?" She shuddered. "Do you truly want to see me put on a shelf?"

"Bad form?"

"The worst." She nodded politely to a matron — a friend of his mother's, he thought — who walked past them open-mouthed. She hurried past and caught the first lady she came to and began tittering like a sparrow.

"I believe I'm causing a stir," he noted.

"By tomorrow, Lady Montrose's story will be that you are opening the house back up for Mother and me, having finally come to your senses, and that you are looking to marry."

He swung toward her, the horror on his face making his sister laugh. "This is only temporary," he told her. "I have no intention —"

She waved aside his protest with a flutter of her fan. "We shall see," she said, looking smugly confident.

Bother, it was only for tonight, he wanted to announce to one and all. Then he was going back to his lair.

He *was*.

He looked up and found a good portion of the company had turned their attention toward him, Lady Montrose's chirping having fluttered through the room with all the haste of a robin on the wing.

His gut clenched. So many people looking at him. He tried to breathe, did his best to quell the dangerous tattoo in his chest begging him to run, ignore how the room had begun to close in around him, how the harmless chatter now drummed at his skull.

Retreat. Run. Flee.

"Pierson?" Roselie prompted, her hand coming to rest on his sleeve.

"I had forgotten —" he began.

"Yes, well it hasn't changed. It never does," Roselie remarked, having settled her hand in the crook of his elbow.

But he wasn't fooled. His sister was binding herself to him like a rudder, determined to steer him forward, like a pilot taking a ship through rocky shoals.

But even with his sister guiding him, Pierson soon found himself floundering.

A cotillion was in full swing — the bejeweled and elegantly clad partners moving gracefully and elegantly through the steps; the grand vision only left his chest tight with anxiety. The perfect steps, the careful manners, the precision with which everyone moved.

They made him look and feel like a blundering ape as he limped along. Damn his leg, and damn their stares as more than one matron glanced at him, each arched brow asking the same question.

Whatever are you *doing here?*

Then all around him the room began to swirl in a cacophony of sounds — the chatter of voices, the music, the clink of glasses and the clatter of trays as servants hustled through the crush.

Wakefield closed his eyes and tried to blot it all out even as fear galloped through his chest, pounding down his resolve. *What was I thinking letting Tiploft prod me into coming?*

He willed his eyes open, and when he glanced up, it seemed half the room was gaping at him. Faces of people he half remembered and so many strangers — all pressed into the one room — closing in on all sides of him.

Once again his eyes screwed shut but now all he could smell was sweat, and spent powder, his ears filled with the cries of the dying and the retort of muskets.

No. No. No. Not Spain.

He was in London, he tried telling himself, willing himself to open his eyes, and yet it seemed they were shuttered tight, barred against his will, leaving him floundering over this pit.

Help me . . . Oh, dear God . . . He was falling. Falling down into a darkness.

Then just before he tumbled, there was an insistent tug at his arm. "Pierson? Pierson, good heavens, what is it?"

His eyes sprang open and he looked to his side.

Roselie. Her dark eyes wide with alarm. Whatever was she doing here? She couldn't be. And yet, here she was, firmly beside him, alive and well, with nothing but concern etched into her youthful features. "Pierson, are you unwell?"

He drew a deep breath and glanced around. London. *You are home. Safe.* "As well as one can be in this place," he tried joking.

She shook her head, her lips pressed together. "Don't frighten me like that. I don't know where it is you go when you are like this, but you mustn't allow yourself such dark moments." Roselie smiled bravely and nodded toward the room as if to remind him, reinforce to him where they were.

"Yes, well, it isn't as if I have my full senses," he reminded her.

She laughed. "You have more sense than you realize. And scare me like that again, and I'll tell Mama that you want us to come back and live with you."

He froze.

His sister laughed and tugged him deeper into the pit. "Bachelors! You are all the same. Now, come along. I'll grant you Almack's is horribly dreary and ever-so-dull, but you asked me to come with you. Remember?"

Yes, he had asked her, but that didn't make the potion any easier to swallow.

"Excellent! There's Uncle Charleton," Roselie announced.

"Where?" he asked, daring to look around again. The room had returned to its normal glittering splendor.

"Over there," she said, nonchalantly tipping her fan toward the far side of the room. "Have you heard the news?" Then she sort of barked a laugh. "Good heavens! Whyever am I asking you — as if you know of anything that is happening." She leaned closer. "Believe it or not, uncle has taken in —"

"— two misses from the country. Yes, I know."

More than he wanted to.

Roselie's lips opened in a wide O. "Have you met them?"

"Yes. One of them," he said, trying to sound as nonchalant as he could.

His sister slanted a suspicious glance at him, but said nothing. Instead, she nonchalantly looked around, her gaze narrowing as she scanned the crowd. Not that Pierson was fooled.

She was putting the pieces together like a diplomat. Clearly, she'd inherited their father's prudent nature — and his sharp mind.

His mother and sister Margaret would never be so circumspect.

However, Roselie's reticence to pursue the subject only meant she'd be patient now. He suffered no delusions that she wouldn't do her demmed best to ferret out the truth before the night was over. "If Uncle is here, then *they* must be here as well."

"They are," he told her. He was quickly realizing he'd underestimated his little sister.

She would put the best spies in the Foreign Office to shame.

Roselie's eyes were bright with interest. "Aha!"

"Aha, nothing. My invitation has nothing to do with uncle's newfound chits," he told her. "And everything to do with Tuck."

"Tuck?" Roselie came to a stumbling halt. "We came here to find Tuck?"

He nodded. "Yes, I told you as much —"

"I thought you were joking. That you'd finally —"

He looked at her, as stone-faced as he could muster.

Roselie huffed a sigh. "If we are here in search of Tuck Rowland, we'd be better off searching the wine cellars of London, or better yet, some Cyprian's bower in Seven Dials, than think to find him here." She paused for a moment. "At Almack's?" This was followed by a bark of a laugh.

Meanwhile, Pierson gaped as he struggled to get over the notion that his little sister knew anything of Seven Dials, let alone some "Cyprian's bower." Where the devil did she hear such things?

She must have known what he was thinking, for she huffed again. "This is my third Season, Pierson. I know."

"Good God! What does that mean?" he sputtered before he could stop himself.

Truly, he didn't want to know.

But still, she told him. "That while you've been holed up in your cave, I've grown up."

"Not too much —" he growled, feeling very much like a bear shaken out of hibernation while it was still winter.

"Enough." She grinned, then deftly changed the subject. "Imagine, Uncle bringing out two unknowns! Why, it is utter folly. Something ruinous will come of this, mark my words."

Something already has, he realized as he looked across the room. "You sound like Mother."

He was rewarded with a rap of her fan. "Don't be dreadful. You are lucky she's off to the theater tonight or you'd have her to contend with." One of her brows rose in an ominous arch, in perfect imitation of their mother.

Yes, he well knew what his mother would make of his sudden interest in society. In Almack's, no less.

"Is that one of them?" Roselie pressed, this time nodding and pointing her fan. "I would so love an introduction. I'll steal the march on that horrible Lady Honoria when I can tell one and all at Lady Belton's afternoon in tomorrow that Uncle's misses have been my dearest friends for ages. Why, we are on the best of terms."

"Best of terms?" he teased. "Of all the falderal."

"I will be by tomorrow," she said confidently.

If she was looking for an *on dit,* Wakefield imagined he could give her one that would scald every ear in Lady Belton's salon.

In the linen closet? Heavens, no!

Meanwhile, Roselie had her sights set on their uncle like a terrier and moments later was tugging her brother through the crowd, nattering on as she plowed forth, firing off questions like a French sniper. "What are their names?"

"Miss Tempest and Miss Tempest."

Roselie's withering stare was worthy of their mother.

"I've only met the one," he told her.

"Which one?"

"Miss Tempest," he replied.

Roselie laughed to be outwitted once again. "You are the most dreadful brother. It is why I love you so."

This confession stopped him. "You do?" He couldn't imagine why.

"Oh, you are a widgeon," she said, taking his arm once again. "You asked me to come with you tonight. Not Margaret. Or Mama."

"Mother? Never."

"I suppose not. Still, you asked me over Margaret," Roselie turned and surveyed the crowd before them. "I will be able to lord over her for years to come that I am your favorite."

"Not if you keep nattering on —"

"I might natter, but Margaret would have had you matched to half a dozen girls before you'd gotten in her carriage."

Now it was Pierson's turn to laugh. "I wouldn't have gotten in."

"You asked me because this Miss Tempest of yours is pretty. She is pretty, isn't she? I cannot tell from here."

Extremely. Temptingly. Perfectly.

Instead he tried to sound bland. "Presentable."

He earned a sideways glance from his all-too-astute sister. "We aren't so far away that I can't tell you are lying. Whatever are you about?"

"Nothing. I hardly met the chit."

"Harrumph," was his sister's reply. *We shall see.*

As they drew closer, Roselie gave him a poke in the ribs. "You had best see Mother's oculist. Or get out of your house more. She's quite pretty. No wonder everyone is mad to meet them."

And it was then that the crowd parted enough that Wakefield could see her. Miss Tempest — surrounded by a bevy of admirers. Yet he blinked and looked again, for he thought he must be mistaken — the lady there couldn't be his Miss Tempest, for where he was used to seeing the practical miss with her plain gown and definitive views on, well, everything, here was an entirely different lady.

Her dark hair was done up in a cascade of ringlets that fell down to her shoulders. She wore an elegant gown with short sleeves and gloves that went up to her elbows, and just there was a hint of the fair, silken skin he'd caressed before. Could still feel beneath his fingertips.

You cannot kiss her. Not again. And certainly not here.

"Is that Lord Rimswell with her? But of course it is. That rakish devil," Roselie said with a bit of a huff.

Rimswell? Wakefield came up short, halting their progress. "Can't be —" he began, for the rest of the words stopped at the tip of his tongue. The words that always tore him in two. *Rimswell is dead.*

And yet the fellow there had all of his old friend's looks — the brown hair, the wide shoulders. But there was a steadiness in the smile that would never have rested easily on Poldie's madcap demeanor. No, not Poldie. This was Brody.

Still, it stayed the viscount's step to look at his friend's brother. His heir. The one who gained the title when . . .

His breath stopped in his chest. That dangerous din began to rise again in his ears.

Oh, Poldie, you demmed fool. Why did you have to do that? Why save me?

Why did you leave me to live like this?

"I can't," Wakefield declared, turning as quickly as he dared. "I won't."

"Oh, good heavens, Pierson, we've come this far," she told him, moving quickly to catch hold of his arm and anchor his retreat. "And whatever is wrong with Rimswell? Yes, yes, he's Poldie's brother, but he doesn't blame you —"

The dark glance he shot her stopped her flow of words. And thankfully this was Rose-lie — she said nothing further.

He glanced back over his shoulder to where Miss Tempest was holding court, the new Lord Rimswell at her side. To his dismay, there were several other prospects as well — all just loitering about in a circle of admiration.

Pups and lordlings all. Well, that hadn't taken long — just as he'd told her.

But then again, this was precisely why he'd lied to Tuck. A pretty new face in London brought out the ne'er-do-wells and rakes like bees to honey. Not that she seemed to notice.

He tried reminding himself that this was exactly how a young lady spent her Season. Meeting eligible young lordlings and rich prospects. And there in the midst of them was the perfect sort — for Brody was charming, well-to-do and most eligible. If he was anything like Poldie, he was also a pleasant sort. Probably kept his house well run and didn't need his closets turned inside out.

Exactly the kind of fellow Miss Tempest should have courting her — even if she claimed not to be in the market for a husband.

Well, it appeared whether she was looking or not, the Lotharios of London had certainly found her.

For Miss Tempest was smiling radiantly at the new baron — and Wakefield couldn't recall that she'd ever looked at him in such a way.

And why should she have? All he'd done was yell and be beastly around her.

That and kiss her . . .

And whatever was he to do now? He certainly couldn't go up and offer his apologies for his earlier behavior in front of her newfound admirers. He couldn't very well ask her to dance to separate her from them either, as he might have in his salad days.

No, he'd have to stand here and watch as Miss Tempest — his Miss Tempest — got swept away into a London society where he didn't belong.

Never would.

Just then, she glanced up and spied him and the look on her face spoke volumes. Shock. Dismay. Alarm.

Oh, he knew exactly what she was thinking.

What the devil is he doing here?

Well, perhaps not the devil part.

"This was a mistake," he said to Roselie, turning to leave.

But his sister's gaze was fixed elsewhere, somewhere over his shoulder, and her expression was a mixture of fury and loathing.

Whatever could have set Roselie's hackles up like a cat on points?

He turned and looked and had a very different reaction, his gut twisting.

"A mistake? I couldn't agree more," she said as she stiffened and turned slightly. "Piers, don't tell me we've come here for *her.*"

"I told you, we came to see that Tuck doesn't disgrace himself." He paused for a moment and tried to gather his shocked sensibilities together.

But to his amazement and relief, he found that whatever he'd felt in that moment when he'd looked at his former love, it had dissipated. Other than a bit of dismay, he felt nothing.

Not a demmed thing. He looked at the lady and for the first time saw her as Tuck always had.

With a full measure of wary disdain.

"Are you certain she's not why we're here?" Roselie asked just before the woman in question stopped before them.

"Pierson, darling! I couldn't believe it when Lord Ilford told me you'd come through the door. But how could you not, now that I've returned." She spared a slight, swift glance at Roselie and then turned all her beguiling powers on Pierson.

He had only one word to say. "Melliscent."

Louisa tried smiling at the all-too-affable Lord Rimswell. He was offering advice on what to see in London, while over his shoulder, Lady Aveley beamed approvingly.

"Yes, I've always wanted to see the Tower," she replied as politely as she could muster. There were other gentlemen clustered around them and they offered their advice as well until her head was swimming.

"The museum, Miss Tempest, you must go."

"Fustian! Astley's is just the ticket."

Good heavens, I wish they would all go away.

Because she wanted none of their attentions. Not when *he* was here.

Lord Wakefield.

But it can't be . . . Her heart fluttered, her lips opened slightly, as if in greeting, as if to say, *Come, my lord, come kiss me again.*

But she had to be imagining things — for the gentleman across the crush of Almack's was combed and shaved. Oh, he certainly looked like Wakefield, and his dark, unruly mane still fell to his shoulders, but someone had dared to try taming it. They'd failed utterly, happily, for it left him looking like he needed a woman's touch, the gentle brush of her fingers through those tangles to set them to rights.

Like everything about the man — he so desperately needed putting to rights.

His coat hung loosely on him — suggesting that the man who'd once worn it had been larger, grander — but Louisa knew only too well of the lean, muscular strength hidden beneath that dark wool.

Yet, what was it Lady Aveley had said? Oh, yes. *You'll never see Viscount Wakefield at Almack's.*

But here he was.

Louisa tried to breathe. Whatever did this mean? Had he come here for her? For all his teasing kisses and blustering ways, had he suddenly developed a *tendre* for her?

No, it was utterly ridiculous, yet here was her heart hammering in joy.

He loves you. He wouldn't have come unless . . . unless . . .

Then the crowd shifted and Louisa saw in an instant why the viscount had breached his own walls to come into the very heart of society.

For there standing before him, holding his attention — and most likely his heart — stood Lady Melliscent. The cool beauty smiled radiantly at her former betrothed.

He'd come not for her. But for Melliscent. Oh, good heavens, she was an idiot to have even thought he cared for her.

Whatever tittering had been going on inside her heart stopped cold. In that instant, Louisa knew that for all the reasons she hadn't wanted to come to London, here was one she'd never expected.

For having come here, having stepped into the madness of the marriage mart, she'd risked everything.

And lost the only thing that mattered: her heart.

And when she glanced up again and saw that Melliscent wasn't alone, her heart plummeted even deeper.

For even if Lord Wakefield had an iota of affection for her, he wouldn't for long.

Not with Lord Ilford standing beside him, looking all too willing to share his newest *on dit*.

Pierson gaped at the woman before him. She couldn't truly think . . .

No, this was Melliscent. Of course she thought he was here for her.

Her grasp on her companion's sleeve fell away, and she reached to take his hands in hers.

But the viscount wasn't about to be pulled into another of Melliscent's tangles, and so he stepped back.

His obvious reticence barely gave her pause, only brightened her smile. "Darling, dear Pierson, I returned to Town, hoping, wishing . . ." She spoke in that breathless tone of hers. The one filled with anxious, restless desires. The sort of half whisper, half plea that begged a man to come closer, to give her his protection.

As if she needed it.

Melliscent was about as helpless as a viper.

"I do believe we met some years ago," her companion was saying. "I'm Ilford." He then glanced over at Roselie and smiled, awaiting an introduction — which would be the mannered thing to do.

"Yes, I recall," Pierson said. And ended it there. Introduce this reprobate to his little sister? Never.

He'd been shot in the leg, not his wits.

So he turned his attention to Melliscent, and realized she was wearing a dove gray gown — half mourning.

"Blaxhall?" he managed.

"Lost," she said with a dramatic sigh, adding a sniff with her handkerchief to her lips.

Not to hide her grief, but most likely to draw attention to her perfect smile, her mouth — wide and curved, the sort that begged to be kissed and explored.

But not by him.

"So tragic," Ilford had added, as if by afterthought. Having perceived the viscount's snub, he was looking about the room, most likely looking for greener pastures. Nor did he appear pleased by Melliscent's sudden defection.

"My loss," Melliscent said, picking up the thread and lending a purr to her words, "has given me such hope, such dreams, like I haven't had in years. Not since you left, since —"

"I thought you left him," Roselie interjected, arms crossed over her chest.

Ilford snorted with delight at this sally, while Melliscent turned a look on Roselie that burned with murder. And then it was gone, flaming quickly and eloquently, as if she remembered her true quest.

"Darling," she said softly, turning all her attention on Pierson. "I heard you weren't being seen in public, but now here you are." She preened a bit. "I told Ilford you were a man of great determination. That when you arrived here tonight, I knew —"

As she continued on, using many of the same cloying phrases she'd plied him with when he'd been a callow fool, he glanced around for Tuck, hoping his friend, of all people, didn't see this unlikely reunion. Pierson could well imagine what he would say, once he got done laughing.

I told you she was a conceited bitch. And you planted a facer on me for it.

It wasn't like Pierson hadn't known the truth, but rather Lady Melliscent Tendring had been the prize of that Season, and he'd been determined to win her — if only to claim the distinction. Crow like a cock at White's and put all the wagers in the betting book to shame.

A fool. He'd been an utter fool.

For he'd won her without any thought of the consequences, much as when he'd enlisted — in the heat of fervor and a raging desire to conquer. He hadn't given his future or what his choices might mean a second thought. Only blazing forward with a reckless disregard for anything or anyone.

Now he looked at the woman he'd sought with such fervor and saw only kindling in her fire — she was the sort of flame that burned quickly and was gone.

Just as she'd deserted him when he'd come home from Spain, still feverish and his leg all but ruined. Taken one look down at his broken body and left.

A man who couldn't kneel before her altar, a man who couldn't champion her heart, was utterly useless to her.

Of course, he'd known all along of her fickle, vain ways. He hadn't cared.

But that was before he'd realized what could grow, there in the hardness of his heart, given the right bit of sunshine.

Given the right woman.

Unbidden he glanced in that direction.

Louisa. And in that moment, he felt the chill of Melliscent's arrival melt.

Lord Ilford glanced that way as well and smiled knowingly. Then he stopped Melliscent's chatter cold by announcing with all the conviction of a man most experienced, "Come Lady Blaxhall, Wakefield has his eye on another." He nodded in Louisa's direction.

Melliscent's brows tugged together, her expression muddled, silently begging the question, *Another? I hardly think so.* "What? Charleton's country maids? Oh, Pierson, you mustn't dabble there. They aren't good *ton.* Isn't that correct, Ilford?"

The fellow dragged his gaze away from

Louisa, but looked quite delighted to share his *on dit.* "Yes. Sad but true. Still, one can't deny they are fetching. And identical as well. Imagine that."

Pierson didn't like the direction of Ilford's statement because it came with a lurid glance and a knowing smirk.

Nor was the marquess done. "My father claims to have *known* their mother — if the old devil is to be believed. Was braying about just that this afternoon at the club — he and his cronies. A graying pack of magpies crowing about their old conquests, and they had rare things to say about Lady Tempest." Ilford smiled slowly, if only to draw out his scandalous tale. "Apparently their mother was all the rage when she arrived in London. Much as you were, Lady Blaxhall, in your time."

Now it was Roselie's turn to laugh a bit, but when she received another scathing glance from Melliscent, she glanced away and coughed into her glove.

Sniffing a bit, Melliscent straightened as if she hadn't the least idea she'd been insulted. Her hair, done in a sleek coil of curls, fell like a pale silk ribbon over one shoulder. "Pretty they might be, but weren't you just saying, Lord Ilford, that their mother behaved in a most indelicate fashion?"

That stopped Pierson cold. He might have been out of society for nearly five years, but he knew a dangerous, ruinous rumor when he heard it.

"This doesn't sound like a fit subject to be discussed in front of my little sister," Pierson told her.

At this, Roselie's gaze rolled upward, but instead of staying put and ensuring the subject remained capped, she instead chose to leave. "Oh, goodness, there is Miss Welford," she exclaimed. "If you will excuse me, I have something I must ask Thomasine." And without waiting for an answer, she scurried away, taking one last look over her shoulder, a wicked grin on her lips.

Wretched chit probably thought he'd repeat the gossip to her when they were alone later.

Hardly.

With Roselie's departure, Melliscent quickly prompted the marquess again. "Do tell Pierson what you know, Ilford. I would so hate for him to become entangled with some ingénue of questionable lineage."

Yes, because I haven't done that before, he mused as he looked at her, remembering how innocent and shy she'd seemed back then.

"Ah, yes, Miss Tempest," the man replied,

dragging his gaze away from Louisa. "Apparently, she's the very image of her mother — and you know what they say about bloodlines. Might have to consider putting my oar in there, though I don't want to end up like poor Sir Ambrose — wearing the horns and watching his wife hie off to Italy to dally with some dancing master."

Pierson, who had been watching Louisa, or rather, watching Poldie's younger brother entertain her with his smiles and that infamous Garrick charm, hadn't really been listening; he'd never been one for the mean-spirited tattle that seemed at times to be the very lifeblood of the *ton.*

But he'd heard the last part.

"Her mother is dead," he corrected.

Ilford nodded. "So you've heard the tale. Yes, well, she is now. But she didn't die as her husband would like everyone to believe — in some ludicrous carriage accident." The marquess blew out a breath and shook his head. "Why is it always some carriage accident that claims a man's lightskirt of a wife when she runs off?"

Melliscent laughed a bit, shaking her head as if the fate of Lady Tempest was nothing more than an amusing farce being played for a Covent Garden audience.

"Lady Tempest is dead, but she died not

on the road to London, but in Italy of a fever, with her paramour by her side," Ilford declared, taking another appreciative glance in Louisa's direction. "But now here are her daughters, and just as fetching. Sir Ambrose is still the fool to send them to Town and think no one would remember. But then again he was always a bookish nob." He huffed a bit and puffed out his chest, rising up on his boots to get a better glance at where Louisa stood. "That one is terribly cowhanded. Trod on my foot three times when I danced with her. But if she's got her mother's blood, she won't be so clumsy when she's lying on her back, now will she?" His brows notched up suggestively and again Melliscent laughed.

But not for long.

Her merriment ended the moment Pierson's fist came smashing into Ilford's face, tapping his claret, and sending the marquess windmilling backward.

CHAPTER 11

Suddenly, Roselie was back at Pierson's side, tugging at his arm. "What have you done? You've gone and ruined everything!"

Not quite.

That was yet to come.

"Have you killed him?" Roselie demanded as she peered warily down at the prone fellow.

"Look, there, he's moving. I only tapped him a bit," Pierson told her.

He should have put a bullet in his chest, if only to stop him from spreading such tales.

But it was probably too late. Scandal — at the depths of what Ilford was hinting at — was like wildfire. Once lit, it wouldn't stop until it had no new places to burn.

Out of nowhere Tuck arrived. A bit rumpled, his jacket askew and looking as tipsy as he had when he'd arrived for dinner. He stepped over Ilford and said quite succinctly, "Dreadful fellow." Glancing back over his shoulder, he added, "Never really liked him. Always underfoot."

"Yes, quite," Pierson agreed. "Where have you been?"

Tuck shifted from one boot to another, as he had when they were kids and had been caught out in some mischief or another, but now added to that was the quantity of brandy he'd most likely consumed. "On the dance floor. Bit of trouble out there. Thought it best I make my bow and resort to a hasty exit."

Roselie gasped as she glanced out at the dance floor, where there was a grand pile of ladies and gentlemen on the floor, all trying to gain their feet and their dignity.

"Tripped on a hem," he admitted. "Though your business here, Piers, will most likely trump mine. You've done me a grand favor, my old friend."

"A favor!" Roselie burst out. "He's gone and ruined everything."

On the floor, Ilford was starting to come to, groaning and rolling about, his hands clapped over his bloody nose.

Tuck slapped the viscount soundly on the back and grinned. "I never thought you could improve Almack's. Well done."

Even as Pierson regained his footing, Roselie whirled on Tuck, in an indignant huff of silk. "Well done? Are you mad?" She spared only a glance at Lord Charleton's heir, as if the answer was rather evident.

Yes, utterly.

"Mother is going to have apoplexy when she hears this." Roselie wagged her fan under her brother's nose. "As if it isn't bad enough that you've gone and ruined my chances, if I am orphaned by all this, you will answer for it."

Ruined. At that word, Pierson glanced up and spied Louisa, standing beside Lord Rimswell and gaping at him.

Like most everyone else was doing. The gaping part, that is.

Where the devil was Charleton, or Lady Aveley? What were they thinking, leaving her unprotected?

Pierson glanced over at the still prostrate marquess and realized he probably hadn't done her any favors in that regard.

In fact, he'd made a mess of everything.

Get her out of here, his better judgment prodded. *Get her out now.*

Yes, exactly. He pushed his way through the room, leaving Roselie and Tuck staring after him. The last thing he wanted was for Louisa to hear Lord Ilford's ugly contentions being bandied about.

It would be bad enough in the coming

days as the gossip ran through the *ton* like wildfire.

Did you know their mother . . .

Pierson shook his head. No. If there was any way to get her out of here before . . .

He'd failed someone once before. He wasn't about to let it happen again.

Yet to his consternation, he arrived at her side just as Bradwell Garrick, Lord Rimswell did.

"What do you think you are doing?" Brody demanded as Pierson took Louisa's hand and began to tow her from the room.

"Getting her out of here," he replied over his shoulder.

"I was just about to do the same thing," Rimswell declared, following behind with the same sort of determination Poldie used to display.

Pierson snorted and spared a glance at Poldie's little brother. "Not if I have anything to say about the matter."

"Do I have any say —" Louisa began.

"No!" both of the gentleman barked.

Pierson could see she was all too close to digging her heels stubbornly into the marble beneath her slippers.

"I won't go without my sister, Lord Wakefield. Not without Lavinia," she told him, trying to pull up to a stop, which was only drawing more attention to them. "She's in the middle of that muddle." She tipped her head toward the nasty stew of overturned dancers Tuck had managed.

How like Miss Tempest to want to wade right in. And it seemed she had gained a champion willing to help her.

He turned to Lord Rimswell, telling the fellow, "Do something useful. Go tell my uncle to fetch the other Miss Tempest out of that" — he pointed toward the mess of ladies, many of whom were now quarreling and pointing fingers — "and take her home. Immediately."

Brody looked ready to argue the point, but being young and full of romantic notions, it probably mattered not to him which damsel he rescued.

Besides, Miss Tempest gave him an encouraging nudge. "If you would be so kind, my lord. I would be in your debt."

The young baron nodded and turned to go find Lord Charleton, pushing his way through the crush.

Pierson retraced his course, Louisa now in tow, until he reached Roselie and Tuck. "We're leaving."

"So soon?" Tuck jested, following in step behind them — though his path was far from steady. "I'd say the evening just got interesting."

"Don't you think you've made it interesting enough?" Miss Tempest shot back.

Tuck laughed. "So this one is your harridan, isn't she, Piers?"

Pierson flinched slightly and decided to avoid looking at Miss Tempest, not that his sister wasn't adverse to continue the wigging Tuck most likely deserved.

"Do shut up," Roselie told him, marching past the man and coming up beside her brother and Miss Tempest. "You've ruined me, you know." So much for his sister turning her wrath on Tuck. "Whyever did you demand I come with you to Almack's if all you ever intended to do was cause a ruckus?"

"Believe it or not, Roselie, I hardly came to Almack's on your account," he told her.

She glanced across him at Louisa. "Yes, I can see that now." Nor was his sister done. "Whatever was Ilford prattling on about that left you with no choice but to screw up his ogle?"

"Screw up his ogle?" Pierson repeated, more scandalized at his little sister's usage of boxing cant than he was by her calculating glance at Louisa. "Wherever do you hear such things?"

"This is my third —"

"Third Season, yes I know," he replied, cutting her off. "I think you would be better served by not reminding everyone how long you've been out."

Behind them, Tuck laughed. A dangerous choice on his part, for given the murderous expression on his sister's face, Rowland might be the next one in line to have his eye blackened.

"So I will point out that you've gone and ruined us both." She cast another glance at Louisa. "I fear we haven't been properly introduced, nor do I have any faith my brother can accomplish the feat, so I am Miss Roselie Stratton. I do believe you are one of the Tempest sisters —"

"Yes. I'm Louisa," she told her. "It is so lovely to meet you."

Both Pierson and Roselie gaped at her very proper response — for here they were making a very improper retreat out of Almack's, down the steps and nearly to the carriage-clogged street outside and Miss Tempest sounded like the finest graduate of a Bath school.

"I might be cowhanded, my lord," she told him pertly, "but I am not rag-mannered."

"I like her," Roselie told her brother.

"I don't think you are alone in that regard," Tuck muttered, though no one was paying him much heed.

Roselie continued on, "Yes, well, I suspect you are going to wish you'd never become acquainted with my brother after tonight. He's done you a horrible wrong, Miss Tempest, by dragging you into his folly."

Then, the lady in question surprised Pierson, her fingers curling a bit around his. "I think he was being rather splendid."

"Splendid?" Roselie heaved another sigh. "You're all mad."

Pierson's heart stopped. And it wasn't from the dangerous tendrils of desire that wound up his arm as Louisa had touched him. No, it was because she thought him a hero.

And there was nothing further from the truth. He was no one's hero. Not hers. Not Roselie's. Not Poldie's.

They had gotten to the edge of the street and Pierson paused to take their bearings, drawing in a deep breath and exhaling it with the panic that was starting to overwhelm him. He couldn't do this. She couldn't continue to believe he'd save her.

Because eventually he'd fail, and she'd be the one to pay the price.

Behind them a flurry of activity erupted.

"Wakefield, I'll have satisfaction for this affront!" Ilford called out as he pushed and shoved his way out the door, a bellicose bear roaring his displeasure.

"Can I hit him this time?" Tuck asked, looking all too gleeful to help out. "That would satisfy me. Immensely."

"No one is going to hit anyone," Roselie told them both.

"Wakefield!" Ilford bellowed as he came down another step. "I'll send my seconds around in the morning, mark my words."

Pierson glanced up at the steps, seeing not the Marquess of Ilford, but the lady standing silhouetted in the doorway. Melliscent.

She looked down at him with something akin to feral pleasure. A dangerous admiration that made the hair on the back of his neck stand up. The look in her eyes was an offer and a promise.

In that moment, he realized how little he knew her. *Had known her.* The woman he once thought to marry. The woman he'd been mad to possess.

Then he glanced over at Louisa and he was struck by the contrast between the two — Melliscent, a cool, cold goddess, demanding of admiration and conquest. And Louisa, her quiet beauty asking for nothing, but giving everything in return.

Which left him considering how little he knew of Louisa.

How well could any man know the mysteries inside a woman?

But one thing he couldn't shake was the sense that Louisa, unlike the woman on the steps, wouldn't have left him broken and tormented.

She'd have persevered out of loyalty. And love. For she would never agree to wed unless her heart was engaged.

Deeply and thoroughly.

Look at how she'd seen to getting Bitty new dresses, and breeches that fit Bob. Nothing missed her attention.

On the other hand, Melliscent wouldn't have even noticed creatures so far beneath her skirts, or worried over Pierson's linen closets, or cared beyond her own sphere.

No, Louisa Tempest was like the plants she carefully tucked into his garden — she would only take root where she was certain of her heart, where she could thrive and grow and blossom, year after year.

Where there was no question of anything less than love.

Meanwhile, Pierson's world came crashing back into his reverie.

"Wakefield, I will ruin you!" Ilford continued to threaten, repeating his earlier challenge. "Expect my seconds to call in the morning."

"No, they won't," Tuck said, sounding more than a bit disappointed. "Never do. He clamors and wails about 'satisfaction' and then decamps for one of his father's Scottish hunting boxes until it all blows over."

"There's always a first," Roselie pointed out, though Pierson wasn't really listening.

Tuck took a glance over his shoulder and shuddered at the angry mob behind them. "What the devil did Ilford say that got you milling about like Gentleman Jim? Thought you'd given up fighting."

"Leave it be, Tuck." Pierson spied his coach and started to wade into the street, Louisa's hand still caught in his grasp and Roselie following, muttering as to her undeserved fate.

"Leave it be?" Tuck shook his head. "That is what you always tell me to do. But it seems I have a horse in this race, cuz. Always have had. Just as I did the last time you told me to 'leave it be.' You recall that one? Just after you came home. *Alone.*"

That word stopped Pierson cold. *Alone.* Yes, he'd come home alone. Without Poldie. He hardly needed reminding of the fact, but here was Tuck, dancing on that razor's edge.

Then again, Tuck's timing was never what

one would call well thought out.

"What are you going to do, Piers? Tap my claret as well?" his old friend taunted as he came closer. "You know I won't hit you back. Or call for seconds. But I will keep asking. What happened to the two of you in Spain? Poldie was my friend as well."

"Is this really the time to be having *this* discussion?" Roselie interjected, shoving herself between the two men, most likely fearing she was about to witness another bout of fisticuffs.

Tuck turned on her. "As if Poldie's death wasn't a boon to you, Miss Stratton. Elevated your heart's desire right up to an eligible *parti,* didn't it? No small favor, eh? Not that Brody has noticed. Not once in all three of your precious Seasons."

His sister sucked in a deep breath, her cheeks flushing with a dark blush, but more to the point, her lips moved to argue the point, to deny the accusations being flung at her, but nothing came out.

Roselie loved Brody?

Pierson swayed at the realization that his little sister had grown up without him, and how much he had missed, lost, by locking himself away.

He shook his head, for as he'd said before, now was not the time for the squabbling around him. His sister's romantic entanglements — or lack thereof — would have to wait.

His own entanglements, as knotty as they'd suddenly become, were difficult enough.

"Begone, Tuck. I don't have time for this," Pierson told him. They'd gotten to the carriage and he yanked the door open. Roselie scrambled in quickly, most likely all too happy to be out of sight. "Or I will hit you."

Tuck, his face a mixture of anger and hurt, stumbled back a few steps, reopening the breach between them. "One day you'll have to answer me, Piers. You'll never be done with all of this until you do. You owe me that much."

Owe him? Pierson wasn't the one who'd squandered his commission money away on a table of loo just before they were to set sail.

No. He'd gone. Fought. And by all accounts, lost everything. While Tuck . . .

Tuck had the audacity to stand there and accuse him?

It wasn't to be borne.

"Then perhaps you should have come along," he replied. "Done as you promised. Seen to him yourself. Poldie kept his word."

"And died," Tuck pointed out, before he

turned on one heel and stalked off.

All the while, as Viscount Wakefield practically dragged her toward his carriage, Louisa was assailed by images of what had just happened — and all in the mere course of an evening.

The loathsome Lord Ilford and his intimations . . . The sight of Wakefield in the doorway . . . The realization of why he'd come to Almack's . . . Melliscent and her icy beauty . . . Wakefield knocking the marquess to the ground . . . Lavinia's cry from the dance floor.

Lavinia!

"I won't leave without my sister," she protested as Wakefield all but tossed her into the carriage. His sister had already scrambled inside, though of her own volition. "My sister — I cannot —"

The viscount's large frame blocked her escape. He was closing the door and rapping on the roof even before he took his seat — as eager as his sister to be gone. "Charleton and Lady Aveley have her well in hand," he told her. "I saw them going toward his carriage just now." His dark gaze was enough to pin her to her seat.

Which was good because the carriage jolted forward.

"Then maybe I should join them and —"
Louisa tried to catch her breath, but the
man sitting across from her left her breathless. Suddenly the carriage was too close —
and she wanted out.

She must get out.

He must have sensed her panic, for he
shoved one of his long legs out in front of
him, blocking the door, leaving her trapped
even as the carriage quickly left Almack's
behind. There was nothing left but for the
shadows of this disastrous night to close in
around her. After all, her life was in ruins.

Lord Ilford would see to that. And not
because the viscount had knocked him
down. But because he was the sort of man
who delighted in such mischief.

But whyever had the man chosen her as
the object of his interest?

If Louisa had been smarter, she'd have
gathered up Lavinia right after she'd danced
with the marquess and bought tickets on
the first mail coach going within thirty miles
of Kempton.

Oh, dear heavens! Louisa bit her lips
together. Lavinia!

"Miss Tempest, I can see you are dis-
tressed," the viscount's sister began. "I'm
certain all of this will —" She stopped and
glanced at her brother, as if seeking his

319

confirmation.

That all this would just blow over.

But the viscount gave a slight shake to his head and his sister pressed her lips together, trying to push them up into an encouraging smile.

"Thank you, Miss Stratton," Louisa managed before she looked out the window and up toward the sky. There she thought she saw the tiny light of a star through the endless London haze. It blinked and fluttered for a second and then was gone.

Extinguished.

Rather like the starry hope that Viscount Wakefield's kiss had ignited inside her.

That she might . . . find love right across the lane. An unexpected bit of happiness all her own.

As she glanced furtively across the carriage at Wakefield's stormy expression, she knew that whatever bliss she had found in his arms was lost forevermore.

She'd pulled him into a whirlwind of scandal and notice. Quite likely ruined his sister's chances as well.

Across the carriage, Miss Stratton shifted, and settled back in the leather recesses. "Well, if you won't answer Rowland, you will answer me," his sister began. "What foul thing did Ilford say? I am assuming it was most foul — or it had better have been, if only to justify that scene you caused." Miss Stratton crossed her arms over her chest and stared at her brother. "Well?"

"I'm not discussing the matter with you. It isn't a fit subject for your ears." He paused for a moment. "For any lady's ears. Even one with three Seasons."

"If that is your decision . . ." Miss Stratton's response trailed off, ending with a little sniff. "You won't be able to put off Mother so easily. She'll be on your doorstep at dawn."

"Dawn?" Wakefield replied, his brows quirking as he smiled slightly.

His sister smiled as well, if only for a moment. "Oh, bother. You know very well what I mean." She turned to Louisa. "Mother never rises before one," she explained. "She says it is unseemly to get up early." Then she turned her attention back to her brother. "But mark my words, when she hears about this debacle, she'll make an exception."

"I doubt word will reach her that quickly."

Miss Stratton snorted and turned her head to look out the window. With three Seasons of experience, she most likely knew just how fast a scandal could travel through the *ton.* "The theater will be getting out any time now, and she'll have the news before she reaches her carriage."

As the two siblings argued the matter, Louisa did her best to sink into the deep recesses of the leather seat and pretend she wasn't there. In this carriage. With Lord Wakefield.

For she didn't want to think of what Lord Ilford must have said to the viscount.

Yet it was all she could think of — unfortunately — and how Wakefield must detest her now.

Then there had been his reaction when she called him "splendid." He'd looked horrified by her admiration.

He hadn't wanted her praise. Not in the least.

All too soon, the carriage rolled to a stop at a residence, and Lord Wakefield pulled his long legs back up and turned to his sister. "This is your stop."

Roselie glanced first at Louisa and then at her brother. "I hardly think it is proper for me to get out first. Mother would not approve."

"Miss Tempest lives next door to me. I will not have the coachman dallying back and forth across Mayfair in the middle of the night to suit your sensibilities, Roselie." He opened the door and got down to let her out. "And Mother need not find out if

322

you don't tell her."

There was a finality to his words that had the age-old ring of tell-her-and-I'll-cut-off-your-pin-money.

His sister huffed a bit. "As if I want to speak a word of this entire evening," she told him tartly. "Miss Tempest, my apologies again. Do know that the only reason I am leaving you alone with my ogre of a brother is because you appear far too intelligent to be easily frightened. But if he tries, please know for all his threats and fisticuffs, he isn't as horrible as he wants the world to believe. No matter how hard he tries." She pulled a face at her brother and sauntered up to the door. "One scandal per evening is the limit, Piers. One doesn't need three Seasons to know that much."

And then she was gone into the house and Louisa was alone with Lord Wakefield.

Again.

He climbed back in and rapped the ceiling with his walking stick.

The coachman was only too happy to continue on — most likely he had his warm bed in his sights.

"My lord —" she began.

Even as he said, "Miss Tempest —"

"You go," he said, nodding to her.

"No, you," she insisted.

"I wanted to say —" he began, and then faltered to a stop, taking a furtive glance out the window.

"Yes?" she urged.

"It's just that I —" He pressed his lips together. "This afternoon, that is —"

"Yes, my lord?"

"I . . . I . . . I planted the remainder of the strawberries for you. So you needn't have to come back, that is, if you don't wish to return."

"Is that what you desire?"

Louisa's lips snapped shut. *Desire.* Goodness, couldn't she have used another word? Such as *want.* Or *need.* Oh, bother, every word she tried spoke of one thing.

Desire. And there it was. She desired Lord Wakefield. For he was, as his sister had said, not beastly at all. But rather heavenly. Even if he was a tad difficult.

Which, she decided, came in handy at times. Especially with the likes of Ilford around.

Oh, Ilford. That horrible man.

Louisa glanced up at Lord Wakefield. "If I may ask, what did Lord Ilford say that gave you cause to strike him?"

To her surprise, the viscount laughed. "You have fewer Seasons to your credit than my sister. What makes you think I would share such tattle with you?" He glanced out the window and then said, "If you must know —"

"I must."

"Well, then, he spoke ill of someone and I cared not for his inferences."

"I had the same experience when I danced with him," she said, notching her head up. "So I trod on his foot. Twice."

Wakefield smiled. "The marquess claims it was thrice."

"Yes, it was three times. The first one was an accident. Well, it seemed an accident."

Wakefield nodded with approval. "I doubt he will ever dance with you again." His words were quiet and dark. And not merely a statement. More like a promise.

Louisa shivered, for she'd never heard such vehemence behind a man's words. "I don't want you to fight a duel with him. Not over me. Can you refuse his seconds?"

"There won't be any seconds," he told her. "It's as Tuck said, Ilford will curse and bluster a bit, but he won't make good on his threat." His fingers curled into a fist, then slowly unwound, and in a flash of lamplight, Louisa saw the blood.

He'd hurt himself defending . . . Well, defending someone. And it didn't matter who, for in an instant, she crossed the desert between them and took his hand in hers.

"You shouldn't have," she murmured, as she turned his hand over so she could see his injury more clearly.

Wakefield would have none of her fussing. He pulled his hand free. "It is nothing."

"I disagree." She dug into her reticule and pulled out her handkerchief, then reached for his hand, which he held aloft and well out of her reach. "Do you realize how foolish you look? Give me your hand."

"It is my hand," he told her, a mulish expression on his handsome features.

Ignoring his protests, she caught hold of his sleeve and pulled his hand back down into her grasp. "A hand injured over my honor." This time she wasn't letting go. No matter how much he blustered.

"I never said it was you."

"Well, I know it was," she said. "And you shouldn't have."

"Why? Because I made matters worse?"

"Oh, I suspect matters were ruined before you planted that facer."

"Not you as well," he moaned at her use of cant.

"I used the term correctly, didn't I?" she asked, suddenly feeling a bit shy, for the warmth of his hand was filling her senses with all sorts of notions.

"Yes. Unfortunately." That last part was added like a scold. No, it was a scold.

"These will need to be washed when you get home, but for now —" She began to wind her handkerchief around his broad, scarred knuckles. This wasn't the first time he'd used his fists thusly. And she glanced up at him, realizing how little she knew of this man. "If you must know, I heard Harriet Hathaway's mother use the expression — at the Midsummer Eve's Ball a few years ago, just after Benjamin Hathaway had landed a most excellent facer on his twin, Benedict."

"Lady Hathaway used the expression *facer* at a ball?" He shook his head. "I *have* been out of society for too long."

Louisa laughed a little. "Perhaps. But I don't think Lady Hathaway can help herself — she does have five rather unruly sons to contend with. Nor would it be a very good Midsummer Eve's Ball in Kempton if there weren't some scandal or another." She leaned closer and glanced up into his eyes. "In comparison I found Almack's rather dull . . . that is, until you arrived."

"I probably shouldn't have," he said, his gaze locked with hers. "I rather made a muddle of things."

She didn't know if he meant hitting Ilford

or just the fact that he arrived at Almack's.

"Not to me," she told him. "But why did you —"

"Hit Ilford? I thought I'd already explained —"

"No," she said, as she finished tying a knot in her handkerchief and neatly tucking the ends in. "Why did you come to Almack's tonight?"

"My sister —" he began.

Louisa went to let go of his hand, but he caught hold of her fingers and held them.

Trapped them.

She quirked up a brow at him. "It wasn't your sister." The words came out in a whisper. A hope.

A wish.

"It wasn't? How can you be so certain?"

He was looking at her again. His gaze searching hers.

Be certain? She wasn't, but her heart . . . Oh, her heart longed to know the truth.

To hear it. From him.

"You refused Mr. Rowland earlier —"

"You heard about that?" He shook his head. "Never mind. Of course you did."

"What changed your mind?"

"You," he said quite simply.

Whatever had possessed him to make such

a declaration? Pierson couldn't even manage to look at her for fear she'd see the truth, even as he tried to defuse his confession. "Well, rather Tiploft did."

"Tiploft?" Miss Tempest smiled. "Dear Tiploft."

"He has a newly discovered talent for interfering. I can't imagine what, or rather, who, has inspired such an alteration in his character. He was quite sensible up until recently." Pierson dared a glance at her.

Of course, she met his gaze squarely, surely. "And you, my lord? Have you changed?"

She had to ask?

Yes, she did. This was Miss Tempest. She always asked the impertinent questions.

And had he? Changed?

Yes, unfortunately. In a thousand different ways. All of them terrifying. All of them impossible.

Better than confessing the truth, he chose to tease her a bit. "Yes, I suppose I have. Having an orderly linen closet gives a man an entirely new perspective on things." He grinned at her and brought her fingers to his lips.

Slowly, hypnotically, he rolled her glove down, leaving her fingers bared to his.

How was it that she could bind his knuckles, tie a handkerchief around his hand, but her bare hand, the feel of her silken skin against his, left him vulnerable, wounded, bruised with something far more dangerous.

Longing.

How could something so simple as her touch pull him to her so easily?

But it did. Her warmth flowed into the ice within him. Her fingers trapped in his grasp made him want so much more . . .

"I don't think —" she began to protest, trying to pull her hand back.

"Don't think," he told her, as he tossed her glove on the empty seat across the carriage, then brought her hand up to his lips, his gaze locked with hers.

Daring her to protest.

When his lips touched her fingertips, when the warmth that seemed an intangible part of her, lured him closer, desire burst forth inside him.

Bottled up for days, one might even argue since the moment they'd met, it sparked to life once again, a blaze of need.

His lips nibbled at her fingers while his gaze told another story.

This is what I would do to you. All of you.

Her eyes widened just slightly, before she

sighed, leaning her luscious body toward him.

Offering herself to him.

"Forgive me," he whispered as he reached out and caught the back of her head and drew her close.

Forgive him? The moment his lips touched hers there was nothing to forgive.

She went quite willingly into his arms, pulling herself up against him.

Letting his kiss pull them ever closer.

His tongue swiped at hers, dared her as his gaze had, even as his hand — the one uninjured from the night — was exploring her, along the curve of her hip, up to her breast and then over her nipple.

"Oooh," she moaned, unable to stop herself.

His fingers curled around the edge of her bodice, and then dipped the silk down, freeing her for him to explore.

Good heavens, she was exposed to him, and was nearly about to panic with mortification, when he dipped his head down and began tracing that circle once again, this time over the tip of her breast, his tongue both rough and smooth as he explored her, sucked at her, drew her into his mouth.

Any thought of all the reasons why this

was wrong — finding herself half naked in the viscount's carriage — were forgotten in the ocean of desire threatening to swallow her.

Tossing her about in its stormy grasp.

Just then, the viscount looked up from his labors, his expression hungry, his mouth tilted in a wry grin. He paused only for that long moment, and Louisa tried her best to catch her breath. But he hardly gave her a chance — rising up and catching her mouth again, kissing her deeply, exploring her, tasting her, all the while pressing her back into the seat until he covered her.

The carriage bounced over an uneven bit, and her hands caught hold of his hips, clinging to him as she tried to find her balance — but it wasn't easily done with Lord Wakefield's lips upon hers, his hands exploring her.

She only spiraled further into the chaotic abyss he was stirring inside her as his fingers began pulling her skirt up, leaving a hot trail along her calf, and then moving slowly upward.

The cool night air hadn't a chance against the heat he was creating between her legs, as if calling to his fingers to come even higher, begging for him to stroke and tease their way past her thigh.

Louisa knew she should be shocked, she should be protesting, but if anything, his lips, his touch had enticed her, seduced her, left her breathless.

Wanting more.

And more was what he had in mind.

He moved closer, if that was even possible, but there he was, his entire body claiming hers, atop her, his fingers having found their way to her very core, and slowly, languidly, he began to stroke her, tease her to open up to him.

However could she speak when he touched her like that? Left her in this delicious state of wonder. Of need.

Her lashes fluttered shut as she blocked out everything, felt herself drawn toward a single point. An aching, begging place, where all she wanted was him to touch her.

And then do it again.

Wakefield was unraveling her, uncoiling the tightly held passions he'd wound around her in the past few weeks.

Every dream she'd had. Every kiss they shared, every time he'd touched her, had left her waiting for this.

This.

This need, this anxious, desperate desire. For every time she'd awakened restless and full of want, his touch now teased her toward unknown treasures. Whispered for her to follow. As if they were bound together by a single thread.

And when he pulled, she came toward him. Closer ever still. Her hips rising up to meet him.

Slowly, deliberately, he pulled at that thread and teased it out of the knot he'd tied with that first kiss.

"Wakefield," she gasped, as her world began to tighten, as her hands fisted onto his jacket, her eyes now wide open and looking at him.

They were still dark, still dangerous, so very full of passion, but she would have followed him, devil that he was, anywhere in that moment.

She was lost and he would show her the way.

"Pierson," he whispered back, his finger delving into her, sliding over her sex and sliding back inside her. Deeper. Harder.

She rocked against him, rode his touch, his strokes.

And when she said his name again, called it, gasped it, it was because he'd taken her over that edge, carried her into a world she couldn't have imagined.

"Pierson!" she cried out, her body quaking, falling, rising all at once. "Oh, Pierson, yes!"

For now she knew the way.

CHAPTER 12

The carriage came to a halt in front of Lord Charleton's residence.

"Demmit," Pierson muttered as he glanced up and out the window.

Beneath him, Louisa struggled up, her hair tousled and her dress askew.

Askew. That was putting it mildly. Hell, it was nearly up over her head.

And he'd done all this — from the sly smile on her lips to the heavy-lidded gaze looking up at him in admiration. Even the smoky desire still simmering in her eyes.

Offering as much as he had given her.

He was hard as a rock, and wanted nothing more than to bury himself inside her. Find his release as quickly as he could and then . . . then . . .

Oh, hell that was the problem.

The "then."

As he looked down at Louisa Tempest, her cheeks flushed, that gorgeous mahogany hair all tumbled and begging to be pulled free from the pins that remained, he knew that as much as he wanted a singular, hastily taken moment of gratification, wanted to tell the coachman to take one more slow turn around the block, he also wanted the "then."

And everything that came after.

Seeing her bright smile every morning.

He suspected Louisa Tempest arose each day, just as dawn crept over the horizon, brimming with delight, only because a full day of meddling lay before her.

And how she would meddle her way through his lair.

Well-cooked meals. An orderly house. Suppers with friends. (Never mind that he had none currently, Louisa would remedy that.) Lively discussions. Even more lively arguments. Improvements. Changes.

Reopening Stratton House. Good God! She'd be in alt over all those Holland covers and all the dust that needed to be swept aside.

And then she'd make it a home again. She'd insist.

A lifetime whirled before him. Marriage. Children. An heir.

And Louisa. Always Louisa. Smiling. Chiding. Loving.

His heart, cold and abandoned, warmed and beat anew.

But not for long.

What makes you think you deserve any of that? That dark whisper invaded his joy with the swift surety of a well-aimed arrow.

That horrible voice, the one filled with guilt and anger, could stem any tide, cut through any bit of hope. A fiendish demon he'd spent so many hours trying to blot out. And yet it always found a way out of the blackness, a way to call him back into the hole into which he'd climbed the moment he'd awakened to find his leg festering, his best friend dead. That soulless demon reached out and caught hold of him, towing him back into its dark clutches.

You don't deserve her. Not you.

Then the darkness tugged and pulled at him, like determined street urchins after the meager coins of hope he'd hidden away in his pockets. He could feel its grasp and knew he was losing.

When he glanced at Miss Tempest, he also knew a horrible truth.

He'd drag her right down with him.

"I don't know what I was thinking," Pierson said as he hastily pulled her skirt back down and clumsily tried to put her back into some semblance of order.

For worse yet, a second carriage had just pulled in behind them and he could hear his uncle's voice bellowing for his butler.

"Brobson! Where the devil are you? Open the door!"

Oh, yes, Charleton was in a rare and foul mood.

Taking another glance at the tumbled and all-but-ruined lady beside him, Pierson knew without a doubt if his uncle caught a glance at his houseguest's starry expression and rumpled state of *dishabille,* he'd be facing a different set of seconds in the morning.

"Oh, bloody hell," he muttered as he quickened his efforts.

With her usual efficiency, Louisa brushed his hands aside. "Good heavens, let me."

And in moments she was nearly in order.

Nearly. For there was no way to remove that blush from her cheeks, that knowing light in her eyes.

He'd done that. And while he wanted to proudly claim it, he didn't fancy his uncle aiming a pistol at his heart.

"I — I —" he stammered. The words that so desperately wanted to come out, stuck in his throat. "Oh, hell!" was all he could manage to sputter.

Louisa looked up at him, her hand reaching out to cradle his jaw. "You are a devil of a beast, Lord Wakefield." Her smile widened, as if it could light up the darkest corners, and then she got out of his carriage and was gone.

Leaving him to gape after her. Whatever did that mean? He was a devil of a beast? Was that good or bad?

The carriage rolled forward down to the next set of doors, leaving him little time to consider the notion as he climbed out.

He told himself not to look for her, but he couldn't help it.

It took all of a second for his gaze to light on her as she followed Lady Aveley up the steps. Then and there, she paused, her hand on the railing, and slowly she glanced in his direction.

She didn't acknowledge him with a nod or a smile or even any indication that she'd seen him.

But his heart knew. It walloped in his chest. *Don't let her go. Fetch her back here, you fool.*

Pierson started to turn, about to race down his steps (as fast as a man with a cane could), with only one thought: *Toss her over your shoulder and bring her home.*

Despite all the obvious flaws in such a ridiculous plan, first and foremost, he doubted his uncle would approve of such an arrangement. Especially given his current mood.

He stole another glance at her just before she entered Charleton's house, and the temptation, the need to have her, nearly drove him forward.

But this time it was Ilford who stopped him.

Bloody Ilford and all his insinuations about the chit's mother.

For had he, Pierson, just treated Miss Tempest any better?

The answer drove him up his steps and into his house. Where he belonged.

Yet as he entered and stood there in the quiet, empty foyer before him, Pierson Stratton, Viscount Wakefield, realized that there was no escaping the matter now.

The only way to save Louisa Tempest from a lifetime of ruin was to marry her.

To have her at his side always. She'd be his light, his spark, what with her busybody ways. Her smile.

Her kiss.

And that was what was wrong. For if he married her, he would surely snuff out that light of hers eventually. Darken her bright spirit.

And that was something he wouldn't allow himself to do. She deserved so much better.

Why was it, at that moment, an image of Brody whirled in his thoughts. Poldie's brother. His heir. A baron now. He was the sort of happy, settled man Miss Tempest should marry.

Not him.

Pierson's gaze turned upward, to the dark, gaping hole of the stairs that led to where it was all shadows and coldly familiar. His room. His bottle. The place where he could shut out the dreams. The visions that had haunted him ever since . . .

He closed his eyes to try and blot that image out.

Poldie, his chest a river of blood. His eyes staring up into the sky, his lips moving to form a single word over and over again. *Live. Live. Live.*

And yet Poldie hadn't. He'd died there. Taken the full force of the bullet meant for another.

Pierson had no right to live a good and happy life — certainly none to the happiness that burst into his heart when he saw Louisa turn in his direction. Nor the anxious joy that nudged at him when he heard the *snip, snip* of her shears in the garden.

Not when Poldie was lying in a cold,

unmarked grave beside an empty Spanish road.

He, Pierson, should be in that hole. Not Poldie.

Looking back up the stairs, he let the darkness beckon him.

Taking the stairs slowly, painfully, he let the blackness close in around him. It was bleak and cold, and he didn't mind at all. For when he found his room, he closed his door and reached for the bottle.

And let the oblivion it offered wash over his broken heart.

Louisa didn't look left or right as she went up the stairs, through the foyer, and up the long staircase to the chamber she shared with Lavinia — hoping to make it there quickly, if only to escape Lady Aveley's or Lord Charleton's notice.

Not that she was going to escape her sister's scrutiny.

Lavinia closed the door behind her with a solid thump. And then remained in front of it like a prison guard, unwilling to let her charge move one step out of her sight. After several long, tense moments of silence, her sister finally spoke. "What was that?"

Louisa stood with her back to Lavinia, try- ing to find the words, but standing as she was meant that she faced the window.

The window that looked across the garden and at his house.

And that was unbearable.

Better to face her sister.

Or so she thought before she turned around and saw Lavinia's expression. Brows arched, jaw set stubbornly.

"Why did Wakefield strike that man?"

"I haven't the least notion —" Louisa began, but stopped right there, for it was impossible to lie to Lavinia.

"He's gone and ruined us. Can't you see that?" Lavinia took a step closer.

"He hasn't ruined us —" *Me certainly, but not us.* Though Louisa could hardly admit that aloud. And then she thought of something else. "However did all those people end up toppled over on the dance floor?"

Lavinia's cheeks blushed to a deep shade of pink.

As Louisa had suspected all along. "You promised not to dance."

"So did you. I didn't see you refusing Lord Ilford."

Louisa shuddered at the memory. "He made it impossible to refuse."

"As did Mr. Rowland. He kept insisting that he must dance with me to 'keep Charleton happy.' And then he just led me out.

Dragged me, if you must know. And then imagine my horror upon discovering it was a cotillion and I was —"

Yes, Louisa knew exactly what Lavinia was. *Ruined.* Mr. Rowland might as well have asked Lavinia to perform at the ballet, as to ask her to dance something as complicated as a cotillion.

Poor Lavinia.

When she glanced up, she found her sister's eyes awash with brimming tears. "Louisa, all I wanted was to make a respectable match," she said in a whisper. "Be married. Prove I'm not like —"

And right there Lavinia stopped, so abruptly it startled Louisa.

I'm not like —

Her sister's mouth fell open and then she closed it quickly, biting her bottom lip, as if that would prevent anything else from slipping out. Even her tears seemed to still.

"Not like who?" Louisa asked, a wary niggle running down her spine.

"Never mind," Lavinia told her, suddenly busy taking off her gloves and then reaching up to unpin her bonnet. "It matters not now. Your viscount has seen to that."

"He's not my viscount," Louisa told her, coming over to help. She found the pin that had been eluding her sister — it was always the one on the left — and pulled it free.

Lavinia turned slightly, and they were so close, there could be no lies between them. "Are you certain?"

"He won't marry me," Louisa whispered. She knew that. The darkness in his eyes had told her that. Oh, he'd looked at her with longing and desire, and for a whisper of a second, she'd thought . . . Well, she'd been foolish to think so.

Her sister reached out and took her hand. "Should he, Louisa? Should he ask for you? He hasn't . . . You haven't . . . You aren't . . ."

How could she answer? She hadn't lost her innocence . . . entirely. Yet as she stole a glance out the window, toward the dark house across the way, she knew she would have let him.

Wished with all her heart that he had.

"Louisa?"

"Oh, Lavinia, I am in such a muddle," she finally confessed, and they were in each other's arms, hugging and holding each other close.

"We should never have come to London," Lavinia lamented.

Louisa pulled back a bit. "You insisted."

"I did, didn't I?" She went and sat down on the edge of her bed and Louisa followed. "Why didn't you talk some sense into me?"

Talk sense into Lavinia? Louisa would have laughed if she could have. "No one can do that, my dear. No one."

"I suppose not." Lavinia sighed and glanced around the room. "Whatever did Lord Ilford say to Lord Wakefield to provoke such violence?"

Louisa shook her head. "He wouldn't say."

"That doesn't mean the rest of London will be so discreet." Lavinia stifled a sob and looked away.

"Vivi," Louisa whispered, using an old, childhood nickname. "What is it?"

"Oh, Lala, forgive me," Lavinia told her. "Forgive her. I should have known. We never should have come here. I was so wrong to think —"

"That no one else knew about Mama?" Louisa whispered, deciding it was time.

Lavinia's gaze flew up. "You know?"

"You know?" Louisa asked back.

And then the two confessed how much they knew of their mother's ruin and what all of London would know come the next day.

"Charleton! This is a disaster!" Lady Aveley exclaimed as she paced in front of the fireplace in his study.

To the baron's credit, he'd managed to

quickly get them all out of Almack's and away from the scandal.

But nothing would stop the storm that had been unleashed when Wakefield had struck Lord Ilford.

Egads! Ilford, of all people! Not that Lady Aveley was surprised. That wretched marquess loved to share his font of gossip and disgraceful *on dits*.

It wasn't very difficult to imagine what Ilford had said — but Wakefield? Good heavens, she expected such antics of Rowland, but certainly not Wakefield.

Still, the outcome was all that mattered, and now Ilford's wrath would be squarely pointed at the Tempest sisters. For given the blow he'd received, the lady doubted he'd impugn Wakefield. At least not openly.

Not and risk a second thrashing.

Lady Aveley sighed heavily and sank into the chair beside the fireplace.

When she looked up, there was Charleton holding out a glass for her.

"I don't imbibe spirits," she told him.

"You do tonight. Drink it," he ordered, handing the glass to her and taking the chair opposite hers. "Is it as bad as it appears?"

"Worse," Lady Aveley told him, stretching her slippered feet toward the warmth of the coals and taking a tentative sip from the glass. It was a brandy, smooth and elegant, and it warmed her in places the fire couldn't reach.

"I have to imagine he knows about Kitty." She glanced over to see if he knew what she meant.

He nodded and went back to examining his drink.

"I should have known someone would bring up that old business."

Charleton shrugged. "I give Sir Ambrose credit. He did his level best with that falderal that Lady Tempest died in a carriage accident —"

"So the girls would never be tarnished by their mother's sins."

"Did she truly sin?" Charleton stared at the coals in the grate, his legs stretched out before him. "She didn't love Ambrose. Married him because Eddowes died. I've even wondered if those girls —"

"Don't say it —" Lady Aveley snapped, even if she had thought the same thing more than once. "Sir Ambrose loves *his* daughters."

"Yes, so he does. Yet what is that worth when so many people know the truth?"

The truth. How was it that the truth could be so abhorrent, Lady Aveley mused. Why couldn't everyone just believe the lie and leave well enough alone? The truth, well, the truth should have been left in Pandora's box where it belonged.

But Kitty had ruined that. She'd never been one to be discreet.

Lady Aveley wished her old friend had taken to heart what most everyone knew: There are no secrets in the *ton* if more than one person knows the particulars.

Lord Charleton looked up from his own musings. "This is all her fault. Lady Tempest was foolish and stupid. She promised Sir Ambrose she'd disappear. Never come back."

Lady Aveley shook her head. "I'm sure Kitty meant to, at least she did when she gave her word." But most likely that promise, like so many others, had flitted out of her head the moment another need — a more pressing one — arose. She'd always been like that — so frivolous and spoiled. She'd probably convinced herself that running away with a handsome dancing master would be yet another grand adventure.

Not seen the ruin that it was.

"Yes, well," Charleton began, reaching for the decanter and pouring out another measure, "she shouldn't have written for money, begging help from all her friends."

This stopped Lady Aveley. "She wrote Isobel?"

Charleton snorted. "Of course she did. And probably half a dozen others. Selfish chit."

Here Lady Aveley had thought she'd been the only one. Then again, she should have known. How like Kitty to solicit help from her "only and dearest friend."

Of course, each of her numerous friends had been the "only and dearest" in that vain moment. But it had left the entire *ton* knowledgeable of her scandal.

Which meant . . .

Lady Aveley closed her eyes and considered what was before her. "This mess is now my problem."

"Our problem," Charleton corrected.

There was a tendril to his words that wound inside her. *Our problem.* The idea left her unbalanced. And when she glanced up, she found him staring at her in a way he hadn't in a very long time.

Tying his fate to hers.

Oh, that would never do.

"I haven't the least notion how I'm to find those girls proper husbands now," she admitted, sitting up and shaking off the warm and cozy air that was descending upon her. It was all too easy to be lulled into the false sense of security by a tumbler of brandy . . .

. . . and George Rowland. She glanced over at her host and recalled how in his own day, he had been ever so like Tuck. Devil-may-care and all too charming.

To her never-ending heartbreak.

Oh, dear, she was getting maudlin. All this talk of the past.

The past . . . When it had been she and Izzy and Kitty. All fresh from school and out for their first Season. How the years had passed so quickly. And now she was the only one left.

And Kitty's daughters. So like their mother in looks and so different in temperament. It wasn't fair that they should be tarred with their mother's sins, and yet here they were — with Lord Ilford more than happy to wipe that brush from one end of London to another.

Setting aside the glass, she smoothed her hands over her skirt. "We were entrusted with these girls. They need husbands. Gentlemen who will treat them with respect and generosity. And now, most especially, with love."

As you never did me, her heart silently added.

"And yet . . ." she finished, looking not at

the baron but at the coals glowing in the grate.

"And yet?" Charleton prodded. As if he didn't already know the answer.

Still, she told him. "Well, I don't know. I haven't the least notion what's to be done. Ilford is not one to suffer humiliation."

Charleton leaned back in his chair and smiled at her. "You can fix all this, Amy. I know you can."

Amy. He hadn't called her by her given name in years. Not since . . . Well, not since another had gained his heart.

But such a moment of familiarity wasn't going to be her undoing. "Don't you try and cozen me," she warned, reminding herself she was a respectable matron, not a fresh-out-of-school girl whose heart raced when a man took such a liberty.

Amy.

"Bah, you make this all sound so dire," Charleton told her. "You had a bit of scandal attached to you when you came out —"

"George Rowland!" she exclaimed, feeling heat rising on her cheeks. Even all these years later, she still blushed over her less-than-stellar coming out.

"Oh, don't get missish on me. We've known each other too long for that. Besides, look how well you turned out. Got Aveley to boot and broke hearts all over London."

Except yours.

Lady Aveley bit her lip and glanced over at her half-drunk glass. *Oh, good heavens, what was in that brandy?*

Giving the tumbler another nudge well out of reach, she reminded him of the obvious. "I did well because I had a dowry that lessened my faults."

"And so do those chits upstairs," Charleton told her, nodding toward the ceiling. "Had a letter from Sir Ambrose just today with the particulars — just in case one of them manages to 'trip up some fool.' " He glanced up, probably knowing how she would react to such a description and added, "His words, not mine." Then he chuckled. "Both of them stand to inherit a small fortune."

"How small?" Lady Aveley asked. A fortune always managed to smooth over minor social missteps.

Unfortunately, Kitty's sins could hardly be called minor.

"I wouldn't worry much over all this," Charleton continued. "If you would stop wringing your hands, you might see that we've got two excellent prospects for the girls right before us."

Lady Aveley's brows pulled together as she tried to comprehend who he was talking about. And then it hit her.

"Tuck and Wakefield?" she sputtered. "Are you mad?"

Lord Charleton looked at her with a bit of puzzlement, as if he was surprised she couldn't see this as the perfect solution. "Not in the least. The pair of them solves everything."

Lady Aveley huffed. "Wakefield is a temperamental recluse, while Tuck is . . ." She tried to come up with the right words and still remain ladylike.

"Yes, well, Tuck is Tuck," Charleton supplied, saving her the embarrassment, but grinning at her all the same — just as he used to when he was fresh from Cambridge. "Why do you think Wakefield sent Ilford flying?"

"I don't know," she replied. "As I said he's unpredictable, he's got a screw loose —"

"Have you not considered all the time that gel's spent over there?"

Her eyes widened. "She's been helping the staff . . . Getting things in order . . ." *Wasn't she?* "Oh, goodness, no!"

Charleton grinned. "Oh, goodness, yes. Which is perfect, because of all the things Wakefield is, he's an honorable sort. Why do you think he was there tonight? At bloody Almack's, for God's sake?"

Lady Aveley got up, because that grin, that mischievous light in his eyes had always been her undoing. "You think he'll come up to scratch?" Her question was more a statement of disbelief.

"I'd wager it. Care to place a bet, Amy?"

Her mouth went dry, but she managed to answer him. "No." She'd wagered her heart on him all those years ago and lost.

She wouldn't take that bet ever again. Instead, she nodded to him and went to leave.

Yet when she got to the door, Charleton asked one more question.

One that stopped her cold.

"Are you still as cowhanded as you once were, Amy? Is that why you didn't dance tonight?"

Her hand on the latch, she paused. Of all the infuriating things to ask, why, she should . . . Why, she ought to . . .

She stopped herself right there. Charleton had always been able to vex her with his teasing — since they'd been children.

Seemed he could still find a way to raise her temper.

Well, no more.

Glancing over her shoulder, she looked at

him with a level gaze that she hoped hid her racing heart. "I didn't dance because no one asked me."

"London fools," he remarked, tipping his glass at her.

"Yes, indeed. Fools," she replied.

One especially.

CHAPTER 13

Five days later

"Is *he* going to get up and eat today?" Mrs. Petchell asked Tiploft when the butler came downstairs for his morning tea. She didn't like cooking for someone who didn't deign to show up for her meals.

"He remains a bit under the weather," Tiploft said in even tones as he settled slowly and wearily into his place at the head of the servants' table.

Under the weather! Mrs. Petchell wasn't fooled. She knew exactly what the man meant. His Lordship was still drunk.

He'd come home from Almack's and ordered a bottle sent up to his room. And no one had seen hide nor hair of him since. Only heard the bell tolling when his bottle went lacking.

Men! Matilda silently huffed. Idiots and fools, all of them. Drowning their problems in a bottle of gin. Or, as the viscount was wont to do, a case of Madeira.

Yet she could see the worry and despair etching lines of concern on the butler's otherwise impervious features.

That a good and respectable man like Mr. Tiploft cared so much for the viscount and was worried sick that this time, their employer's despair could not be rectified, said enough about the recluse upstairs to keep her from packing her bags and leaving.

Besides, Matilda Petchell knew a thing or two about men and how to drive them out of their caves.

"Leave this to me, Mr. Tiploft," she told the butler as she went to the larder. "Leave this to me."

Pierson awoke to the most wretched smell he'd ever encountered. Even on the sun-baked battlefields of Spain.

Dear God, had someone left a corpse in his room?

He opened one eye and spied an innocent-looking tray on the bed stand beside him. Cautiously, he raised the silver dome over the plate and just as quickly put it back. He rolled over and emptied his stomach into the chamber pot.

When he finished tossing up his accounts, he knew he had two choices — stagger over to the bell and then wait for Tiploft to arrive and carry that wretched tray out of his room.

Or flee.

Stealing one last look of loathing at the tray, he made his choice, taking the most expedient route out of his room, catching up his dressing gown and ignoring the fact that the cold floor was biting at his toes.

If anything, it helped to hurry him along.

When he opened the door, he was greeted by an ear-splitting yowl.

R-r-r-ro-oew. Hannibal looked up at him and went to open his mouth again.

"Do not," Pierson warned the ugly creature.

Thankfully, that worked, for the cat stopped, and then went jauntily down the hall toward the stairs.

The viscount followed, if only to escape that horror in his room. But it wasn't easy. Halfway down the flight, his head spun, his leg ached like the devil, and when he thought he might throw up again, he caught hold of the railing and willed his stomach back into order.

But since the entire house seemed to smell as if it had been converted into a morgue, he suspected he was fighting a losing battle.

Right then, a slight figure brushed past

him and when he glanced in that direction, he found a young girl in a mop cap gaping at him as if she were looking at a monster.

"Milord," she squeaked, and then scurried up the stairs, bucket in hand.

A maid? When had he agreed to hire a maid? Well, if he had, he certainly hoped she could find the source of this stench and clean it up. Better yet, he wished she'd left him the bucket.

As he reached the foyer, an upright young man stepped forward, eyeing him as if he were a housebreaker. "Who might you be?" the fellow asked, reaching into the hat stand near the door for one of Pierson's walking sticks.

Hannibal, who had followed him downstairs, continued on into the dining room without any such confrontation, the viscount noted. Rather something when a cat had more precedence in a house than the lord and master. But it was Bob who came to his rescue and saved the day, poking his head out of the study. "Put that down, Clarks, that's himself."

"My lord?" It was more a question than a greeting from the man.

Meanwhile, Bob caught the viscount's arm and towed him into the study, explaining as they went. "That's Clarks, the new footman. He's not as daft as he seems." The boy took a look up at him and his expression was one of sympathy and understanding. But, like most children, he accepted Wakefield's less-than-stellar appearance for what it was, and appeared pleased that he was simply back among the living.

Not that Pierson felt like he was — living, that is. His head was pounding and he could barely keep his eyes opened, especially with the sting of sunlight pouring in from the opening in the curtains, where Bitty stood peering out the window. The bright light cut a swath through his aching head that he was sure was akin to being shot again.

That and the stench that had chased him downstairs was only more pungent in here.

If he didn't get some fresh air soon, he'd make an even worse fool of himself in front of the children.

"What are you two doing?" he asked, crossing the space toward the window — he needed to get it open and quickly.

"Watching the young miss, milord," Bob said.

The young miss? Pierson paused, then stepped back a bit. Oh. Miss Tempest.

How could he forget? Even with all the alcohol he'd consumed, she invaded his dreams, his hallucinations.

Tempting him. Calling to him. Cursing him for his failures.

And now here she was again. He spun to face Bob. "She's not coming to the door, is she?"

"Oh, no," whispered Bitty.

Pierson glanced over at her, for he'd nearly forgotten she was here, such a silent little mite that she was. "Then what is so interesting?"

"She's going riding," Bitty told him.

"Oh, aye," Bob said, not at all hesitating to resume his watch, parting the curtains without the least thought of subtlety. "Say what you will about that Jemmy out there, but he's got an excellent set of cattle."

Pierson snorted. "What do you know of 'excellent cattle'?"

Bob didn't even blink, but nodded toward the street as if that was proof enough.

The viscount went to the other window and parted that drape slightly, enough to see out, but not so much that he had to close his eyes to blot out the bright spring morning that came flooding in.

It was morning, wasn't it?

He wasn't certain.

But when he looked down in the street, demmed if the boy was right — the horses were well matched.

"She's so lovely," Bitty sighed, having come to stand right beside him.

Pierson nearly jumped, especially when the little girl reached out and took his hand, as if she thought he needed a reassuring presence.

He had to admit, he didn't feel quite as off with Mrs. Petchell's urchins on either side of him.

"Isn't she?" Bitty urged.

"Isn't she what?" he asked, finally daring to raise his gaze from the horses to the lady being helped into the carriage.

"Lovely," Bitty prompted.

"She's something," he muttered back. For indeed, there she was, all dressed up for a ride, her bonnet all but hiding her face, leaving only the curve of her delighted smile for him to see.

A smile being given to another.

The ache in his chest, he told himself, was because he hadn't eaten in a day.

It had been a day, right?

"Where do you think they are going today?" Bob asked his sister.

Today? Pierson shook the cobwebs from his addled thoughts. As in there had been a yesterday?

"What the devil day is it?" he asked, letting go of Bitty's hand. He'd nearly forgotten she was holding on to him.

"Monday," Bob said.

Pierson shook his head. No. That was impossible. "Are you certain?"

"Aunt Matilda made us go to church yesterday," Bitty said with a bit of pious indignation. "You were still . . . sleeping."

Always the diplomat, this Bitty.

Bob just snorted as if he hadn't heard anything so amusing. He glanced up at Pierson, once again taking in his appearance. *Sleeping.* The boy snorted again.

All the while, Pierson was coming to the realization that this was indeed Monday . . . and that the world had moved along quite well without him, long enough for him to acquire a new maid and a footman.

Meanwhile the children had continued their debate as if he weren't even there.

"Probably going riding in the park," Bitty offered.

"Nah," the boy scoffed. "They're off on an assignation."

"Not on a Monday," Bitty shot back, sounding most authoritative on the subject.

Pierson nearly opened his mouth to argue the matter — that any day of the week would do for an intimate interlude — when he realized what the devil these children were debating.

"A bloody wh-a-a-at?" Pierson sputtered, looking from one to the other.

"An assignation," Bob repeated slowly as if he wanted the word to penetrate the viscount's Madeira-soaked brain, and, to make matters worse, then added a cheeky wink to his confident statement.

"What would you know about such matters?" Pierson asked.

Immediately he wished he hadn't.

The boy drew himself up to his full height, stuffed his thumbs in his belt loops and rocked on his heels. "About the same as I know about horses."

Which didn't do much for Pierson since the lad had been spot-on about the cattle.

His gaze shot back to the street outside. An assignation? Over his dead body. Or rather the soon-to-be-dead body of the bastard who dared.

He strained to spy who this interloper, this rare devil, might be, but the man had his back to the house.

"Do you think she might be in trouble, milord?" Bitty asked, her little brown brows furrowed, making her look like a sparrow who'd lost her nest. Worse, an expression that made him feel utterly responsible for fixing her worries. "She hasn't got no one else with her. Not a maid. Not that kindly

Lady Aveley. No one but *him*."

Pierson's gaze swiveled back to the street, this time taking in the entire tableau before him.

Curricle, check. Fast horses, check. Gentleman of dubious intentions, check.

Lady without a respectable, or even a questionable, companion. Check. And check again.

His gut clenched into a tight, bitter ball. This was all wrong. And he blamed this mysterious rake who had her smiling . . . and now laughing — had he ever made her laugh thusly? He couldn't think of a single instance, and that alone had him considering murder.

Oh, that innocent fool. Yet he knew full well he was just as guilty, for hadn't he done much the same thing . . . take advantage of her?

But it was quite another matter when someone else began unraveling his Miss Tempest. Yes, his.

Nor did his mood improve when the man turned around.

"Bloody hell," he swore at the familiar sight.

Tuck.

"Oh, aye, milord," Bob said, rocking on his heels again, taking great delight that

Pierson had just confirmed his observation. "Same knave who came round yesterday."

"And the day afore that," Bitty added.

Pierson groaned. Had the world gone mad? What was his uncle thinking allowing this? Or Lady Aveley? Wasn't anyone seeing to Miss Tempest's welfare?

He spun from the window and marched toward the door, bellowing at the top of his lungs. "Tiploft! Tiploft!"

Tiploft came hurrying up from the kitchen, Mrs. Petchell on his heels. "My carriage!" Pierson ordered. "And be quick about it."

Then Pierson went toward the door.

"My lord, no!" came the anguished cry from Tiploft.

Pierson stopped, hand on the latch and turned around. All four of them were gaping at him and when he turned to continue on his course — out the front door and into the street — out of the corner of his eye, he spied his reflection in the mirror.

Unshaven. Unkempt. Gaunt. And looking like the corpse he'd thought he'd smelled.

He gave himself a sniff and shuddered. He *was* the corpse he'd suspected Mrs. Petchell of having sent up.

That, and he hadn't a stitch on under his wrapper.

"A wash and a shave, I suppose," he corrected. "Oh, and some clothes." He'd never
get Miss Tempest out of Tuck's curricle if
he looked (and smelled) worse than some
Seven Dials cur. "But let's be quick about
it." Then he turned to Bob. "My curricle. I
want it brought around now."

Setting off up the stairs, his leg reminded
him how little he'd done over the past week,
but he had better things to worry about now.

Like one very important matter.

He'd gone and lost her.

In his haste to go up the stairs, he missed
Mrs. Petchell's aside to Tiploft.

"Liver and onions. Does it every time."

Louisa flinched as the door slammed shut.
"Lavinia —" she began, but it was of no
use. Her sister was already on the stairs, the
determined click of her heels as she fled
their latest argument.

Over the debacle at Almack's. And about
staying in London. About everything.

In the five days since Lavinia and Louisa
had revealed to each other that they had
both known the truth about their mother,
instead of drawing them closer, they'd
become strangers. The terrible secret divid-
ing them.

That Lavinia had known of their mother's

disgrace and still insisted on coming to Town for the Season was, in Louisa's estimation, unforgivable.

This afternoon's row had begun not long after Lady Aveley had returned from another round of not-so-successful morning calls. She'd come through the door, her usual sunny expression set in a mask of worried lines.

Which was not unexpected. First, the salver that had initially overflowed had run dry. Then had come their tentative foray back into London society Saturday evening to a simple soirée.

Though it had turned out not to be so simple.

They'd arrived with high hopes that all of Lord Ilford's bellicose threats had been for naught.

But, unfortunately, this time the man had been good to his word. They'd entered Lady Gourley's drawing room to a silence that could have chilled every last bottle of champagne in London. No one would speak to them — they were given the cut direct by one and all. Despite Lady Aveley's best intentions and her good name, not even the memory of dear Lady Charleton could get the *ton* to move from their ill-judgment of the Tempest sisters.

370

And as they were leaving, they had heard one matron sniff loudly as they passed and say to her companion, "Scandalous creatures — the both of them. Whatever is Lady Aveley thinking?"

Lavinia had come home in tears.

So this afternoon, when Louisa had once again broached the subject of returning to Kempton, Lavinia wouldn't hear a word of such heresy.

Leave London in defeat and disgrace? Never!

"That is not what Lady Essex would do," Lavinia had proclaimed. "Nor will I be undone by gossip. We can overcome all of this — just you wait and see."

Louisa had nearly pointed out that Lady Essex's mother had been a model of decorum, but then remembered something about the esteemed lady's mother being a former opera dancer, which hardly served the moment.

"Just because all your hopes are dashed," Lavinia had said in a willful moment of spite, before storming out of the house, seeking solace at the lending library around the corner where Lord Charleton held a subscription.

Louisa glanced out the window, where, over the garden wall, she hadn't seen so much as a curtain move in days. She'd come up with a thousand and one reasons why Lord Wakefield had abandoned her.

And knew the one that was true. He didn't want her. He never truly had.

According to Bob, "himself" had decamped to his lair and "wasn't fit company."

Besides, with Lady Melliscent now available . . . A widow must be much more preferable to the daughter of a . . .

Louisa spun away from the window. *Oh, heavens, Mother. How could you? Abandon us like this. Leave us to face your misdeeds?*

And Lavinia . . . she'd known all this time and never once . . .

Then again, so had she.

Yet Louisa knew her current woes were her own fault and certainly couldn't be laid at another's doorstep.

This was all her own doing. And undoing.

She'd behaved much as her mother had — without a thought to the consequences.

For the simple truth was, every time Wakefield looked at her, touched her, kissed her, she was lost.

How was it that the viscount knew exactly how to tap into her very soul? Tease out that cork that she'd used to tamp down every passion, every secret wish?

One glance and he unbottled her desires.

Bother the man. And his undone house. And all his beastly ways.

Still, what had she done? Driven him deeper into his lair, when he'd only just begun to come out.

So if Wakefield was lost, and their Season was adrift, there was one thing Louisa could do. Taking a deep breath, she gathered up her bonnet, pelisse and gloves, determined to mend fences with Lavinia. It hardly served for them to continue this brangle. To live at odds.

As Lady Essex always said, "One problem at a time."

Stealing a last glance out the window toward the house over the wall, Louisa set off for the lending library.

Lavinia been going there nearly every day since the debacle at Almack's — and since her sister only ever read the *Miss Darby* novels, romantic drivel of the worst order, in Louisa's opinion, she was starting to have suspicions about her sister's sudden interest in literature.

As it was, something else gave her pause. A few steps down the block there was a curricle in front of Lord Wakefield's town house.

And worse, there was the viscount himself trying to get up into it.

Glancing over her shoulder, she considered walking around the block in the opposite direction, but then she considered what Lady Essex would say to such cowardice.

Balderdash! A lady always holds her head up.

So Louisa took a deep breath and continued her course, determined to walk right on past, until, that is, she came alongside him as he was making yet another attempt to climb up into his curricle, and lost both his walking stick and balance in the process.

She stepped forward quickly, putting her arm under his, and held him fast until he found his footing.

He glanced down at her and nearly tumbled again as he recoiled from her. "Miss Tempest? What the devil are you doing there?"

It was hardly the response she expected. A mere "thank you" might have sufficed.

Then again she nearly wished she'd let him fall to the ground, for just wrapping her hand around his elbow, brushing up against him to steady him was too much of a reminder of what it had been like to be in his arms.

To be kissed by him.

To have him tease her until her world

unraveled.

Now here he was, gaping at her. "Where did you come from?" he demanded.

Something about his outraged tone needled her. "If it is any of your business, from Lord Charleton's house." She went to move around him, but he reached out and caught her by her elbow.

"No. I distinctly saw you get into a carriage and leave with Tuck."

She glanced down at his fingers still wound around her arm and frowned. "Mr. Rowland? I think not," she told him, shaking her head. He'd been one of the instruments of their fall from grace and was certainly the last person on earth Louisa would be seen with. Besides, there was a more obvious point. "However could I be in a carriage when I am standing right —"

Then her outrage caught up with what he'd been saying, put all the pieces together.

What had Lavinia said? *I can overcome all of this — just you wait and see . . .*

And then Wakefield. *I distinctly saw you get into a carriage and leave with Tuck . . .*

"Oh, good heavens, no!" she gasped, shaking her arm loose from his grasp and looking up and down the street for any sign of her sister.

"But I saw you —" he insisted.

"You didn't see me," she told him. "You saw my sister, Lavinia."

He took a step back. "Oh, good Lord, I forgot. There's two of you."

"Yes, and one of us is apparently out riding with Mr. Rowland." Any thoughts of reaching an accord with her sister were shelved. Along with her fiction of going to the library.

Oh, she was going to kill Lavinia! What was her sister thinking? Riding about with such a knave?

Thank goodness there were still men like Lord Wakefield who was willing to stop . . . willing to go after . . .

Louisa paused as a second revelation crossed through her thoughts and she looked up at the viscount. "Wait, you thought Lavinia was me."

"Well, yes. I didn't realize that you —"

"— are a twin," she said offhandedly, not wanting to move away from her revealing discovery. "You were planning on rescuing me from Mr. Rowland."

She couldn't help herself, she smiled at him. All but forgot the indignities of the past five days.

He managed to look exceedingly put out by the suggestion, but Louisa wasn't fooled,

not even when he added a stumbling protest.

"I — I — I was not —"

And a hastily planned rescue from the
looks of it. For here he was, his cravat barely
tied, his chin scraped of whiskers with more
than one nick, and his hair still damp from
being scrubbed.

All evidence that he'd come after her in
all due haste.

She crossed her arms over her chest and
tapped her boot to the pavement. Oh, he
could protest all he wanted, but the evidence
was right before her.

Worse, inside her chest, a tiny hope
sparked back to life.

He'd come to rescue me . . .

"Well, I might have been under the impression —" he began, running a hand
through his hair.

She cocked a brow upward.

"My uncle's honor —" he added lamely.

At this she just laughed. Lord Charleton's
honor had hardly been in the forefront of
Wakefield's thinking the other night in the
carriage. "And what were you planning to
do once you lured me away from Mr. Rowland?"

A whirlwind of possibilities ran through
her thoughts. Suggestions, ideas, promises.

Kiss me? Make love to me . . . Unravel me.

"Nothing!" he protested.

Not quite the answer she'd been hoping for, but then again she was cautiously optimistic this rescue was still in the planning stages.

"So you did dash out of your house to come rescue me," she said with all confidence.

"Not in so many words," he protested. "That is I —"

Oh, bother the man. As much as she would prefer to stand here and wait for a declaration from this obstinate viscount, she hadn't the time.

And she knew what needed to be done. And quickly.

Louisa huffed a sigh and walked around the carriage, climbing up and into the driver's seat, then glanced down at him. "Do you mind if I borrow your carriage so I can go rescue my sister?"

"I do indeed," he huffed.

"Then you had best get up here and come with me. For I have every intention of borrowing it, whether you approve or not."

"Then whyever did you ask?"

"I was attempting to be polite," she told him. "Now am I borrowing it or stealing it?"

"You wouldn't dare," he said, standing his ground.

But this was Louisa, and of course she would.

CHAPTER 14

"This is nothing less than blackmail," Pierson told Miss Tempest, as he gritted his teeth and managed to climb up into his curricle. That he made it up and into the seat surprised him, almost as much as when he settled into place, in a spot he never thought he'd find himself again — driving a carriage.

Yet he wasn't driving.

To his horror, Miss Tempest had wound the ribbons through her gloved hands and was giving them an experienced wag, sending the obedient horses down the street.

"What the devil are you doing?" he demanded.

"Since you've refused, I must. Drive, that is," she told him. "Besides, you said my sister is in devilish company. You seemed in a great haste to go after Mr. Rowland when you thought it was me —" The little busybody had the nerve to pin a knowing glance on him.

"I was just . . ." He rather hated the fact that once again she had him in a tight corner.

"Be that as it may, your rescue is now of my sister."

Yes, so it appeared. He glanced up and found that they were passing a young buck in a stylish-looking phaeton. The fellow gaped at Louisa before giving Pierson a pitying glance.

Oh, this will never do. He reached over and took the ribbons from her. "If we must rescue your sister, then I am driving."

"As you wish," she said quite willingly, settling into her seat. "Since it is most likely for the best."

"I don't know, you seem quite good at driving," he admitted as he adjusted his hold.

"Thank you," she said, nodding politely. "However, driving is always enhanced when one goes in the right direction . . . My lord, you just drove past the turn to the lending library." She glanced over her shoulder and then back at the horses.

"The lending library? Is that where your sister said she was going?" Pierson couldn't help himself, he laughed.

"I don't see why that is amusing, especially when the lending library is back there," she said, reaching over for the ribbons.

He batted her hand away.

"We should turn back," she persisted.

"Your sister isn't at the lending library."

"And how do you know that?"

"Well, for one, I saw her get into a carriage with Tuck."

"Mr. Rowland, indeed! I can't imagine Lavinia going with *him*. No, you must have mistaken the matter. It is impossible." She sat with her arms folded over her chest.

"And if such circumstances are, as you say, impossible, why are you insisting that we go rescue her?"

She took a glance at him. "Harrumph!"

"So I thought," he said, feeling a momentary bit of control over the situation. Not that he expected to maintain it for very long. "Your sister is not at the lending library, because that is exactly the same lie Tuck and I would tell our tutor when we wanted to get out of our lessons. How long has she had this interest in the 'library?' "

She glanced sideways at him, eyes narrowed. Apparently not the news she wanted to hear. "You must be mistaken. Lavinia would never —"

Yet she stopped short of completely denying the possibility.

"Tuck and I shared a tutor when we were

young," he explained. "Dry, horrible old fellow. And so when it was fair out and we hardly wanted to be inside, we would confess a desire to go to the lending library, and our tutor, who didn't like walking so far, would grant us permission to go."

"But you didn't —"

He shook his head. "No, we didn't. We'd gallivant about Town, finding mischief and generally doing what boys do when left to their own devices." He laughed a bit at the memory. He hadn't thought of old Dr. Smithson in a long time. "Once we got lost and had a devil of a time finding our way home. We knew we would be caught out, and by the time we returned, our absence had been noticed. But Tuck had a ready reply."

"Which was?" she asked, though she didn't look like she wanted to hear the answer.

"Oh, yes. He had some bang-up tale about how we'd found ourselves caught up reading Homer, *The Odyssey,* I think it was, and lost track of time."

Miss Tempest scoffed at such a thing. "And that was believed?"

"I don't know, but Lady Charleton spied us sneaking home, managed to get us inside without anyone else seeing — and when they did notice our return, she had a way about her that left everyone else inclined to be lenient." He paused for a moment, thinking about his aunt. "I'm certain she knew we hadn't been anywhere near the library, but made excuses for us anyway. She loved Tuck dearly — thought of him as a son, especially since it was obvious he was going to be Charleton's heir. My aunt, your godmother, was a remarkable woman."

"I never met her."

Pierson glanced over at her. "No?"

"No," she said with a wistful note.

"That's unfortunate." And he meant it. He suspected that if Aunt Isobel had lived, she would never have allowed him to wallow about, or feel sorry for himself, or hide away in his darkened lair.

She would have done much as her goddaughter had done over the last fortnight — cajole him back into the world.

Speaking of which, Miss Tempest began prodding him again. It seemed she never missed an opportunity to meddle.

He was finding that he rather admired that about her. Her persistence.

"Lord Wakefield, *if* my sister is in Mr. Rowland's company —"

"If? No. She *is.*"

There was a long sigh from his companion. Make that her demmed persistence.

"While I am still of the opinion that not even Lavinia would be so foolish as to keep company with Mr. Rowland, and *if* she isn't at the lending library, where do you think she might be if she is in Mr. Rowland's company? Where does a gentleman take a lady in the middle of the afternoon?" And after a moment's pause, she added, "Do say something respectable."

That was the problem. Being that this was Tuck, the situation was most likely anything but.

Pierson ground his teeth together. What the devil was Rowland thinking? Especially when the chit was staying in their uncle's house. Under their uncle's protection.

Which might have been something to consider before you found yourself alone in a carriage with the chit the other night, eh Pierson?

He ignored that ironic little voice of reason.

"Let us try the park," he said, hoping that gave Tuck enough time to get the second Miss Tempest back to Charleton's house.

That seemed to reassure her, for she sat back, her hands folded primly in front of her. But this silence and her stiff stance unnerved him a bit.

He thought back to the last time he'd been

with her — in the carriage, holding her.

Well, more than holding her. And he supposed he owed her an apology. Should explain his actions. Perhaps starting with why he hadn't come to call.

No. No. No. That would never do. *Yes, well, I am so sorry, Miss Tempest, I've been indisposed.*

Make that drunk as an emperor and trying my best to forget you, he corrected.

Oh, that was hardly the way to start such a conversation.

Nor did the silence weigh well on Miss Tempest, for she spoke up before he had a chance. "How long has it been since you were out driving?"

She made it sound like they were on some pleasant jaunt to the park.

"Not since —" He stopped right there.

But she wasn't afraid to say it. "Since before you went to Spain."

"Yes."

"You appear to like it," she pointed out, as he crossed through traffic with nary a blink.

"I do. Rather, I did," he quickly corrected.

"You shouldn't have stopped."

He could hardly tell her the real reason — he hadn't thought he could get up into a carriage — at least up and into the driver's seat — without making a complete cake of himself.

But here he was.

She'd forced him into trying, what with her blackmail.

He glanced away, because it was just one more way she'd widened the cracks in his fortress walls.

Bothersome chit.

As they journeyed a bit farther, she sighed heavily.

"Whatever is wrong?" he asked. Oh, demmit, why had he done that? When was he going to learn not to make these sort of queries?

Because she always answered them.

"I find London so sad," she said, her mouth setting in a serious line. "I had thought it would be all grand homes and gardens and beautiful spaces, but it isn't."

"Then I had best not take you to Seven Dials or Southwark if you find Mayfair not to your liking."

"Oh, the houses are lovely, and grand, but it is the poor creatures on every corner that I did not expect. Why isn't anything done about that?" She nodded toward a man leaning heavily against the corner of a building, one arm wound around a crutch.

One pant leg hung flapping in the breeze,

where he'd lost a leg. Nor was there any mistaking his tattered jacket.

A Hussar.

Close by, a pair of children held out their caps, hoping to catch any coins that the poor soldier missed.

"That might have been Bitty and Bob — if you hadn't taken them in," she said as they passed. She glanced over her shoulder at the waifish imps, watching them most likely until they were out of sight.

"What would you have me do?" he asked. "Take every beggar in London into my service?"

"No, your house isn't big enough," she pointed out.

Practical minx. But that didn't mean she hadn't other means to meddle.

She sat up straight and gazed at him. One of her looks that pinned him in place, made him sit up and pay attention. "But you could help them."

He barked a laugh. Because as she'd noted, there was misery on every corner.

And London had a lot of corners.

"It would take a fortune," he told her, not looking at the man curled up on the sidewalk, his dark green jacket flung over him like a blanket.

She reached out and put her hand on his

sleeve. "You could gain them that fortune. You could be their voice."

He didn't quite see what she was suggesting. "Are you saying I should beg for them?"

"No. I'm saying you should take your place in the House of Lords and demand it."

Pierson nearly choked. She didn't ask for much. The fortune would be easier to manage.

"You could be their voice, my lord. Look at Bitty and Bob and imagine their fate if they hadn't their aunt. Hadn't you. Force those fusty old lords to help the men who have served. Make them remember not only the men who have lost limbs, their livelihoods, but their families as well."

No, she didn't ask for much at all. *Save my sister from ruin. Save every limbless fellow and all the orphans.*

But the worst part of all was that he knew she was right.

And demmit, if she hadn't chosen to plant a seed exactly where it could grow.

Meddling bit of muslin. He glanced over at her and could see she was most likely beginning to map out his entire political campaign. But if there was one thing he had learned about her, she could be diverted.

"I bumped into a new maid as I was coming down the stairs —" he began.

Immediately, he had her attention. But not as he expected.

"Dear heavens! You didn't frighten Caddy, did you? She's a good girl and comes highly recommended, but I fear she's terribly shy." This scold was followed by an accusing glance.

He looked away, for now he was the one who was ruffled.

Frighten the gel? Whyever would Miss Tempest say such a thing? Did she think him a complete ogre?

Then he thought back to that encounter on the stairs and flinched. Well, the maid had looked a bit pale.

"You did, didn't you?" Miss Tempest said, for nothing slipped past her sharp gaze.

"I might have given her a slight start," he admitted. Recalling the girl's gaping expression of horror, he supposed he'd rather traumatized this poor Caddy. But he wasn't about to run up a white flag just yet. "Apparently I have a new footman as well," he added. "Do I have your interference to thank for my new maid and footman?"

She glanced away, but not before he noticed the pretty blush rising on her cheeks. "Maids and footmen," she corrected.

Maids and footmen. As in more than just this Caddy and Clarks. "So you've been meddling in my house again, haven't you?"

She had the audacity to appear affronted. "How could I, when you've forbidden your staff to let me enter?"

"Hasn't stopped them apparently," he muttered under his breath.

"Mr. Tiploft asked my opinion on the matter," she admitted, then rushed to add, "Since Caddy and her sister Betty are the daughters of Mrs. Petchell's cousin, while the Clarkses are her nephews on her husband's side. Mr. Tiploft wanted to ensure they were all suitable choices without offending Mrs. Petchell."

Good heavens, considering what his cook had sent up for him today, he'd hate to see what she'd do when "offended."

"Am I to employ all of Mrs. Petchell's wayward relations?"

At this she sniffed. "Better that than the thief you had previously. You are lucky to have a single teaspoon left in your house."

She had him there. Nearly.

"Since you are so intent on seeing me fully staffed, are you also paying all their salaries?"

That got her attention.

"Oh, dear me, no!" Her eyes grew round

with alarm. "I just assumed . . . you would . . . That is if you can afford . . ." She paused for a second, then lowered her voice. "You can afford them, can't you?"

He leaned over. "I can."

Her relief welled out of her. "Thank heavens, because my pin money would barely cover Bitty and Bob."

"From the amount Bob eats, your pin money must be most generous," the viscount commented. "I am beginning to think a few missing teaspoons isn't much to consider when faced with an empty larder."

"You wouldn't turn him out for eating too much, would you?"

Pierson laughed. "What sort of beast do you think I am? No, don't tell me — that question was merely rhetorical and I suspect you would be more than willing to forgo good manners and give me a full accounting of my failings."

She laughed and glanced away — for most likely she'd begun to compile her reckoning — or worse, had done so already and been happily waiting for just such an opportunity.

"You needn't worry," he said hastily, because he certainly didn't want to hear what she thought of him. "I will not turn out those two guttersnipes. I've grown far too fond of Mrs. Petchell's cooking. And if

I must have her entire clan beneath my roof if only to enjoy the delights of her roast beef, then so be it."

Though today's offering had been a bit of a shock, a harkening back to the days of Monsieur Begnoche. If Pierson had to guess, he suspected the old gal had served him up that dreadful liver stew on purpose.

She had cooked for the previous Lord Aveley, after all. And he had been known to have his fair share of infamous bouts.

Miss Tempest sat up a bit straighter and adjusted her bonnet. "I think you will find them all competent and excellent additions to your household. I was most impressed when I interviewed them."

"Aha! So you admit to meddling in my life," he pointed out.

"You call it meddling, I call it something to do," she told him.

When he stole a sideways glance at her, he found her brows furrowed together. Oh, God help him, she was plotting again.

"What is it now?" he dared to ask.

"Can you afford a valet?"

Pierson coughed. "A wha-a-a-at?"

"A valet. While footmen and pot boys aren't overly expensive, I suspect a good valet does not come cheaply."

"No, they do not," he informed her most

solemnly. Then he thought about what she was really saying. "Why do you think I need a valet?"

The look she gave him — one that swept from his top hat to his boots — was most telling.

Still, that didn't stop him from asking, "What?"

"It's just —" Her fingers fluttered about as if they weren't sure where to point first.

He glanced down at himself. Certainly he was no Beau Brummell, but he wasn't completely unpresentable.

Well, mostly. "What?" he repeated. Demanded.

"You need tidying," she said, her wide blue eyes all earnest and serious.

Tidying. Well, yes, he supposed he did. But that wasn't exactly what she meant. Her words, her earnest glance held so much more.

Leave it to Miss Tempest to get to the heart of the matter.

His heart, to be exact. He knew exactly what she was saying. He didn't need a valet (well, he probably did, but that was beside the point), he needed her.

Desperately.

And looking into her eyes again, she needed him as well. That was the part that frightened him. Down to his boots.

Miss Tempest needed him. Longed for him. Desired him.

That part terrified him.

Why couldn't she be like everyone else in London and see how unworthy he was? It was as if, no matter how hard he tried to convince her otherwise, she refused to see anything else.

In her eyes, he saw reflected a man he didn't completely recognize. There was some of the rake he'd been before. Before he'd bought his commission . . . before he'd needed tidying, as she so eloquently put it.

Yet there was also the man cast firmly in the darkness. The stranger who pulled at his soul to wade deeper and deeper into that mire. To hide in the shadows where no one could see his shame.

His secrets.

Except her.

Somehow, Miss Tempest saw him in his entirety. The rake. The damaged soldier. The rarely noble viscount.

They weren't all pieces to her — like so many others saw him.

Society, who recoiled from his injuries with their furtive glances and pitying looks.

His mother, with her eyes filled with regrets.

Tiploft, who longed each day to see the lord and master of the manor arise and come forth.

Tuck, who saw . . . too much.

But not Miss Tempest. She was like a general on the hill. The one who saw the full scope of the battlefield. Had the power to lead him out from beneath the barrage of cannons and sniper fire under which he'd been hiding.

His silence must have been unnerving her, for she started to chatter on. "Take that jacket. It doesn't fit. And your hair. It is ill-kempt. A valet would see to those things. Not allow them to go unattended."

Pierson couldn't help himself. "Like my linen closet?"

Those gorgeous eyes of hers widened — first with determination and then the realization of what he was really implying.

"Oh! This has nothing to do with your linen closet," she told him, folding her gloved hands in her lap and staring demurely ahead.

"I certainly hope not. So might I assume that 'linen closet' is some new cant that I've missed picking up in my absence from society?" He did his best to keep his features schooled in all seriousness, even as he watched a mixture of chastisement and, though she'd never admit it, delight, wage war at her lips.

And then after a few moments, she turned toward him. "I'm sorry, my lord. But a linen closet is still a linen closet."

"That's unfortunate," he told her.

"What is unfortunate is yours. It is still unfinished."

"The closet or the kiss?" he dared, as he pulled the horses to a stop to wait for a break in traffic.

She straightened up. "I hardly think now is the time to discuss kissing."

Liar. He could tell by the blush on her cheeks that she was considering the notion.

Besides, he knew Louisa Tempest. She didn't like anything half finished.

Including a kiss.

Which he was tempted to steal right here and now, but from behind them, a driver shouted his annoyance. "Move along there. Haven't got all day!"

"No, we haven't," she added, nodding toward the entrance to the park.

Of course, yes. The park. He gave the reins a wag and all too soon they were driving through the crush of society out on afternoon parade. He guided the horses into the flow and settled back.

But immediately, Pierson realized something wasn't right. "I know I haven't been out much in the last few years —"

"Rather not at all," she corrected.

"Yes, thank you," he noted. "As I was saying, even having not been out much, I don't recall being snubbed everywhere I went."

For indeed, every carriage they passed, every rider who trotted past, after a moment's recognition, made a very deliberate effort to give them the cut direct.

"It isn't you; it is me," she said quietly, looking down at her hands, which were now knotted together in her lap.

Pierson glanced around at the hostile reception. "You?"

"I suppose you will find out eventually," she said. "I'm no longer considered proper. Not since Almack's."

"Not proper? Of all the —" Then he stopped.

You did this. You ruined her the other night and then fled as if half of Boney's army was chasing you.

He swung to face her. "I'm so sorry. This is all my —"

"Don't," she said, her gaze still fixed on her hands. "You had nothing to do with any of this. There are other . . . circumstances."

Pierson looked up and around them, feeling the full weight of the scorn being heaped

398

in their direction.

Whatever could cause such disdain? Then he stilled.

What had she said? *Not since Almack's.*

Then he remembered, those ugly words haunting forward from that night.

Lady Tempest is dead . . . in Italy . . . with her paramour by her side . . . if she's got her mother's blood, she won't be so clumsy when she's lying on her back . . .

It wouldn't have mattered how many marquesses he'd struck that night. Such damaging, scandal-ridden gossip — rife with adultery and lies — would trump any other mayhem.

He took another glance around and realized the full extent of her ruin by the misery in her eyes.

"That bastard!" he said without thinking.

At this, she reeled back, her mouth gaping open.

"Oh, good heavens!" she gasped. "So that is what Lord Ilford said to you. He told you about —" Yet she couldn't finish the sentence.

He was of half a mind to deny it, but Miss Tempest was no fool. Instead he shrugged a bit. "I suppose my striking him didn't help."

"Unfortunately Lord Ilford and Lady Kipps have taken great delight in seeing that . . . everyone knows . . ."

Kipps? Not that pup that had always been loitering after Preston and Roxley.

Still, he had to ask. "Kipps got married?"

"Apparently," she said. "I don't think the lady is his mother."

"And what has this Lady Kipps got to do with this?"

"She was in the middle of a dance floor when Mr. Rowland ruined my sister. If that was all this was, I daresay we could weather such a thing."

Pierson blinked. Certainly he was a bit under the weather, but still he couldn't have heard her correctly. "Tuck ruined your sister on the dance floor at Almack's?"

Then that part of the evening came back to him. Louisa insisting that someone rescue her sister from the tumble on the dance floor. Tuck coming up to him just after he'd struck Ilford. What was it he'd said? Oh, yes.

Bit of trouble out there. Thought it best I make my bow and resort to a hasty exit.

Bit of trouble indeed! It had looked like a mail coach had toppled over and emptied all its passengers in the process.

That had been Tuck's fault?

Then again, if anyone could manage such

a debacle, Alaster Rowland was the man to do it.

"Yes, exactly. If he hadn't been there, Lady Kipps would never have ended up atop Lady Jersey."

Oh, if his head wasn't spinning before, it was now. But he tried to follow. "This Lady Kipps fell on Lady Jersey?"

"Yes, but only after Lord Pomfrey tumbled onto her."

This was where his less-than-perfect faculties did not aid him. He closed his eyes and tried to line up all the players, and then set them in motion like a perfect column of dominos. "And Tuck did all this?"

Her snort rather confirmed that. "You can't imagine —"

"I'm beginning to."

"And it all began when Mr. Rowland let go of Lavinia to come to your aid —"

His aid? Oh, his pride couldn't allow such a thing. "I was never in distress," he pointed out. "You might recall, I wasn't the one on the floor."

Her glance implied she would have preferred that he had been — on the floor.

"As it was," she said, continuing, but he noted, choosing her words a little more carefully, "Without Mr. Rowland's hold on

my sister, she tumbled into Lord Pomfrey
—"

"Who fell into Lady Kipps —"

"Yes, and then the countess stumbled and fell —"

"Taking Lady Jersey with her."

Miss Tempest sighed. "Unfortunately. There were others who ended up in the hodgepodge, but they are hardly of note."

"How unfortunate your sister didn't dance with Lord Ilford and you with Tuck," he said, still trying to put that night's events in order.

"I hardly think that would have changed the situation. At least not the other dilemma . . ."

Meaning her mother.

"Besides, I had no intention of dancing with Mr. Rowland, Lord Charleton's heir or not," she had continued. "He was bosky."

"Bosky? Listen to you." He laughed to hear the very proper Miss Tempest use such cant.

That was the real problem with her. One moment she was tied up in her stringent notions of organization and staffing, and the next, she was being utterly improper.

Then again, when she came close enough to him so he could smell her perfume, see the soft sheen in her hair, the tiny hint of freckles across her cheeks, it was easy to forget what proper meant.

And today she was definitely sited in the proper camp. "No reason to find that amusing. He was bosky, I say." She glanced at him as if to challenge him to deny it.

How could he? "The only way to get Tuck into Almack's, I imagine." It was meant to lighten the mood, but it hardly worked.

"Excuse me?" Her brow winged up.

"Well, you wouldn't expect Tuck to go there and not be drunk, would you?"

Her shoulders drew a taut line. "I would."

Yes, she would.

And that was the problem. Miss Tempest in all her proper and tidy ways wouldn't understand the very untidy and irrational notion of drinking oneself into a stupor.

Getting lost so in a kiss you forgot your manners, your honor.

Pierson gave his head a slight shake, then glanced over at her and wondered if she knew how he'd spent the last few days. He hoped not, but considering how meddling she was, she probably did.

And he was struck by how much he wished she didn't.

Yet here she was — no matter what she thought of him. Asking him to help her find her sister.

Worse, if he was to hazard a wager, he'd have to say she thought him quite capable of saving the day.

Miss Tempest, I am no hero, he wanted to tell her.

Meanwhile, she'd continued her lament. "It isn't all that bad that we must leave," she was saying, glancing up at him from beneath the brim of her bonnet. "Especially now that it is all over Town that we are . . ." Again her voice trailed off, but she plucked up her chin and finished the best she could manage, ". . . not good *ton.*" She sighed. " 'Tis better to go home than watch poor Lady Aveley despair that no one will acknowledge us or invite us anywhere."

He hadn't been listening as carefully as he ought, for he was still trying to think of some way to locate Tuck.

And the other Miss Tempest. That and get this Miss Tempest home, where she wouldn't be subjected to the harsh censure of every member of the *ton* they passed.

Oh, that, and salvage all this mess. Put a smile on her strawberry-colored lips, put that light back in her eyes.

But it was then that her words sank in. Exactly what she was saying. And what it meant. To him.

"Go home? Leave London?" Pierson shook his head. "No, no, that will never do."

CHAPTER 15

"Stay in London?" Miss Tempest shook her head. Vehemently. Then she made a point of glancing around, urging him, as it were, to survey the landscape as well. "Can't you see that is impossible?"

He didn't need to look around to know the situation was unbearable, he could see it in the humiliation in her eyes. That sad, terrible light, oh, that he knew.

But leave? No! Couldn't she see that he needed her?

Terribly. Vehemently.

Because, he realized in that oh-so-desperate moment, he loved her. From her pert strawberry lips to the breakage that swelled in her wake. To her meddling ways.

Oh, especially those meddling ways.

Love.

Such a small word to tip his world upside down. Crumble the last vestiges of his defenses.

He, Pierson Stratton, the Viscount Wakefield, loved Miss Tempest.

And he knew there were three things that needed to be done.

Get her back to Charleton's and well away from the slings and arrows of society. Which would leave him free to go find Tuck in his usual haunts. The sort of places one didn't take a lady.

Then, he'd go have a little discussion with Ilford. Not so much a discussion, but rather a good thrashing.

After that, he supposed there was one more thing he would have to do. He would have to let her go.

Back to her beloved Kempton. Back to where she could shine brightly, meddle to her heart's content and no one would look askance at her. She could hold her head up and be the lady that she was.

This time, he looked away, because the idea of standing in the window and watching some traveling barouche take her from him left him reeling. He wouldn't be able to do it.

Not even with Bitty and Bob at his side. Especially not with them. If Bitty started crying, Pierson made no guarantees that he wouldn't turn into a veritable watering pot as well.

Yet when he looked up and around, as if seeking help, who did his gaze fall on, but the perfect gentleman to help him.

Brody.

Why was it that at this very moment, Poldie's brother pulled up alongside them?

"Wakefield," the baron said, nodding politely. The younger man's face brightened with a smile when he recognized Pierson's companion. "Miss Tempest! What a delight!"

And like Poldie, there was no guile in his address, no false bright notes. The man was genuinely happy to see her.

"Rimswell," Pierson said in greeting, trying not to flinch as he used Poldie's old title. "Could you help me out, my good man?"

"Always," the man replied, his eyes widening at this unprecedented request.

"Could you take Miss Tempest home to Lord Charleton's. He's on —"

"— Hanover Square," Rimswell finished for him. "Yes, I know. Be more than delighted to be of assistance."

But there was one person who was far from delighted. And she turned her outraged expression on Pierson.

Not that he had expected her to go easily.

"Have you not forgotten our errand that needs seeing to?" Her brows rose, as if to nudge him.

Pierson wasn't about to be nudged. "I have not. But I can complete it more efficiently if you are home. Besides, weren't you just saying that the sun has left you quite fatigued?"

The lady didn't look tired in the least. Furious and angry, yes. Nor did she see the point of playing along. Not at first.

"I said no such —" But then her protests stopped as she glanced over her shoulder at Lord Rimswell. She could hardly complain further in front of the baron, especially when the fellow had that look of an overeager pup on him. Sir Galahad with an honorable crusade before him. She took a deep breath. "Our errand —" she pressed quietly.

Pierson leaned closer. "I shall see to it. Now go with Rimswell. Please."

She looked ready to protest further, but stopped, when yet another carriage rolled by.

He didn't recognize the lady in the carriage, but he did the gentleman driving. The Earl of Kipps. Pierson had to guess that the woman next him, a pretty-looking bit but with the sharp eye of a merchant and a cruel twist to her lips, was none other than Lady Kipps.

But even without the lady's husband there

to give her identity away, the deep blush that rose on Miss Tempest's cheeks was evidence enough.

That, and her sudden and hasty acquiescence. "Yes, well, perhaps I have been out too long, Lord Wakefield," she agreed, slanting a glance at Pierson, before accepting Brody's hand and making the transfer to the seat beside him.

"I will have you safely home in no time, Miss Tempest," Brody vowed, tipping his hat to Pierson before giving the ribbons a practiced wag.

Never one to leave a moment unmeddled, his Miss Tempest called after him. "Our errand."

As if he could forget.

Pierson smiled for half a second, and then his eyes narrowed. He had an errant heir to find. A marquess to murder. And his heart to bury.

Louisa glanced over her shoulder and watched Lord Wakefield move quickly out of the park as if the devil were on his heels.

And why wouldn't he want to be away from her? When every pair of eyes they passed gazed at her, and now at him, in scorn.

Guilty by association.

She should never have forced him to come along with her. Yet . . . for a moment when he'd been protesting her leaving London, she'd thought . . . well, hoped, he had come out with her today for reasons other than her "blackmail," as he called it.

That he truly had come blustering out of his house, half shaved and still damp around the edges to rescue her from Tuck.

Rescue her. Those words sent a shiver of desire down her spine.

He'd come out to rescue her.

Much as he'd arrived at Almack's like a knight in shining armor.

Could he . . . She stopped herself right there. The very idea left her breathless.

For all the problems she'd brought to his doorstep, could Lord Wakefield actually hold a *tendre* for her?

Louisa pressed her lips together and looked away. Oh, that would never do.

Because he'd have to be completely mad to fall in love with her and here she'd always vowed that if (and that was a rather large *if*) she married, she certainly wouldn't marry a man who wasn't sensible. She wouldn't fall in love with some beastly fellow just to be married.

And yet . . .

For all Wakefield's adamant protests that

she couldn't leave London, he'd failed to mention the one reason that mattered most.

That he loved her.

As worried sick as she was over Lavinia's disappearance, she nearly laughed at the very thought of Lord Wakefield making some flowery declaration of love.

He was not a man for speeches. At least not those kind.

But she could see him standing up in the House of Lords and giving a voice to those whose cries went unheard, day in and day out. That's why she'd made the suggestion. Urged him to take his seat.

Besides, she'd seen the grief on his face as they'd passed that poor man with only one leg. That he was lost and homeless hadn't escaped the viscount.

As much as Lord Charleton applauded how she'd been able to draw the viscount out of his lair, one look at his face when he'd seen so many of his fellow soldiers in such desperate straits — well, it hadn't felt like a kindness.

"I wish he didn't blame me so," Lord Rimswell said to her.

"Excuse me?"

"I said, I wish Wakefield didn't blame me," the baron repeated.

"Blame you? Whatever for?" If anyone was

to blame, it was she.

"For being Rimswell. For being Poldie's heir."

"I'm sorry, my lord. I don't quite understand. Who was Poldie?" Even as she asked the question, she realized that name was familiar. She'd heard it before. And while she tried to remember where she'd heard it, Lord Rimswell made his explanation.

"My brother was Baron Rimswell before me. He'd been Rimswell since just after I was born."

"Your brother?" She paused. "You inherited your title from your brother?"

"Yes. I know Wakefield finds me a poor substitute for Poldie, as well I know I am," he confessed. "Poldie thought of Wakefield more like a brother than a friend. I was merely the spare who wanted to tag along."

"I doubt that, Lord Rimswell," she told him.

"You are most kind to say so." He sat back in his seat and held the reins with an easy grace, but his gaze was fixed on a spot far from London. "Don't get me wrong, Poldie was a grand fellow — oh, not nearly as choice as Wakefield or even Rowland, but in his own way, he cut a swath through Town. The three of them larked about all the time."

"You are the second person who has told me that, and yet I have a hard time imagining Lord Wakefield ever 'larking about,' " she told him.

Rimswell laughed. "I suppose so. He's not the same man who sailed for Spain. But I'll never forget the two of them, standing on the deck of that ship, all done up in their coats and ready to whip Bonaparte into submission. They quite swaggered."

Louisa smiled at this. She couldn't help herself. As the baron described his carefree brother, she swore she could see him, there beside Lord Wakefield.

"So your brother wanted to go?"

"Oh, yes, nothing would stop him," Lord Rimswell told her. "When he bought his commission, my mother was furious, but Poldie was adamant about going. 'If Wakefield can do his bit . . .' he told her. ' 'Sides, I can't let him go alone. He needs me.' He believed that, Poldie did. That Wakefield needed him. Believed it with all his heart."

Then Louisa remembered where she had heard Poldie's name. When Wakefield and Mr. Rowland had argued outside the carriage at Almack's.

Poldie kept his word, the viscount had said. *And died,* Tuck had said with a regret in

414

his voice that had been heart-wrenching to hear.

"Yet Mr. Rowland didn't go to Spain," she said, trying to put the pieces together. She felt as if she was on the verge of discovery. As much as Lady Aveley avowed that Wakefield had come to his beastly state when Melliscent had thrown him over, Louisa had suspected there was something more to the man's pain than a jilted betrothal.

"Tuck was supposed to go, at least as far as I know, but in the end it was just Wakefield and Poldie. I don't know the circumstances, so I can't blame the man, not like Wakefield does."

"Is that why the viscount is so —"

"Like he is?" Rimswell teased. "Yes, I expect that's part of it. Oh, I know there are those who think it was all that Lady Melliscent business, but it wasn't. He was broken before she left. The plain fact is, he came home without Poldie and he can't forgive himself. Can't forgive me for inheriting. Can't forgive Tuck for whatever reasons."

"Oh, heavens, how horrible," Louisa said more to herself. For now it seemed she had found her answers.

But hardly the solution to it. She bit her lip in consternation and looked away.

"Wakefield shouldn't blame himself,"

Lord Rimswell continued. "Poldie made his choice. Wild horses couldn't have stopped him. For Lord knows, my mother tried and she's about as determined as they come."

Louisa couldn't help herself, she laughed a little. "Have you tried to talk to Wakefield?"

"Can anyone?" the baron laughed, shaking his head. "That much about him hasn't changed. He's always been stubborn. But still, I tried when he first came back. Knew he'd taken Poldie's death hard — we all did. Brought over his letters — my brother wrote constantly — and all of them talk about Wakefield — his heroism, his regard for his men. His bravery. Poldie quite idolized him. Knew he would come home and do great things."

They were nearly to Hanover Square, and as they drove into the square, the baron continued. "What is odd is that Poldie never once wrote about coming home. Never wrote of missing our cook, or clean sheets, or the other comforts you'd think a man would miss. Not Poldie. It was as if he knew there would come a moment when the choice would be made for him, and he was resigned to it. Knew his fate and would play the hand before him."

"He must have been an extraordinary man."

"Actually if you'd met him, you might have thought him quite ordinary. Still, I had hoped that if Wakefield would read his letters, he would know that whatever happened there, however Poldie died, it wasn't his fault. At least not in Poldie's eyes."

"That might be exactly what the viscount needs," Louisa agreed.

At this Rimswell snorted. "Yes, but good luck trying to get the fellow to see sense. He had his butler throw me out when I tried to leave them for him. Banned me from the house."

"He's banned me as well," she told him. "But I ignore his bluster."

"I think you rather like it," he said.

"I don't know about that," she said, though a part of her thrilled to think of the passion Lord Wakefield inspired. His bluster, his beastly ways, made his kindness and his passion that much more amazing.

Yet what if those letters could heal some part of Wakefield's wounded heart? Louisa, as ever, was unwilling to leave such a thing unfinished. She had to try. "Might you give them to me? Your brother's letters, that is."

The young baron grinned and pulled the carriage to a stop in front of a house. "I'll

417

do one better. I will give them to you right this very minute."

He dashed into the house and returned a few minutes later with a bundle of worn and tattered letters carefully tied together with a navy blue ribbon.

"I would so love to see Wakefield restored," he told her as he entrusted her with his brother's legacy. For a second she thought he might relent and take them back, so precious were his brother's words, but then he took a deep breath and gathered up the reins. "Yes, for Wakefield. It's what Poldie would have wanted."

After delivering Poldie's letters to Tiploft, who had promised quite faithfully to see that His Lordship would receive them, she hurried home, hoping to find Lavinia already there.

"Has my sister returned?" Louisa asked Brobson as she came in the door.

The poor fellow's brows puzzled together, and she could all but hear the question in his thoughts. *Whichever one is this one?*

She knew the dear old man couldn't tell the two of them apart. "Lavinia —" she prompted.

"No, miss," he told her.

Louisa went up to the room they shared

and took off her pelisse and gloves. She was pulling the pins from her bonnet and putting them away, when she heard the front door opening. She hurried downstairs to find Lavinia just coming in.

Make that swanning in as if she had all of London bowing at the hem of her skirts.

"Where have you been?" Louisa demanded.

This stopped her sister's grand entrance in its tracks.

"Why, at the library. You knew that," Lavinia said, hurrying toward the stairs.

And, most notably, not looking Louisa in the eye. They weren't twins for nothing. Louisa could tell when Lavinia was lying — all it took was one look into those all-too-familiar eyes.

But right now, her sister was doing her best not to look Louisa in the eye.

Which told the entire story.

She drew close to Lavinia. "You were not at the library —"

"Why of course I was."

"You were seen, Lavinia." That was all Louisa had to say for her sister's gaze to come flying up.

"Seen? Whatever does that mean? I went to the library." She was all defiance now, hands fisted to her hips.

"Lord Wakefield saw you getting into Mr. Rowland's carriage, Lavinia."

If she expected her sister to retreat, or even blanch with the knowledge that she'd been caught, Louisa was wrong.

For Lavinia quickly countered. "And how would you know that? Were you over there again? With him? Alone?"

"No!" Louisa managed, taking a tentative step back. This was hardly going as she'd planned. "He and I . . . That is, he offered —"

"Yes, I suppose he did," Lavinia said, now completely on the offensive. "He always seems to be on hand to offer."

Louisa bristled, yet before she could make a hasty retort, Lady Aveley appeared on the landing above them.

"Girls! There you are. I had hoped to find you together. Excellent." She smiled at them and began to come down the stairs.

The sisters shot each other hot glances, vows that this was hardly over.

But it was, in ways that they could never have suspected.

"However was the library?" Lady Aveley asked Lavinia.

Lavinia smirked at Louisa and then turned to face the matron. "Delightful. Though I am afraid I lost track of time — I started reading Homer's *Odyssey* and couldn't put it down. Such a gripping tale."

Louisa groaned. Oh, good heavens, couldn't Mr. Rowland have helped her — at the very least — come up with a more believable lie?

Not that Lady Aveley noticed, for she only smiled brighter, as she came to a stop in the foyer. "I have had a letter from your father." She held up the note, the familiar handwriting giving Louisa a bit of a start. "He has asked Lord Charleton to provide you with a carriage as far as Tunbridge Wells, and he will have your coachman meet you there."

"Leave London?" Lavinia whispered.

"Yes. Your father thought these arrangements would be the most expedient," Lady Aveley told them.

"No!" Lavinia told her, backing away. "I won't go."

"My dear, I know this is —" Lady Aveley reached out to her, but Lavinia jerked back, her face stricken, her eyes already brimming with tears.

"No! I won't go," Lavinia repeated as she backed into the post at the bottom of the stairwell, using it to support herself. "You cannot make me. The Season . . . It isn't fair —"

"Is over. At least for us," Louisa said, with

all certainty. How could she not be anything but certain when she could still feel the sting of the park.

"Not for me. I refuse to go. I won't leave. Not yet," Lavinia told them, before she burst into tears and went running for the refuge of their room.

Louisa made a move to go after her, but Lady Aveley shook her head. "Let her go. She's right. It isn't fair. It never has been."

Her Ladyship turned and walked away, her head held high, but there was a slump to her shoulders that told Louisa all too well that Lavinia wasn't the first lady in London to discover how cruel the *ton* could be.

Pierson had spent the better part of the day and into the evening looking for Tuck . . . And Miss Tempest's sister, to no avail. Nor had he been able to locate any sign of where Ilford might be.

He'd returned to find Tiploft waiting for him. "My lord, I do apologize. He arrived not long ago and took the liberty of —"

His loyal servant needn't say anything further. The viscount knew exactly who he meant.

"Tuck," he said, more as an accusation than a greeting as he entered the dining room. He'd known exactly where to look.

Tuck wouldn't waste his time pacing about a library. Not when supper was set and waiting.

Nor was Tuck simply waiting for his host. From the looks of things, he was well into his third helping, settled in his seat and reading something. Tuck glanced up and grinned. "Where the devil have you been, cuz?"

"Looking for you all over Town," Pierson said as he strolled toward his chair. Then he looked down at the scattering of paper in front of Tuck.

All in a familiar hand. Gooseflesh spread across his arms and it seemed as if every bit of air had been sucked from the room.

"What are those?" he managed, even when he already knew.

"Letters," Tuck replied, setting the one he'd been reading down among the jumble.

Pierson glanced back at the pile, the broad strokes of the pen so much like their author. No, this wasn't right.

He gathered them all up as quickly as he could and carried them to the fireplace.

He quite expected Tuck to rise up and stop him, but all the man did was make a quiet request.

"Please don't. If you bear any bit of love for Poldie, don't do that."

If he bore any love for Poldie? How could Tuck even say such a thing. Poldie had been like a brother to both of them.

He glanced down at the letters and felt the tug to open them. To read Poldie's words, to hear his voice rise out of the ink and paper. Yet that, oh, God, that was too much.

"I can't. I can't read them," he confessed, the words faltering over his tongue.

"Then let me tell you what they say —"

The gooseflesh shivered again and if ever he had felt a moment of fear, it was right now.

Tuck got up and took the letters from him. Sorting through them, he smiled at one and began to read.

Wakefield found us a rare cook. A fellow from Bristol who can make a feast out of a rat. Though he had the nerve to try and convince us it was rabbit.

He couldn't help himself, Pierson laughed. As much at the memory, but also at the way Tuck managed to recreate Poldie's affable charm and thick Northern accent.

Tuck set it down and chose another.

Wakefield saved my life tonight. Pulled me

off my horse and down behind a tree just as the French snipers began picking us off again. I never noticed a thing before that moment, but he did. I'll get him killed before this march ends and I'll never be able to live with myself.

Pierson didn't even realize it, but his eyes had welled up with tears. Suddenly he was back on that road, and right there with Poldie. As usual, his friend had been chatting away about some Spanish bit of muslin, with not a care in the world, as if the French weren't right on their heels and harrying them the entire way to the coast.

"The next day it was him," Pierson said quietly, a sheen misting his vision. "He saved me. But —"

"Yes, indeed," Tuck said, glancing away, as he dashed at his eyes with his sleeve and went back to reading.

You should see him, Brody. Wakefield is magnificent with the men. He can rally them through chaos, and has held our unit together these long days of marching. The people of England will be well served when he takes his seat in the House of Lords.

Pierson's gaze flew up. For wasn't that

425

exactly what Miss Tempest had urged him this very afternoon? Now here was Poldie making the same charge.

"No more," he told Tuck, reaching for that letter.

"No," Tuck said, shaking his head. "This is the last one he wrote and you will listen."

Promise me, that if I don't make it, you'll follow his example. Seek his advice. He's the finest man I've ever known. He deserves every honor, every happiness.

"No more, please, no more," Pierson told him, his heart breaking.

"As you wish. Couldn't read anything more if I wanted to. Those were his last words, Piers. His final wish. That you find happiness."

Pierson shook his head and turned his back to Tuck, trying to sort out of the tangle of emotions rolling inside him.

Demmit, Poldie! How could you?

He glanced over his shoulder at Tuck. His friend had sat down and was stacking the letters back up and tying them with a navy ribbon. "Why did you bring those here?"

Tuck shrugged. "I didn't. They were here on the table when I came in."

"So you —"

"Of course. I knew that hand immediately. Knew you might go into one of your stubborn tempers and burn them." He paused and looked Pierson directly in the eye.

Tuck was right. That's exactly what he would have done.

"Where did they come from?" the viscount asked, taking his chair and collapsing into it.

"According to Tiploft, your Miss Tempest brought them by earlier."

"How the devil —" he began, but he didn't need to finish. He'd sent her off with Brody. And then, if he was still the wagering sort, he'd guess she'd meddled.

Pouring himself a glass of wine, and then, after a second, filling Tuck's glass, he looked up. "Did you know?"

"Yes," Tuck told him, picking up his glass and letting the wine swirl a bit. "Rather, I suspected. He wrote me as well, you know. Never one to hold a grudge, that Poldie."

"Never," Pierson agreed, a shiver lifting an unseen weight from his shoulders. It was as if the burden he'd been carrying since Spain no longer had a place to reside in his life.

He raised his glass, and Tuck followed suit.

"To Poldie," they said together.

And in that moment, a good portion of

the estrangement between them melted away as well. Pierson looked over at Tuck and his friend nodded in silent acknowledgment.

"Yes, well," Tuck said, nodding toward one of the covers on the table. "Do try the roast lamb. Mrs. Petchell has outdone herself."

"You mean there is some left?" Pierson asked.

"Always," Tuck told him. "Always."

And while Pierson filled his plate, Tuck leaned back in his chair, glass in hand.

"Why are you here, Tuck?" he asked.

"Thought I'd save you the trouble of all that driving and come to call. Heard you were looking for me." He paused and shook his head. "Don't like the idea of anyone nosing about my rooms. Simply not done, my good man. Not without an invitation." He sat up and passed the platter of pork chops. "These are most excellent."

"Thank you."

"You're welcome," Tuck said. "Demmit, Piers, what did you think to find?"

"Not what. Whom," Pierson corrected. "What were you doing with Miss Tempest's sister?"

"Which one?" Tuck asked, his eyes alight with mischief. "They are devilishly hard to tell apart."

"It doesn't matter which one," Pierson told him. "Whatever you are about, stop."

"Can't," Tuck told him, cutting into a chop.

"Can't?"

"Won't," the man insisted.

"Now see here," Pierson said. "Charleton will have you staked out on the nearest piling on the Thames and leave you for the tide and the fishes for leading one of Sir Ambrose's daughters astray. And nor would I blame him."

Tuck glanced down at his nails, turning his hand one way, then the other, completely unmoved. "So is that why you went bolting out of your house to go looking for me? Didn't want me stealing a march on you, eh?"

This was a turn in the conversation Pierson hadn't anticipated. It was Tuck's behavior that was in question, not his. Besides . . . "How did you —"

"You need to remind those urchins of yours to remember under whose roof they live before they start gossiping."

Bitty and Bob.

Pierson's hand went to his forehead. Of course.

"Yes," Tuck said, once again grinning and raising a glass in a mock toast. "You can't imagine how well informed those two imps are." He paused for a second, his head tipping a bit as he examined Pierson. "Well, perhaps you can."

"This isn't about me," the viscount told him, sitting up straight and taking control of his own table. He'd deal with Bitty and Bob later. A week of cleaning out the cellar would be just the thing to teach them a lesson on the wisdom of letting their tongues wag in front of Tuck.

Or any visitor.

"Not about you? Oh, but it is," Tuck replied. "What the devil are you doing, Piers, kicking up a fuss to find Ilford? You've gone and sent that fox to ground what with all your stomping and saber rattling in all the clubs and his dreary haunts."

Pierson ground his teeth together rather than admit that Tuck might be right.

Nor was the man finished. Tuck leaned forward. "Going after Ilford all by yourself? *Tsk, tsk, tsk.* Badly done."

He might have felt chastened before, but now his old familiar ire caught a fresh wind. "You don't think I could?"

Tuck held up both hands. "Oh, I know you could. That's the problem." He reached for his napkin and settled it on the table, then pushed his empty plate forward. "Once you found him, then what were you going to do? Kill him?" He shook his head. "Then once you'd put him to bed with a shovel, what do you think would happen?"

Pierson took a steadying breath. *Demmit.*

When had Tuck gotten so sensible? The old Tuck would have helped him drag Ilford down to the river and toss him into the Thames without a second thought. Probably been the one to remember to carry along a few rocks for the marquess's pockets.

Worse, Tuck had grown far more than just sensible. He'd gained a measure of wisdom that left Pierson staggered.

"You have a chance here, Piers." Tuck needn't say what that chance was.

The viscount knew. Miss Tempest. *His* Miss Tempest.

"What are you thinking? Letting the likes of Ilford ruin it for you?"

His old friend's words were hitting far too close to home. "There is no chance there. She's bound for the country —"

Tuck merely laughed. "Don't try some bouncer on me. You went racing out of this house today because you love that gel."

"I hardly raced."

"Yes, well, I got my information from those brats of yours."

"They are not mine."

"Tell them that," Tuck replied, smiling as he poured himself another glass of wine. "As for the other Miss Tempest, you have to trust me when I say I have the chit's best interests at heart. You'll see."

"I doubt it. Besides, they must leave town now, Tuck. There is no other way of it," Pierson said.

"Bother that," Tuck declared. "I'll make those two the talk of the Town before the Season is done."

"I think Ilford already managed that."

"He can go to the devil."

Now it was Pierson's turn to laugh. "You told me I couldn't kill him."

"So I did," Tuck admitted. "Sometimes I forget myself."

Just then there was a scratch at the door, followed by Tiploft's entrance. He came in carrying a tray and wearing a somber expression. "You are summoned to Lord Charleton's."

Pierson glanced over at Tuck. "Told you. You're in the suds now. Charleton will cut off your quarterlies, if not your —"

"My lord," Tiploft said in an uncharacteristic interruption. "It isn't Mr. Rowland."

He looked up at his butler. "Pardon?"

"It isn't Mr. Rowland who is summoned

next door," Tiploft told him. "You are, my
lord."

CHAPTER 16

Sometime after supper, Louisa followed a maid down the stairs to Lord Charleton's study.

"His Lordship said you were to meet him in there," the girl said, offering a tremulous smile before beating a hasty retreat.

As bad as all that, Louisa mused as she drew in a deep breath and went to the door.

The room was cast in ominous shadows, with only a solitary candle burning on the desk, while a soft glow radiated off the coals in the grate.

The large winged chair the baron favored was turned toward the fireplace and all she could see of him was his hand curled around the arm of the chair.

Taking another deep breath, Louisa stepped into the room and launched in. "I fear I've failed you, my lord. I did my best to help your nephew, but I've only made matters worse for him."

To her never-ending regret. Dragging him into society's glare. Into the middle of her scandalous ruin.

How he must detest her.

As well he should.

As for Lord Charleton, he said nothing. Just sat there with his back to her.

His silence gave Louisa the fidgets. Her father was prone to such moody displays when he was displeased.

What was it Papa always said? Something about the truth.

"I had hoped Lord Wakefield might find a measure of happiness in . . ."

My kiss. In holding me in his arms. As I found with him.

Instead, she continued, "In having his house in order. At the very least, he approves of Mrs. Petchell. Or so I believe." Though he hadn't at first. She couldn't help herself, she smiled at the memory of him blustering across his yard all determined to send the woman packing until a pair of orphans had tugged at his heart. "It's why I fell in love with him," she said aloud without thinking.

And once she said the words, she pressed her lips together and wished them back.

But did she really? Really want to take that declaration back?

She loved the viscount.

"Everyone calls him beastly and rude and uncivil, and he is all those things —"

The hand on the arm of the chair tightened its grasp until his knuckles practically glowed white.

Well, Lord Charleton could hardly be insulted by the truth. He'd said as much himself about his nephew.

"Yet Lord Wakefield is one of the most honorable men I've ever met. He's also — and please don't laugh — excessively kindhearted."

She smiled to herself, recalling Bob's excitement the other day to learn that he was to go to school.

Himself insists. Says I'm as bright as a copper. Me, miss! Me!

"How could I but help to fall in love with him?"

Still the baron said nothing.

"I know it is said that his heart was broken when his betrothed cried off and left him, but I don't think that is the matter at all. I think it is the loss of someone else entirely that plagues him still. There is no replacing such a hole in one's heart, but surely one day he will learn to live with it. I had rather hoped I might —"

Louisa had edged forward as she spoke

and now stood at the edge of the candle-light. Just beyond lay the shadows in which Lord Charleton sat.

"Please, my lord, say something," she said, as she came around the chair.

Yet her plea hadn't been made to Lord Charleton, but another.

For there sat Wakefield. Ensconced in Charleton's chair with Hannibal in his lap.

And tears in his eyes.

"What did my uncle ask you to do, Louisa?"

For once, the lady was without words. She gaped at him, but he could see her thoughts racing, the questions running through her shock at finding not Charleton, but him.

"What did Charleton ask you to do?" he repeated, this time standing up.

Hannibal yowled and complained to be abandoned so abruptly, and showed his displeasure, giving his half a tail a lofty wave and stalking out the door. *If you cannot give me the attention I deserve . . .*

Wakefield stopped in front of Miss Tempest and with one finger tipped her chin up so she looked at him. "What did he ask?"

"To keep up what I was doing," she whispered.

"Which was?" His hand curled beneath

her chin, gently caressing her.

"Annoying you, I suppose," she told him, her gaze never wavering from his. "You had ordered me out of your house and he —"

Wakefield could see where this was going. So she'd taken to the gardens.

And drawn him out like a moth to a flame.

As no one else could.

That was the part that left him a bit gobsmacked. Just as Tuck had earlier. As Poldie's letters had. None of which he would have gained without her. Without her dogged interference.

Her love.

There it is. That is happiness. Damn Ilford. To hell with the Lady Kipps of the world. Love this woman. It is all she needs.

All you need.

Her. Miss Tempest. This busybody, chatty miss with her heart on her sleeve.

Even now, he could see her mind at work, the bit of panic in her eye. *Did he hear what I said?*

"Yes, I heard you," he told her softly. "You love me."

"I — I — I didn't realize," she began, her gaze fluttering toward the chair. "That is. You weren't being very honorable by not announcing —" she protested, pushing him back with her hands on his chest.

He caught hold of her wrists and held her there. "By not announcing myself? And look at what I would have missed. Besides, you said I was honorable. And kindhearted. Whatever are you doing, telling such Banbury tales?"

"They are both true," she shot back, this time notching up her chin on her own, once again defiant.

"Beg to differ," he told her, drawing her close, winding one arm about her waist so he could hold her, and the other hand began picking at those dreadful pins in her hair. "If I were honorable, I wouldn't be doing this."

Whyever would a woman with such a gorgeous head of hair want to pin it up in some ugly knot? So he set those silken strands of mahogany free, one pin at a time.

"You shouldn't," she whispered as her hair began to fall about her shoulders. Chiding him because she should, not because she wanted him to stop.

Because each time he pulled a pin from her hair, he could feel a sigh slip from her, feel her body ease closer to him, sense the tremble of her heart.

"I'm ever so glad you love me," he told her.

"Why is that?" Her words were a whisper

of hope.

Pierson leaned closer and began nibbling on her neck, letting his lips and tongue trace over her skin. She was soft and supple and wavering within his arms. "Because I find myself in quite the same state," he confessed.

Her lashes fluttered open as he made his confession. "You do?"

How could he not fall in love with her? *La Tempesta* with her meddling ways and orderly closets and kisses that tasted of strawberries and desire.

A woman who looked at him and saw straight to his heart.

But his silence was hardly what she wanted. "Do say something."

"There is nothing more to say," he told her as he went to the door.

"Please don't go," she whispered, urgency in every word.

"I'm not," he told her as he got to the door. And then made the decision that opened his heart.

By closing one more door.

And throwing the latch shut.

"Where is Louisa?"

The question gave Charleton a start. He spun around and found Amy coming down the steps.

Never Lady Aveley to him. She would always be Amy in his mind.

"Ssshh!" he warned, and took her by the arm and led her up to the first landing. "You'll ruin everything."

"Ruin?" Amy's brows arched with alarm.

Probably not the best word to use in front of a matron charged with the care of two young ladies.

"Where is Louisa, Charleton?" This time her words were an insistent demand, all starched and proper.

"Which one is Louisa?" he teased, blocking her path.

"Don't play coy with me," she shot back, trying to look over his shoulder at whatever was to be found in the foyer and beyond.

He supposed it was the shadowy beyond that had her at sixes and sevens.

"I was just in their room and Lavinia informed me that you requested Louisa in your study. And now I find you here lurking about —"

"I hardly lurk—"

"Lurking, I say. You haven't looked so guilty of something since you spent a fortnight catching frogs to let loose at Lady Duddington's ball. What are you doing, Charleton?"

"I've arranged —"

Downstairs, the sound of boots crossing the floor could be heard, then the slam of the study door as it closed, followed by the very distinct sound of a latch being thrown.

Amy's mouth fell open and her face drained of color. "Was that —"

"Wakefield?" the baron nodded. "It was, indeed."

"Don't tell me that Louisa is —"

"In there?" He glanced over his shoulder at the closed door and grinned. "I couldn't say. Not when you've asked me not to."

"Oh, what have you done? This is highly improper!" Amy went to move around him, and he caught hold of her arm and held her fast.

"I certainly hope so," Charleton told her. It was such a small thing — to take hold of her. But suddenly, everything that had happened in the last fortnight had boiled down to this choice.

To live in the past, or look forward once more.

Oh, it hadn't been easy to reach this place — ever since his house had been flung open, it had been nothing but torment. Girlish laughter ringing through the halls. The doorbell being pulled from morning to night with invitations and notes.

And perfume! The house seemed to breathe with it.

All painful reminders of the life, of the love, he'd lost.

And then had come Almack's and the horrible ruin of that evening. He'd awakened the next morning and realized that he'd failed these girls — horribly. Against Izzy's wishes, against everything she'd desired.

Oh, Isobel, what would you make of me now? It was then that he'd finally unlocked the drawer where he'd hidden her letter.

And for some time he'd merely run his fingers over the familiar script, so curved and beautiful.

As she'd been.

Eventually, he'd taken a deep breath, and with trembling fingers opened her missive.

The first words had been a shocking reminder of who his wife had been. While he preferred to remember her soft smiles and kind words, he had forgotten why she had enchanted him in the first place. Her very forthright manner.

I am gone, Charleton. Forevermore.

That statement, clearly all Isobel, had been like losing her all over again.

He didn't know how long he'd stared

blankly at those words, trapped in the same state of denial he'd been in for nearly two years.

She wasn't gone. Just lost. Yet there were her words, so utterly final.

For some reason, he finally laughed. Oh, Isobel. So very practical. She would have loved Louisa Tempest.

And it seemed she had, for her god-daughters were foremost in her thoughts.

Help them find love, Charleton, as I found my heart with you. That is the greatest gift you could ever pass along in this world — the continuation of love.

"Oh, Izzy, I've failed you. I've failed them," he told her.

Why had he been so demmed stubborn? Then he continued to read, instructions she'd underlined, as if she knew he would do his utmost to admire her penmanship and ignore their message.

Your heart was meant for love, Charleton. Please, my dearest, give it to another, for I can no longer share it with you. And a heart that is not shared with others, be-loved by another, only withers and dies. Laugh with another. Love another. Take her to your bed. Make her your wife. You were never meant to marry me, and yet you did against everyone's wishes.

Now surprise them all again, and marry anew.

While he had scoffed at the very notion of marrying again when he'd read the words the first time, now it was another line that haunted him as he dragged himself back into the present.

You were never meant to marry me . . .

He hadn't been. His future had been pledged to another since childhood.

That is until Isobel had come dancing into his path.

But it wasn't Isobel he held at the moment, but Amy. His childhood companion. The girl next door.

"Charleton, you must go in there and stop this," she was saying.

He glanced over his shoulder at the closed study door. "Why?"

"Why? Because Wakefield is in there with Louisa. Alone."

"I think her bloody cat is in there."

As if on cue, Hannibal came around the corner and began scratching the post at the bottom of the stairs.

When the beast finished, he glanced up at

them with an expression that said, *What?*

"This is ruinous," Amy persisted.

"How else are things to move along if they aren't alone?"

"Move along?" The lady appeared horrified. "This is not the way these things are done, Charleton!"

"George," he told her. "You used to call me George."

Beneath his fingers, she quailed and then suddenly pulled her arm free of his, as if she'd just realized that he was holding her.

Wherever was the indomitable, impossible, Miss Amy Strathaven he'd once known?

The one who had helped him catch those frogs and carry them across three fields to get them into Lady Duddington's ballroom just as the first dance was being called.

His scandalous, devilish Amy.

He glanced over at her and saw her as he hadn't in years. She looked much as she had that night all those years ago, her hair done in a simple braid, wearing nothing more than a plain gown.

No ornaments, no pots of paint for Amy. No unnecessary frippery. Just her fair cheeks and her bright eyes.

And suddenly his body tightened. His breath stilled.

Now surprise them all again . . .

"I will not condone this," Amy declared, going to push past him and in desperation, Charleton did the only thing he could think of to stop her.

Something he hadn't done to her in years. He caught her in his arms and pulled her close.

Her startled gaze flew up to meet his. It was a terrifying moment of indecision. For both of them.

And it was then he realized how much he had changed in the past fortnight. How much he had lost in the last two years. And he knew he wasn't about to let that continue one moment longer.

So he pulled Amy closer and bent his head to capture her lips.

Louisa watched the viscount stalk back across the room.

She counted every step. For each one brought him closer. Brought him back so she could find herself in his arms, feel his lips on hers.

She had yet to tell him they were leaving. That she and Lavinia were being sent home, but she didn't want to think of such things.

Right now, right this very moment, all she desired was to be kissed.

When his arms folded around her, Louisa went quite willingly, her hands splaying out across his chest — hard and muscled — and then his lips trapped hers and he was kissing her again, his tongue running over hers. Each swipe, each teasing exploration left her hungry, wanting so much more.

She wanted to touch him. Her hands slid boldly under his jacket and she pushed it over and off his shoulders. In an instant he'd finished the job, shrugging it off and sending it flying over the back of the chair.

Undoing the buttons of his waistcoat, her fingers caught hold of his shirt and tugged it from his breeches. Then holding her breath, she ran them over his bare skin. Up his chest, over the crisp dark hair there.

It was heady and delicious all at the same time.

His hand caught hold of the hem of her gown, pulling it up, until his fingers could cup her buttocks and tugged her up and against him, where he was long and hard. He held her there and she found herself moving against him, for it was like having his fingers there, easing this madness that was tightening inside her.

Her hands went to work, opening the buttons at the front of his breeches, tugging at the stubborn ones until they came open and brazenly she slid her hand inside — where she immediately found what she had sought.

His manhood. Hard and ready for her. She drew it out — not that he needed much coaxing — and ran her fingers down the entire length, and if it were possible, he grew harder and longer, filling her hand until he seemed ready to burst with need.

The viscount made a sort of strangled sound, and she continued stroking him, opening her mouth to him so he could kiss her deeply, plunging his tongue into her mouth as she stroked his length.

Mesmerized by the length, the soft rounded head, the veins beneath her fingertips, Louisa sank to her knees.

The advantage of having spent so much time in Lady Essex's house was that it had gained her access to Her Ladyship's library, including the handful of books on the top shelf.

French books. *With prints.*

She might not have known the foreign words, but pictures . . . Well, pictures were hard to mistake.

And one had always fascinated her. Perplexed her. Could this be pleasurable? She put her mouth over the rounded end of his manhood and sucked him inside her.

"Oh, God!" he gasped. "Oh, damnation."

His hips rose and thrust at her, and Louisa continued to run her tongue over him, cupping his balls in her hand, licking him as he continued to gasp and groan above her and then it was for him as it had been for her in the carriage.

At least she assumed so, for suddenly he began to gasp, his eyes closed and his body thrust forward, and he reached his climax. She reeled back a bit as his seed shot from him. She continued to stroke him until he dropped to the carpet in front of her, kneeling before her.

"Devilish minx, you quite stole my march," he teased, and then pushed her back on the carpet, so he covered her, their mouths once again fused and his tongue tormenting her.

Not just his kiss, his touch. For he explored her eagerly, teasing her nipples into taut tips, then lower, where he found the curls between her legs — without hesitating, she opened herself to him.

She wanted his touch, wanted him to find that spot where her need left her begging and hungry. Anxious and half mad.

And when he touched her, teased her open, slid his finger over the wetness and inside her, her hips arched up, welcoming his touch.

"Oooh," she gasped, as his finger slid over her again, swirling in a circle and then pressing down right where it was the tightest and vibrating against her until she was nearly at her peak. "Please —"

Yet he stopped and when she wrenched her eyes open, ready to protest — most vehemently — she found him moving down her, exploring with his mouth the spots his fingers had already ignited. Her neck, her shoulders, a heated trail over her breasts.

Her protests died quickly as a blaze of desires ignited inside her. She shivered in a heavenly state of delirium — so close to her completion and yet held there on the pinnacle by this master of seduction.

Cupping her breast in his hand, he drew her nipple into his mouth and Louisa nearly cried out to be suckled so. One hand teased her cleft, the other held her breast so he could suck at her — it was all too much.

Well, not *too* much . . .

For here he was about to take her to that passionate brink and she reached upward, her hips rising, her breath catching as she dared not even exhale . . .

Yet he stopped, and let himself go farther down, until his lips blew a hot, steamy kiss over her sex, leaving her gasping, and then it was his tongue on her, lapping at her, drawing her into his mouth and sucking at her sex.

He'd slid his fingers inside her again, easing their way in, but it was his mouth, teasing over her, that left her gasping for air, reaching upward, nearly at that brink.

And yet . . . He paused, just before she thought she was going to find her release. Oh, the very devil, she thought as she found him grinning wickedly at her.

Oh, yes, she could see that "stealing his march" was a most grievous sin indeed. He was paying her back. Torturing her with seduction. Leaving her in this limbo of desire and need.

She'd have to remember to steal his march as often as she might . . .

If there ever is another chance . . . something deep and sensible inside her protested.

I don't care. Let me have this night.

She reached for Lord Wakefield, her hands guiding him upward, until his mouth claimed hers again in a long, slow kiss.

"Make love to me, my lord," she whispered.

Make love to her?

How could he not? Pierson was hard again, his senses filled with her — her touch, her scent, her very taste. She was strawberries and fire and desire, and he wanted nothing more than to be inside her, to watch her face as she came to her crisis.

To join her in that moment.

He knew he was breaking every rule. He was ruining a girl under his uncle's protection. Exactly the same outrage he'd been railing on Tuck against.

One might argue he'd already done that — ruined Miss Tempest — but this time, to do this, had more permanent implications.

To do this meant everything.

And when Pierson looked into Louisa's eyes, he saw just that. Everything.

His future, his heart, his love.

How could he not make love to her tonight, when he planned to do so every night until the stars stopped shining?

She was his, forevermore.

Sometime in the wee hours before dawn, Louisa woke up. She lay curled up in a ball, much as Hannibal might, on the settee in Lord Charleton's study.

After a few moments of confusion, the preceding hours flashed through her thoughts.

Lord Wakefield closing the door, locking them in.

His kiss.

His touch.

How he'd brought her to . . . Louisa shivered with the memory of how he'd finally carried her to that blissful state.

In his arms, before the fireplace. She glanced over at the spot on the carpet.

Where after she'd made him promise, he'd covered her body with his and made love to her. Entering her slowly and carefully, breaching her maidenhood, and then with kisses and caresses, and his manhood filling her, stroking her, until she'd breathlessly reached her pinnacle, wave after wave of pleasure washing over her. And just as quickly, Pierson had found his release.

"Is Louisa your given name or a nickname?" *he murmured in her ear, as he once again nuzzled at that spot behind her ear.*

Oh, bother! Did he know what his lips did to her?

He kissed that spot yet again. Yes, apparently he did.

"No, my given name is Louisa."

"Miss Louisa Tempest," he repeated, grinning. "Most excellent."

"How so?" she couldn't resist asking, even as he began kissing her in another spot, this one a bit lower.

"Because now there will be no mistake of what name I need to have the archbishop put

on the Special License —"

After that, the rest of the night had rather turned into a blur of pleasure and passion.

What had he said? Louisa sat bolt upright. He had said Special License, hadn't he?

Which meant . . . Dear heavens, Lord Wakefield had proposed!

Well, not precisely, she realized. More like made up his mind and told her.

She didn't know whether to be annoyed at his presumption or overjoyed. Then she glanced down and saw something lying on the carpet that she hadn't noticed before.

Getting up, she tiptoed over to that place, and found a single rose lying where he'd made his proposal of sorts.

Louisa picked it up and smiled. And then made her way upstairs to her bed to dream of the nights to come.

CHAPTER 17

Bright morning light nudged Louisa awake. At first she blinked and then rolled away from the window, covering her head with a pillow.

Dear heavens, when had the sun started rising so early?

The unfamiliar ache between her legs wrenched her fully awake.

Oh, yes. She remembered the previous night with as much clarity as the sunshine streaming into the bedchamber she shared with her sister.

Lavinia?

Louisa swiveled in the direction of her sister's bed and found it empty. To her everlasting relief.

However was she to face Lavinia this morning?

Well, funny thing, Vivi, Lord Wakefield ruined me last night, but be assured he means to marry me.

Stopping herself right there, she had to ask, he did, didn't he?

She turned over her pillow and there was the rose that had been his parting gift.

His promise.

Yet the sight of Wakefield's — no, Pierson's — rose didn't cheer her as it ought. Instead she saw only Lavinia's dashed hopes for marriage.

While, she — Louisa — the one who hadn't wanted to get married was . . .

Oh, bother, she certainly couldn't say anything until she was certain of the viscount's intentions.

It was all rather like his linen closet, still undone.

So she got herself dressed and did her morning ablutions even though she suspected it was closer to afternoon.

Taking a deep breath, she went downstairs and found Bitty dashing around a corner from the back stairs.

"Miss! Oh, miss!" she called out. "Mr. Tiploft sent me. You must come at once. Quickly." Bitty caught hold of her hand and tugged at her.

"What is it, Bitty?" Louisa asked. "Is something wrong with the viscount?"

"It will be if you don't come right away."

Louisa, ever so worried, hurried along,

though she still found herself being towed — Bitty pulling at her like a draft horse with its barn in sight.

"Hurry, miss," the girl urged as they dashed up the steps.

When they got into the foyer, Clarks, the new footman was waiting. He nodded toward the parlor opposite the viscount's study. "In there."

The door was partially open, so Louisa took a deep breath and walked in.

And to her horror, the sole occupant of the room wasn't Lord Wakefield.

But Lady Blaxhall. Melliscent.

"Well, well," the lady said, her delicate brows arching with a high-winged tip. She was gowned in a bright lavender silk that shimmered in the light, a shade that could barely be called half mourning, but which suited the lady.

And Louisa assumed Lady Blaxhall never wore a color that didn't suit her perfectly, no matter the circumstances.

"What do we have here?" Melliscent came strolling forward, examining Louisa as one might survey Hannibal's latest offering. "Miss Tempest, isn't it?"

"Yes, Your Ladyship," Louisa replied, making a belated but polite curtsy.

"Aren't you quaint," the lady said as she

circled around Louisa.

Louisa moved as well, a niggle of fear running down her spine that the very notion of turning her back on this woman would be dangerous.

"I suppose that brat came and fetched you," she was saying.

"Bitty isn't —"

"Don't correct me," Lady Blaxhall told her, dismissing any other objection with a fluttering wave of her gloved hand as she moved back to the center of the room. "Though I can't imagine why that urchin would think you could be of help, that is unless —" The lady paused her catlike movements and stilled. "She thinks Piers —" But like her dismissal of Bitty, she laughed at whatever notion she'd considered. "How ridiculous."

And this time when the lady turned toward her, her gown trailing behind her like a swirling cloud of subtle fury, she pinned a narrow glance on Louisa.

So this is how Hannibal's prey feels, Louisa mused, trying to summon every bit of courage she possessed. But in the face of this woman's poise, her unquestionable beauty and her lofty place in society, Louisa's valor wavered.

Melliscent's scathing glance seemed to ask

one mocking question.

Whyever would he prefer you?

She must have answered her own silent question because her lips turned slightly in a smile and she drew closer, head tipped as she looked Louisa over. "You've let him, haven't you?"

It was the last question Louisa would have ever expected. However could the lady have known? "I — I — I hardly think —"

Melliscent shrugged off her feeble protest. "So like your mother. Or so I am told. Unfortunate." She strolled over toward the window where the sunlight silhouetted her figure.

Good heavens, this woman could show to every advantage no matter the situation, Louisa thought.

Melliscent sniffed at the air, as if she suddenly found it most unpleasant. "Weren't there any dancing masters available, my dear?"

It was as if the lady had slapped her across the face. It would have been kinder.

But it had the unexpected effect of snapping Louisa out of her quiescence. "How dare you!"

"I dare because I am a lady," Melliscent shot back. "And how unfortunate for Piers that he had to be entangled by your poor breeding."

Poor breeding, indeed. The lady should see herself in the mirror right now — for her icy beauty was not well served by this ugly assault.

"He doesn't love you," Louisa told her. "He never has."

The lady laughed, and again made another dismissive wave. "Do you think I care for such things? What a little fool you are."

"He won't have you —"

"Because he's had you? Is that how you think it works?"

"But he —" Louisa began, her bravado crumbling. She'd been about to tell the lady in no uncertain terms that the viscount loved her, but she couldn't.

For Wakefield had never said as much.

Something Melliscent must have sensed, for the lady smiled. "Has he told you he loves you?"

"Not in so many words —" she said, but even to her own ears the statement was hardly a foundation.

"Yes, not in words," Melliscent replied. "I imagine he didn't use words to convince you to give yourself to him either." She laughed again, and this time it was tinged in a cruelty that cut through the rest of Louisa's confidence.

He did love her. He must. He'd asked her to marry him.

Hadn't he? Louisa took a step back and bumped into the doorjamb.

Her face must have revealed much of her confusion, for Melliscent was back on the attack.

If the lady had been missing an eye and most of one ear, one might have thought her Hannibal's closest relation.

"And if there is a child, Miss Tempest, please don't come back here. Men deplore such desperate tactics. You'll have to go find someone as easily duped as your supposed father."

Supposed father? Whatever was she saying?

Then it hit Louisa exactly what the lady was suggesting — that she and Lavinia were by-blows just like any child she might be carrying.

A child? Her hand went to her belly, and she looked up, only to find Melliscent's hard, mocking smile was too much to bear.

"Didn't that occur to you? How unfortunate," Melliscent said, sounding anything but sympathetic. "He'll marry me, my dear. For the simple reason that I am good *ton,* and you are not."

"No," she whispered.

"I do thank you though," Melliscent continued, "for prodding him back into Society. He was utterly useless to me before. But now your work and your place here is finished. I won't have the stain of your bloodlines tainting what is mine."

Tears welled in Louisa's eyes, and botheration, there was no way she was going to turn into a watering pot in front of this evil woman.

So she turned and fled, past Bitty and Clarks, and even Mr. Tiploft.

"Miss Tempest?" the butler asked, apparently quite surprised to see her.

So he hadn't sent for her. Louisa paused and looked at a guilt-faced Bitty, who stood there, eyes wide with horror and her little hand stuffed in her mouth.

"Oh, miss . . . I only thought that —" Bitty began, but Louisa resumed her flight — out the door and down the stairs, blindly dashing with only one thought — to reach the sanctuary of her room.

And then back to Kempton as quickly as she could find a coach.

Pierson awoke to the sound of the bell downstairs, and the yowl of Hannibal outside his room.

Where once neither would have been a

welcome beginning to his day, now he found himself smiling.

Even when he spied the half-eaten rodent Miss Tempest's — no, make that Louisa's — cat had brought with him.

"Thank you, Hannibal," he told the cat as he let the beast in. "But I am famished for something else."

My bride.

Even though he'd barely had any sleep, it was as if he'd finally gotten the respite he'd been seeking for years.

Oh, his leg still ached and he still had to reach for his cane, but what he noticed far more was how bright and persistent a sliver of sunshine could be when it sought a way into the darkness.

Like a certain lady he knew.

He grinned as he shrugged on his breeches and a shirt, along with his jacket, and went downstairs, for he'd heard the front door open a second time and couldn't help wondering what had brought such a parade to his doorstep.

Besides, he had a visit to make to the archbishop's office, and then pay a call to his uncle and his solicitor. And a jeweler as well.

He grinned again. Perhaps he'd change that order around and call on Charleton first, where perhaps he could steal a kiss from a certain lady.

When he got to the landing on the stairs, he could have sworn he saw the last bit of a skirt dashing down his steps, but it was the shocked and sad expressions on the faces of his staff that alarmed him more.

"What the devil is going on?" he asked.

"My lord —" Tiploft began.

But before his butler could continue, another voice chimed in.

"Piers, darling, there you are. Oh, dear, I see I have called too early. You look a wreck."

Melliscent.

He turned around slowly. "What are you doing here?"

"Why calling on you, of course," she said, coming forward and linking her arm into his. She went to pull him toward the parlor, seeking privacy, but he refused to budge.

"What do you want, Lady Blaxhall? I have some rather pressing business today that needs my immediate attention."

"Lady Blaxhall? How foolishly formal you are being. Dearest, you can call me Melliscent again. I'm free. Free to be yours all over again. As for your business matters, I doubt there is anything more worthy of your attention than me," she purred.

How he had once loved the sound of her

voice, how it stroked a man's sense of self-importance, how it had once made his best intentions, his good sense, take flight.

She was still pulling on his arm, still tugging at him to come with her, this time a little more insistently, and now, with his eyes wide open, he found her attempts cloying and distasteful.

Very distasteful.

Pierson shook her hand off his arm. "Lady Blaxhall, you seem to be under the impression that I want your attentions. I do not."

"That isn't what Lord Ilford —"

"Ilford? What has he to do with this?"

"He told me last night that if I was to call on you, you'd be more than happy to see me — that your disastrous attentions on that unworthy girl —"

"You mean Miss Tempest —"

"Is that her name? Such an insignificant creature. Hardly fit for —"

"I mean to marry her," Pierson told her.

"Oh, Piers, how you jest," Melliscent laughed, until the lady realized no one else was sharing in her mirth. "You cannot — that is, how could you?"

"Because I love her."

"Love her? She's naught but the —"

This time Pierson caught hold of her arm. "Say another word against the lady, and I shall throw you out the door myself."

"But . . . But . . ."

He glanced up at the footman. "Clarks, the door please."

The man grinned as he opened it. Wide.

Melliscent's beautiful face contorted into a horrible rage. "How dare you!" she burst out, shaking off his grasp. "You will discover the truth about that dreadful little schemer. Believe me." She sniffed and straightened up, chin high in the air. "And when you do, and you come crawling and begging back to me, do not think I will give you an easy reception."

With that, the lady proceeded to sweep from the foyer, nearly plowing over Bitty.

Tiploft caught the child and set her to rights. "My lord, I fear Her Ladyship —"

"I don't blame you, Tiploft, for letting her in. She's an overbearing . . ." He was about to say "bitch," but thought better of it in front of Bitty, so he finished by saying, ". . . marchioness. Though from now on, she isn't welcome."

"Yes, my lord. However, I think you should know —"

"Whatever it is, my good man, it can wait," Pierson told him. "I need to bathe and have my best coat brushed and ready. I need to call on my uncle."

"I think you might want to make that call sooner —" Tiploft began.

"Sooner? Oh, no. That would hardly be prudent." Pierson spared a glance in the mirror on the wall and flinched a little at the sight before him. "Lady Blaxhall was right about one thing, I'm hardly presentable this morning and I can't go over to Charleton's and ask for Miss Tempest's hand in marriage looking like a beggar."

"But the little miss, my lord —" Bitty piped up.

"What about her?" Pierson asked.

Tiploft answered. "As I have been trying to tell you, Miss Tempest was here. And she had what I believe was a rather unpleasant encounter with Lady Blaxhall."

"Louisa was here?" Pierson glanced toward the door. "Why didn't you tell me?"

"I've been trying, my lord," Tiploft said.

"Dear God, I can't even imagine what that bitch said to her," he sputtered, forgetting Bitty's innocent ears.

"I can," Clarks said, with a low whistle.

Everyone ignored him.

Pierson hurried toward the front door, but when he got to it, he could see a carriage still out front.

Melliscent.

Most likely waiting for him to come running after her.

So he spun around and headed for the dining room and the French doors that led into the gardens, his fury at Melliscent only outpaced by his concern for Louisa.

Yet to his relief, he spied her as he came through the doorway in the garden wall.

She was sitting on the bench with her back to him. Relief washed through him at the sight of her.

"Louisa?"

She seemed to flinch, then as she began to turn toward him his heart clenched slightly in expectation of that moment when she would look at him.

Their gazes would meet, and she'd smile, a quiet greeting full of love meant only for him.

It was such a staggering thing.

Louisa loved him. And he her.

Yet when the lady in the garden turned around, the face that greeted him was so very familiar, from the pert red lips to the bright blue eyes, to the rich mahogany hair, piled artfully atop her head, but the light in her eyes was all wrong.

And there was no smile.

"My lord?"

"You aren't her." He took two steps closer — and realized everything was wrong.

Oh, this lady was identical to his love, but she wasn't Louisa.

"Lord Wakefield," the girl said, nodding slightly and making a quick curtsy. "I must commend you, not many can make the distinction between me and my sister so handily." Her lips curved into a smile that was so very different from Louisa's. "I can only surmise that you love my sister very much to be able to tell us apart at first glance."

"Where is she?" he asked, looking around Charleton's neatly kept garden. "Where is your sister?"

"Over at your house, I imagine," she said quickly, then her brow furrowed. "Isn't she?"

He shook his head.

"Lavinia! There you are," came a greeting from the mews. "Prompt and eager to begin our . . ." His words trailed off as the man came the rest of the way through the gate and spied Pierson standing there.

"Tuck," the viscount said in greeting.

When he looked over at Miss Tempest, he found the girl had blushed a deep shade of red.

Whatever were these two doing in cahoots?

"You were saying you wanted to see my sister?" Lavinia asked, shaking out her skirt and not looking at Tuck. "I can go get her," she added, nodding toward Charleton's house.

"Yes, if you would, please." Pierson decided whatever Lavinia Tempest and Tuck were doing, he'd get to bottom of it once he'd found Louisa. Still, when Lavinia Tempest hurried inside the house, Pierson turned immediately to his friend. "Rather odd, you being here, Tuck."

"A happy coincidence," Charleton's heir offered, rocking on his boot heels, and watching the door as if he, rather than Pierson, were waiting for Louisa

"Care to enlighten me as to how this 'happy coincidence' came to be?"

"Another story for another time," his friend told him as the garden door opened and out came the sisters, Lavinia towing her twin. Even from here, Pierson could see that Louisa had been crying.

Damn Melliscent for her interference, he thought as he rushed to capture Louisa in his arms.

"Yes, well, our work is done here, puss," Tuck was saying, as he caught hold of Lavinia's hand and led her out toward the mews.

Pierson took one glance at the pair and thought he ought to protest, but one snuffled mew from Louisa, and Tuck and his folly were forgotten.

"Whatever Lady Blaxhall said, it was a lie," he told her, holding Louisa out so he could push the wayward strands of hair from her face.

Her eyes were red-rimmed, and her nose a bit runny.

He thought her the most beautiful creature ever. But he also dug into his pocket and found her a handkerchief.

She blew into it noisily. "Oh, if only what she said was a lie. I am not good enough for you."

"Good enough? What utter rubbish! You are my heart. My perfect match."

"You're just being kind," she sniffled.

Pierson laughed, loud and hard. "Louisa Tempest, have you ever known me to be kind?"

Her eyes flickered for a moment, for she was about to argue the matter, but then she too saw the humor in all of it and laughed as well.

"Foolish girl," he told her, retrieving his handkerchief from her grasp and making quick work of removing the smattering of tears on her cheeks.

"But she said —"

His brows arched up. "Not another word

on the subject —"

"But —" she persisted.

He leaned over and kissed her. Soundly and thoroughly. Until she couldn't make a sensible retort. "There. That's much better," he teased. "Now I need your advice on a matter of propriety —"

"Me?"

"Of course. What is the proper amount of time for a gentleman to call upon a lady after he's ravished her? Two or three days?"

"That depends on the gentleman," she replied. "In any case, you are decidedly overdue."

"I said days, not hours," he teased.

"Yes, I suppose you did," she replied, her nose tipping tartly. "But I will still assert you are overdue."

He laughed at her teasing indignation.

"Well, I can't see how we could be married any more quickly. Why, I doubt even the archbishop will see me before three —"

She took a step back from him and crossed her arms over her chest. "Married?"

"Well, yes. Of course," he told her. "We're to be married."

"I don't recall agreeing to be married."

This took him aback. Whatever was she saying? Of course they were going to be married.

"Further, I don't believe I've been asked," she continued.

"Of course I did," he shot back, and then he recounted the previous night and realized that perhaps he had just presumed . . . Oh, bother, he had proposed, hadn't he?

"I don't recall any sort of proper proposal," she was saying.

There it was. The crux of all this. *Proper.* From a lady who could be anything but.

"Oh, demmit, Miss Tempest, you are determined to drive me mad," he said, dropping down to one knee and catching hold of her hand. It hurt like the very devil to get down like this, but he wasn't about to let her slip from his life on some infuriating technicality. "Will you marry me?"

"I don't know," she told him pertly.

"You don't know?" he sputtered, staggering back up and facing her.

"No, I do not. I will not marry a man who doesn't love me. And like your previous 'proposal,' I have yet to hear a declaration of love from you, my lord." Now her pert nose was most decidedly tucked in the air, all smug defiance, but he could see the sparkle of mischief in her eyes.

He nearly laughed. Like a properly ordered linen closet, Louisa Tempest would have nothing less in a marriage proposal.

Tidy. Neatly organized and everything in its proper place.

And in this case, a well-stated request and a heartfelt declaration of love.

Not necessarily in that order, he imagined. Well, if that was what the lady wanted. He would do so every day for the rest of his life if necessary.

Pierson took a deep breath and did his damnedest. "Love?" he declared. "Miss Louisa Tempest, you have taught me the very meaning of the word. You have brought me back from a darkness that no man should find himself lost within, should ever endure. You are my heart, my soul, my passion. I love you as I have never loved, and will never love again." He paused, and took her hand, bringing her fingers to his lips.

She shivered slightly as he kissed the tips, tenderly, slowly, letting his lips and tongue tease her a bit.

Then he drew back slightly and finished with one question. "Will you do me the honor of becoming my wife?"

And then she did the unthinkable. She stood there for far longer than necessary considering the matter.

"Well? Did I leave something undone?" he demanded, feeling a growing impatience to have this decided.

"Yes," she told him in her usual forthright manner. "There is something missing."

"What could I have forgotten?" he blurted out with all his old bluster and rough manners.

She laughed at him and rose up on her tiptoes so she could whisper into his ear, "I believe you've forgotten to kiss me senseless, so that the only word I am able to utter is yes."

And so, Pierson Stratton, the fifth Viscount Wakefield, kissed Miss Louisa Tempest until she was weak in the knees and wavering in his arms. Until the stubborn little miss was whispering a breathy, gasping (and most emphatic) "Yes."

And then he kissed her again.

Just to be certain.

AUTHOR'S NOTE

Dear Reader,

I hope you have enjoyed Louisa Tempest's story. The Rhymes With Love series has been such fun to write, and I've looked forward to tackling the Tempest twins' adventures.

As you may have noticed, I have left a few loose ends, and believe me, I can hear your questions now. Whatever are Tuck and Lavinia doing sneaking about? What happened with Charleton and Lady Aveley after that kiss? What about all those nefarious foes: Lord Ilford, Lady Kipps, and don't forget, Charlie Bludger!?

There just wasn't any way to tie both stories together (and not be like a thousand pages long) so I've had to split their two stories, and I promise you will find all your answers in Lavinia and Tuck's story, *The Knave of Hearts.*

Their unlikely romance will give us all a

chance to revisit some of your favorite characters, including Tabitha, Daphne and Harriet. I'm pretty sure Lavinia is going to need their help if she wants to find her true love. And of course, Lady Essex will arrive to lend a hand as well.

And then who will get their story told next in the world of Kempton? I haven't quite decided yet . . .

Thank you again for all your kindness and support. Truly, writing is only rewarding when you have fans as dear as all of you.

My best wishes to you and yours,
Elizabeth Boyle

ABOUT THE AUTHOR

Elizabeth Boyle's passions include her husband and two sons (or as she calls them, "her heroes in training"). In between the kids's activities, camping and gardening and trying to keep up on her ever-growing knitting pattern collection, she continues to write new and exciting romances.

The employees of Thorndike Press hope you have enjoyed this Large Print book. All our Thorndike, Wheeler, and Kennebec Large Print titles are designed for easy reading, and all our books are made to last. Other Thorndike Press Large Print books are available at your library, through selected bookstores, or directly from us.

For information about titles, please call:
(800) 223-1244

or visit our Web site at:
http://gale.cengage.com/thorndike

To share your comments, please write:
Publisher
Thorndike Press
10 Water St., Suite 310
Waterville, ME 04901